FLORENZER

FLORENZER

A NOVEL

Phil Melanson

Liveright Publishing Corporation

A Division of W. W. Norton & Company
Independent Publishers Since 1923

For information about permission to reproduce selections from this book,
write to Permissions, Liveright Publishing Corporation, a division of
W. W. Norton & Company, Inc., 500 Fifth Avenue, New York, NY 10110

For information about special discounts for bulk purchases, please contact
W. W. Norton Special Sales at specialsales@wwnorton.com or 800-233-4830

Manufacturing by Lake Book Manufacturing
Book design by Beth Steidle
Production manager: Lauren Abbate

ISBN 978-1-324-09503-3

Liveright Publishing Corporation, 500 Fifth Avenue, New York, NY 10110
www.wwnorton.com

W. W. Norton & Company Ltd., 15 Carlisle Street, London W1D 3BS

1 2 3 4 5 6 7 8 9 0

Rejoice, O Florence, in thy widening fame!
Thy wings thou beatest over land and sea,
And even through Inferno spreads thy name.

—DANTE ALIGHIERI, *INFERNO*

C. 1321

Translated by James Romanes Sibbald

You are a Tuscan, and Tuscans love cocks.

—ANTONIO BECCADELLI, *L'ERMAFRODITO*

1425–26

Translated by Michael de Cossart

Dedicated to Cosimo de' Medici

For Andrew.

CAST OF CHARACTERS

IN THE REPUBLIC OF FLORENCE:

Lorenzo de' Medici, *heir to the Medici Bank and de facto ruler of Florence*

Giuliano, *his younger brother*

Bianca, *his eldest sister*

Nannina, *his older sister*

Lucrezia, *his mother*

Piero, *his father*

Cosimo, *his grandfather*

Clarice Orsini, *Lorenzo's wife; a Roman noblewoman*

Lucrezia
Piero
Maddalena
Giovanni   *their children*
Luisa
Contessina
Giuliano

Tommaso Soderini, *Lorenzo's uncle and advisor*

Agnolo Poliziano, *Lorenzo's secretary; also, a poet*

Francesco Nori, *manager of the Medici Bank's Florence branch*

Sigismondo della Stufa, *Lorenzo's friend*

Jacopo de' Pazzi, *a wealthy banker*

Guglielmo de' Pazzi, *his nephew; also, Bianca de' Medici's husband*

Bernardo Bandini dei Baroncelli, *a debtor to the Pazzi Bank*

The Signoria of Florence, *the city's most important governing council*

The gonfalonier, *its leader*

Leonardo da Vinci, *an artist, among other things*
Piero da Vinci, *his father; a notary*
Francesca, *his father's second wife*
Margherita, *his father's third wife*
Caterina, *his mother; a peasant*
Andrea del Verrocchio, *an artist; Leonardo's master*

> Sandro Botticelli
> Domenico Ghirlandaio
> Pietro Perugino

Andrea's apprentices, past and present.

> Antonio del Pollaiuolo
> Piero del Pollaiuolo
> Cosimo Rosselli

other artists working in Florence

Iac Saltarelli, *a goldsmith's apprentice; also, a prostitute*

Atalante Migliorotti, *a musician; Leonardo's apprentice*

Ginevra de' Benci, *an heiress and wife-to-be*
Giovanni de' Benci, *her brother*

Fioretta Gorini, *a professor's daughter*
Antonio Gorini, *her father*

Jacopo Bracciolini, *a scholar*

IN ROME, IN THE PAPAL STATES:
  Francesco Salviati, *a Florentine priest in the service of Francesco della Rovere*

  Pope Sisto IV, also known as Francesco della Rovere, *leader of the church and the Papal States*
  Pope Paolo II, also known as Pietro Barbo, *Rovere's predecessor*
  Girolamo Riario, *Rovere's supposed nephew; also, captain of the papal army*

Pietro Riario, *Rovere's nephew and Girolamo's supposed brother; a cardinal*

Raffaele Riario, *another of Rovere's nephews; a cardinal*

Giovanni Battista da Montesecco, *head of the papal guard*

Francesco de' Pazzi, *Jacopo's nephew and Guglielmo's brother; manager of the Pazzi Bank's Roman branch*

Beatrice, *a pious widow*

Maddalena, *a cook*

IN THE DUCHY OF MILAN:

Galeazzo Maria Sforza, *duke of Milan*

Bona of Savoy, *his wife*

Caterina, *his bastard daughter*

Ludovico Sforza, *his brother; later, the regent of Milan*

IN THE KINGDOM OF NAPLES:

Ferdinand I, called Ferrante, *king of Naples*

IN THE REPUBLIC OF VENICE:

The doge, *the elected leader of the Venetian Republic*

IN THE DUCHY OF URBINO:

Federico da Montefeltro, *lord of Urbino and later, its duke; a condottiero*

IN CONSTANTINOPLE, IN THE OTTOMAN EMPIRE:

Mehmed II, called the Conqueror, *sultan of the Ottoman Empire*

FLORENZER

PROLOGUE

August 3, 1464

ON HIS FIRST MORNING IN FLORENCE, THE BOY GOES TO A funeral. Yesterday, he sat on a dray, dangling his legs off its end. He watched the farmhouse sink into neat rows of Tuscan grapes, the village tavern fall from view, the sparse bell towers retreat behind cypress-studded hills. All he's ever known, gone in a day. Twenty miles eastward he traveled, and now he's arrived in a different world.

This city is startling, rich and rude. The river runs red with butcher-stall blood. The air is sweet with sugared almonds and choked by churning bonfires. There are tall towers of bone-white marble; they rise from filth-strewn streets of dirt. And in those streets, people pass wearing shining satin and brocades in cloth of gold, in undyed worsted and threadbare serge too.

Now, the boy lives here. He's being threaded into its strange fabric.

He's lean and lithe, with a pleasantly long face framed by thick, shoulder-length curls. He has a strong nose, just like his father. A small, almost delicate mouth he's told he inherited from his mother. He's dressed in a shade of brown pretending to be black, same as everyone else. A quick glance, and he's indistinguishable. There's no mark of greatness. He's only twelve years old.

But creases plow across his forehead, incongruous with his young face. He furrows his brows when he stares—and he is always staring: at the starlings overhead, peppering the clouds; at the endless turning of a watermill; at the sweat-specked, half-dressed bodies of the fieldmen back home, or what was home. He commits his curiosities, his stirrings, his whims to paper, loose sheets he tucks beneath his mattress. He is beginning to gather secrets, like the nub of charcoal hidden inside his left boot and the many-times-folded piece of paper beneath this over-large tunic his father has forced him to wear.

He is following his father through a crowded piazza toward a long—a very long—stone church. His father strides, but the boy ambles, and

1

every new sight slows him more. A passing wheelbarrow filled with blushing, egg-shaped apricots. A stalk of pale yellow melilot reaching defiantly toward the August sun. And the faces all around him—so many of them to draw! At the farmhouse, there was only his grandfather. But he's dead now. He thought he was going to live with his mother, with her family. Instead, his father has brought him here, to Florence.

He wants to explore, to see the domed cathedral that every Tuscan praises. He wants to sketch bronze statues and long bridges. Not to go to Mass with his father, to stand and kneel and pray for the soul of a man he never knew. An inconvenience, his father had called it. The boy wasn't sure if his father meant the man's death, or his own arrival.

Memorize the details, he tells himself. Remember the one-toothed man and his grizzly beard. The girl sneaking her hands beneath her veil to pinch her cheeks. All these shades of near-black: the slice of raven-feather silk under a woman's mantle; the dusky sable trim of a man's lucco; the faded, scuffed leather of his own boots. He already knows that black is never simply black; it always bleeds into other colors. He just doesn't yet know the names for these shades, doesn't know vine black from bone black.

He can learn. His grandfather said so, told him there are workshops in this city where artists take in young pupils, train them to be painters or sculptors. His father, however, has different designs for him, expects the boy to become a notary, like him. To pore over ledgers, assemble testaments, write contracts. He could do that, he thinks. He's clever enough. But he also knows it's in his nature to wander, to wonder—at the swirling water in a draining tub; at the heavy, curling lashes of a beautiful boy; at this church in front of them, how it was possible to stack all those stones.

"Keep up."

He barely hears his father over all this noise, the hurried footsteps, flapping pigeons, shouting vendors.

When his father repeats the words, he hurries to his side. "Can I stay outside?" the boy asks. "I didn't know him, the dead man. I don't know anyone here."

Thick fingers curl around his arm. "You know me," his father says, turning him back toward the way they came, where the dark parade of mourners has parted for a single family. A man with a cane taking slow, stiff steps. Two veiled women following him. Children marching behind them. A boy—perhaps a few years older than him—keeping himself ahead of the rest. He's wearing a cloak, clasped in gold at the neck. Its velvet shimmers. Its color, its black, is different from any other in this piazza. It's pure, depthless. But the boy's face is horrid. His nose is flat, his jaw low and square, his brows uneven. His skin is the shade of withered artichoke.

It's the most extraordinary face the boy has ever seen.

"You may not know them, but they're the most important family in this city," his father says into his ear.

His hand crawls toward his belt. Beneath his tunic, the paper itches. "But why do I have to go?"

His father stands in front of him. Surveys him, as if he were a rabbit, neck broken, splayed across the counter of a butcher's shopboard. A catch with little meat to the bone, one with a price to be bartered.

"It's expected," he says, as if it's a suitable explanation.

Why, the boy wants to ask, to provoke. He knows he's being petulant, knows he's a problem his father doesn't know how to solve. What he hopes for is that his father will give up trying. Leave him here in the piazza, with his charcoal and paper.

But his father's lips are bunching together, like a fist. The boy's drawings will have to wait. He'll have to try to remember the odd-faced boy.

His father pulls him toward the church. "Come, Leonardo."

—

THE LAST AMEN IS SPOKEN, and Lorenzo rises from his knees. All down the nave, thousands upon thousands are coming to their feet. Men from every guild in the city: bankers, blacksmiths, and judges; wool-men and silk-men and linen-men too. Makers of paintings, makers of swords, makers of shoes. Men who sell salt and oil, and men who sell slaves. And then there are still the men not in guilds. Nearest the altar, the old-blood nobles and the new-blood priors. In the rear, the laborers and the paupers. And then, in a section of their own, all the city's women: the wives and widows; the matrons and handmaids and wenches. Some daughters are veiled, hiding their pearl-ringed throats. Others are bolder, bare-faced with lead-painted cheeks.

All of them, every man and woman, clutch a cloth to their faces. Embroidered silk handkerchiefs, simple linen squares, or rough and unravelling serge. Dipped in camphor, pressed rosemary, even vinegar. Anything to stave off the dreaded sickness. They all know a plague has come to Florence, and still they've come here, to this church, dim and hot and thronged, to honor his grandfather, Cosimo de' Medici.

There he is, on a bier before the high altar. Wrinkled face shrouded by linen, white and starched. Seventy-five years he had. A long life, a productive one. The people here would say he made Florence matter to the world, that he spent his wealth making it beautiful, that he made them all rich too.

Of course, nothing is so simple. Lorenzo is only fourteen, and he already knows this; he is being educated in the methods of the family bank. How they keep half this city—half the world, even—in debt. How pope after pope, English kings and French kings and so many of the peninsula's dukes all came to his grandfather, and his father before him, for the gold to build their palaces and wage their wars. Because, in truth, his grandfather was wealthier than them all. And he understood that wealth is a relative, mutable thing. That if money could be made from turning his gold florins into ducats, francs, and sterlings, then he could mint authority too. So with his coin, in this kingless city of councils and republican ways, his grandfather fashioned himself ruler in all but name.

Now he is dead. His funeral is finished. Already the priests are retreating to the sacristy, the doors creaking open, the congregation clotting together and tiding toward the transept.

Lorenzo watches them approach, one by one. Shuffling around each other, shouldering themselves to the front. Giving their obeisance as if it meant their debts would be forgiven.

Most fail to notice his grandmother. She is just a widow to them now. They ignore his sisters too. Meek Nannina gazes at the floor, but Bianca, the eldest, keeps her head high. She takes a defiant step forward.

To Giuliano, his younger brother, the mourners offer a brief nod. His brother is good-natured and loyal, handsome too; he is sure to return each nod. He keeps his back straight, his hands pressed in prayer. Lorenzo knows his brother is worried their mother is watching him.

She isn't. His mother's sharp gaze swings over the crowd with the gravity of a headsman's axe. She, in her long and heavy brocade, stands taller, stiffer, prouder than his father. To her, to Lucrezia, the congregants genuflect and whisper condolences. In this city, everyone knows to take their appeals to her.

Now they come before him. Plague be damned, they draw close, they kneel. He's grateful he can hide his face behind a handkerchief, soaked in some fragrant oil. What scent? He doesn't know. His nose is crumpled, faulty; he has no sense of smell.

When the people rise, they peek at him over their own wrinkled cloths, their eyes so obvious in their curiosity. He knows how the nobles and peasants joke about his face. And he also knows they all say he'll soon be leading the family, that his father is a sickly man.

It's true. His father's fingers, made cherry red and knobby by gout, grip an ebony cane. Anyone can see he only has a few summers left.

Lorenzo meets his mother's small, nearly black eyes beneath her webbed veil. She leans toward him, grabs his hand. "Look," she whispers, her breath hot. "Look at your grandfather, at all he's done."

He turns toward his grandfather, prone and small, resting on a bier. He had a long life, a rich one, and yet all he is now is a corpse, lying on a straw mattress, sprinkled with white and purple flowers. Just another body ruined by plague.

His mother's grip tightens. "We must hold on to this. You must protect what you'll inherit above everything else. You must be strong. Promise me, Lorenzo."

He searches for her eyes behind the veil. "I promise," he says, his voice thin and high.

He means it. He wants more, more than this, more than anything his grandfather imagined. He wants his funeral under the soaring dome of Santa Reparata, not here in dank San Lorenzo. He wants not thousands but tens of thousands gathered. He wants a pope to kneel beside his wrinkled body, to commend his soul to heaven. He wants permanence, legend.

Whatever it takes, he thinks, he'll do it. Anything, to be magnificent.

THE CHURCH REEKS. The censers have sputtered the last of their frankincense, unmasking the motley stench of the congregants: the rosewater worn by a widow, the stale ale on a drunkard's breath, the cheesemonger who still smelled of his wares. The good and bad brewing together, souring Salviati's gut.

He's standing before the Medici boy and his family, in the shaggy line of men waiting to pay their respects. He presses an old cloth against his face, searches for its rosemary scent. It's fading, too weak for the awful air around him. He prays, silently, not to catch the pestilence.

"Rome stinks too, you know," his cousin says. "Worse than a whore's piss pot."

He buries his grin in his cloth. "Then I hope they have more censers burning in the Vatican." A tall, sad crucifix hangs above the altar. His stomach heaves again. "We forget ourselves."

Jacopo rubs at his gray brows, chastened. Salviati's cousin's steps are slow and deliberate. His cape, black satin, hangs on him stiffly, as if it were threaded with lead.

They are not just cousins but friends too, and sometimes he forgets he is only twenty-one and Jacopo is twice that in years. That his cousin has stood through too many funerals, has already buried both of his brothers.

Then again, he, too, has sat through many funerals. His father's, for one. And he'll have many more to come if he's to join the church.

Jacopo turns to him. His eyes are pale blue, gentle and kind. "It is a noble thing you want to do. I only wish you were as selfish as the rest of us so you could stay here."

"I'm in your debt. Your support—"

Jacopo waves his hand, silencing him. But he knows Jacopo needs to hear his gratitude. His cousin runs his family's bank, a bank whose scale is second only to that of the dead man's. Like any talented banker, he knows his cousin keeps a careful ledger in his mind, that he expects his investments—such as Salviati himself—to one day prove profitable.

"My offer still stands," Jacopo says.

"And I promise you I'm still considering it."

A lie, God forgive him.

They move closer to the body, the sole of his right boot flapping with each step. The too-sweet stink of rot is creeping into his nose. The priests have uselessly covered the body with wildflowers, anointed it with oil, molded its face to have a semblance of piety. But Salviati has been study-ing the ways of priests. He knows how a body is prepared for a funeral. That the man's chest was carved open, filled with herbs, then sewn shut. Stuffed like a pheasant.

It's all an elaborate pretense, he thinks. Cosimo was a banker; he was rich and vain. The Bible says usury is a sin, and Cosimo knew he was a sinner. That was why he paid for so many monuments to the Lord—he was trying to salvage his soul. But Salviati is certain: such efforts are futile. God always sees the truth.

Wood rattles against the floor, stirring him from his thoughts. A cane lies before Piero de' Medici. The man tries to reach for it, but his wife swats his hand. The young heir, Lorenzo, doesn't move. A flock of velvet-wearing sycophants clamor to grab the cane, and from the group, Jacopo emerges victorious.

His cousin presents the cane to Piero as if it is a scepter. While his condolences to Piero are cursory and brief, they're only a preamble. Now comes the bankers' talk: the price of English wool, a new tax on wine—unctuous, crude conversation. Unsuitable for a church.

Jacopo is grabbing his arm, pulling him out of the crowd and toward the family seated before them. "I wish to introduce you," Jacopo says. "My cousin, Francesco Salviati."

"An honor, my lord," he hears himself saying.

Piero stares at him. His eyes, rimmed with red, flaky skin, look back to Jacopo. "A Salviati, you said?"

His cousin smiles gently. "I've offered him a post within my bank. But he's reluctant. He wishes to go to Rome, to join the church. One banker to another, what do you say to this? Help me convince him to stay."

Piero isn't listening. His gaze has returned to Salviati, falling on his clothes, his too-dark skin. "Are you certain he's your cousin, Jacopo?"

The fug around him thickens; it gathers in his lungs. He avoids the stares, but he still feels them, searing, all of them—the father and mother, their sons and daughters. His cousin too, who lets out an uneasy laugh.

He turns instead toward the young heir, a boy draped in fabric worth more than all of Salviati's possessions. A boy who also carries a storied name in Florence, who also was raised in a palace within its walls.

But this boy isn't a bastard.

The young heir's black eyes flit to him. They rove over his doublet, too faded. They linger on his hair, too coiled.

Salviati flinches. His shallow breaths are quickening now. The back of his mouth is filling with spit. He's going to be ill.

He pushes his way through the crowd with a clammy, clawing hand. He opens the church doors and stumbles, blinded by the sun. He leans against the side of the church and vomits onto its stone.

Weakened, he wipes his mouth. There's a puddle of mess between his legs. Spatter is flecked over his one good pair of black hose.

He turns toward the piazza. It is bright and crowded, as it is every day. This city has nothing for him. No amount of his cousin's gold will change that.

He has to leave. Florence is sick, he thinks. He sees it now: God has made His judgment on this marble Sodom.

Save the monuments, and let the plague take the rest.

Part One

THE
DRAPERY
STUDY

1471–1473

I

"PAY ATTENTION, LEONARDO."

He doesn't hear his master. His mind is on the statue directly in front of him that comes to his shoulders. A boy, cast in smooth bronze with clay and wax and iron underneath. He's not thinking about the pose he's meant to be holding. He's wondering how such a heavy object will be lifted. He sees not the workshop but gears with great, oily teeth. Thick, braided ropes spooling around a wooden winch. Men with calloused hands pushing the bars. Sweat beading across their broad backs like dew.

Not for the first time, he considers if he's erred by choosing to apprentice as a painter. If his ambition should have been to make machines and not Madonnas.

"Your hand."

Andrea's sprightly, plump face is next to him now. His master takes his left hand and gently returns it to rest against his hip. Then Andrea steps back to the statue, where another of his apprentices is waiting.

Domenico runs a finger down his long, wide nose. He does this when he grows impatient. All the apprentices have learned each other's habits, Andrea's too—how their master is dreadfully cross before breakfast; how if he bites the end of his brush, he's frustrated, liable to tantrum. After years of living in this workshop, of sleeping alongside one another in the quarters upstairs, they know nearly everything about each other. Even that which they didn't want to know or have known.

It has been a whole afternoon of this: Andrea's final fiddling; Domenico waiting to place this or that piece of gold leaf; Leonardo standing, his legs apart, his hand on his hip, his eyes trying not to drift toward the statue.

It's a David, the boy who slayed a giant with only a slingshot and his faith in God. He stands with a sword in his hand, Goliath's severed head at his feet. He's youthful, bold, a little arrogant too. He's real to life, as if a metal heart cooly beats beneath his bronze ribs.

Leonardo can mark his time in the workshop by the David. It was nothing more than the vaguest promise when he arrived. He was still a boy then. Still a foreigner to Florence, still skittish as a doe in its never-still streets. In the workshop, he asked questions. Proudly showed Andrea his drawings. Felt as if he had finally found a home in the city.

Then, near the end of his first year in the workshop, Andrea asked him to serve as the model for his David. Leonardo was young; he was svelte and handsome—a natural choice for a boy warrior. So he didn't demur. The apprentices always did any task Andrea assigned to them, without complaint. They knew it was a privilege, the rarest kind, to work for one of Florence's busiest artists.

On that day, Leonardo had dutifully stripped off his tunic and quickly rolled down his hose. He posed before Andrea and the rest of the apprentices, all of them ready with their papers, their pens. He stood—silent and patient—one hand on his hip, the other holding a dull, half-rusted sword.

Pens scratched, they tapped vials of ink. The sun had crawled across the floor, it ambered. His mind, then as it does now, wandered. And he let it roam—to any thought, any thought at all, that might make him forget his naked state. The doors, bronze and gleaming, outside the baptistery. A yellow-breasted songbird that flittered about a brass cage beside a stall at the Mercato Nuovo. The zabaglione Sandro had promised to bring him on Easter, that he'd said would be the sweetest thing he'd ever tasted.

He looked at Sandro then. He was one of the oldest apprentices, a man among boys. His chin was dimpled. His hair fell over his brow in rust-colored waves. His irises were green like mint cut with cream.

He had felt it all at once, his body betraying him: the heat flaring beneath his cheeks, the lone bead of sweat running over his ribs, the slight stiffening of his cock, which was just beginning to darken with hair.

He'd heard a laugh.

He'd heard a whisper. "He's meant to be a warrior, not a buggerer."

He saw the twist of Domenico's lips, saw Perugino stifle a snigger, saw Sandro refusing to look away from his paper.

He hadn't understood it, not at first. He always knew he was different. But he thought all of them were different in this way. That this difference was why they chose to be painters and sculptors, rather than notaries or merchants.

He was wrong.

Now he stands in the same pose, in the same workshop.

But it is only Andrea and Domenico watching him. Sandro is gone; he has his own workshop. And Leonardo, thankfully, is posing today in a plain, belted tunic. He's nineteen, unrecognizable from that child who arrived at the workshop. The dark hair, nape-length in his youth, stretches beyond his shoulders, resting on his broadened back. His nose has grown longer, even more like his father's. His barbered chin juts.

Years have passed, and he's learned how to grind pigments fetched from places he can only imagine. He knows how to thread silk and embroider brocade as good as Florence's best weavers. He can carve details into wood, can gild gold leaf.

But he is still only an apprentice. He has no work to his name. He still avoids going to the public baths with the other boys. He still lives a sexless life.

And in all this time, the David before him has gone from poles of iron to clay to wax and now to gold-foiled bronze. David, who has lingered and taunted him every day of his apprenticeship is now leaving. Finally off to the Medici who commissioned him.

"It's done," Andrea says. He glides his fingers along its arm, around the sharp angle of its elbow.

The apprentices turn away; they allow their master this final moment. Domenico retreats with the gold leaf, back to a pigment-stained cupboard in the workshop's rear. Leonardo steps down from the crate he was standing on; he rests the sword on an empty table beside the statue.

"You're tired of this. I know," Andrea says. "But you made for a good David."

He tries to smile. It was nearly impossible to begrudge his master, with his bright and wide cheeks, his jocular disposition. Andrea has taught him every skill an artist needs. He's been kind to him too.

Andrea steps closer, leans in. "What do you think?"

"I think it's beautiful."

Andrea's voice lowers. "What do you really think?"

Leonardo considers the work, lets his gaze draw toward its mistakes. Here, where the knee doesn't protrude enough. Or there, where the shield's edge curves too little. But it was too late to fix such errors, so he concentrates instead on its marvels. Goliath's head, huge and monstrous, at the boy's feet. How the giant's hair falls in wavy, damp strands. How its neck is so brutally severed. It raises the hairs on his arms.

"It's your best work. Truly."

His master nods; he quickly wipes away a tear. Leonardo wants to reach out a hand, to let it rest on his back. He savors these moments when Andrea asks him such questions, him and no one else. When, for the length of an Ave, Andrea is more than avuncular. Almost a friend.

Then they remember themselves. The teeming workshop around them. The apprentices sketching, molding, weaving, cleaning, waiting for orders. And Leonardo remembers that he works for this man—unpaid, in exchange for a lumpy mattress to sleep on and meals by morning and afternoon. That he must do whatever his master bids. That, in truth, he's a servant.

"The statue will be leaving tomorrow," Andrea says. "I want you to come with me to the palace. It's nigh time for you to find your own work. It would be good for you to see how that's done."

He says nothing; he's struck stupid. Nearly six years, and he's never visited a client.

Andrea smiles at him, satisfied. "Tell Domenico and Perugino to come too."

THE FOUR OF THEM STAND in the palace courtyard, Leonardo to Andrea's left, Domenico and Perugino to his right. All of them looking their best: their hair washed and combed, their boots rinsed of dirt and polished, their tunics pressed and neatly belted. Leonardo has worn his favorite today. It is shorter than most, ending just above his knees. It's twilled wool, dyed lilac. Not a popular shade, for men or women. But it pleases him. He's become friendly with the dyers after years of errand-running for Andrea; they color his tunics according to his whims, and in turn he gifts them sketches in charcoal.

Domenico smirked when he saw Leonardo wearing the lilac tunic. But he doesn't care. How could he today?

The courtyard is surrounded on all sides by shadowed arcades. Leonardo not only gets to stand here, to be worthy of being admitted to this place, but he gets to admire it too: the uniform arches and their ribboned reliefs, how they gracefully, effortlessly lift up the palace's countless rooms. He gets to see the true scale of this building, so tall that it must block the sun from reaching the courtyard's stones for most of the day.

Andrea was wise to come at midday. In this moment, the David is brilliant.

But there is another David here, behind them. It is, after all, a perennially fashionable subject in Florence. But this one, the one he knows was cast by a dead sculptor called Donatello, Leonardo has never seen. And he doesn't dare turn to compare it with his master's work. Not when Andrea is watching him.

"Now this is a giant slayer!" a sharp voice shouts.

Here is the man he hears has more gold than anyone on the peninsula, whose commissions keep Andrea's workshop open, who decides everything in this city. His doublet is emerald velvet. His hose are stark white. But it is his face that steals Leonardo's attention. He'd thought it was a figment of his childish imagination—what he remembers seeing that first morning in Florence. A gargoyle he had conjured out of the fear of being thrust into the city. He tried to see this face again in the ensuing years, but he has only seen Lorenzo from a distance, in fragments—on a dais during a tournament or between the shifting bodies of costumed revelers on a festival day.

Now he sees Lorenzo again, sees him closely. His face is the same as the image he stamped onto his memory. The brows, uneven and mismatched, as if they were carved by a novice sculptor. The bottom lip jutting beyond the upper, giving up a constant pout. His tiny, impenetrable eyes and dark, ropy hair.

Andrea greets him, walks him around the statue, points here and there.

"I know it was my father, God rest his soul, who asked you to make this. But I could not be more pleased. It's the David Florence deserves. I've only kept the other one because it was a favorite of my grandfather. But I find it embarrassing, truthfully. David is meant to be our city's hero, is he not? Crushing Goliath, crushing Rome. I cannot fathom why Donatello took a warrior and turned him into a sodomite."

He knows he shouldn't, but he has to see it. He turns.

A boy, standing with a sword, naked except for his boots and hat.

Skin so supple, muscles so lean and taut. It is a delicate, beautiful thing. It's unlike any statue he's ever seen. It makes his blood quicken, makes his fingers curl, wishing for a phantom pen. But he wills himself to turn away from it, back to his master's work and the man inspecting it.

"It's you," Lorenzo says, his dark eyes meeting Leonardo's. Staring at him, unmistakably.

"It's him, Andrea. Am I right? In the statue."

Now everyone turns to him.

"Yes. You miss no detail, do you?" Andrea says, his voice honeyed. "This is Leonardo, a most talented painter. All these boys are. Allow me to introduce to you Domenico Ghirlandaio and Pietro Perugino."

Lorenzo doesn't acknowledge the others. His gaze stays fixed on Leonardo. "Would I know your work?"

"Not yet," Andrea interjects. "He's still an apprentice. For now."

"Perhaps one day I'll be hiring him."

"Perhaps," Andrea says, nudging Leonardo forward.

"It would be an honor." The words fumble around his tongue; they come out quiet and strained.

Lorenzo's eyes rove from Leonardo's face to his tunic, to its hem above the knee. The tunic, dyed pale purple, which he foolishly, stubbornly chose to wear today.

He smirks. "We'll see."

Leonardo bows his head, deeply, as if he were standing on the gallows. His trembling hands are pressed together, like a beggar's.

Lorenzo thanks Andrea and leaves them as suddenly as he arrived.

Andrea gives his statue a last, wistful salute, then he ushers them back to the Via Larga. He grabs Leonardo's arm as he passes, leans close to his ear. "He knows you now. Don't let that be a waste."

II

THERE ARE WHISPERS ON THE WIND. QUIET AT FIRST. NO louder than the silver-green rustling of an olive tree. Heard only after the farmers have rolled into the city with their carts, after the pealing of the noontime bells. They're loudest in the markets, where they hover between the grocers' stalls and breed like black flies in a basket of soft, rotting figs.

The whispers are saying the pope is dead.

He was found in his bedroom, they say. In his palace in Rome. His body was sprawled across the stone floor. His white cassock was crumped above the knees, revealing milky, hairless calves.

It was the pope's chamberlain who came to his side. Who knelt beside the body. Whose nose wrinkled at the stench. And the chamberlain saw that ceremony was upheld. He took a silver hammer and struck the pope's forehead with it, calling his name: Paolo. Again, with another thud to the skull: Paolo, Paolo.

The pope's leg twitched, but his eyes stayed unblinking, his mouth gaping as if he were a hooked fish. He was truly dead, God rest his soul.

The chamberlain made the proclamation, and whispers carried it out of the Vatican palace. They crossed the Tiber's bridges and crawled over Rome's hills. They wandered into arcades, baths, and taverns. But it was in the markets that they settled, grew.

Here, linens go unwashed and broad-leafed herbs remain unsold, for gossip and suspicion, those old friends, must be indulged. The whispers turn into explanations, into stories; they become the city's currency. Fresh rumors are soon more valuable than a bullion of gold. Their trade is incessant, day and night, and now two narratives have emerged.

IN ONE, IT'S SAID THAT, on that humid July afternoon, the pope experienced a craving for his favorite fruit. A page boy was sent from the pope's apartments to the kitchens. Melon! he shouted. The pope wants melon!

The kitchens were prepared for this: all summer, a pile of the fruit was kept on the counter. A cook fetched one, inspected its netted rind, hoped he'd picked the ripest. He carved it into jade-colored slices, passed one to the taster—a suspiciously thin man—who tested the fruit to ensure no evil agents had tampered with the Holy Father's sustenance. The melon was then placed on a golden platter and carried upstairs by the page boy.

But on that hot day, one melon was not enough for the pope. The fruit was cool and sweet, a divine relief. Two melons, then three did not satiate His Holiness—he wanted more. The page boy hesitated upon the request for a fourth melon, but what could he do? If the pope wished for more melon, the desire was providence: it had to be satisfied.

The Holy Father, his reddened cheeks sticky and shiny with juice, was halfway through eating his fourth melon when a pain sharper than indigestion stung his heart. He grimaced, he belched, he dropped his plate. He fell from his chair, pale green vomit rioting from his lips, and expired.

MANY BELIEVE THIS STORY. It is spoken by wives and husbands, by cardinals, by spies.

But some remain incredulous. Yes, the pope was fat, they say. But it was not his appetite for melons that brought his end. They proffer a different explanation. They say on that July afternoon, a cardinal had arrived to entreat the pope for a new benefice. But the pope was not in his presence chamber as expected. He was not sitting in his salon; he was not in his chapel. He was not even nibbling on melons in his dining room.

In a corridor out of sight, the attendants huddled together. They knew the pope grew drowsy in the heat, that sometimes he fell asleep, knelt beside his bedroom window in between his Aves. But they also knew the pope raged when servants entered his bedroom unbidden.

Naturally, they chose the newest attendant to call on the Holy Father. And this attendant was young; he came from Venice where men are quiet and severe. So when he approached the pope's bedroom, he didn't recognize the noises he heard, the whines and the slaps. He thought some devil must be harming the pope to cause him to make such sounds, and he swung open the door without knocking.

There was no devil. The pope wasn't dozing in an armchair. He was propped against his writing desk with sweat dribbling down his brow and a smile stretched across his face. There was even rouge covering his cheeks—a habit that was already the subject of much talk—so the attendant couldn't tell if His Holiness blushed when he saw him. But he heard his last cry: a final, primal moan. He saw him jolt, clutch his chest, then collapse to the floor. And then the attendant saw the page boy who was behind the pope, who was left standing with his oily prick waving in the air.

—

"SO WHICH DO YOU BELIEVE?"

Salviati looks up from the book in his lap. "Your uncle would say we must not wag our tongues with nasty gossip. But it must be the melons, no?"

The cardinal's nephew nods. He's standing again, waiting by the east-facing windows dimming with dusk's approach.

Salviati returns to his book, the Augustine, hoping the conversation is over. His finger traces the dense lines, searching for a familiar sentence.

"Paolo was a buggerer if I ever saw one," Girolamo mutters. "He was from Venice, was he not?"

He closes the book, keeps his finger wedged between the pages. Again he looks up at the nephew. Everything about him is long: his legs, his face, even his auburn hair.

"He was," Salviati says, already anticipating the response.

"Don't they burn sodomites there? Cook them like hogs, over a fire?" He laughs. "Explains why he left."

Salviati stays silent. How might Girolamo explain why Salviati left Florence, he wonders.

He casts the thought away. The Lord is good, he reminds himself. He is blessed. He smiles at Girolamo. "Sodomy is the lazy man's rumor. It's no more inspired than saying someone has a—" He stops, not daring to say the word on his tongue.

No matter—Girolamo isn't listening; he's turned back to the window, standing sentinel over all of Rome's churches, palaces, ruins lying downhill. Waiting to see white smoke rise from the Vatican.

"How long is this to take?"

"There was once a conclave that took nearly three years." He pauses to savor the whip of Girolamo's head. "But Pope Paolo was elected in two days. Hopefully your uncle and the other cardinals will decide soon."

"Pray for it."

He certainly will. It was tiring to play nurse to a man his own age. But this was the cost of being in the service of the prosperous Cardinal Rovere. Rome had blessed him with a new beginning, but he hadn't known the Vatican was a slaughterhouse, that diocese and appointments were its cuts of beef, that cardinals and bishops snapped up the sirloins, rumps, and rib meat, and Salviati and the other novitiates were left with the offal.

Thanks to Rovere, Salviati secured a modest diocese frequented by carpenters, smithies, and pious wives. And Rovere has had the decency never to ask why Salviati sought refuge within the low ranks of the church despite having a respectable Florentine name. In turn, Salviati has never questioned why the cardinal keeps his lewd, pagan nephew nearby.

Girolamo abandons his post at the window for a sideboard across the room, where a servant has wisely replenished their wine. The pitcher is silver, its handle gilded. It's gaudy and obvious, like everything in this salon: the gemstones and pearls littering every surface, the portraits of stern-faced nobles crowding the walls. The whole palace is like this too, the entire building a shiny scar along the crest of the Janiculum Hill. All of it ill-suited for a cardinal, in Salviati's opinion. Especially one who used to be a miserly Franciscan.

Then again, if he'd been forced to suffer years of mendicant living, he, too, would want to indulge once it was over. The cardinal deserves this, he tells himself.

Wine splashes into one chalice, then another. "This is terribly dull," Girolamo says, teetering toward him.

A chalice is thrust in his face. Pale gold dribbles down its stem and falls onto the embroidered cover of the book in his lap. *The City of God.* The letters dampen and darken. He shouldn't worry, he thinks. It's not his book. He couldn't afford such a luxury.

"Drink with me," Girolamo says.

Salviati doesn't move. Refuse it, he thinks.

But why? To leave this palace and wander down the hill? To cross the river and step back into his swampy little pocket of the city, onto a street where it doesn't matter if he's a priest, he'll still be spit on? To climb the crumbling stairs to his cramped, rented room, where he has no armchair, only a narrow bed? What then would we do?

He obliges the nephew, raises the chalice, and sniffs the wine. Trebbiano, heady and floral. He sips, lets it soak his tongue.

Girolamo is sitting across from him now, pouting over the rim of his cup. The last of the daylight falls across his face. That hooked nose, those thin eyebrows arching like a hilltop—his resemblance to the cardinal is unmistakable. The whispers say Rovere built this palace for his sister in exchange for her claiming Girolamo was her son. And, yes, saying a cardinal has a bastard is gossip nearly as trite as calling someone a sodomite. But this is the rare rumor Salviati takes as true.

"So who will be the next pope?"

Salviati could repeat what he has overheard, but that isn't what Girolamo wants to hear. "Your uncle is well-liked," he says. "What he lacks in tenure as a cardinal, he makes up for in piety."

"And what might happen if he were to be elected?" The words are tentative, bashful.

"He'd move to the Vatican. Find you some duchess or princess to wed. And your brother could easily be made bishop."

"May he get a diocese far away from here," Girolamo says. "Constantinople, perhaps."

He shouldn't have mentioned Pietro. Girolamo's younger brother is courteous and clever, wise and well-behaved enough to have followed his uncle into the church after moving to Rome. Better for him, he looks nothing like the cardinal; he is his true, not alleged, nephew.

Girolamo sets his cup, already empty, on the floor. "I should be with him in the conclave. Not Pietro."

"He knows the other cardinals, knows their games."

"So could I, if he only gave me the chance. So could you, even." His drunk, glassy eyes ponder him. "And what about you? What would you want from all of this?"

"I haven't considered it." A lie, God forgive him. But safer than saying he's prayed for Bessarion or Borgia or any of the other cardinals to rise before Rovere. He likes his life as it is. His church, far from the Vatican. A modest thing of patchwork stone, with a sturdy bell tower that comforts him when he marks its rise above the low roofs as he goes to give Mass. He likes his congregants too—they may not tithe much, but they are honest folk. Like the widow Beatrice who brings him ubriachelle every few weeks.

"I don't believe you," Girolamo says.

"I'm grateful to continue serving your uncle however he sees fit." But if Rovere becomes pope, he'd be subjected to more long afternoons with Girolamo. More darting around palaces. More ugly salons. More moonshine in the water.

"It's different for you. You chose to come here. You did that, at least," the nephew says, pawing his wet chin. His doublet's bright blue has darkened to indigo near the armholes; its dye has blotted the white sleeves of his chemise. He looks like a player, alone on a stage, who has forgotten his lines.

Girolamo had to know how his finery was failing him. After all, he used to be a cloth merchant in Savona, before his uncle summoned him here. Salviati can imagine that life for him: Girolamo locking up his shop at the end of the day, lumbering down to the rocky beach, listlessly watching the empty horizon. Like Salviati, he wasn't a man of Rome. He was only beginning to learn its rules.

Perhaps he's misjudged this man. He wonders if he can help him and lead him back to the Lord. Perhaps this was why Rovere asked Salviati to keep him company: to turn him into the prodigal son.

"And what would you want, were he to rise?" Salviati asks.

"To win something of my own, on my own. My brother, he's good at making people like him and getting what he wants that way. I've always had to fight."

"That makes you stronger," Salviati says, though he's not sure he believes his own words. "I could've remained in Florence. Worked at a bank. But I wanted a different future for myself. God rewards those who strive for something greater."

Girolamo staggers to his feet and snatches away Salviati's cup, still half-full of wine. "And you've done quite well for yourself, considering."

Considering what? He wants to ask it, doesn't dare. Besides, Girolamo has already wandered away to fill their chalices once more.

Salviati can't stomach more of it. He walks to the window, still clutching his book. He stares out through the glass at Rome under a muted sky. Down past the huddled roofs of Trastevere, past the Tiber, farther still beyond the ruins and twisting alleys. He searches for the fingerlike bell tower of his church. He squints and scans. He needs to find it.

Then, to the north, he marks something else: white smoke rising into the night.

III

HUNDREDS OF LETTERS, ALL WITH THE SAME ANNOUNCE-
ment: Cardinal Rovere has been elected pope. God bless his soul and
his reign.

Outside the pope's palace, couriers take these letters, tuck them
inside leather satchels. They depart Rome under a dim, white-smeared
sky, exiting through every gate, onto roads leading away from the city
like spokes from the nave of a wagon wheel. They ride all the way to
France, to Burgundy, to Aragon and Castile and Portugal. Some take to
the sea, to England with its chalky cliffs, to Kalmar, to Ethiopia.

But the news first reaches the fractured lands of the Italian peninsula: a smattering of duchies and kingdoms and republics, all of them
with their dubiously held borders, different dialects, and peculiar laws.
The earliest to hear are Viterbo and Spoleto, cities within the pope's
own misshapen lands. Then, to the south, a letter reaches King Ferrante
in Naples. Other couriers are dashing northward, days of riding still
ahead. To growing, squabbling Perugia. To the brick towers in Siena.
Or over the Apennines to Imola and Forlì, loosely held cities coveted by
all their neighbors. They follow the eastern coast to the Doge's Palace
in Venice, or the western coast to Genoa. Some travel farther still, up
the hills toward Duke Sforza in Milan. And then there is the one way-
wise courier, thin and tan, who rides toward the center of the peninsula,
to Florence.

He arrives in this lightsome city from the south, greeted by the smaller
homes of the Oltrarno. He and his tired gray horse follow the clogged,
muddy streets to the pink-watered river that cleanly slices the city in
two, and then he crosses the Arno on a bridge crowded with butchers'
shops. The city's streets become more narrow, more ancient. All around
him, people walk, dart, saunter, run. The men wear cloaks dyed deep
blue, blood red, faint yellow. The women wear veils hemmed with jas-
per or pearl.

He draws closer to the towering dark brick battlements of the Palagio, where Florence's priors bicker inside musty rooms. But he doesn't stop here. His letter isn't meant for the city's council. He must go farther, into the quarter of San Giovanni.

He crosses a piazza, and a shadow falls over him. His horse slows as a bell tower rises before him, emerald, rose, and ivory white. A baptistery shines with doors that seem to be made of gold. And then there is a cathedral, larger than anything he's ever seen, its stone lifting up a tiled dome so wide it seems to reach beyond the city, so high it seems to pierce the ribbonlike clouds. He is stilled, and this courier is no oaf: he has traveled across the continent, has seen turreted castles on snowy peaks in the Hapsburg lands, has seen a temple lifted by women carved into stone on a hill in Athens. But he's never seen anything so massive, so astounding as this cathedral.

He wants to loiter, but he cannot tarry. His destination is close. He spurs his horse northward, and the palace comes into sight, its soft gray stone dwarfing all its neighbors. The street before it, the Via Larga, is wide, very much so, but it is still crowded: men wearing sweat-stained caps pace with crumpled letters in their hands, and grime-faced women swaddling infants cry out to the closed windows.

The courier guides his horse around them all and dismounts beside the palace's archway. His feet move from crushed dirt to washed cobbles as he enters a spacious courtyard. Here, more men are waiting, though they are well-dressed, like he is. More finely, even.

A statue distracts. A boy, sculpted in bronze. He's young, carefree; his skin is so smooth—but there's a sword in his hand, a severed head beneath his foot.

Firm fingers grab the courier's elbow, startling him. He meets the impatient face of a household servant. He opens his satchel, explains that he carries news from Rome, and the servant brandishes an open palm. He reluctantly surrenders his letter. His work is now finished.

The palace servant flips over the letter's coverture and looks at its seal, recognizing the keys of San Pietro. This servant knows it would be a kindness to offer the road-weary courier some bread or wine, but he also knows this letter cannot wait. So, he nods to the courier, a wordless dismissal, then he carries the letter into the palace, up the stairs, two at a time, and then through a long trail of empty rooms ending at the door of his master's bedroom. He lowers his head and knocks.

"Enter," a woman says.

LORENZO DOESN'T LOOK at the servant's face as he enters. He marks the paper in his fingers, extends his hand. His mother does the same.

The servant hesitates. It's amusing to see him fret over whom he should give it to. He wisely chooses him, avoiding his mother's still-raised, talonlike hand. Then he retreats from the room.

Lorenzo lets the letter fall into his lap. He slouches more deeply into his velvet armchair, rests his head against its high back, bracing himself for what's to come. The servant's interruption was only a brief respite from his mother and her incessant complaining.

She's still standing across from him, still refusing the chair he offered her. She's statuesque: hands clasped, beige brocade stiff—even her beady eyes don't flick to the servant scurrying out of the room. They remain on Lorenzo until, not a second after the door shuts, she resumes her tirade.

"You should be glad that wasn't one of the priors. You should be glad it's only me seeing you like this."

He is rather slovenly this morning. His hair hangs in greasy strands across his forehead. His chemise clings wetly to his skin. He knows he reeks, even if he can't smell it himself. And inside he feels worse: a thunderous throbbing in his head, last night's wine uneasy in his gut.

"The Signoria never arrives until the afternoon." His voice is raspy. "I'll be presentable by then."

"By then, half the day is already gone," she says, wrinkling her nose. "All these balls, they're a waste."

"I'm sure the lyre players and the silk guild would disagree," he says. "Besides, the plague is gone; trade is up. We should be celebrating. The city is great again."

"And how long will that last if you empty its purse throwing masques?"

"With that thinking, we should've made Santa Reparata's dome out of thatch," he says, laughing. "What good is success if it can't be enjoyed?"

She doesn't answer. Instead, she inspects his hair, his fingers, his slippers. "You can't sustain this way of living."

"I agree," he says, for he is so terribly bored. For nearly two years, he has suffered the Signoria's daily visits to his bedroom, where they entreat him in careful words and dulcet tones about the city's coffers, about trivial matters in hillside towns within the republic's borders. The nine men of the council speak to him with deference, but Lorenzo knows his authority remains as thin and delicate as gold leaf. Like his father, he leads the city with no promised right.

"You have obligations," his mother says. "The Signoria—"

"Tiring and petulant is what they are."

"And the bank."

"That's even worse." He says this knowing it will irritate her—but, in truth, she is the only person to whom he can say such a thing. To everyone else, he must pretend: that he understands the fluctuations of the florin's value, that he is the wise and gracious banker every local business, every foreign court thinks he is.

And he is good at this, at performing. Every day he acts as if he is Florence's ruler, just as the Signoria eagerly acts as if it controls the city, and the many guildsmen act as if they matter too. All of Florence is a game of pretend, and to borrow his mother's words again, it can't be sustained.

"I didn't raise my children to be careless," she says, her voice taking on that awful haughty tone she always used with his father.

"You didn't raise us, Mother. You trained us."

He stands, and the letter falls to the floor. He doesn't notice it—he's whelmed by the sickening slopping of wine in his stomach. But he can't let his mother see that, so he walks to the window, fumbles with the lock. When it opens, late-summer air pours into the room.

He turns around. His mother is looking at the floor.

"Are you going to open that?" she asks.

"But we're having such a lovely conversation."

"The seal, Lorenzo."

The stamp, with the keys of San Pietro, is facing up. He knows what this letter is, knows it will announce the new pope. Does he care? Very little. Cardinals are a treacherous lot; one cannot be much better than the rest. Besides, Rome and Florence are like two embittered widows—polite by letter but forever holding grudges.

Rome and Florence, Venice and Milan, Naples too—they were all this way. As the peninsula's major powers, they were all bedfellows in one moment, rivals in the next. But for some time now, they've all remained civil, their disputes bloodless. Each knows their tenuous peace, now nearly two decades old, is better than wasting their wealth on the battlefield.

A new pope, a new leader of the church's lands—he could keep the peace; could dash it too.

Lorenzo fetches the letter and breaks the crusty wax. He won't allow his mother to read it first.

"Who is it?" she asks.

"The cardinals have chosen Rovere."

"The fisherman?"

He nods, laughs. Yes, it's an insult—but it admits an intriguing truth: this pope is not a Roman by birth; he must have ambition to have risen to such heights. Lorenzo? He has ambition too. Perhaps he and this pope could share a vision. They could toss out the old ways and mark a new one where there were not five major powers but two: Florence as the peninsula's shining heart and Rome, its prayerful hands. This new pope could see him as what he should be—not a banker, but an equal, a prince. All he needs is an introduction.

"Summon the Signoria," his mother says. "Have them organize a delegation to send to Rome to congratulate Rovere."

"I should find a better outfit if they'll be coming." He raises his hand toward the door. His mother doesn't stir.

"What about Giuliano?" She asks this casually; he knows well that his mother never asks questions—she only demands.

"What about him?"

"Perhaps he should join the delegation. It could help him."

"You really see him as a cardinal? He's far too well-behaved."

"A cardinal today could be a pope tomorrow."

True. It's something his family has never had, and if it were solely up to him, they wouldn't try. He likes having his brother close by, not flung off to Rome. It's a sordid city, all ruins and beggars. Giuliano is better than that.

"I don't think that's wise," he says. "To send only him and not me too?"

"You're more than a diplomat, Lorenzo. Don't belittle yourself."

"But it wouldn't be degrading for Giuliano?"

She huffs. "When change arrives, how you're seen matters, more than anything."

"Precisely," he says. He thinks of the bronze David in their garden, the frescoed Magi in their chapel, the morello silk or the silver-threaded brocade he wears in every parade. Without them, Florence would be ugly, it'd be lifeless.

"Have you given thought to your wife?" she asks.

An unexpected parry, one that knots his tongue. "How is Clarice relevant?"

"You'd presume to leave her alone for weeks?"

"She's in no condition to make such a journey."

"Obviously," his mother scoffs. "I would never suggest such a thing. But you know she'll be cross if you go to Rome without her. She's desperate to go home again."

"This is her home."

She tuts, but there are only so many matters he can concern himself with in a day. This isn't one of them. "I need to dress," he says, more loudly than intended.

She steps toward him. "Stay with your wife. Be a comfort to her. Let your brother go to Rome instead. He needs more. Give him this."

He sees through her designs. She doesn't care if Giuliano travels to Rome—she only cares to keep Lorenzo under her eye in Florence. She prefers him as one of those marionettes that the Sicilians play with. She's threaded his lips with string, and now his mouth only opens on her command, to speak her words. And he's let her do this, has let her meddle and dictate—for years.

"I'll go to Rome. Clarice will understand."

"Very well," she says, smiling coolly. "You'll take your uncle with you, yes?"

"He's nearly seventy," he says, but he'll lose this argument. Tommaso was her old, crooked spy. He'll send her little reports from Rome, complaining that Lorenzo didn't attend enough masses, that he spent too much on a banquet. "He'll slow us down," he adds.

"Perhaps you could use some slowing down. He was your father's best adviser, after all. If you let him, he could be yours too."

Besides her, she means. But she cannot go to Rome, no matter how badly she wants to be there, telling him what to do.

"Anyone else?" he says curtly.

"Guglielmo would be a wise choice."

"If you'd like." This, however, was an easy appeasement: Guglielmo was not only his brother-in-law; he was a friend too. "He's good company, besides."

"I don't care if he keeps you entertained. I care about his family."

"Bianca has nothing to do with this."

"Not your sister," she says, her fingers twitching. "His family. If you take Guglielmo, then we can keep Jacopo from joining, though he'll still clamor about it, I'm sure. We don't need the Pazzi Bank making any more inroads in Rome. Especially within the Vatican."

"If you say so."

"Don't be glib. This is what you need to be thinking about. Nothing is a simple yes or no. There are myriad choices in everything. The accounts we keep and the payments we call in. The villas we build and the towns we place them near. Even the paintings we choose to hang on our walls or the clothes we choose to wear."

He has stopped listening. "I know all this. You—"

"Of course you do," she continues without taking a breath. "But remember that it's not only yourself you have to worry about. You'll need to appeal to the pope on behalf of your brother too."

"Giuliano can speak for himself. We'll both join the delegation."

Her jaw slides, her fingers ball into her palms. He wonders if he was wrong, if she might force her way into joining them. That she'll walk with them to the Vatican so she can primp their hair and fuss with their doublets before they meet the pope.

"You will do no such thing. The two of you, on the road together? Something could happen, God forbid."

Still this old tale. Three years ago, when his father was still alive, Lorenzo was riding back from their villa at Careggi. On a wide, wooded road, he came upon some lackeys paid by a group of discontent nobles to kill his father. He can still recall it: the roar of the cicadas teeming in the bushes along the road. But he outrode the men, returning to the villa. He saved his father. Himself and his brother too, probably. Nothing came of it.

"We'll be with the rest of the delegation," he tells her now. "There's no reason to be concerned."

"No reason? You'll be beyond our lands. Anything could happen. And then what would come of us here? What about your family?" She takes the letter from his hand, folds it back into its coverture. "No, it can only be one of you gone. The other must stay here. You choose who goes."

He doesn't need to dwell on it. He'll apologize to his brother later. "I'll go. I'd like to make a new friend."

IV

A BOY, SITTING ON A STOOL. HIS FACE TURNED AWAY, HIDDEN behind a swirling nest of blond curls. A bolt of heavy, undyed damask gathered around his pale belly. It drapes across his thighs, falling between them into folds, so many little folds.

He's not looking at the boy. He's looking at the fabric, the creases, caverns, and chasms, all in the space between his legs. It slopes down to his calves and spills over them. The curving hem rests on the floor as if it were a lily pad on a still pond.

He skims his brush against umber, darkened with vine black. He dabs the linen canvas, which he washed first with dun and then with white. Strokes it, again and again.

Today, the workshop is filled with this sound: the wet patter of horsehair against canvas. Almost all the apprentices are gathered here in a tidy half-moon around the model. But Perugino is not beside them; he has tucked himself into a recess by the storeroom, where he is preparing a panel for an altarpiece. And Domenico is not here; he is visiting a silk trader's home in hopes of painting a fresco for the family's chapel.

"Note the shade of his hair, boys," Andrea says, walking behind the apprentices. "Darker than the color of straw but far from bronze. Painting it, you'll want to mind how much orpiment you use. Restraint is key."

But he's not painting the boy's face. There's no orpiment on his slab—only whites, browns, blacks. The shadows are what draw his attention today, for shadows are where the truth of any matter lives. They are never simple, never a single color, though most people—even most of the apprentices in this room—are content to see only black. But he never sees simply black. He sees gradations, a thousand shades.

This boy wrapped in taffeta is a stranger to them all, Leonardo included. Andrea has plucked him from elsewhere—a goldsmith's shop, he said. Their master needs to paint a young angel, and he wants his angel to have curls the color of honey. Unfortunately, the boys in his own workshop have brown, black, even copper—but not blond—locks.

"Turn your face to the sun," Andrea tells the model. "The light is beautiful today."

Now Leonardo can see the boy's face. Sun-rosed cheeks. Barely parted lips, shining and pink. Long, curling lashes, faint and delicate as gossamer.

"More toward your left," Andrea says.

The boy shifts. His eyes, brown with bright flakes like mica, meet his own.

He flushes, looks away—back to his work, his ghost of an image. He brings his brush back to the darkness pooling by the left foot. He deepens the darks. He shades furiously.

Andrea's footsteps approach, tapping slowly, evenly. Leonardo's fingers tighten around his brush, for he knows what is about to happen; it has happened a hundred times before. His master will lean in close to his canvas, draw a deep breath, and compliment his work. And Leonardo will feel warm having won his praise, but its glow will be fleeting, for, like always, it will be buried under the lead-heavy glares of the other apprentices.

"It's good." Andrea says, but he doesn't move closer. His voice is flat; his hands remain at his sides. "Whom is it for?"

"What do you mean?"

"Who asked you to paint this?"

"I thought you—"

"I never asked you to work on this today. I don't need you painting me studies. I need you to be bringing in work."

Every apprentice is peering over their easels. Even Perugino has paused before his panel in the back of the room to learn who caused Andrea to raise his voice. And the model, he's still holding his pose— but he must be thinking he's lazy, timid, talentless.

The Ave bell at Sant'Ambrogio rings.

"That's our time for today." Andrea turns to the boy. "You may get dressed."

The model stands, careful to keep the damask close to his bare body. His muscled arms press against the fabric. His fingers, singed at the tips, clutch it.

He's taller than Leonardo expected. Sturdier too.

The model shuffles toward the far wall, where his oat-colored tunic hangs from the back of a chair. Without a glance behind him, he lets the fabric fall from his body. Collects his hose, rolling them over his hay-haired legs, pulling them over his supple, round backside.

Leonardo's brush quivers, its tip wet. He wants to forget about Andrea's words, about what the apprentices will surely whisper over supper. He wants to keep watching this boy, in this quiet moment, and draw him.

But he dresses too quickly; the moment is already lost.

Leonardo rubs his brush against a stained rag, listening to Andrea thank the model. He wipes the pigment from his smeared stone slab, waiting to hear the boy's voice in reply, wondering if Andrea will speak his name.

Instead, he hears the clink of coins dropping into a purse, then dwindling footsteps.

Leonardo lifts his easel and follows him. Outside, he leans his work against the workshop's wall, where its many layers can dry in the sun. Perhaps he'll work on it again, add lead white to mark the taffeta's sheen. Or he might leave it out here for days, for rain to ruin or someone to steal. Most likely, he'll forget about it altogether.

He presses his stained fingers against his stiff neck, turns to face the sun. Mule-drawn carts rattle past, casting clouds of dirt. Down the Via dell'Agnolo, a slender silhouette dissolves into the low afternoon light. He waits for the dirt to settle, for the golden curls to shine once more as the model retreats. But the boy is not moving. He stands in the street, looking back toward him, toward his painting.

A smile curls on the model's pink lips. Before Leonardo can take a single step, he leaves.

"THAT BOY DIDN'T LOOK LIKE a smithy's apprentice."

The careless whisper wakes Leonardo. He stays still beneath his bedquilts.

From supper to the hearth's last embers, the younger boys have chattered incessantly like a brood of chicks. He begged sleep to rescue him, but that was in vain; all the apprentices slept in a single, long room above the workshop.

"No, he is," another says. "My brother's friend works for the same goldsmith. But he told me he rarely sleeps at the workshop."

"He sleeps on the street?"

"No, no." The voice is eager now. "He said that most nights he goes to the Buco."

"The Buco?"

"It's a tavern near the Baldracca, full of lechers and men with wicked tastes. And this boy works there. Men pay him for his company."

The boys laugh.

"What does he do?" a quieter, younger voice asks.

"What do you think? He bends over and lets them bugger his hole."

They titter again, louder this time. Leonardo stares at the wooden rafters above him, half veiled by the smoky gray-blue dark.

"Isn't it dirty?"

"I don't know. And I don't want to know."

"Do you think Andrea knows?"

"What do you think?"

He bolts from bed, silencing the boys. He doesn't know why he is standing, doesn't know what he is doing. He quickly dresses and walks through the maze of mattresses, not lifting his gaze from the faded, clay-colored rug running the length of the room. When he shuts the door behind him, he pretends not to hear their torrent of laughter.

He steps downstairs to the workshop. He prefers this space at night, when the day's rabble has been silenced, when the sketches, sculptures, and paintings that devoured the preceding hours are docile and still.

His study has been brought inside, laid on a table beneath a window. It's good, after all. He knows this. The drapery seems to shimmer, it seems soft to the touch. And beneath it, legs, knees, feet looking so real, they seem as if they might stroll off the canvas and into the workshop. But they can't. The figure has no hands, no head. There are no lungs breathing, no heart stirring or eyes staring.

He hears soft footfalls and turns to see Andrea stepping beside him. His master studies the drawing, rubbing at his night-thick stubble, rounding his slight moue. As if he were looking at a merchant who was too slow in counting his coin.

"I was harsh earlier. For that, I apologize. This is good. Technically excellent. But what purpose does it serve? I look at this, and I feel nothing."

"It was a study," he whispers.

"And yet you already have the skill to do something real if you allowed yourself the chance. Domenico and Perugino, they know this; they're already finding their own work."

"They're older than me. They were already apprentices when I arrived here."

"And yet you paint better than them," Andrea says. "Don't deny it."

Leonardo fingers at a loose curl, pulls it until it's long and taut. He won't deny it. He knows it's true.

"My father was a brickmaker, you know. A good man but not a great one. He took clay, molded it, fired it into brick. When you think about it, it's not dissimilar from the work I do now, though when I was younger all I wanted was to be entirely different from him. But I work with bronze, not clay. I make sculptures, not walls. And the only reason I get to make work unlike his, the only reason I can afford my own way of life is because I have the favor of a wealthy family, and I work hard to keep them pleased."

"I don't know anyone like that."

"Yes, you do."

"The Medici would never hire an apprentice."

"Perhaps not, but one of your father's clients might. He saw that you came here to train. He'll want to see you find work too. You're his son, after all."

Andrea's palm rests against his back. He steps away from its touch, stares at his sketch—into its darkest shadows, where the ink has yet to dry. Andrea doesn't understand, and he can't explain it to him.

"He lends his service to many people, Leonardo. Not just men like me. Families rich enough to worry about wills and what they'll leave behind. Who can afford to pay a young, promising painter for a devotional that will ease their guilt and make them feel pious."

He feels his master's hand on his back again. This time, he doesn't stir. "Find yourself a commission. Then you won't need to be an apprentice any longer."

But all he knows is being an apprentice. He's never made a painting that was his alone. Only details, exercises. Like the work in front of him in the moonlight. Taunting him.

He could make something from this, he thinks. Give it hands, a clean face. He could turn it into an angel or even a young Christ. He can begin to see it: a hazy vision that he could transform into his first painting. Not one for Andrea, not one shared with the other apprentices. Something that is wholly his own creation.

But, to do that, he'd need to see the model again.

V

IN THE COURTYARD, A ROW OF COACHES, THE HORSES BRAYING and kicking. The nine men of the Signoria standing beside them, shaking their scarlet robes to ward off clouds of flies. And then, his family, all of them waiting along the columns to send him off.

"Shall we?" he asks Guglielmo.

"Let's," his brother-in-law says, sweeping back his long, fair hair.

They first bid farewell to their wives. He puts a hand on the swell of Clarice's belly, strokes the soft forehead of their infant daughter swaddled in her arms.

"Give my father my love," Clarice says. Her pale hair is braided, netted with rubies that play with the daylight. But her wide face is still and blank.

"I will," he says, kissing her cool cheek, knowing she won't forgive him if he denies her another trip to Rome.

When she retreats out of the sun into the arcade's shadow he turns to his sister. But Bianca is still huddled close to Guglielmo cooing goodbyes. She kisses him once, twice, three times, then gently pushes him away.

She grabs Lorenzo's arm, presenting her plump, lead-white cheeks for a kiss. "I'll blame you if I hear he's misbehaved," she says. "We both know his brother's a nasty little man. Mind that he doesn't spend too much time with him while you're there?"

"I'll do my best," he says, grinning.

She laughs. "Then expect me to be cross with you when you return."

Beside them, their mother clears her throat. Their smiles vanish.

His mother is squinting in the daylight, pointedly without veil or mantle, stiffly wrapped in a sleeveless gown of rose silk. "I expect a letter as soon as you arrive," she tells him. "Another after you've met with the Holy Father. Don't think I'll wait until you've returned to learn how it went."

"I know you won't," he says. Besides, if she doesn't hear from him, she'll still hear from his uncle, her spy. She lives in contingencies.

She picks a speck of dust from his shoulder. "Don't dress too richly when you meet Rovere. He comes from the Franciscans, and they like their austerity. End your remarks with 'Your Holiness,' and not 'Your Grace.' Make sure to remind him what an honor it is for our family to serve as the Curia's bankers. And above all, be safe." She reaches for his face, cups his cheek with her bony fingers. She forces a dry-lipped kiss onto his cheek. "Now, go say goodbye to your brother."

Giuliano's head hangs low, his loose, brown curls spilling forward. He fingers the gold-threaded hem of his twilled kermes cloak.

"I wish it could be both of us going," Lorenzo says, patting his brother's arm.

Giuliano lifts his face only slightly. His skin is sunned and smooth, his features strong but harmonious, like carefully chiseled marble. So different from his own.

Then his brother looks at him, and his brown eyes are wide and watery. "You don't even like Rome," he mutters.

He doesn't, in truth. "You will be there soon enough. I'll impress upon the pope your eagerness to join the college."

"Promise it."

"What?" he says. It wasn't like his brother to make demands.

"Promise me that I'll be a cardinal in a year's time."

His brother's wet glare is relentless, almost mendicant. It winds his insides. "I'll see it done," he tells him, then he quickly steps away.

For once in his life, he's grateful to have the Signoria waiting for him. There's little to say to them, though. He thanks them for seeing him off, then he walks toward his coach. Slaves in fraying sarks hurry to brush away the horses' shit from his path.

Before stepping up to the coach, he glances back—not to his wife or his brother or even his mother but to the nude David alone in the courtyard's center. He's had the newer sculpture moved to the garden behind the palace. Replacing the Donatello was an argument with his mother from which he chose to spare himself.

The boy's bronze sword glows in the sun.

"I'll return to you like David!" he shouts to the group, then he climbs into the coach.

THEY RIDE: OUT OF SAN GIOVANNI, through Santa Croce and Santo Spirito, then out the city gates. The old Roman road carries them past the dwindling villages of the republic, over green hills furrowed by vineyards, and down into valleys teeming with blooming woodbine.

Through it all, Lorenzo thinks of how he'll introduce himself to this new pope. Not only as his banker but as a trusted friend and dependable ally. Not as a mere leader of Florence but as its rightful prince.

Then, for the first time in two years—since before his father's death, even—he leaves his lands. Into the rival republic of Siena, and as the days grow in number, into the church's own lands. With each afternoon, the coach grows hotter, the cushioned seat flatter. Soon, the ancient road crumbles; it batters the wheels, sends the horses huffing, turns them foamy mouthed. Finally they crest a last hill, and Rome lazes before them.

He remembers: he hates this city. How it is like a drunken former foot soldier, obsessed with his past. He hates the herds of goats grazing about the many ruins, the slow and turgid Tiber, the decrepit walls of San Pietro, and all the tasteless palaces too. The pope's? His is the most offensive of all: a leviathan with scabbed stone and mismatched walls and sprouting ramparts. It's here he must go.

Inside, the palace is cavernous and high-ceilinged; the presence chamber long and half-shadowed by swirling smoke and dust. The delegation—with Lorenzo always a stride ahead—approaches an incense-hazed dais. On it, he sees the contours of a tall throne. The sudden shine of jewels. The silhouette of a figure, looming wide.

He knows he is expected to kneel, and so he does. Beside him, his men lower themselves onto the stone floor too. Old Tommaso wheezes as he follows suit.

He waits. They wait. For a greeting, for a prayer. To be told to stand.

There's only the feathery whisper of waving flabella and the soft sputtering of censers.

He looks up. The large fans cast away the smoke. He sees the pope now, sees that he is rounder than he expected; the man clearly eats his fill of fish. His eyes are thin, his lips even thinner. An aquiline nose carves his face in two. His neck is flabby and wet, like a jelly left out after supper. Sweat trickles down his jowls and drips from the ermine trim of his tiara, three-tiered and sapphire-crusted and teetering above him.

God must be blind, he thinks. This man isn't Atlas, holding up the Christian world. He's an old man—older than Lorenzo's late father, even—struggling to keep his head upright.

The pope extends a fleshy hand, tanned and sunspotted. Lorenzo doesn't hesitate; he quickly brings his mouth to the pope's oil-slick fingers. It doesn't matter how feeble this man may be, as long as he can make him his ally. It might even be better for Lorenzo if he's weak.

The pope smiles, and his lips vanish. "Let us pray," he says—Lorenzo thinks so, at least. His words are sibilant, the end of one word disappearing into the start of the next. Only halfway through the prayer does he realize the pope is speaking a paternoster.

He leans closer, trying to read the pope's lips. Then he sees: the man has no teeth, just a flat tongue slathering over soft pink gums.

"Amen," the pope says. "Rise."

Finally Lorenzo stands, his knees surely bruised from the stone floor.

The pope begins a speech. He introduces his nephew, a bishop, who dutifully repeats his lisp-swallowed words. He speaks of his plans to rebuild Rome, and the celebrations he wishes to host for the Jubilee in three years' time. He talks of how he'll restore the church's standing across the courts of Europe and bring a new crusade against the infidel Turks who stole Constantinople too.

To all of it, Lorenzo nods along. They are fine plans, beautiful plans. But he doesn't care about their details. He'll support them all, if it means the pope will see him not just as another man from Florence.

"It is all why we are most grateful that you, Lorenzo, have made the long journey from Florence to be with us here," the pope says, and his nephew repeats. "Your support has meant a great deal to us. We wish to present you with a gift."

The pope waves his hand, and two attendants bring forward a pair of busts: Augustus and Agrippa. Their features are stern and classic, the marble faultless. He will give one to his brother, he thinks. The Agrippa, as Augustus is more fitting for himself.

"It is an honor to support Your Holiness," he says, the words quick, his blood running fast. The delegation with him—they don't matter now. The pope has seen that.

"And it warms our hearts to hear this," the pope says. "Our plans are holy, but we also know they are ambitious. Costly too. We hope we can continue to look to you as our most loyal and most favored banker."

His smile falters. "Banker," he says. "Yes." The censers continue to gurgle; their smoke burns his eyes. He holds back a laugh. This pope is no different from all the white-draped humps who came before him.

To his left, he knows Tommaso is watching him, waiting for him to continue, already drafting in his head the report he'll send to his mother.

He gathers himself, smiles again. "Your Holiness, know that it is my family's greatest honor to continue serving the Curia's needs. Given this unique bond between us, if it is not so bold of me to ask: might I implore Your Holiness for his guidance on a personal matter? And if it is pleasing to you, might I suggest that my delegation retires? I know they still tire from the long journey here."

Rovere hums contentedly. "Of course, my child."

Lorenzo turns to Tommaso. "You all can take your leave. And can you see that these busts are safely placed with my belongings?"

His uncle scowls, but he says nothing.

Lorenzo places his palms together as the rest of the delegation genuflects. When they leave the chamber, he looks up with the most reverent of faces to the pope once more.

"It's my brother, Your Holiness. He's heard the Lord call to him. When he told me this, he wanted to run to the nearest church and begin learning the ways of a priest. But he is young. I told him that his goodness is too great to be relegated to a local parish. I told him Rome is where the best priests are made, where he might learn from someone as holy as yourself. I promised him I would ask if you thought he might have a future here."

"We see," the pope says. He waves a pink, plump hand toward one of the figures lurking behind his throne. "Salviati, come here where I can see you."

A man emerges from smoke. He wears a black cassock, loose threads at its hem. His face is tanned, deeply so, his tight-curled hair tonsured. His hazel eyes are steady, knowing.

"Salviati is our Florentine," the pope says.

Lorenzo knows the name, but this man is a stranger to him.

VI

HE WAITS FOR THAT FLICKER IN MEDICI'S EYES, TO BE REMEM-
bered from Florence. He's come so far from that funeral years past, when
it was him, not Medici, kneeling. Now he is a priest in Rome. A priest in
the pope's privy circle, no less.

But Medici only dips his head to him, and briefly. As one nods to a
page boy who has poured more wine.

In truth, it is not so surprising. He still wears faded linen, while
everyone around him sports richly dyed satin or Lucchese twill. He still
listens to other men mince; he watches them peacock. He's still only a
mere priest. Nothing more.

Medici knows this. He can see the derision so clearly on his ugly face.

"Salviati," Rovere barks.

His heart rattles; his mind has wandered. Kneeling, he looks up to
his master. "Yes, Your Holiness?"

"What do you think?" he asks. "Is it time to have a new Florentine
among the cardinals?"

His thumb rubs the coarse weave of his sleeve. I'm here, he thinks.
Right before you.

Yes—it's a single word, easy and brief, a mere sound from the
lungs. Instead he finds himself saying, "There is Cardinal Calandrini,
Your Holiness. He's from Sarzana, I believe. A coastal commune of
the republic."

He catches Medici's bitter, black glare.

"Would you call him a Florentine, Salviati?"

No, he thinks, but already more words are coming loose. "There's Cardinal Piccolomini too. He studied in Florence before coming to Rome."

"Enough," Rovere says.

"Forgive me," he mutters, the words hot with shame.

He has sinned. He has forgotten himself, forgotten his station, forgotten whom he kneels beside. He has coveted that which is not his.
Which only God can grant him.

His gaze sinks to the purple carpet beneath his knees. He wishes he could dig himself into it, as if it were dirt.

"Your Holiness, I can only humbly ask for your consideration," Medici says in his oddly high voice. "And it is my sincere prayer that having my brother in Rome with you will make our bond ever stronger."

"Yes," Rovere says, holding on to the word.

Salviati smells it: the pope's sweet sweat, trapped beneath his finery. He looks up and watches the Holy Father pull his wet face into a broad, disquieting smile.

"We will pray on it," he says.

THE AUDIENCE FINISHES. So quickly does everyone disband. Medici, gone after a final bow. The pope, wobbling back to his private apartments, eager to take off his tiara. His nephews trotting after him, like loyal hounds. Even the page boys vanish as soon as the many candles have been snuffed.

To Salviati, no one says a word. He is left alone, kneeling on the plush carpet. When he rises, he stays by the throne. Its back is tall, its arms gold-leafed, its crimson seat made flat by Rovere's wide frame. There's no mysticism to it, no sign of the divine.

He leaves the chamber, wading through the lingering clouds of frankincense, and exits the palace, passing all the coaches and their well-behaved horses. He stops on a crest, where the city unfolds before him. In the late-afternoon sun, the bell towers on the Vatican Hill stretch into long, bladelike shadows over the banks of the Tiber. He'll walk down this hill, cross the river, walk farther still. He'll go to his church—to think, to pray, to repent for the day's sins.

Fingers tap his shoulder. He turns.

It's Pietro, the pope's nephew, short-breathed. "You're not taking a coach?" he asks, astonished by such an idea.

"I try to stay humble."

It was easier than saying that a coach was too costly to hire. That a driver wouldn't dare venture into his dilapidated neighborhood, where the swampish air is thick with mosquitoes and the streets are never swept and the entrails of butchered animals are left in the dirt to be salvaged or to rot.

Pietro smiles at him. He always seems to be baring his perfect teeth. "Might I have a word before you go?"

His fingers ball, the knuckles crack. He's botched it. He knows it. Pietro had followed Rovere back to his apartments, and the pope had complained to him about Salviati and his insolence. He had sent him here to dismiss him. What use did he have to the pope anyway?

"One expects a priest to be pious, but few are also shrewd," Pietro says. "I'm glad you saw it too: Medici's designs beneath all his flattery. He already married into this city. I don't think we need him installing his brother among us too."

He has no words.

Pietro puts his hand on his arm. He holds it there. "You were right to try to dissuade my uncle. Whether he listens, that's another matter. But you have good instincts. You're proving your value to my uncle, and that shouldn't go unnoticed."

Pietro glances at his hand, still on Salviati's arm. "But we have to set that aside. A concern has been raised that I have to make plain to you. Your appearance at court."

"You don't need to say it," he says. "I'll go." He has dreaded this moment ever since Rovere's elevation.

"It's just a matter of some new cassocks."

Pietro's face is pleasant, sympathetic. He's blessed in not resembling his uncle.

"I don't wish to offend, but my uncle believes it's important to maintain a certain magnificence in public." He pinches his sleeve. "Linen blacks won't do. Get yourself to a silk tailor, and the matter will be settled."

"I understand, Your Excellency."

"Good," he says, whispering despite there being no one around them. "I like you, Salviati. My uncle does too. We want you here at the palace, not watching over Girolamo. You just need to look more fitting."

It was so easy for Pietro to say such a thing; he has his family's wealth to rely on—and that was before his bishopric and the benefices that came with it. He could have fragrant, floral jellies to finish each meal.

He could, and did, order bolts of taffeta and velvet; could line his cloaks with fox fur and sable.

Salviati? He lives on a nominal priest's salary, barely enough to cover his bedroom and his board. Yes, his surname carried the reputation of Florentine wealth; but he had left that behind. He had no silks. He had thought Rome wouldn't care about such pretensions.

He reaches out a hand, touches the soft sleeve of Pietro's white rochet. How swiftly Rovere made him a bishop, he thinks. Perhaps he could do the same for him, if he were to dress the part.

"What's the name of your tailor?" he asks.

HE RETURNS TO HIS WALK. Down Vatican Hill, past churning brick furnaces and their buffeting smoke, past Castel Sant'Angelo. By the time he has crossed the river, his feet are already hot and aching, and there's still much farther to go until he's home.

His steps slow as he reaches Ponte. Here, the ruins recede; the clustered shacks give way to statelier homes. This is a fine part of the city—one where he's never had reason to idle. He follows the neatly swept street leading from the bridge, a street studded with banks. He passes open doorways, glimpses quiet rooms with green-clothed tables. Then he reaches the Pazzi Bank.

Not once has he come here in all the years he's lived in Rome, avoiding it as if its very air carried remnants of Florence's plague. And a bank is no place for a priest. Usury is a sin, after all.

Then again, all the popes took huge sums from the Medici; they have for decades. The cardinals too. They all borrow and build and spend.

He tells himself: I can step inside this place, if it's out of duty for Rovere. Usury must be permissible if it's in the light of the Lord.

The accounts keepers gawp when he enters. They say nothing; they do not stir—not until he tells them who his cousin is, and then he is swiftly ushered deeper into the building—past small, stale rooms of bankers bent over their sums and dues, past stacks of heavy ledgers.

He enters a back room with a vaulted ceiling and dark-hued tapestries hanging from its walls. At the center of the room is a large oak desk with two chairs before it, one already occupied. And behind the desk, as he hoped, sits the branch manager, Francesco de' Pazzi.

In truth, Francesco is the other reason he's kept far from this place. He's known Jacopo's nephew since childhood; they were born just months apart, they both lost their fathers too young, and they both left Florence to build a new life in Rome. But he's always found Francesco to be a foul, pugnacious soul. A boy who stole coins from his mother to bet on games of calcio, who forewent his Virgil and instead learned the ways of brothels, who laughed when Salviati first spoke of joining the church.

However, the Francesco before him appears respectable. His fair face is freshly barbered, and his doublet is well-tailored, a pleasing pattern of blue-and-yellow silk—although it does grow taut below the chest.

Francesco shakes his hand at the man sitting across from him; he shushes him. "Here to take my confession?"

Salviati tuts. "If I were here for that, I would've come at first light. It'd take all day."

The man across from Francesco turns. It's a face Salviati has already seen today with the delegation: Guglielmo de' Pazzi. Leaner than his brother, hair more blond than brown. The brother handsome enough, decent enough to marry Medici's eldest sister.

"I'm glad we get to see each other again. And outside the Vatican too. It's so dusty in there," Guglielmo says, smiling. "But I have to say, the cassock suits you."

"That's kind," he says, taking a step backward. "But I should apologize. I've shown up unannounced. I don't mean to rob what little time you two have together."

"Nonsense," Francesco says. "Guglielmo was boring me with tales of fatherhood. Spare me, please. To what do we owe the pleasure of this rare visit?"

Francesco gestures to the empty chair before the desk. Salviati demurs.

"I've come to talk business."

"The business of God or the business of money?" Francesco asks.

The question irks him. "A matter of personal finance."

Francesco laughs. "The Florentine too holy to bank has finally come calling." He waves a hand to the chair again. "Will you please sit? You look as if you're about to flick holy water on me."

He takes the chair reluctantly, reminds himself that this is what Rovere wants. "Trust that I don't come here lightly," he says. "I'm in need of a loan."

Francesco smirks. "Forgive me Father, but what sin has led you to this place? It must be something awful. A bad night at the gambling dens? A too-good night at a brothel?"

"Stop it, Francesco," Guglielmo says. "Let him speak."

"I need new clothes for court. Better ones than these. Money to hire a coach. A house too. Nothing grand, but respectable enough to entertain friends of the court."

Francesco wags a finger. "Is this some sort of test? Am I supposed to remind you that thou shalt not covet?"

"With Rovere's elevation, more is expected of me."

"I see. Have you written to my uncle about this? You were always his favorite. Over either of us, even. His own nephews. Don't you agree, Guglielmo?"

"He does think highly of you, Salviati. I'm sure he'd give you anything you ask."

"No," he says too quickly. "Jacopo has already done too much for me." And he had: he paid for his seminary costs, despite Salviati's protests. But Jacopo was also his sole confidant, the one person who values him, who prays for his rise through the church. He can't stomach Jacopo knowing he's here, begging for more money. That his generosity wasn't enough. "I want this to be fair. It's the only way I'll do it. No favors."

The brothers look at each other.

"I don't like this," Francesco says.

"Trust that I don't either."

"Give in, Francesco," Guglielmo says. "Jacopo would want you to help him."

"This is my branch. I'll decide what's best," Francesco says sharply. He points another finger at Salviati. "Let me tell you something, one Florentine to another. There are only two groups of people in the world. Those like you and those like me. It's your role to come here, to beg for money, and it's my duty to give it to you—at a cost."

"And I will make good on it. You have my word."

"I know how much a priest makes, Salviati. You'd earn more as a tailor."

"Everything's changing. Rovere's pope, and I'm in his privy council. I'll have my own benefices soon enough."

"There was one pope, now there's another. Very little difference to me. Real change is a thunderbolt. It burns down buildings. So pardon me if I remain skeptical of your so-called changed circumstances." He raises his hands. "But I'm not here to preach. That's your job.

"If you want the money, I'll give it to you. But if you fall upon misfortune and I call in payment, I will not help you. Guglielmo here will not help you. Even my uncle will not help you. Because he will do nothing, ever, that interferes with the laws of banking, with settling accounts."

The man is insufferable, but there's a reason Salviati has come here and not gone to some other bank: he knows this devil, knows how small he is, knows he still answers to his uncle, knows his bank will always be second to the Medici's.

He can take this man's money because he's better than him.

VII

HE'S ON HIS OWN. OUTSIDE THE WORKSHOP, ITS FRONT crowded with still-glistening, haloed faces. Walking westward, toward the bloody, setting sun. Feet fast, for he knows Andrea is watching him leave, that he expects him to return with the hope of a commission.

Mules huff and wheels rattle past: farmers, their cheeks stubbled and sunblistered; their carts holding pale, wilted greens and gashed plums. The daily retreat from the Mercato Vecchio, out of the city and back to their homes, wives, brothers, sisters, children. Some to their mothers and fathers too. Ahead of him, the stone homes stretch taller; the bell towers, square or steepled, thrust higher still. And then Santa Reparata appears, its dome a rufous crown, blocking out the sinking sun.

None of it astounds him today. There's only dread sitting heavy as lead in his gut, the thrumming thought that he's going to do something wrong.

He presses on. Past the windowless, silent Stinche, the prison huddled and lonely on its small island, rounded by a moat. Past the Bargello, where trials are held and men executed, and past the Badia too, the monastery where his father rents an office.

Six years ago, he walked this same path, but in the opposite direction. Alone, he carried all his life's belongings in a small wooden trunk to Andrea's doorway. Now he walks, empty-handed, back to his father. No longer is he that boy whose mind brimmed with ideas, who was so eager to become an artist. And now his father lives in a different house.

He sees it ahead of him, down the Via delle Prestanze. A respectable two-story home in the shadow of the Palagio. Much larger than the narrow home they lived in when he first came to Florence. He knows his father cares deeply about appearances, even if he can only afford to rent this place.

His steps slow.

He tells himself: I will go to this house and knock on its door. I will shake my father's hand and kiss my stepmother's cheek. I'll tell my father of Andrea's compliments, of his wish for me to win a commission of my own. I'll ask, gently, politely, if he has any clients who would like a portrait or a devotional. If he's chary, I'll beg him—just as I begged him six years ago to let me join an artist's workshop. I'll tell him that the payment, the subject—they don't matter. That I only need the work.

He loiters before the door, his hands reluctant to reach for the iron knocker.

He wonders: What if his father says no? Worse, what if he cannot do the work his father finds him? For he knows he can sketch, shadow, and blend, but he doesn't know what he'd do with a panel of his own, doesn't know what he'd paint. Nothing stirs him. Except for that boy, draped in taffeta.

He tells himself: I will write my father a letter instead. It will be better that way.

He retreats from the door. His limbs lead him away, down the street and into the piazza beneath the Palagio. He doesn't turn back to the workshop, not yet. He hasn't figured out what he'll say to Andrea. Instead he walks, head down, to the piazza's southern side, toward the only neighborhood in Florence to which he has never ventured: the Baldracca.

Soft chimes sound in these cramped streets. He follows the sound deeper into narrowing alleys. A woman walks toward him. Her cheeks are two small, lead-white moons. Her dress is painted, not embroidered, with ivy and roses. Her steps are slow and deliberate; she wears platformed chopines. They lift her hem above the dirt; they're stitched with small, pewter bells.

She looks at him as she passes, her lips pursed pertly. Only a brief glance, and she continues on. She knows he's not here for her.

He wishes he had her confidence, her certainty. About anything in his life.

He continues through the maze. He passes more prostitutes waiting in doorways, passes men strolling past them, pretending not to stare, acting as if they won't end their nights with one of them, lifting up their dresses—that act he has never done, that he'll never do, that repulses him.

He reaches a tavern hidden in a knot of winding alleys. The Buco, the tavern he knows from the apprentices' rude jokes. An establishment said to serve a particular kind of customer—to offer them ale to drink, yes, but also use of the bedrooms upstairs. The place where he might find the model from the workshop.

He's seen that boy, night after night, against the dark curtain of his closed eyes. Legs wrapped in drapery, freckled arms and reddened hands, a halolike tuft of golden hair. But these are only fragments. They frustrate him, tease him. He wants to see the whole vision: the model in front of him, bare and perfect. He wants—needs—to draw him.

The windows are fogged and glow a pleasant orange. The wooden door shines from a recent coat of paint. It's a modest, comforting edifice, not unlike the hillside inns on the road from the country.

He wonders if he's come upon the wrong place, but then he sees the signpost swaying in the hot, late-summer breeze. He steps up to the door.

He's only here to draw, he reminds himself. To rent a room for a few hours, as if it were his workshop for the night. He only wants to see the model, to have him sit before him unmoving. To admire him.

He reaches out his hand.

A groan, guttural and free, stills him. He steps back from the door, wraps his hands around his chest. Looks up at the signpost creaking. Then he hears it again, a sharper sigh of pleasure slipping into the gathering night from an upstairs window.

His feet dash away, following a different path, rushing toward its end, where the river cuts across the city. He climbs from the street down to the banks of cracked, dried mud. The scent of fatty sausage greets him, ashy woodsmoke in its wake. He walks along the Arno toward bonfires and makeshift camps. Here, lively under the moonlight, are the city's misfit figures. Fife players with bushy white beards, straight-haired women reading palms for a coin, gaunt children kicking pebbles. He wishes he could set down an easel and paint them in the light of day. Something would be absent though.

He continues westward, his feet slowing until he reaches another bridge. Ahead, the moon-blanched reeds sway gently in the warm breeze that refuses to submit to autumn's approach. No fires burn in this part of the riverbank. The figures drift in darkness. Men—all of them standing underneath the bridge or crouching low by the river. They wait, they search, and sometimes they follow each other and disappear into the reeds. This dance, it is wordless and subtle, its movements are slow and careful, but there's feeling in all of it. It's what he wants to do with his own work, if he ever gets to paint something on his own.

He has walked here many times, always upriver from the reeds, never passing beneath the bridge. He knows what happens behind the screen of those reeds, even if he has never seen it. Sometimes he hears it. A cry, like the one he heard inside the tavern. The unexpected, wet sound of skin slapping skin cutting above the rush of the white-capped river.

Tonight, he steps underneath the bridge. He knew he was going to. His curiosity is an insatiable thing.

The tract of shadow is narrow yet cavelike. Water drips from the vaulted stones. His feet slide over scummy rocks. Ahead, under the pale light of the narrow moon, the reeds tremble. He walks toward them, steps into the thicket, the stiff grass stroking his bare legs. He hears water lapping at the shore, hears his shaking breath. And then he hears another breath. He stops, hears a second—deeper, raspier. He should turn back now, but he wants to see the picture that makes these sounds.

He parts the papery stalks with his hands. Amid the dull, beige reeds, two men are huddled together. One of them, his long hair threaded with silver, is standing. His hose are crumpled by his feet. He's pressing forward into the backside of the other man, who kneels before him with his palms in the soil. Leonardo, silent, studies them, the muscles carving shadows, the cordlike sinews visible one moment, gone the next.

The marshy earth beneath his boots feels as if it might suck him in. He closes his eyes, tries to steady himself, but in the darkness he feels every ugly reality of his body. How his tongue hangs in his mouth, how his cock presses stiffly against his tunic.

The wind rises, crashing through the reeds, a cicada roar.

He opens his eyes. He hasn't moved. The heaving men are still in front of him. Closer, even. The man standing upright turns his head. His eyes, the whites as bright as milk, look at Leonardo.

The gaze is like a knife in his chest.

He tramples through the reeds, away from the river's edge, away from the men. He runs back under the bridge, not daring to look into the dark. He retreats upriver, incessantly tugging down his tunic, trying to hide his shame.

Ahead, the bonfires have been snuffed out; only faint embers remain. The vagabonds have crawled beneath their quilts; it's only Leonardo still awake here tonight. Alone in this time suspended between yesterday and tomorrow.

He shouldn't feel this surprise, he tells himself. He knew what happens in the tavern, knew what happens by the river. He knew he wanted to see it.

There's no comfort in this, in knowing what his body craves to do, what he knows he cannot do. He is a painter; he cannot step into the tavern or back into those reeds. That would make him into something else.

What he's seen tonight—it's something to tuck away.

VIII

HE LOOKS AT HIMSELF, IN PAINT. HIS HANDS ARE IN PRAYER.
His neat hair is haloed. He's wearing a red-dyed cloak with billowing
sleeves of blue beneath it. Kneeling on patterned marble like he did at
the Vatican.

He doesn't quite see the resemblance, truthfully. His hair is shaded
too lightly, his head is too small. But the painter has done one thing correctly: he's preserved his face's olive-brown hue. His brother, however,
is unmistakable. His alabaster skin and his rolling brown curls. His
high cheekbones and his straight nose. His wide brown irises, devoutly
watching the Virgin and the infant Christ.

He wouldn't say that he's jealous. His brother simply has the better
face for portraiture.

"And where will this be?" he asks.

"In Sant'Ambrogio, as part of an altarpiece," the painter says.

"I hope they appreciate how blessed they are to have this, Sandro,"
Giuliano says.

Ah, he thinks, that's the painter's name.

"The gentleness of the Madonna's face, the draping of her sleeves—
it's beautiful work."

"I'm grateful for your praise," Sandro says. "You of all people."

His brother does have a talent for judging paintings. He knows
which details to comment on, knows what to praise to keep the artists pleased. Lorenzo wonders how many of them will follow his
brother to Rome.

The door swings open without a knock. Their mother, her chest
blotched and heaving. "The babe is coming," she tells him.

"I'm sorry to leave you like this," he says to the painter, short and
thick in the chest.

He's not sorry to leave, in truth. He is tired of these meetings with
young artists, of complimenting their middling work. But he has had
little else to do in these past months. Everything has been dull since
he returned from Rome; everyone was so eager to settle back into their

56

habits. His mother lingered and proffered unasked advice. The Signoria came to the palace and sparred with him over petty matters. The bank managers sent him letters about accounts growing and payments lapsed. His brother followed him from banquet to banquet, asking each day, Has the pope written?

He had not. A consistory had come and gone, and the Holy Father had only raised two of his nephews to cardinals. Lorenzo should write to him. Remind him of his brother's piety. Remind him, too, of his family's money that he was now spending on these many nephews.

This was his life now: waiting—for his letters to travel across the peninsula, for the eventual replies; for a moment to prove himself, to become a prince.

He follows his mother through the palace, and then he hears it: an infant's wild cry.

At least now something has changed.

"Come," his mother says.

He doesn't move. He knows he should welcome this event, especially if he has been blessed with a son. But he's so young; he's only twenty-three. Most of his friends have yet to marry, and here he is, about to take his second child to be baptized.

He grasps the brass knob with a damp hand.

"If it's not a boy, you'll put another one in her," his mother says. "And quickly."

He opens the door and hot air buffets his face. The hearth is churning, the wood crackling, sparks spitting. The windows are shuttered and fogged, water running like tears down the glass.

A handmaid hurries past him, copper-blotched linens bundled in her arms. Now he looks over to the bed, where a heap of quilts and pelts hides Clarice and the child from view. Around his wife, women are gathered, all of them kneeling, fussing, toiling. Like a painting of the Adoration but one with no kings.

He steps closer to the bed, and his Madonna appears, not haloed, but with limp hair and a pallid, wet forehead. Nestled against her striated breasts is not some beatific savior, but a creature mottled red and purple with greasy white slurry matting its hair.

With bowed heads, the handmaidens retreat from the bedside. The midwife stays to swaddle the babe in white silk. Clarice faintly smiles, tells him, "God has given us a son."

"Praise be," his mother says behind him.

The midwife presents the bundle to him, and with a sickening lurch, he sees his life splaying before him, a stack of playing cards spread across a table. Over and over again, he'll greet an infant in this bedroom with the same hearth burning, the same bed dampened. Only he and Clarice will change—his face growing lined, her hair growing brittle.

"Take him, Lorenzo," Clarice says. The softness in her voice is gone, her smile has fallen. She, too, knows she'll suffer this moment again.

He holds his son. In his arms, the infant, his heir, twists. He searches for himself in the babe's flushed face. His hair is fair, like Clarice's. There's the ghost of something familiar in the boy's nose, in his long chin—but he can't place it. The eyes, blinking, are a deep brown. They seem to look up at him, to search him with a stern, judgmental stare.

He knows the resemblance. His mother.

He shifts the child in his arms, and his son wails—a ringing, full-bodied cry. Lorenzo looks first to Clarice and then to the midwife, but neither moves. The child jerks, and he fears he'll fall out of his arms.

"Calm him, Lorenzo. Say something to him," Clarice says.

He hands the child to his mother. He doesn't know what words to give his son.

HE DECIDES TO WRITE THEM INSTEAD. A record of his life and his family's history.

He hides away in his bedroom, the door closed to the distant crying. He hoards volumes bound in soft, green lambskin and old quartos lined with sums. He thumbs through dates of births, deaths, and marriages; he reads letters and ledgers of loans. He turns the uncreased pages back and forth, trying to assemble so many disparate parts into something with meaning, with purpose—real or contrived, he doesn't care. He just wants coherency. To understand.

At his desk, the bust of Augustus watches him ready paper and uncork ink. In front of him is his daily stack of letters: the blatant entreaties for financial rescue, requests to bless this or that marriage, reports of trivial disputes in Tuscan hill towns. He pushes them all aside.

Now his desk is clean, washed with morning sunlight. He begins.

The first lines are given to his great-grandfather, the man who founded the bank, who won the Curial account and made his family Florence's most preeminent. He continues with his grandfather, not only a banker, but the city's leader too. He describes the perilous moment when the old families turned against him and had the Signoria imprison him in the Palagio, how they were ready to take his head, but instead they fatefully exiled him from the republic. A year later, when his grandfather returned to Florence, he triumphed over them all, taking their treachery, melting it down, forging a harder, stronger grip on the city from it.

About his father, his son's namesake, he writes less. A few lines about that brief attempt on his life on the road to Careggi, a short mention of his ill health.

He looks up from the wet words. His desk now rests under muted light, the sun gone from the panes of sky seen through his window. The paper waits for his pen, waits for him to write of his own life.

But where did that truly begin? His earliest memories are useless fragments: the brocade oranges stitched into the canopy in his father's bedroom and the sound of his breath rattling; his mother, standing above him in a garden, her silhouette blocking the sun. None of that matters—that wasn't life. Life was made of events, seismic moments that shape and shake.

He sets aside his pen and thumbs through a quarto stacked beside his papers. A catalog of payments made by his family to the city: alms for hospitals and convents; funds to design the sacristy in San Lorenzo; more funds toward building Santa Reparata's brick dome; commissions for frescoes and paintings and bronze statues; and taxes, of course—so much in taxes.

He indulges his curiosity and sums it all. The number staggers. He wonders if one family in all the world had ever spent so much. He records this sum on the paper. He says it was money well spent. Certainly, it was enough to earn him his place as Florence's prince.

The page waits again, still half blank.

He begins by writing of the funeral he arranged for his father, of his inheritance, of marrying Clarice. He scratches the paper with details of his visit with the pope. He doesn't mention Giuliano though—he'll write of his cardinalship once they've heard from Rome.

The pen hovers above the page. The ink dries.

He fingers the sheets. His grandfather's life consumed two pages, his father's one. His own? Two trim paragraphs.

—

THEN, LIKE HIS GRANDFATHER before him, he gets his own summons to the Palagio.

"What did you do?" his mother asks, clasping his hand.

"Nothing," he says truthfully, for nothing had changed.

"The Signoria wouldn't summon you to the Palagio for nothing."

This is also true. The council always came here, to the palace, but now they want him to go to their musty old council hall. He didn't think this lot had such gall. He'd be impressed, if he wasn't its recipient.

"When your grandfather was summoned, they—"

"Jailed him. I know." He does. The family history's still stuck in his mind, the record tucked in his desk drawer.

Her grip tightens. "You must have erred somewhere. You can tell me. I'll understand."

She's frightened, he realizes. Needlessly so.

"It must be some minor misunderstanding."

"But you must know what's caused it."

"I don't."

She releases his hand. Her arms swing wide. "How can you not know?"

It's a stupid question. On the Ponte Vecchio, the butchers slaughter scores of swine in a single day. The steaming blood drips onto the stones, drains into the river. Most days, by noon, the Arno runs red. If someone were to look at the river, frothing with blood, and ask which pig turned it red and which butcher held the knife, could anyone answer?

"Any simple favor could've gone awry," he tells her.

She shuts her eyes. Presses her palms together. "You'll take your uncle with you to the council."

"I wouldn't have expected otherwise."

"And you'll leave your brother here."

Of course, he thinks. She needs a spare.

AT THE PALAGIO, A BISHOP from the country spouts off—to Lorenzo and his uncle, and to the Signoria. "Now a man has been thrown from a bell tower—over alum, no less!"

But alum is quite valuable, he thinks. The factories along the Arno use it to cleanse the matted wool the English send them. The dyers use it to set their rich colors onto soft silk. The tanneries use it to cure their leather. Even he makes quite a profit managing alum mines on behalf of the pope.

He keeps this all to himself, however. It wouldn't help. Besides, the bishop has yet to cease talking.

"Volterra's councilors want to share their gratitude to be within the republic and to have your protection. But they also believe that this dispute over the mine's ownership was a matter that could have been more carefully resolved by themselves. That Florence's involvement was unnecessary."

The bishop looks at him. The priors look at him. Even his uncle looks at him.

So this is the rub. He remembers only fragments from the letter, an appeal for him to decide to whom the mine belonged. It was one of his many decisions that day, far from the most important. He almost laughs at the absurdity of it all. A man had died—a regrettable event, of course—but he died in a Tuscan city a half-day's ride away. A sleepy place he doesn't care about, that none of the priors care about either. This wasn't some attempt at a coup, not something that was going to get him thrown in the cell up in the Palagio's bell tower.

"What we've just heard is inexcusable. An abhorrent disrespect for our authority and for the sanctity of life," he says, loud and—he hopes—impassioned.

The sun blazes into the meeting hall through a triad of wide windows, and the nine backlit men of the Signoria, sitting in their chairs, watch him as if he's performing a Lenten play for them. The table before the priors is massive, carved walnut. It's adorned in the front with nude, mischievous-looking dryads, wooden tits and all. But the priors are so serious, looking so uncomfortable in their heavy scarlet robes—the velvet moth-eaten, the ermine collars matted.

The gonfalonier sighs. Lorenzo knows him; he's a friend of the family. He's the leader of the council—for now, at least. The Signoria's terms are only two months long.

"This was avoidable," he says.

Here's the opening salvo, Lorenzo thinks. Already he's caught a menacing glare from one of the priors—some guildsman he doesn't recognize and doesn't care to know. While Lorenzo culls a pile of suitable candidates prior to each election, with the council's short terms, it is impossible for him to know everyone.

Another prior, with a toadlike face weighed down by sagging jowls, leans forward. "A man has died, and a town is in revolt. What I'd like to understand is why we weren't consulted on this dispute."

Lorenzo smiles curtly. A predictable rebuke, one he prepared for. "Respectfully, the request to arbitrate came to me, personally. Not to the council. And the commune ignored my decision."

"You don't—" the prior begins, but the gonfalonier silences him.

"You were asked to arbitrate because they saw you as a representative of the republic's government," the gonfalonier says, each word measured. "The issue should have at least been brought before the council for debate."

Lorenzo laughs, knowing he shouldn't. "Does the council wish to open my letters for me too? Serve as my secretary? Mine has been getting the most terrible hand cramps from writing so much. I'm sure he'd welcome the assistance."

The gonfalonier blanches. Another prior chuckles.

A sensation ripples through him: a sordid sort of excitement. He likes this, being impetuous. Reminding them that no matter what he does to offend, he's untouchable.

Tommaso's fingers cinch Lorenzo's elbow. "Gentlemen," his uncle says, his voice throaty. "Let's not squabble about what has already transpired. Let's speak of what we'll do." His uncle keeps holding on to him, like he's a cane.

"Thank you," the gonfalonier says. "On one hand, we have a town within our borders in revolt. On the other, perhaps there's been an unnecessary transgression of our authority."

"Volterra is a part of our republic. We have the authority," Lorenzo says. "What does it say to our other cities if we don't reprimand them when they act against our leadership?"

The gonfalonier leans forward and peers at Lorenzo. "What do you propose?"

Lorenzo looks past the priors, through the large windows. The great cupola of Santa Reparata curves over the priors. Decades have passed since its construction, yet it remains the city's pride. It dwarfs them all.

"A simple show of force is needed," he says to the council. "Send in a small number of troops. It will protect the mine's rightful owners, and it will ensure that the commune acquiesces."

"Show force?" the toad-faced man says, slamming his hand down on the table. "You caused this madness. We should be sending an apology and brokering a compromise."

Now, of all times, the bishop interjects. "A show of force is unnecessary and provocative."

Sodding clergy. Useless, unless a man is looking for absolution. And he had done nothing needing forgiveness.

"This is about more than Volterra," Lorenzo says. "Yes, we've enjoyed a period of peace for some time now—but that's only lasted because we've kept our own subjects under control. If we do nothing to admonish Volterra, then Siena—or worse, Rome—will see us as weak. They'll be all too eager to send soldiers to creep into our lands from the south. They'll steal away towns at our borders for their own lands. Then they'll feel emboldened. We can't risk that. We have to make an example out of Volterra. Show them that our decisions are absolute."

"Your decisions," a prior says. "Not the republic's."

Lorenzo takes a single, careful step backward. "If that's how you see it, then I'll take my leave and respond how I see fit."

"Enough," the gonfalonier says. "We're still a republic. The council will decide by vote. The question is: Do we raise troops or not?"

They prepare to vote, to drop dried beans into a glass jar: black for yes, white for no. A silly show, one that always makes him grin.

The priors rise from their chairs. Some finger the beans in their palms, pretending they haven't already made up their minds. Others mingle by the window, conferring in whispers. Lorenzo strolls past them, calm and assured. He knows what must be done. All it takes is for him to meet the eyes of each wavering prior. A particular, protean glance he learned from his mother. His dark gaze is many things: reminders, promises, assurances. It causes one prior to remember his outstanding debt. Another thinks of his youngest daughter, who has yet to be wedded. With the gonfalonier, however, a more direct approach is needed: Lorenzo steps beside him, tells him—quietly, of course—that he can raise the necessary payment for the troops from his bank's coffers, rather than the city's. The gonfalonier smiles at this.

The voting begins. The gonfalonier is first: he drops a black bean in the jar. Toad-face is quick to mark his dissent by adding a white bean, but this doesn't matter—Lorenzo knows he will win. Two more black beans are added to the jar, then another white bean. Followed by a third white bean. At the fourth, his stomach squirms. By the sixth, he's in disbelief.

Six fools, he thinks.

The gonfalonier hesitates. "It's decided. We'll pursue a diplomatic resolution with the commune. No troops are needed."

Lorenzo turns to his right. Tommaso is merely standing there, fingering the wisps of his white hair. A pigeon would be better company. His mother would at least see this resolved differently. That must be why they ban women from the Palagio; if she were here, they'd never have peace.

She'd have another plan, he thinks. So should he. But the priors are already rising, dispersing toward their chambers to take their naps. The gonfalonier is approaching him, his steps slow.

"I wish I could've swayed them. But you understand, yes?"

The gonfalonier is coddling him, as if he's a child being told he can't have any more sugar plums. But Lorenzo's not looking at him; he's looking at the proud rise of Santa Reparata. With the council out of the way, it looks larger, the dome's tiles more violent in color.

"I understand," he tells the gonfalonier, still looking at the rufous dome, leering over them all. He knows now what he will write in the record of his life, the lesson he must impart to his son.

What moves this city? The gonfalonier would say it's the Signoria. The priests would say it's God. Lorenzo would like to say it's him, but he knows he can't yet say this with full honesty. Here's the truth: coin is the one thing this city pays allegiance to. It puts these men on the council, it pays for its paintings, it pays for its churches. The Signoria and their votes? They don't matter. Money makes the decisions here. And no one has more of it than he does.

IX

EVERY DAY, HE RISES WITH THE DAWN. NOT THE EARLY, WARM rays that filter through the cloth windowpanes, but the first slit of ultramarine that peers above the horizon. He dresses without a candle, chooses the day's tunic by the feel of its weave. Down in the workshop, he navigates around metal limbs and spread-legged easels. On his table, sometimes his candlestick's wax is still soft from the night before.

Work begins. He fetches a glass jar of pigment from the wooden shelves. Lapis or bone black or Siena earth, depending on the day. He moves aside loose papers and torn notes, makes room for a slab of marble, discolored to a motley gray. On it, he grinds the pigment with a stone until it's nearly dust, stifling his coughs from the noxious air. Some days, he beats egg yolks and water, sprinkles this mixture with pigment, swirling until the tempera becomes bright and less gummy. Other days, he adds pigment to ambery linseed oil, watching as the colors, miraclelike, form more brilliantly than they ever could in powder form. He prefers this way, how swiftly he can will layers of oil to become shadow.

He makes his first strokes as light begins to color the workshop. Around this time, Andrea comes out from his bedroom and begins to rummage about, trying to remember what work he must do. They don't greet each other; they're both better suited to silence, which is short-lived, for soon the boys are thudding down the stairs, jostling each other as they sit at the long, plain table in the rear, where Emilia, the kitchen maid, has laid out jam and warm, seeded bread. By the time Leonardo eats, the bread will be cool, the jam jar empty.

He has little in common with the remaining apprentices, has no reason to break his fast with them. Domenico is gone; he plans to open his own workshop, now that he's registered at the painter's confraternity. And Perugino is now painting back in his hometown.

Leonardo returns to his seat after breakfast, quickly resuming his work, while the other apprentices mill about the workshop, preparing their pigments or looking over their sketches. They talk among each other, but never to him. He knows how it riles them that he works earlier, harder, longer, later than any of them dare. How they mock him for examining each sheet of paper by sunlight and by candlelight. They think him haughty, but he's learning—learning to question everything. The others, they don't seem to notice how one sheet of paper may have an oat-colored tinge, the next tinted palest blue. It'll be painted over, they'll say, what does it matter? But Leonardo knows no amount of lead white can hide the truth of something.

A hush falls on the workshop. The soft, damp patter of brushes. The gentle scratch of pen against paper. Now Leonardo allows himself a glance at his fellow apprentices, leaning dutifully over their work. Passable work, at best. The truth is that they're all too late. Brunelleschi has built his dome, Giotto has painted his frescoes at Santa Croce, and Donatello has cast his last bronze. The best artists are dead. Leonardo, the other apprentices, even Andrea—they're doomed to work under their long shadow. None of them will match their predecessors' greatness. Yet Andrea still doles out praise to his pupils' middling work, perhaps so they don't see how insignificant it is, perhaps because it's easier for Andrea to compliment his apprentices than to acknowledge the pervasive mediocrity of his own workshop.

Leonardo thinks this, but the slow tap of his master's feet behind him still quickens his blood. When his master praises him, it still brings a hot, sudden flush to his cheeks.

The cloth in the windows grows opaque once more. The boys leave. Leonardo stays, lights his candle again. Now is the difficult time, when his wrists become tender and his blinking eyes strain. But he must keep working—now, of all times. If he stops, he will walk the nighttime streets, he will wander until he finds himself back in the Baldracca or down by the riverbanks. So he paints, draws, sculpts, hoping it will swallow him.

He dabs and shades until his work shifts from ordinary to feeble. He stops then, steps away from his table, guided by the uncertain glow of a short, fat candlestick. He blows out its flame before going upstairs. In the bedroom, he creeps atop his straw mattress. Lies there dazed, his mind exhausted—and that is a relief, a necessary one. Sleep comes swiftly, and soon dawn returns once more.

BUT NOW A DAY ARRIVES that will be different. There's no portent of this in the dawn light: it's unremarkable and gray. Nothing is new in the way Leonardo rises or tiptoes downstairs. Today, he grinds vermilion, the pigment bright, almost violent against his marble slab. He cracks an egg against a clay bowl. Still drowsy, he lets the yolk slip through his fingers, and he tries again, careful this time to only let the viscous white slip fall away. The yolk, a sun in his palm, rolls off his hand and into another bowl, where he dilutes it with water. He adds the finely ground pigment until the mixture is radiant. He still thinks it looks duller than oil, but he has to use tempera. It's not his painting.

He turns to the easel. It's a small painting, no larger than his chest. A hopeful Tobias in a blue cloak, following the archangel Raffaele, his wings spread wide. It's full of movement and lovely embellishments, done by Andrea: the intricate gold brocade on Raffaele's sleeves and the drapery of his cloak, so many silk ridges and shadows.

The rest of it isn't worth a fart. Raffaele's wings look disjointed. The landscape in the background is flat, and there's a castle back there too, something that looks like it was drawn by a child. Then there are the hands—the sodding hands! Raffaele and Tobias both have their thumbs outturned, the index fingers ready to point. They are identical within the same painting. Leonardo even knows which sketchbook of poses they were copied from.

Of course, Leonardo didn't do this. It was another apprentice. But it still irks him to share a panel with such lazy work. He'll be adding strokes to his part of the painting and feel his eyes drift to the hands. He wants to complain, to call it wrong—but it's not his place to say so. This is Andrea's work, meaning it was at Andrea's discretion which parts of the painting he delegated to his most promising pupils.

Leonardo's task is the carp, carried by Tobias on a string. A tiny detail in a small painting. Small enough that at a few paces' distance, it can't be seen. But if he believes the parable, without the carp, Tobias's father would never regain his sight. Leonardo tells himself this daily. But when the daylight fades and the candles burn out, he knows his contribution to this painting is merely a dead fish. One he must suffer painting with tempera because his master doesn't even know how to use oils. A painting whose colors will fade in some dingy church, for Andrea has never been asked to paint for the Medici or the priors or even the monks. They all prefer his sculptures. Leonardo does too.

He brings his face close to the carp. Its sad, shimmering mouth droops open, choked by the rope tied around its gills. Caught and carried onward to somewhere unknown.

He searches the details for his errors. The fins are almost featherlike, the eyes glassy, the scales iridescent, each different from the rest. He spent so many afternoons at the Mercato Vecchio sketching beside a fishmonger's stall and swatting at flies. They were worth it—the fish is good. Very good, if he'll allow himself the compliment. His painting has eclipsed his master's abilities; he has little left to learn from the man. And this isn't vanity. Andrea has said so himself, repeatedly. Told him he's too good to remain an apprentice.

He can't dwell on that. There are still so many ways he can improve the fish. Just yesterday, he realized it merely hung from Tobias's string; there was no explanation of how it got there. So today, with his brush tipped in vermillion, he brings his hand to the carp's belly. He paints a wound, fingernail thin. He even adds the smallest drops of blood, falling toward the dirt.

He looks at it, pauses. He hopes this is right, but he can't be sure. His father never taught him how to fish. Doesn't matter. There's a story now. A plausible one. Even if it's wrong, isn't that better than the absence of one?

"Still the fish?" Andrea asks. He puts on a pair of spectacles. "It's excellent. You're done with it now, yes?"

"Almost."

Andrea's cheeks sag. He removes his spectacles, rubs at his eyes. "Grab your sack. Bring your purse with you too. You're coming with me."

THEY WALK TOWARD the city center, the climbing sun on their necks. He matches his master's steady gait, wondering where he might be leading them. To sketch one of the many saints in marble and bronze that leer from the walls at Orsanmichele? To the Mercato Vecchio to haggle over peaches or to the Mercato di Santa Maria to purchase more madder or verdigris? But then, at the Via Larga, they turn to the north, away from all that.

Now they join a stream of carts and coaches, men on horses, men on mules. They watch their steps, dodging puddles, dung, refuse.

"I met with your father yesterday to discuss a contract," Andrea says.

His feet stall, but his master keeps walking.

"He asked after you, of course. Said it had been many months since he had last seen you. You can imagine my surprise, of course. I was under the impression he was helping secure you a commission from one of his clients."

"I wanted to finish your carp." It's all he can think to say.

"My carp? Your fish is done, Leonardo. You finished it weeks ago."

He disagrees.

"You should know it's a weakness," Andrea says, the words barbed. "The people in this city who will pay for your work, they won't care about the folds of a Madonna's dress or the scales of a fish. They only care about two things: that they get their work as soon as possible, and that it is what they wanted."

Leonardo thinks of the carp. How its tail is too stiff. How it isn't yet real. "But what if they're disappointed by the work?"

"Could they ever make something better themselves? No, and they know that. So their opinion doesn't matter as long as they pay you. There's little use in trying to be Florence's greatest painter if you can't afford a jar of pigment."

They reach the piazza, where to their right, the cathedral swells and soars into the sky. Next to it, the bell tower rises in its tricolor marble, delicate and patterned like a many-faceted jewel. He'll say it: they're impressive, but neither is his favorite building in this piazza. Yes, the dome's a feat—one whose secrets he badly wants to understand—but there's a certain brutish ease in making something so large. Of course people will gawp at it, of course it will impress; it's impossible not to look at it when it pokes at the heavens.

He prefers the baptistery to their left. Lower to earth, yes, but more magnificent—if someone stops to look. Three sets of bronze doors, sculpted into scene after scene so detailed that if he stares too closely, he feels as if he could fall into a rippling, gold sea. It's a different kind of artistry. One of truth and nuance and a thousand little choices. The kind he one day hopes to make.

"Answer me a single question, Leonardo. What do you want to do with your life? You're not a boy anymore."

"I want to paint. I want to work. I want to understand things. Everything, really. I want to build things too."

"And you can. All of it. But you won't accomplish a thing of your own if you stay hidden away in my workshop."

Andrea shields his eyes; he looks up high at Santa Reparata—above the low, half-finished front clustered with statues, up to the dome, and higher still to the copper orb and cross, leafed in gold and resting at its peak, shining in the morning sun.

It's Andrea's work. Leonardo was standing in this same spot on the day it was placed on top of the cathedral. The rest of the apprentices were there too, clapping each other's backs, hooting as the orb was lifted onto the dome's peak. They told Andrea how perfectly round it was; they praised its sheen. To Leonardo, though, it was only a pretty ornament. The installation was what fascinated him. He crouched in the piazza, away from the boys. Sketched the barrage of oxen, of pulleys and levers that hoisted the heavy thing up to the clouds. For days and days, he turned back to those pages in his notebook wanting to comprehend how it worked.

He wonders now if his mind was better suited to understanding gears and wheels and cables, that clean and clear kind of knowledge. If he might already have work of his own, had he spent the last seven years designing tools, rather than painting fish.

"We must remember that we're lucky to live in a city that prizes beauty above arms or timber or raw cloth. A city that will spend to see beautiful things made. Like that dome. Brunelleschi built it, but soon most people won't remember his name. Doesn't matter. They'll still know that dome. All we can hope for is to make good work. Something that can survive longer than we will. And I pray that when you get your chance, it's something more than a little brass ball."

Andrea turns to him, eyes narrowed, creases building just above his nose. An examining look, a sculptor's look.

"I've watched you for years, Leonardo. Seen you grow from boy to man. I understand you more than you might realize. I know you creep down to the workshop to paint by night. I know you don't keep the company of the other boys. Solitude can be a good thing for an artist. It can clarify. But you also can't imprison yourself at your easel. You can't look only at the details. You can't be afraid. You have to be out in the world. You have to see the good and the bad of it. Otherwise, you'll never make anything real."

Words flood from his mouth. "But what if I become distracted, away from the work? What if I might be meant to be someone other than a painter? What if the work is never good enough?"

"Don't be foolish." Andrea's hands cup his cheeks, the fingers rough and scarred. "I see what you have within you, Leonardo. Talent, unmistakable. Using it is the only way men like us—who won't inherit riches, who might never marry—can one day walk among the men who matter in this world. You will be a painter, Leonardo. A great one. I can't let you waste that talent."

He watches his master's blurred figure step away. He wipes at his eyes with his sleeve and follows him through the narrow pathway between the baptistery and the cathedral.

"You're to register. Today," Andrea says. "I've been too patient with you. You should've gone with Domenico and Perugino. They're already working. Sandro, I hear, is even meeting with the Medici. After today, that could be you.

"When you register, you can pick a new name for yourself, if you wish. I know I wanted something different from my family name. You'll sign your new name, and then you'll no longer be my apprentice. You can go out and find your own place. Finally be on your own."

ANDREA LEAVES HIM at the door of an ancient, poorly lit hall. Inside, the floor is stone, the walls bare, the whole thing smells of damp hay.

The clerk, sitting at a long table, doesn't look up when Leonardo opens the wide wooden doors, nor when he steps into the hall, not even when he stands before the man. The clerk is leant over a neat pile of papers, his quill moving tirelessly from line to line. It reminds him of his father drafting his contracts and letters, all in fluid, unblemished script. Right-handed writing. Leonardo doesn't know how it feels to write the normal way, what it's like to never have to worry about smudged words. He's training himself to write backward with his left hand.

When the clerk's quill runs dry, Leonardo clears his throat. "Excuse me, sir. My master has sent me here."

"And he is?" the clerk says, still staring at his ledger.

"Andrea del Verrocchio."

"You're fortunate. I have many records here of your master's work. But why are you here?"

"He's deemed my training complete."

Now the clerk looks up at him. "You're quite young to be finishing your apprenticeship."

He knows.

Behind his smudged spectacles, the clerk blinks once, twice. "So you'd like to register."

"As a painter, yes."

"A master painter, you mean?"

Seems quite the leap to go from apprentice to master. "If that's the proper term."

"It is," the clerk says flatly. He drags a heavy ledger, bound with red leather, from the corner of the table. He opens the book, sighs. Thumbs the thick, crackling pages. All the city's painters—the prolific and the destitute—are in this ledger. All the city's frescoes and portraits and altarpieces are summarized here, reduced to names and florins paid.

The clerk extends a clean, open palm. "Thirty-two soldi."

He doesn't understand.

"Your dues," the clerk says.

"But I haven't worked yet."

"You still need to pay to join the confraternity. Unless you wish to remain an apprentice."

Leonardo kneels, rummaging through the loose papers and chipped charcoal nibs inside his leather sack, all the while trying to ignore the clerk's impatient stare. He finds his coin purse, tries to count the coins by touch alone. He feels plenty of the small denari, a handful of soldi—but certainly not thirty-two of them. Then he feels it: a single, large florin. His father's monthly allowance to him.

He places the gold coin on the clerk's palm, along with a pile of soldi. It's barely enough, and it leaves his purse deflated.

The clerk counts the coins, and with a twist of his hand, hides them from sight. He turns his ledger to face Leonardo, taps a yellow-nailed finger on an empty line. "Write the name under which you wish to work."

The clerk dips the quill in ink and holds it up to Leonardo. When he grabs the quill with his left hand, the clerk pouts.

In the ledger, there are names, so many of them, all in neat rows. He hasn't thought about what he'd like his own to be. He knows that Andrea took his master's name, that Sandro's was a mere nickname—something about him being barrel-chested.

Leonardo? He has no clever names, only the ones he's heard the apprentices call him. Bastard, that's an easy one. Fawner, if they're feeling bitter. Fop, when he wears his pastel tunics. Sodomite, when they think he's not listening.

But to himself? He's only ever been Leonardo.

He brings the quill to the thick paper, presses hard to write his name. The letters are stilted, awkward.

Leonardo di Ser Piero da Vinci, he writes.

X

HE'S ARMORED IN FLAWLESS STEEL, STRADDLING A COAL-
black horse, a sopping, brocaded caparison beneath his thighs, a
ruby-crusted sword sheathed at his side. Riding down the Via Larga, the
throughway today a stream of mud—past the cathedral, onward still,
past the storm-gloomed Palagio. Over the Arno, its surface stabbed by
stubborn summer rain, hooves wetly clopping against dirt and stone,
the sound echoed by two dozen more horses, steered by friends and fellow bankers, old-blood nobles and former priors.

How good he must look at the front of them all.

But the ill weather has emptied the roads. The Oltrarno's streets are
still. No one to see him leave; no grand send-off. Only his mother had
stood in the courtyard, her clothes clinging to her frame, shrinking her.
She looked first at his brother on the horse beside him then to him. He
waited for her to say goodbye, to pray for their safe return, even for a final
admonishment, muttered under her breath. She said nothing.

Into the country he goes. His country. Verdant hills, vineyards, valleys. Sprawling farms, veined by plowed earth, and orchards of thick-
trunked trees with branches budding with cherries, red as blood.
Narrow bell towers circled by stone-walled towns. Roadside taverns
with chimneys huffing black smoke. He's blessed; Tuscany is a rich land,
a fertile one.

Today, he rides for Volterra. For weeks, the town had ignored the
soldiers outside its gates; they starved as grain was blocked from enter-
ing. But their larders finally emptied of the last jars of syrupy dates and
the remaining few hunks of hard cheese. At last, they've surrendered.

The siege was an expensive lesson for Volterra, for Lorenzo too. He
had hired the troops from Lord Montefeltro in Urbino, a small duchy
due east of Florence; he personally paid the condottiero for all twelve-
thousand men. When the Signoria learned of this, they shouted and
stammered—but that was all they could do. It was his money. If they
were to claim he was nothing more than a private citizen, they had

no say if he chose to spend his wealth on armies rather than portraits or frescoes.

The priors realized he had prevailed, that they could only acquiesce. And he made it easy for them to accept: he told them he had no desire to see the peninsula's peace upended; he stressed to them that he had instructed Montefeltro to lead a gentle siege, a civilized one. The twelve-thousand men? They were just for show. He wanted no deaths, no cannon fire, no skirmishes at the gates. He simply wanted the Volterrans to accept Florence's authority.

Now they finally have. And he, graciously, is travelling to them, alongside a delegation of Florence's finest men. Not to celebrate his victory, but so Volterra can see: how they were wrong to question him; how, as leader of their land, he simply wants them to prosper as Florence has. As he has.

THE RAIN FOLLOWS THE DELEGATION all morning long. It turns Lorenzo's cheeks clammy, it pools inside the pointed ends of his sabatons, pruning his toes. It darkens the sky, the grassy hillsides. It surges the brooks and creeks. The horses now whinny as they clamber over half-drowned bridges. The road ahead of them dissolves in a flood.

They change their route and instead approach Volterra from the south. Here, the familiar cypresses dwindle, the hills ease into long, flat plains. The songbirds, the squirrels, the frogs all vanish, and the clouds descend, growing thick. Flashes of lightning reveal cratered earth, striated with saffron-colored moss. Round pools bubble with steaming, murky water.

A horse comes alongside his. "What is this place?" Giuliano asks him.

"Morba." He knows the name from childhood, from conversations heard through his father's bedroom door. His mother fussing over his father's gout, telling him he must recover in a place to the south. "Father came here," he tells his brother. "There are hot springs, supposedly good for your health."

Giuliano balls a gauntleted fist against his nose. "I don't see how. It looks like hell."

He thinks: What will he say of Rome?

Water dribbles from his brother's nose. Underneath his helmet, his dark curls are pressed to his forehead, turned flat like pressed leaves. Still, he is somehow handsome and valiant-looking. He has it easy that way.

"I'm glad you're here," Lorenzo says. "That we have this time together before you leave."

"The pope hasn't—"

"Don't fret. He was always going to elevate his nephews first. But at the next consistory, he'll repay favors to those who have supported him. And given the tens of thousands he's already borrowed from us, you will surely be next."

"You said this would be settled within a year."

"And a year has not yet come and gone. I'll write to him again, if you wish. Reiterate your enthusiasm. I promise you'll have this."

He tries to imagine Giuliano, his locks gone, his hair tonsured. In garish scarlet, rather than this steel. Wandering around the Vatican, being chased about with censers. Seems a tragedy, a waste of his good looks. But his mother says the church is the prudent destination for second sons.

"If you want it, that is."

Giuliano's head whips. "Of course I want it. I need to make my own name too."

"And you will. You could head the church, and I'll be leading Florence."

But his brother doesn't smile at this. His mouth has twisted into a grimace.

"What's the matter?" Lorenzo asks.

"You can't smell it?"

"What?"

"The stench."

White clouds rise from the cracked land. They hang about them, denser than fog, vanishing the horizon. The men closest to him, the ones he can still see, are holding handkerchiefs to their faces. His uncle, his brother, his bank manager Nori and his friend Sigismondo, even his rival banker Jacopo de' Pazzi—who is always so ingratiating—all look as if they're about to retch.

Today, it's a blessing he can't smell. Nothing to do but keep riding across the bilious earth.

VOLTERRA APPEARS, A DISTANT SUGGESTION. Up high, half-streaked with clouds, on a lone hill rising from the low plains. They climb a cliff-edge road that circuits the hill in tighter and tighter circles, like a spooling ribbon. The horses huff. The rain abates, but water still drips from boots, capes, helmets; the clothes beneath remain stubbornly, coolly damp. The city towers remain out of sight, hidden above chiseled-looking cliffs, above the hill that now seems more like a mountain, that lifts them up above the rain-soaked plains, above the skim of mist that hung over the horizon. Now cerulean sky spreads above them, too bright.

Details emerge from the haze, as if a veil is being lifted. Opened barrels and empty, frayed fiaschi of wine. Boot prints and the trails of cart wheels in the rich earth. Ahead, above, the walls of Volterra are now rising suddenly, glistening bronze-like in the sudden sun that slices across the summit. Around the walls, the army's camp sprawls, a mass of tents and sooty bonfires and weatherworn sleeping mats that covers the road, that continues down the slope, like a patchwork pall draped over the hill.

The road flattens. Their pace slows. They continue, single file, navigating around men swigging wine, men already dazed from drink, men deeply asleep. Lorenzo straightens his back, nods kindly at each man they pass. He waits to see a glint, a recognition in their dirt-rimmed eyes, but they only stare dumbly back at him, all of them brawny and covered in grime, all of them with swords lying next to them in the grass.

He shifts in his saddle, looks back at Giuliano, at the rest of the men too. They are only two dozen among twelve thousand.

It's foolish to worry. These men are his, he reminds himself. He bought them.

ONWARD THEY GO, through the open gates. No one is waiting to greet them; the town is lifeless, the streets empty, the houses all boarded up. There are wide slips of loose earth. Splintered beams of wood. Piles of rubble. Volterra had endured days of heavy rain too.

Jacopo de' Pazzi has noticed this as well. The banker is scanning the collapsed homes; he's pricing out the flood's damage, calculating the loans the townspeople will need for repairs. Lorenzo wishes it was Guglielmo with him instead of his uncle, but Bianca is soon to have another child and wanted her husband close.

Embarrassment stabs him right in the lungs. They've arrived in polished steel with leather and silk underneath. They came to smile, to mark the end of an unfortunate misunderstanding. But now they look like gloaters.

He marks a tail of black smoke, twisting around a bell tower—the first sign of any life. He spurs his horse toward it, following a muddy road. The delegation staggers as debris crowds the road, but he presses onward at its front, eager to dismount. His throat has run dry.

He looks back. The others have stopped; they're gathering around his brother. Giuliano isn't speaking, isn't looking up the road, to him. He clutches at his helmet. He leans over the side of the white horse. He vomits.

Lorenzo rides back and waves the rest of the men away. He presses a wineskin into his brother's hands. Tells him, softly, how the ride was long, how he needs to drink. Giuliano, heaving, takes the pouch but doesn't drink. He stares back at him, the skin beneath his eyes pallid and shining. He shakes his head. Points to a spot behind Lorenzo.

At the roadside, in the coursing water, a plait of blonde hair bobs. He doesn't look at the face—he looks down to where crooked fingers fail to cover an ugly slit of a wound, the cloth around it tattered and stained.

It doesn't make sense. He was promised a bloodless surrender.

"We should continue," he shouts to his men. He spurs his horse onward.

Bright sun falls across the road and onto the bell tower emerging farther ahead. It catches the taverns with battered doors and the homes with no one inside. It shines on the bent, still figures abandoned at the roadside. On stabbed chests and bruised faces. Skirts bunched and torn.

He grips the reins tighter. This isn't what he paid for.

They reach a piazza, where finally there is life. Townspeople circle a bonfire, wider than it is tall, spitting sparks; they crouch over cauldrons, gather and guard their sparse belongings, sleep atop heaps of soiled fabric. None of them turn toward him, toward any of his men.

The thick smoke billows, scorching his eyes and abrading his throat. He coughs, he wheezes. The rest of the delegation clutch at their noses and gag.

He wipes the soot from his face, dismounts. His sabatons land hard on the setts, scattering crows into the air. He's unsteady; his feet are damp, aching, and swollen. He feels feverish underneath his armor. He pats his waist for his wineskin, then remembers he gave it to Giuliano. Nori, always attentive to his needs, God bless him, hands him his own. But the wine is hot and tastes of ash.

He looks ahead at the churning bonfire. He sees men crawling atop each other in the flames. He shakes his head, drinks more of the acrid wine, tries to dispel the strange vision. Then he notes the bare, blackened feet, curling and narrow, among the planks of wood. It's a pyre, not a bonfire. Like the ones that burned in Florence's streets during the plague.

"The Signoria will be furious," his uncle says. "You promised them no one would be harmed." He's shaking, looking as if he might fall to the ground and die on the spot.

I shouldn't have come here, he thinks.

"That's what I demanded of Montefeltro. He—"

"You hired mercenaries when you could have sent diplomats," Jacopo says, his blue eyes weary but steady. "What did you think would happen?"

"It's not what was agreed upon," he says, his voice hardening. "There wasn't meant to be any killing."

"They did what you paid them to do."

"The commune is here," Tommaso says, trying to silence them. At the base of the bell tower, a small group of men whispers to one another, watching them. He recognizes the bishop wearing his purple zucchetto, damp from the rain.

"We need to explain," Jacopo says. "Apologize, most of all."

The smoke has dried his mouth. His tongue feels swollen. "Apologize? They were the ones who first disobeyed. Not us."

"Disobeyed you. A citizen. Not the elected council."

"They ignored the republic's authority. That's insurrection."

"Does that matter now? After all this?"

"Of course it does," Lorenzo says. "If you disagree, then why don't you speak to them?"

"I will not own this," Jacopo says, defiant.

The wind shifts, carrying another black cloud from the pyre. He and Jacopo look away from each other, water welling in their eyes as they blink furiously.

Lorenzo walks, his sabatons clanging, back to his horse. He mounts, turns to his brother. "Come, Giuliano. We're leaving."

He doesn't look to see if his brother has listened; he is already riding off. Out from the piazza he goes, through its ashy haze, coughing hard as he rides, trying to lose the taste of char on his tongue. Down through the town, more quickly now, the hooves hammering the dirt, scattering the mud, casting it onto the buildings—burnt-out, broken-in, barricaded, he can't tell—all passing in a blur.

They all forced him to this point, he thinks. All of them. The Volterrans, who brought this on themselves. Montefeltro, who ignored his orders. Tommaso, who outlived his use. Jacopo, who was so arrogant.

He spurs his horse. Rides faster, away from it all. Rides harder, his thighs aching, his saddle beating against his bones. He hears only the growing rush of his race, and—yes, there he is—his brother chasing closely behind. He feels cool tears streaming down his cheeks as he flies out the city gates, past the hired arms who leap out of his path, who shout curses at him that he happily returns.

The road empties, it steepens, and he plunges down it, to the hellish plains, to, farther yet, Florence.

XI

THE RAIN IS RELENTLESS, THE WATER PERSISTENT, FINDING A new way into his house with each passing day. It slips between roof tiles or underneath windowpanes. It soaks the chimney bricks and crawls across beams and seeps down walls.

He first saw the ceiling stains in the downstairs salon, empty save for a soft blue couch. Yesterday, water pattered off the untarnished pans, hanging along the kitchen wall. Today, it invades his bedroom with its mattress covered by neatly folded quilts and a cypress-wood cassone at its foot.

Salviati fetches the pail from the salon, places it beside his writing desk. The water plunks against the iron bottom. Again and again. An unfathomably loud sound.

He should move to another room. But every other room will already be dark; the sun is on its descent. Here, at least, he can glimpse its last glow through the westward window. On his desk, he can see his cousin's letter yawning open, teasing him.

It's a social invitation, he reminds himself. Nothing more. Jacopo is visiting from Florence, and he's invited Salviati to join him and Francesco that evening. In truth, there's no mention of money in the letter, not even the slightest allusion to what he's borrowed from his cousin's bank. Since he arranged the loan a year ago, Francesco has sent him no invitation to sup, has paid no unannounced visits, has not spoken a single word about repayment. And in that absence, it became so easy for Salviati to pretend: that there was no reason to worry about money; that he was living a respectable life in a respectable house; that he was indeed rising in the church.

He picks up the letter, reads it again. He can explain himself, he thinks. The loan was meant to be a temporary arrangement, though he supposes all loans are meant to be such things. He could tell Jacopo how carefully he spent the borrowed money, how he kept a ledger of every purchase made. Was he really so indulgent? Tailored cassocks, some doublets, one or two cloaks too. This moldering house—a modest thing, in Trastevere, where the streets are still dirt. Only the most essential household staff. Quality, not quantity, he told himself. A cook, named Maddalena, who had a heart-shaped face and came to his masses; who, one evening, he had seen sleeping on the church steps. A servant boy, Carlo, who loitered outside derelict San Pietro, cap in hand, day after day.

He puts the letter down. How pleasant it had been: to sit in a house with more than one room, to have a hot supper ready when he returned each evening, to have a boy to carry his letters to the Vatican. These were not extravagant pleasures. And they gifted him so much time, time he spent at the church, his church, which he had neglected in Rovere's first months as pope. Once again, he took the confessions of the widow Beatrice, watched her face soften as he gave her absolution. He had a new closeness with God, a warming satisfaction that he was finally living the way He intended for him. And this feeling wasn't confined only to his church. After all, at the Vatican when the pope complimented his new clothes, was that not God's approval too?

He sensed his ambitions nearing, for it was such a prosperous time. Rovere had made Piero a cardinal, had made Girolamo the captain of his army. He was next, he thought. A simple bishopric. He prayed for it every night. He still prays for it.

The months numbered. His purse lightened. He began to worry that God was withholding his bishopric. That he was punishing him—for his avarice, for failing to be humble, for putting his advancement before the salvation of his congregation. Most of all, for resorting to usury. It didn't matter that all the cardinals and even the pope did the same; he was meant to be better than them. Borrowing money was the Florentine way of living, and he had left that city for a reason.

Now, still without a bishopric, he has no benefices coming to him. When Francesco eventually calls in his payment, the pittance that was his priest's salary will be as useful as a pillow filled with a single goose-feather.

And he thinks that day has finally come.

He stands from his desk and meets his reflection in the tall mirror along the wall. His cassock, dark wool, mocks him. He's going to a tavern tonight. Of all places. He should have demurred, but Francesco already thinks he's holier-than-thou; he didn't want Jacopo to find him joyless too.

He pulls off his cassock, tosses it onto his bed. He reaches into his wooden chest, digs until he feels a soft twill weave. He takes out a doublet, handsome and tan. Unworn. He puts it on, along with a cloak, and turns toward the mirror. The cloak drapes all the way to his ankles, gently hanging over his body, disguising his leanness that has only worsened of late. Beneath it, the doublet's color is a pleasant change from his usual dark browns; it transforms him. If the light is low enough in the tavern, his tonsured hair might not be visible; he might even pass as a merchant. When Jacopo shouts at him to repay his loan, any man watching will think Salviati is simply a man of business, struck with the misfortune of a bad season. The onlookers won't dwell on it, won't joke about it, for they'll know this pain.

Looking in the mirror, he tries softening his countenance, tries smiling. But over his reflected shoulder, he can still see his discarded cassock twisted across his bed quilts. He knows what he's doing by wearing this outfit: he's hiding, and it's useless trying to hide from God. He shouldn't be going to a tavern to meet with bankers. He should be going to Sant'Agata to confess what he's done.

He leaves his bedroom and walks down the creaking stairs to the stone-floored kitchen, where Maddalena is mending a pair of his hose by the light of a squat tallow candle. He stops in the doorway to watch her work. The warm, flickering light deepens her swart cheeks that have grown fuller since she came to work for him; it turns purple the full, bottom lip that she bites as she sews. She told him she came from Sicily when he asked her.

"I'll be late returning tonight. No need to keep a candle lit."

She nods. "I was thinking about tomorrow's supper. I could find us a capon, if you'd like."

"Just sausage is fine," he says, trying to find the smile he practiced in his mirror. He can't afford capon. In truth, he can't afford to keep her as his maid. He's already had to dismiss the boy, and he knows it must look improper to live here, alone, with an unmarried woman. He knows most men would say she's beautiful, but she stirs nothing within him. That particular restraint of the priesthood has never been a challenge for him.

When he looks at her, he feels only the guilt of knowing the fate that will befall her—the same fate that seemed to await every woman in the Testaments: to care for a man, only to have him abandon her.

Through the door, out into the garden, the trees shade blue. The hour grows late. There's no time to seek forgiveness from a priest, not tonight. He'll have to find absolution by humbling himself before his cousin, by pleading for his forgiveness, kneeling on a sawdust-covered floor. He'll bear Jacopo's reproach because he deserves it. And every day forward, he'll work tirelessly to repay his debt. That will be his penance for all of this.

THE TAVERN IS A GODFORSAKEN PLACE. A cellar unmarked on its outside, accessed by a narrow flight of crumbling steps. Inside, the ceiling is low and arched. Grime-glassed lanterns glow a dim yellow. Men huddle close to one another at small, round tables. All of them are guarding something in their hands: playing cards. And at the center of every table, there's a messy pile of coins waiting to be won.

"Before you complain—Francesco chose the place, not me." Jacopo catches him in a firm embrace.

He should leave this place, but he can't. God has brought him here because he's no different from the gamblers and drunkards playing their illicit card games; in the Lord's eyes, he, too, is a sinner.

"You look good, cousin," his cousin says.

Jacopo's good humor is unexpected, disarming. He has missed this man, the closest thing to a friend he's known in his life. "As do you," he says.

Truthfully, the years have made war with his cousin's face. It is thatched with wrinkles, stubbled with gray hairs.

"I thought priests weren't supposed to lie." Jacopo laughs, but when Salviati doesn't smile, his face sinks. "Relax. Let's have a drink."

Jacopo leaves him for the barmaid. Alone, he lets himself dissolve into the scenery. To his left, there's a table for bassetta. Men gather round it, all flushed, all shouting over each other. He doesn't know how it's played, doesn't care to learn. He heard one cardinal played and lost thousands, a year's benefices, in a single game. More than his own loan, lost for sport. He can't fathom it.

Jacopo returns, handing him a tankard with froth dribbling over its rim. They sit on two stools along the wall, away from the tables.

"Francesco?" Salviati thinks to ask.

"He sends his regrets. Ate some bad trout, he said."

That, at least, will soften his humiliation.

"I'll pray for his recovery," he says.

"Don't waste your prayers. He's a reprobate if there ever was one. I sent him here to manage the local branch, perhaps bring in a new account or two, but all he seems to do is go feasting and hunting and whoring, night after night." Jacopo drinks, then wipes the foam from his chin. "Mea culpa. I shouldn't be complaining of such things in front of a priest."

"Unless you're at confession," Salviati says.

This is his opening, he thinks. The next words are so simple: I, too, have something to confess.

"I do have something to complain about to you, cousin."

Salviati grips his tankard, holds his breath. But then Jacopo looks at him with those eyes—still a serene blue even in the dim—and smiles. "You're terrible at writing me, so I know very little about your life in Rome. Tell me everything."

His mind rushes, spins, as if he's had six ales instead of one. Jacopo must know nothing of the loan; Francesco has unexpectedly kept their secret. But that still doesn't change his purpose here tonight.

"Where to begin?" he mutters.

"You're still with Rovere, yes?"

"I am, and his ascension has been a blessing. But my own has been slower. Not that I'm ungrateful. The pope has far more important matters than my own advancement. But I feel as if I'm wandering the desert, nothing on the horizon no matter where I look.

"And I know that's foolish. That I have no right to be dissatisfied in any way. I'm in extraordinary circumstances, far beyond what I thought was possible when I arrived here. But I'm tethered, my whole future yoked—"

"By the whims of another."

Salviati nods. He doesn't have this rapport with anyone in Rome.

"This may be no comfort to hear, but your situation—it's nothing unique. We all live at the pleasure of someone more powerful. You might call him pope. Or God. For me, his name is Lorenzo."

"I never liked him."

"I liked Cosimo. He was a reasonable man. Indulgent, yes, but in the right way. Lorenzo, I can't grasp. He's civil toward me, invites me to join a delegation to Volterra—then, afterward, nearly my whole family is left off the ballot for the council. Even Guglielmo, and he's married to Lorenzo's sister. And I don't know anyone who could do that but him. As for why? I can't think of any decent reasons beyond pettiness or vanity."

Jacopo drinks deeply from his tankard, then lets out a long breath. "Everyone still speaks of Florence like it's the grandest city in the world. But is it? Perhaps once, when I was young. But now?" He shrugs. "Tell me: do you miss it?"

"Never," Salviati says. There was nothing for him to miss.

"You were wise to leave when you did. I was too foolish to see it then. Rovere, he's building something here. Rome is rising. Lorenzo? Florence? I don't know."

Change the subject now, he thinks. Don't listen to this prattle. He left this all behind, yet it still tugs at him.

"What do you think of the brother?" he asks.

"Giuliano? I don't, truthfully. Handsome lad. Keeps his mouth shut, unlike his brother."

"Lorenzo made quite a plea to the pope to make him a cardinal, and Rovere seemed pleased with the idea."

That turns his cousin's head. "Really? That'd be a clever move. What do you make of his prospects?"

"That's beyond my sphere."

"Yet you've worked your way into the pope's inner circle."

"It's not what it seems," Salviati admits. "I'm little more than an attendant."

"That's foolish talk. You clearly have the pope's favor, so why aren't you using it? You say you're waiting for your promotion? Make yourself indispensable. Listen to everything he says. Be at his side, always. Wash his holy ass if you must. Eventually there will be a moment of opportunity, and you mustn't hesitate. You must seize upon it. What you did to get there? You'll forget about it as soon as you get what you deserve.

"Think. You could've been one of my bankers. But you said no to that, and I'm glad you did. You had larger designs for your future. Look at you: you're on the cusp of something great. So don't balk now. You say the pope likes the idea of a Florentine cardinal. Why can't that be you?"

"God willing," he says, the words barely louder than a whisper, yet their slip surprises him. It's the truth of the matter, isn't it? His path could go to dust before his feet, leave him with his modest parish, as a priest whose little income is drained by an ever-growing debt. But, by the grace of God, he might still win a bishopric—or, yes, perhaps a cardinalship—with benefices that would make his loan seem like a paltry sum. And what help would confessing his loan to Jacopo, would earning his cousin's shame, be to either outcome?

Jacopo stands, peers into his tankard. "First, we need more ale. Then, we play bassetta."

"I can't do that."

"Relax, cousin. If no one knows, what's the harm?"

"I can't afford it."

"You're being modest," Jacopo says, touching Salviati's sleeve, rubbing its fabric between his fingers. "Clearly you're doing well for yourself."

The ale sloshes in his gut. "You'd have to teach me."

Jacopo smiles. "It'd be my pleasure."

"Just one game."

"That's all we need. Shouldn't we be lucky with God on our side?"

XII

HE KNOCKED. HE WAITED. HE KNOCKED AGAIN. NOW HIS
father is standing in the open doorway.

"Don't just stand there. You're letting in the cold," he's told.

He follows his father through rooms lit by candles, their flames wavering in a cool, persistent draft. He passes a stairwell leading to bedrooms he has never seen: the room his father shares with his stepmother; the others empty, he presumes, though he knows his father has his designs for them. Might one of them be set aside for him? He doesn't think so.

He keeps behind his father, matches his quick, steady steps. He realizes he now looks down on the man; he can even see the top of his cap—squirrel-lined, made of a stiff weave. Different from the shapeless linen thing he used to wear. He sees, too, that his doublet is velvet. Expensive.

He wonders if it might not be such an imposition to ask his father for money.

They come to a dining room, the table set with pewter plates and cups. His father sits at its head, and Leonardo walks toward the chair to his right.

"That's Francesca's," his father says.

He takes the chair opposite, and his father pours himself wine. "You wrote that you have something to share."

"We can wait for Francesca," Leonardo offers.

"No use. Go on."

He reaches for the pitcher of wine, grips it tightly as he pours. "I registered at the painter's confraternity. I'm a master painter now."

"What does that mean?"

"That I'm no longer an apprentice. That I can work on my own."

"And that makes you a master?" His father brings his cup to his wry lips.

He has nothing to say. Did he not have the same thought when he registered at the guild? He still had no work, no money for pigments, for panels. Certainly not enough to rent out a space for a workshop.

Francesca walks into the room bearing a platter of sausages and arti-chokes. She sets down the food and comes beside Leonardo, brushing his cheek with a brief, stilted kiss. They're strangers to each other, really. He was already at Andrea's workshop when she came into his father's life. Still, when she sits across from him, he sees that she has a kind smile. That she's perceptive, too, for she only needs a single glance at her hus-band's face to know she must quickly place the thick sausage and drip-ping artichoke onto his empty plate.

His father begins eating while he and Francesca fill their plates. "They're not hot. We expected you a half hour ago."

"I'm sorry, I was—" He stops. No use telling his father that he walked past the house a dozen times before approaching the door. It was only when his hands went numb that he finally coaxed himself to knock.

His father looks at him, blinks. Then he returns to his food. "So you're done working for Andrea. What now?"

"He says I can open my own workshop."

"The other apprentices that have finished, is this what they've done too?"

"Some do," he says, taking a bite of artichoke. "Sandro and Domen-ico have their own spaces now. But others sometimes paint in someone else's workshop, just not as an apprentice."

"These ones who don't open their own place, Andrea thinks you're better than them?"

"Yes," he says, looking down at his plate and pushing the meat aside. When he turns back to his father, he sees that he's glaring. Not at him—at the uneaten sausage.

"So how do you make this happen, opening your own workshop?" his father asks.

"I would need to rent out a space of my own. Purchase the necessary supplies. Bring in commissions, most of all."

"Your allowance can help with the costs, at least."

"And I'm grateful for it. Very much so," he says, balling his napkin in his fist. "But it's not enough to start a workshop. I already had to spend over a florin on my dues alone."

"Not enough?" His father puts down his fork and knife. "Most men your age have already been working. For years. They've been saving their money so they can open their own shops, so they can buy a house of their own too. They're thinking about family. They're not acting like boys."

At the far end of the room, the hearth weakly hisses.

"I didn't mean to offend," Leonardo finally says.

"I know. You've never meant to offend. That's precisely the problem, isn't it?" His father shakes his head. "You know what most of my work is these days? Wedding contracts. Nice, pretty girls with a dowry that can change a man's situation. You're grown now, still a young man, yes, but old enough to start thinking about such an arrangement for yourself. A decent dowry could solve your predicament. That money could get you started."

Cold sweat trickles down his back. "I don't know if I'll want to wed."

"Nonsense. Every man does, save for the priests."

"Not Andrea."

"Perhaps I was mistaken to send you to him, if he's put these fancies in your head."

"He hasn't. The words are unexpectedly loud. "I enjoy being on my own," he adds in a quieter voice. Though the thought of it scares him.

"If you insist on being obstinate in this matter, then I suppose you'll just have to sell a painting to bring in the money you need for a shop."

He rests his knife on the plate. He considers his father's soft doublet. Well cut, neatly hemmed. His father has coin, has the clients, he tells himself. He can do this for him.

"A painting takes time. Months, if not longer. And I'd still require the right introductions to win my first commission."

"Did you come here for money or for introductions, Leonardo?"

Both, but he daren't say it.

Francesca places a hand on his father's arm, rubs it gently. His father's stern expression eases, softening into something he doesn't quite recognize. "I can't give you money for the workshop, but I know some of my clients are looking for artists to hire. If they're in need of a painting, perhaps I could mention your name."

He smiles. Andrea was right. "Thank you. Truly."

"What name are you working under?"

"What do you mean?"

"I manage Andrea's contracts. I know Verrocchio isn't his real name. What's your artist's name?"

"It's the same."

"Come again?"

"Leonardo," he says. "Leonardo di Ser Piero da Vinci."

His father takes off his cap, tosses it onto the table. "Why would you do that?" he asks, combing his fingers through flattened, loose strands of black hair.

The hat rests against the edge of Leonardo's plate, a smear of grease wetting the tips of its fur trim. He picks it up—it's surprisingly plush— and tries to wipe away the mark.

"It's my name," he says.

"No, it's not. It's *my* name. You are Leonardo. Only that." He snatches the cap from his hands. "You can leave."

He looks up, expecting to meet that familiar, cold stare. But his father is not looking at him—he's turned to Francesca, whose hands are gathered in front of her small, flat belly.

She'd make a good Madonna, he thinks. She just needs the child.

Leonardo stands. When he looks down at his father, he notes the strong ridge of his nose, the one they share, the nostrils flaring with each breath.

"Wait," his father says, his chair scraping against the floor.

Leonardo listens to him walk, heavy-footed, out of the room and up the stairwell.

He should leave. That he thought his father would be impressed that he's a master painter? What a laugh! He will never be what his father wants. He's always been too peculiar, too prone to daydream. To his father, he is wayward and recalcitrant. A stubborn mistake. No amount of overpainting or whitewash could conceal that.

Pewter clatters. Francesca has stood; she's gathering the grease-streaked plates from dinner.

"Let me help," he says, picking up his plate, his knife and fork.

"No. You're a guest here." Francesca tugs the plate from his fingers. "He does care for you. I hope you know that. All he wants is something to be proud of."

No, he wants to tell her. All he wants is a true-born son, one who can follow his example and become a notary. But to say such a thing would be a cruelty.

They say nothing more to each other, for at the sound of his father's returning footsteps, Francesca retreats from the room.

When the two of them are alone, his father sighs, pressing a single florin into his palm. "I don't want to see you become a pauper."

"Thank you," Leonardo says, thinking of how the coin might sustain him another month, maybe two. But it certainly wasn't enough to rent a workshop.

"You'll still get your allowance. But nothing more than that. You have to make it on your own. It'll do you good. Make you learn."

Learn what? he wants to ask.

HE LEAVES WITHOUT SAYING GOODBYE, the same way he left all those years ago, from a different house, as a different boy. That country boy who didn't yet know the throughways and side streets of Florence, whose mind was crowded with so many questions, who only wanted to find a way to take his imaginings and render them real. That boy was merely curious, a sky-gazing dreamer who thought he could transform himself into anything. Now he knows more, too much more.

But is that even true? He might now know that vine black has a warmer, brownish tone to it, that lamp black is the truer, deeper black— but what does that matter out in the city without his brush? He knows only useless things, substanceless things, not anything that matters. Not where he's walking, not what he'll do tomorrow, or the next day, or in the weeks, the months, the years to come.

He stands, unmoored, beneath the Palagio. He should go back to the workshop, but he can't bear the thought of Andrea's disappointment, of having to trudge up the stairs and climb back into his narrow bed, beside all the tittering apprentices.

In the piazza, the colors are darkening, westward reds and yellows staining to darker hues. By day, this is a crowded place, priors and bankers and guildsmen marching every direction, men he needs to impress, from whom he needs to win work. But tonight, there is no one. Only him, and who is he? A master painter? No, he isn't master of anything.

His bag slides from his shoulder. He opens it, digs out his coin purse. Inside is the florin his father gave him, along with a few soldi and denari. A sum of no significance. He turns toward the piazza's south side, where the dirty streets of the Baldracca tangle like a thicket. A good place to go to become nobody.

When the Buco appears before him, the tavern is unchanged, its windows fogged and glowing. Tonight he doesn't stand to look at the details. He walks to the door and opens it before he has time to doubt himself.

The interior is unremarkable. Long tables with surfaces darkened by spilled ale. Tired-looking men nursing their tankards. Air flecked with sawdust and a trace of chimney-smoke. It's a disappointment, really.

Then the men look up from their ales. Their backs stiffen; they turn gently in his direction. Behind their tankards, their mouths curl with a faint suggestion that requires no words. He catches round hazel eyes, catches narrow brown eyes—all of them lingering too long, curious and unabashed. The kind of look he always tries to keep himself from making.

He flushes. He knows this sensation; he's felt it on his abandoned nights of walking the riverbanks. He's wanted. It shouldn't be unexpected—he's good-looking, younger than most of the men here. But this feeling, and its arrival, is a surprise. So is how good it feels.

At the rear of the room, there's a staircase, a row of men staggered on its steps. All of them his age, give or take a few years. All holding a tankard of ale. But they're not sipping from them, and Leonardo notices this detail, notices how they hold them at such a careless angle that their contents should be spilling.

Then he sees him—on the highest stair, almost out of view. He's a year older, now more man than boy. But he's still so familiar. His fingers, red and calloused, curled around an empty tankard. His legs, delicate yet muscled, that Leonardo etched into his memory, sketch by sketch.

He jolts. What a fool he must look, standing, blush-cheeked, just a step from the door. He turns away from the men on the staircase, walks toward the bar, where before he can even rest his hands against the wood counter, a woman turns to him, asks him what he wants.

"An ale," he tells her, looking at her hair—red, almost vermilion.

Too quickly, she fills a tankard and smacks it down in front of him.

"What else?" She nods at the men standing on the staircase.

He wets his lips. "The tall one, with the curled hair," he says, without having to look.

"A room too?"

He nods, uses some of his coins to pay the matron. It's a good bargain, compared to his dues.

She calls the boy—Iac, his name is—and he walks down the stairs. When he smiles at Leonardo, there's a calming recognition in it. Iac curls his arm around his elbow. Wordlessly, he guides him up the stairs and into a bedroom, shutting the door behind them.

The room is plain but pleasant; it smells of woodsmoke and marjoram. There's a wide bed with a neatly laid stack of quilts on top. There's a purling fire in the hearth, warding off the night's chill. It's quiet, almost silent—so starkly different from the bedroom at the workshop.

Iac lights the candles at the bedside and sits along the edge of the bed. He looks back at Leonardo, who has not moved, who remains within arm's reach of the door.

"What would you like?" Iac finally asks, kicking one boot off, and then the other.

Leonardo's teeth quietly chatter. "I don't know," he mutters. The words for what he wants seem so base and ugly.

Amusement flickers in the boy's features. "I'll undress. Would you like that?"

He doesn't know if he's said yes, if he's even nodded, but a belt falls to the floor and Iac pulls his brown tunic over his head. Golden hair lolls onto freckled shoulders. Ridges of ribs appear with an intake of breath, only to vanish a moment later. This—his body—is what Leonardo remembers. The gentle curve of its torso, the long delicate neck—he knows all these shapes, he has sketched these lines. By candlelight, so many times has he stared at their inky shadows. But here is something new: sparse, hay-colored hairs, rounding his navel, leading downward.

Iac rolls down his hose, and Leonardo shuts his eyes. He listens to the bed creak, to Iac's feet, bare on the stone floor, grow closer. He feels a hand on his hip. A tug, as his belt is undone, and a clatter when it lands. Now there is one hand on his shoulder, and another is reaching beneath his loosened tunic and tracing the seam of his hose. He thinks he should tell Iac to stop. He wants to apologize for how his body, stiff and vulgar, has betrayed him.

But he doesn't tell him to stop, and when Iac clutches him, he opens his eyes.

He sees Iac watching him, watching him in the same, curious way he did on that afternoon outside the workshop, looking back at his study, looking back at him.

Leonardo's left hand, always so steady, is trembling. He takes Iac into his palm, and the sight of this stirs him more. Without thinking, he begins to move his hand. He tugs softly.

"Would you like to lie with me?" Iac asks.

"Yes—if that's what you'd like too."

"Yes." Iac laughs. "I'd very much like that." He reaches down, stills his hand. Then he steps away to grab a small vial from a table. "Olive oil," he explains. "I'm going to put some on you, if you agree. Like this." He sits on the edge of the bed, then pours the amber liquid into his palm, streaking it across his belly, his cock.

Leonardo—he is staring at this dumbly; he is thinking how much like linseed oil it looks; he is imagining oils blending into it, the boy's body turned into a painted panel. And Iac notices this, Leonardo's awe-struck face, for he stops touching himself. Says, "We can use spit, if you'd prefer?"

"No," he manages to say. "The oil."

"Good. Come here."

Iac grabs him with a slick hand and guides him closer to the bed. He shifts aside the quilts, moves farther back onto the mattress. He spreads his legs, pulls Leonardo to kneel in the space between them. Then he oils Leonardo's body too, turns it softer than satin.

He takes Leonardo's left palm, pours more oil onto it. He leads his hand beneath him, between him. "You feel that, right?" He pushes Leonardo's fingers, urges them to search. "Put it there."

He obliges, blundering at first. But Iac is a patient teacher. He strokes Leonardo's chin, wraps his legs around Leonardo's back, coaxes him closer.

And then he feels it: a sensation different from anything he's ever known. A feeling not to understand, one he knows he couldn't paint, not with a thousand pigments. He falls into it, and it rushes past, as if time itself has been oiled. He and Iac, they stroke, they clutch, then—in a gasp, a spasm, a damp, hot rush—it's over. So much more quickly than he expected.

A steadiness drapes over him now, toe to crown, like a pall. A calm haze crawls across his mind, blurring away everything else. He's not thinking about his father; he's not thinking about Andrea; he's not thinking about where he's going to live or how he'll afford pigment. He's thinking about nothing, and it feels wonderful.

Then words, whispered into his ear, dispel the peace: "You're different."

This is his curse, he thinks. Everything he has just felt was nothing more than a brief reprieve from that truth. He rises from the bed, his nose wrinkling at the stink of sex.

A hand, soft and warm, grasps his fingers.

"You drew me," Iac says. "I remember."

He looks back. Iac's face faintly glows in the last of the firelight. On his lips is a smile, a guileless one.

"I remember too." He climbs back onto the bed, reaching toward Iac with his left hand. He traces the boy's nose, his mouth, his jaw. He imagines his hand wetted with linseed, each fingertip dusted with pigment, madder and massicot, vine black and umber.

He sees the boy before him transmuted onto panel. New visions are spinning in his head. He wants to paint them all.

"What's your name?" Iac asks.

He doesn't hesitate. "Leonardo."

XIII

HE STANDS STRADDLE-LEGGED ON THE PLAYING FIELD. HIS
whole body shines from his bare, heaving chest down to the silk of his
billowing, loudly colored hose. In this moment, he thinks he is no different from the rest of the players—his skin is bruised, his eyes are fierce
and focused, craving the inevitable violence of the game.

His brother tried to dissuade him from playing. His friends tried to
lure him away for weekends of falconry instead. He didn't listen, and
now they—Giuliano, Guglielmo, Sigismondo, even his new secretary,
Agnolo—have come to watch his match.

Calcio is a hot-blooded game, despite the cold. Played on the frost-
hardened dirt of an emptied piazza. The players don't wear armor, they
don't wear gloves—they don't even wear shirts. They punch, they brawl,
they claw for the ball. Their winter-dried skin tears, their chapped lips
split. When they shout, their breath fogs.

The stitched leather ball, the two netted goals, the uniform hose—
Lorenzo has needed this. Something brash and obvious when everything else in his life has become so murky. Plead to a pope to make your
brother a cardinal, and he'll ignore your letters. Remind a town who
owns their mine, and they'll toss its owner from a tower. Pay a soldier to
siege a town, and he'll pillage it instead. What use are promises when no
one keeps to them?

In calcio, words are worthless, and the aim is clear: score at any cost.
This, he understands.

The match begins. Feet kick, dirt swirls. Lorenzo sees the ball wrestled among a storm of players. Then a man in the blue hose of the oppos-
ing team comes running toward him. The ball is between his feet; he's
preparing to dash for the goal.

The man's nose, bulbous and red, is easy to aim for. When his fist
meets the man's face, it's not the pain that startles him—it's how vis-
ceral the impact is: the scabbed skin along his knuckles ripping open;
the quiet but discernible pop of the man's nose collapsing; the hot and
syrupy blood running between his fingers.

The man touches his face, and the ball rolls away from him. Lorenzo dashes for it. He pushes his own men out of the way, for it's clear none of them see it. Anonymous kicks jolt his shins, but still he runs—runs until he can feel the ball against his toes. Now he curls the ball away from the tangle, kicks it toward the far end of the piazza. Here, there are no legs to jump over. There's only the tattered net ahead of him. He barrels toward the center, curls his leg back, prepares to kick.

At his midpoint, a tearing. His body is thrashed, it pulls against itself in every direction. Churning pain courses up his spine and suddenly he is looking sideways at the brittle weeds sprouting from the dirt. But he can feel the ball between his feet. He can still score. He pushes himself upright, vomit riling in his throat, and he readies a kick.

A fist. He sees it the moment before it meets his jaw. Long enough only to grit his teeth, to hear grains of sand crunch between them. Then his vision turns to smashed glass. He's kneeling now. He doesn't know when that happened. There's blood in his mouth. His tongue laps at it.

Something is wrong, so he stands again. This time, he sees only a blur of smeary red fingers. He staggers backward. His left eye struggles to blink against the stinging fluid pouring over his vision.

He doesn't see the final blow. One moment he is standing, the next his body is limp, descending toward the ground. He feels cold, stony dirt spraying his chest. And then he feels nothing.

HE WAKES TO A DRYNESS in his throat. Then comes an approximation of pain dithering in his fogged head. Water laps against his cracked lips, drowns his tongue.

He can't swallow, can't form the words to say so. The water leaks, tepid, from the corners of his mouth. The back of his head is damp too.

He moves his hand, and his bones seem to grind against each other, unaligned, as if he is a broken majolica plate poorly glued together again. His face is tender everywhere he touches; he feels his wounds and their tacky residue.

He opens his eyes. He is home. In bed, splayed atop his quilt, a sweat-damp pillow beneath his throbbing head. His brother is standing at his bedside.

"How?" The word rips from his chest.

"You were thrown to the ground. The man cried when he saw it was you. Wouldn't stop even when we told him you would've done the same to him."

"Did we win?" His speech is slow and labored.

"I don't know. We all carried you home before it finished. But I sent the others away, except Agnolo. I didn't want Mother or Clarice to notice."

This was wise. "Thank you."

Giuliano fills a small bowl from a pitcher on his bedside table and brings it to his mouth. This time, he can swallow it.

"You kept getting back up," his brother says.

Lorenzo tries to smile, but Giuliano is shaking his head. "Even after you were hit, you kept trying to stand. You wouldn't stop."

"I wanted to score," he says.

"I know."

The bedroom door groans, and his brother's head turns. Lorenzo can't raise himself up to see, but at the familiar, quick patter of feet, the throbbing in his head grows stronger. The room dims as his mother's silhouette blocks the window and the waning daylight. Giuliano retreats from the bedside, and now she's hanging over Lorenzo, overlarge, her face gentle but plaintive. Like a frescoed Madonna on a church ceiling.

"You should know better. Both of you," she says, her voice weary and resigned. "Leave us, Giuliano."

His brother obeys.

He expects a certain look on his mother's face; one with gritted teeth and flared nostrils. Instead, her expression is vague, her soft features forced stiff, like a bolt of fabric pulled taut.

"I don't expect you to understand," he says.

"It's easy to understand. But I didn't think you'd be so reckless. Jousts? I don't like them, but there's honor in them, traditions to be upheld. Even a tilter has the sense to wear armor. But calcio? It's a brutish game. Stupid and pointless."

"It's a game for men. You—"

"You think I can't take violence? A woman bleeds more in her life than any man could stomach."

He thinks of wan Clarice with his infant son in her arms. Her hand-maid, carrying away bloodied sheets.

His mother sits on the edge of the mattress. "You went out there today and let the others make you into just another player on the pitch. You can't allow them to do that to you."

"You sound like you're talking to father," he says, hoping to wound.

"Hardly," she says, unbothered. But then she stands, her hands ball. "Your father never had the opportunity to make such mistakes. He was twice your age and riddled with gout when it was finally his chance to lead. He only had five years. You've already enjoyed three. And this is what you're doing with them?"

He can't listen to this, not now.

"I have time," he says, then shuts his eyes, hoping she'll disappear. He feels her body leave the mattress, hears slow footsteps, wonders if by some miracle she has indeed left him, that he can rest again until every-thing stops hurting.

Something soft and cool grazes his forehead. She's not gone. She's scrubbing his face with a linen towel wrapped around her fingers. "Just because you have more time than your father did doesn't mean you get to make more mistakes. Your youth, it's a boon and a bane." She wipes at a gash along his cheek, scrubs at it as if she were scouring the bottom of an iron pot. "First Volterra, now this? Be sensible, Lorenzo. Let me help you."

Something trickles into his eyes, burning them. "You think I need help?"

She puts down the cloth and wipes her hands against the quilt. "I won't always be around, you know. Let me in, while I can still be here. Especially if your brother is soon to be in Rome."

"Who knows when that will be. I've waited over a year, and—"

His mother places a letter in his hand, bottom side up, showing the pope's stamped insignia.

"It came this morning. After you had left for your little game."

A miracle she didn't break the wax herself, he thinks.

He'd rather not open such a letter before an audience, but he has no choice. He breaks the seal, his fingers stiff and clumsy. He reads through the pope's words once, and then out of disbelief, reads through them again.

"Are we to have a cardinal in the family?" his mother asks.

"There's not a blasted thing about Giuliano," he says, holding up the paper. She snatches it from his hands and reads it herself. Her eyes narrow as she parses the words, then they return to the top of the letter. Like him, she reads it twice.

It's a request for money. Not from Lorenzo personally, of course, but the bank. Such demands are routine; typically, they're sent directly to the bank's branch in Rome, so Lorenzo rarely sees them himself. And this is far from the pope's first request—he has already borrowed plenty. Lorenzo's been kept well-informed of the pope's wish to refresh Rome before the celebrations of the Jubilee. New roads, new bridges, new churches. Like dressing a goat in taffeta, he thinks.

This request is different. It has come to him, in Florence. It's significant and far from holy. The money is for Girolamo Riario, who has been offered the countship of Imola as part of his new bride's dowry. Or, at least, the promise of the countship, provided he pays his new father-in-law, Galeazzo Sforza, duke of Milan, forty thousand ducats.

"I never liked Galeazzo," his mother mutters.

Few do. Lorenzo once heard he executed a man by nailing him, alive, to his own coffin. But one must overlook such rumors for the sake of diplomacy. "Milan is our best ally."

"*Was* our best ally, you mean. He's cozying up to Rome."

He considers this. Florence, Rome, Milan, Naples, and Venice. Their constant, exhausting dance. If Galeazzo was souring on him, if he preferred to league Milan with Rome instead of Florence, that would leave Lorenzo with King Ferrante as his only ally. Naples has a powerful army, sure, but it was far from Florence—and Rome's lands rested uncomfortably between them. And then there was Venice to worry about too.

"Galeazzo only married off his bastard daughter to the pope," he tells his mother.

"True, but now he's also willing to give Imola to the pope's nephew, when you already offered to purchase it."

"Son, not nephew."

"Really?" she asks, smirking.

"If you saw the two of them, you'd know it. God as my witness."

His mother sighs. "I liked Imola for us."

He did too. It's a well-sized city on the trade roads between Florence and Venice. A pleasing, logical expansion for his republic.

"Forty thousand," he says. "When I offered Galeazzo a hundred thousand."

"I told you that was foolish."

So did his bankers. They said he was mad, that a hundred thousand was more than a fifth of the wealth made by all of England in a single year. Don't tell Edward that, Lorenzo had warned, or the king would ask to borrow even more.

"He must be thinking only of Caterina's dowry, of wanting to save some coin on the cost. He likely didn't even think about Florence in all of this."

"And that is precisely the issue," his mother says.

She's not wrong.

"Why are we fussing over Sforza?" he says. "It's the pope who's asking us for the money, who's insulting us."

"Insulting? I think he's made quite a clear proposition. If we want a cardinal, we'll give him the loan and let his son have Imola."

"That's an awful lot to pay for a scarlet mozzetta."

"It is," she admits. "I imagine the pope knows that. But he also knows the potential for us if Giuliano joins the college. It's something no other family in Florence has."

"Nowhere in his letter does he mention Giuliano. And this comes after all my letters, reminding him of Giuliano's desire. After all the loans we've given him for his nephews' palaces."

She picks up the towel, takes it to the bedside ewer, rolls up her sleeves. He blinks at the sight. Around her wrists, the skin is crusted, flaky, and wine-colored. She rinses the cloth, wrings it, and after the peachy water runs off her fingers, he sees that they, too, are blotched red.

He opens his mouth. "What is—"

She has caught his stare. "Shall I call for Agnolo to write your reply?" she asks, pulling down her sleeves, though her hands are still dripping. "Or do you need your rest?"

He watches her, saying nothing. Anger or pain, he can't tell which, flares inside him.

"I'll take care of this," he says.

"It's disappointing to lose Imola, but there will be other towns to fold into our lands. At least Giuliano can have a future in this. It's costly, yes, but it will be worth it in the end."

"The pope is demanding that we give him money so he can set up his son, whom I should remind you is the captain of his army, in a fortress right at our borders. Why would we ever consent to such a thing?"

"This is the pope, Lorenzo. We provide his loans. You can't refuse him."

"Why not? He ignores my letters and then finally writes to me only when he needs to borrow money. It's disrespectful."

His mother's hands flutter in front of her, like a moth trapped indoors. "The Curia is our largest account."

"He's belittling us and therefore all of Florence too. I won't take it."

She sits again on the edge of the bed, grabs his left hand, clasps it between her moist fingers. "Think about your brother. He needs this. Hear me on this, Lorenzo," she says, almost pleading.

"He'll understand. This is larger than him."

"You promised him. You can't break that. You can't do this."

"But I can. And I don't need you telling me what I can or can't do anymore."

He pulls free his left hand, though it aches, throbs. He reaches for the letter at the edge of the bed, and pain courses up his back, down his arm. His mother stands from the bed, her eyes unfocused. She wraps her hands around her bodice. Takes one step back. Another. Then she leaves him.

XIV

GOD DAMN THE MAN!

The thought is sudden, frightening. He wishes it gone but it persists, burning inside him like bile. To think such a horrible thing—to curse a cardinal, of all people! It's not just wrong of him. It's wicked.

He silently mutters an Ave, but he can't unhear all the inane chatter wafting about him. Nobles, bishops and merchants, wives and courtesans—all of them blathering around a long dining table. And at its head is Pietro, smiling of course, his cheeks are red from wine, the shade clashing with his scarlet zucchetto.

Forgive me, he thinks, bowing his head. His own face greets him, reflected on the surface of the plate in front of him. The image dazzles, plays tricks. His clipped hair ripples. His clenched jaw looks as hard as metal. His skin is burnished, shaded to deepest, most precious bronze.

He touches the plate, leaving a greasy fingerprint on its rim. He lifts it. No, not bronze—this plate is solid gold.

"Hear! Hear!" someone shouts.

Chalices, clearest Venetian glass full of gem-red wine, are raised all around the table. To Pietro, who has brought them all to his palace tonight, who has hosted this banquet to celebrate his newest post: the archbishopric of Florence.

Salviati hadn't dared to ask for it. But it would've suited him. Made Jacopo proud. Enriched him enough to pay back the bank too. Instead, Rovere has gifted it to his favorite nephew. As if the cardinalship and the fleet of bishoprics he already held weren't enough.

Thunder, somewhere distant. The dining room flashes with white light. It shines upon the silver trenchers heaped with pheasant and geese and trout. The lustered bowls with saffron jellies. The gilt-trimmed mirrors and the silk-upholstered chairs. All of it ill-befitting a cardinal—and this room is more restrained than most. He's heard the bedrooms have piss pots made of gold.

The toast continues. He knows he should lift his chalice, even if it's empty. Instead he sits with his hands resting on the table, while Pietro's head turns, owllike, from one side of the table to the other. When his gaze passes over Salviati, his simpering mouth twitches.

But Salviati isn't the only one who has failed to raise his glass. Girolamo, sitting next to him, has glowered all through supper, has wallowed for what feels like months. Medici denied his loan, and he was no longer to be the Count of Imola.

The toast finishes, the conversations gather again.

"He gets whatever he wants. Gets whatever money he needs," Girolamo mutters.

"He has his benefices," Salviati reminds him.

"And what has he done to earn them? Constantinople? He's never been. Neither has he gone to Valence. But he still gets to scoop up his tens of thousands in gold, all without leaving Rome. Meanwhile, I don't get the one title promised to me."

"You have your wife. Don't forget that."

"An eleven-year-old. What good is she?"

Across the table, some nobleman hides his face behind his wineglass. The blonde-haired woman next to him pats her handkerchief to her blotched neck.

"Imola was supposed to be my future. Something of my own, away from all this."

"And it will be yours, when the Lord sees it right and shows Medici the error of his ways. You must be patient."

Girolamo rolls his bleary eyes. Salviati heard it too: how cloying he sounds, how false. He had been patient too—and for what? God wasn't watching out for either of them; He was letting them suffer purgatory.

A fleet of servants enters the room, parading golden-brown tarts and soft yellow zabaglione. A bowl is placed before him, and he pushes it away. His stomach is unsettled.

Everyone else devours the dessert. The man across the table digs his spoon into the custard. He leans forward, holding the heaped spoon aloft. "Might you seek help from your uncle? Surely he can find a solution for you."

What a stupid thing to say, Salviati thinks.

"My uncle?" Girolamo laughs. "He thinks it's a matter for the bank to resolve. He says all he can do is pray on it."

Ah, yes. Rovere's favorite phrase.

The woman with blonde hair puts down her wine, pouting slightly. Her eyes gently, cautiously look at Girolamo. "Is there another bank you could go to?"

He feels a rush, as if he's been given smelling salts. The rest of the room, the insectile chatter—it all falls away. There is only this woman, so sage. Brought before him like a messenger angel.

Another bank—it was so obvious, and yet it could work.

"It's more complicated than that," her neighbor chides.

She says nothing, only looks down at the small bowl of zabaglione before her, scoops a silver spoonful and slips the custard between her lips. But Salviati sees the truth: this woman is a Cassandra, and unlike the man beside her, Salviati is wise enough to listen to her.

She's right—there are plenty of other banks, many of which would be eager to serve the pope. Foremost among them? His cousin's, of course. The plan is already weaving together in his mind, intricate like a fine tapestry. He could help Girolamo, he could help his cousin, and most importantly, he could help himself.

Then, a snag. This way of thinking is greasy, he thinks. Like the rich meal he's just eaten, it coats his tongue and churns in his gut.

He looks at the Cassandra, custard clinging to the corner of her mouth, the bowl before her nearly empty. All down the table, men and women are shoveling more food into their mouths, racing to indulge. It's gluttonous, repulsive.

Through the window, lightning sparks across the sky. In the flash, he imagines a bolt striking the roof, setting fire to this palace. Flames lapping at the hanging portraits of self-satisfied men on the walls, the gilded ceiling melting, fat drops of gold falling like rain, Pietro and Girolamo clutching their throats in the gathering smoke, the fire then dwindling to muted embers, and from the hazy rubble, Salviati emerging alone, his cassock merely singed. He'd step into the rain, each drop wiping away the soot on his skin. He'd be free then—no longer beholden to Girolamo, to Pietro, to the pope.

He should go home, he thinks. Kneel beside his chamber pot—red clay, not gold—and retch. If the impulse won't come naturally, he can slide his fingers, stinking of garlic, into his mouth and past his tongue.

Prod until this terrible mess spills out of him. Stay on his knees, bringing his saliva-wet fingers together in prayer. Ask God for forgiveness. To show him another way, a more honest one.

But once those prayers were spoken, his loan would still be waiting for him. His ruin a day, a month, at most a year away.

So what if, for once, he took his cousin's advice? Didn't hesitate, grabbed the opportunity at hand. He deserves it, doesn't he? Far more so than the terrible company at this table. And he can't keep waiting for his turn. He is not Rovere's blood, after all. No matter how well he's served him, he won't rise unless he forces it.

And what if this was what God wanted for him? His move to Rome, his time with Rovere, and now this prophetess before him—what if all of it was providence?

He takes his spoon to the pillowy custard. Brings to his mouth. Breathes in its gentle scent of cinnamon and sweet wine. He lets it sit on his tongue, smiles at the taste. He swallows.

He eats the rest of the dessert slowly, luxuriating in every spoonful. Once his bowl is empty, he places his hand on Girolamo's shoulder, whispers a quiet apology to his neighbors. The two of them must retire for the evening, he says. And then he helps Girolamo to his feet, tries to hide that the man can barely walk.

He glances back a final time at his Cassandra. She is watching him leave, a discomforting, pitiful frown on her face.

NOW HE MUST HAVE THREE CONVERSATIONS.

First: Girolamo—upstairs, just after leaving the feast. He guides Girolamo, stumbling and wine-breathed, to a bedroom. Once he's ensconced under the canopy with a pillow already beneath his head, Salviati fetches a towel and dips it into an ewer. He sees the piss pot at the bedside. It's true—they're gold.

"Sober up," he tells Girolamo, throwing him the damp towel. "I know how to get your forty thousand."

Girolamo laughs. "And my cock's a foot long."

"My cousin's a banker, you know."

"Forty thousand would empty most banks."

"Not the Pazzi Bank."

Girolamo sits up. For the first time in weeks, he's smiling.

They make their plans right then—Salviati standing, Girolamo half slumped over his bedquilts. They discuss how the bank must be approached, how the offer must then be brought before the pope. They talk about Pietro, how they might counter any reluctance he may slip into the pope's ear. Once it has all been thought through, Salviati sits on the bed beside Girolamo; he asks him to promise him something in return for his ingenuity.

He knows not to be greedy. A bishopric is a fine start.

SECOND: THE BANK—THE NEXT MORNING. A day ago he would've crucified himself before returning here. Now he strides into the back-room, calmly ignores the rows of clerks.

"I come with good fortune," he says to Francesco, taking the chair across from him.

The banker leans back, his doublet straining against his growing belly. "Unless it's your loan repaid in full, I'm not interested."

"How about a new account? A significant one."

"What's significant to you is picayune to this bank."

He breathes in the room's damp paper stench and grins. "Would you consider the largest account in the Christian world to be a trivial thing? I can write to Jacopo if you don't think it worthy of your time."

"Go on," Francesco says softly.

"Medici refused the pope an important loan. If you could fulfill it, I could see to it that the pope comes to believe that he should move management of the Curial account to the Pazzi Bank."

"How much is the loan?"

"Forty thousand ducats."

"I'll need to write to Jacopo."

"Go ahead. I know your uncle is disappointed in your progress here. Think how impressed he'll be when you bring him this account. Say it was your idea, for all I care. No need to mention me."

Francesco laughs dryly. "Maybe you should've been a banker."

"I only want what's best for the Holy Father."

"And yourself, I'm assuming. You can't be doing this solely out of Christian spirit. I have one question, and I want an honest answer."

"Ask it," he says, thumbing the crucifix at his neck.

Francesco leans closer. He's wearing camphor, too much of it, and yet he can still smell the stink of his sweat beneath it. "Why are you doing this? For me, of all people."

"Because you're going to forgive my debt."

THIRD: THE POPE. Letters have darted between Rome and Florence, and Salviati's instincts are proven right. His cousin can't neglect an opportunity for his bank to eclipse its biggest competition.

So Salviati comes to the Vatican. Kneeling before the Holy Father and Girolamo and Pietro, he speaks of the Pazzi Bank's interest in furnishing the loan that Medici had so rudely refused to honor. And, as he talks, Girolamo carefully prompts the right questions so the pope doesn't ask the wrong ones.

The whole forty thousand? Yes, the whole forty thousand.

Are the terms attractive? They are most attractive.

Does the Pazzi Bank have interest in an ongoing relationship with the Curia? They would be most honored with such an opportunity.

Rovere mulls it all with ostentation, his forehead scrunched into many folds, his long, sun-spotted fingers tapping the gilded armrest of his throne. Then he looks skyward, hands pressed in prayer, lips fluttering like a fish. It's all pomp and performance, but it's necessary. Without it, Rovere's just a man—not God's voice on Earth.

"We are most pleased," he finally says. "Let your cousin know we gratefully accept his offer."

Pietro's hand clasps the pope's shoulder. He leans forward toward his small ear. Speaks in a whisper they can all hear, "Is it wise to offend Medici?"

The pope's smile falters. He always listens to Pietro. But they've planned for this.

"We needn't worry about offending him. He's just a banker," Girolamo says. "After the kindness and generosity you showed him, he still had the audacity to disrespect you. Denying the brother a cardinalship isn't a strong enough message. When a dog snarls and bites its owner, is it not wise to chain the pet until it learns to behave?"

It's quite a sight: the two supposed brothers on each side of the pope, making their entreaties; the Holy Father, sitting between them, unable to turn his head for the heavy tiara on top of it.

"Peace in our kingdom is what's most important," says the pope. "Then again, he has failed us our banker."

Where's God's guidance when this man needs it? Salviati thinks.

The pope turns to him, as if he's heard his thoughts. "What do you think, my Florentine? Will we have a problem in Florence if I am to change banks?"

Seize it, he thinks.

"This is about more than money, Your Holiness. Medici has caused grave offense to you, your family, and the papacy. And I believe what we must protect above all else is your magnificence."

The pope smiles again. "You are a wise one, Salviati."

"Well said," Girolamo adds. "I, for one, cannot find the words to express the depth of my gratitude to Salviati. Uncle, I'm glad he's righting this wrong made against you. But don't you think such a trusted and pious advisor is too important to remain only a priest? That perhaps there might be a bishopric in his future?"

The pope surveys Salviati, from the crown of his head down to his black lambskin boots.

"Yes," the pope says. "That's a fine idea. We'll pray for it."

"Thank you, Your Holiness," Salviati says, bowing deeply, grinning broadly.

This is paradise. He feels nothing but a radiant goodness inside of him. It's fine as gold, soft as silk. He's burning, gloriously burning with his love for God. He's a red-draped seraph floating into the air, soaring over the clouds high above San Pietro. Holy, holy, holy, he wants to sing. He, at last, is rising.

Part Two

THE
MADONNA
AND CHILD

1474–1476

XV

HE WAKES, BUT HE DOESN'T STIR. HIS HANDS REMAIN ON THE warm, bare flesh of his thighs. His long, thin toes stay still beneath the coarse, gray quilt.

He doesn't need his sight, not yet. He knows this bedroom, can summon its every intimate detail. This mattress, its hay that dryly rustles with even the smallest of movements. The sole, squat window, and its twin rotted-wood louvers, always kept shut, even on the hottest August day, hiding his secrets from view. In front of the window, the poplar table, low and long and with a splintering rear leg. On its surface, the narrow-necked urn filled with the olive oil that has made his body a discovery, a delight. Next to it, the clay ewer holding water, always cold, that he then uses to wash his slick skin.

He knows the smell of this room too: a certain musk and dried marjoram.

Waking here is a luxury, one he doesn't want to end. Out there is the work he hasn't finished, the commissions he let go to Sandro, Rosselli, Domenico, or one of the Pollaiuolo brothers. Here, he is only Leonardo. Nothing more.

He opens his eyes. Sees his fogging breath and the bluish, pale dawn, the color of winter. Beneath the quilt, his skin is sweaty, hot. Surprisingly so. Along his left side especially.

He turns.

Beside him, Iac is asleep. He studies his face, the features that are indelible in his mind. The ears, soft and delicate. The small, always-moist lips. The curls of hair, tight spirals like the Arno's eddies, that fascinate him.

It is always him. Only him. Every night that he's come to the Buco since his first visit that was, what, two years ago now?

But never has he waked to find Iac still next to him. Usually, Leonardo drags himself across the moonlit city back to the workshop. On the nights when he does indulge himself in sleeping here, in the mornings he always finds a wrinkled gap where Iac's body lay just hours before. He doesn't resent this. He understands the nature of their relationship. He knows Iac has to earn, that he's trying to save every soldo until he finishes his apprenticeship and can register as a goldsmith.

That Iac is still here in this bed beside him—it strikes him with an uncomfortable, unfamiliar feeling. There was no warning; nothing was unusual about the previous night. He paid the same sum of coins to the matron, followed Iac up the stairs to the same bedroom as always. They undressed quickly, ran their tongues down the other's neck, over the ridged terrain of his ribs, down farther still across bristled hair and supplest skin. They touched each other in those familiar places, favoring the hidden nooks they mutually discovered. And when they came, one then the other, it was across each other's chests.

He watches Iac: rubbing his nose with a closed fist, his lips softly pouting. He hasn't seen him this way, by daylight, since the afternoon he modeled for the workshop. This glimpse—it's an unexpected gift.

Iac makes an innocent tableau. Unpretentious and unposed. A perfect subject, one he could transform in ten thousand ways. Paint him into a David, his face sprayed with giant's blood. Or as a Narcissus, enamored with his reflection on a glass-smooth pool. Even as Christ himself—but before his baptism, his miracles, his desert wandering.

No one would want such works, though. Androgynous boys are out of favor now. The rich, they want paintings of men with armored chests and sinewed arms. They want angels, saints, and Madonnas—especially Madonnas. Or they want portraits. Of themselves, of their wives, of the women they wish were their wives.

Leonardo doesn't decide his subjects. He likely never will. A painter never owns their own brushstrokes. By the time the panel is prepared, each smear of pigment is indebted, the brush wielded invisibly by the painting's eventual owner.

He could draw this boy though. Just for himself.

He slowly peels the quilt from their bodies. He looks to his brown leather sack slumped on the floor. He just needs the notebook and the charcoal inside it, just needs to move across the room without waking Iac. He stands, and the cold bites his skin. He hesitates, naked beside the bed. He imagines Iac's eyes fluttering open midsketch, imagines them growing wide with alarm, with betrayal. He could think it's a violation, for Leonardo to draw him like this. And he doesn't want Iac thinking he's just another subject to him.

No, he can't ruin this. This has become a necessity. To fuck or to be fucked, depending on the night. Not for the moment when he gasps aloud but for what follows: the dull nothing that fogs his head, that all too briefly stills his mind, always turning, always sloshing like a watermill.

This habit—yes, it is illicit and costly—but it has served him well. He doesn't know what he'd do if he had to quit. What would become of him.

He steps across the room and dips a towel into the ewer. He wipes away the flaky traces of their sex, then, still damp, he searches for his hose.

"You're leaving?"

He stills, facing the wall. Nude, hose crumped in his hands. "I should've woken you sooner. I'm sorry."

"I'm not. I haven't slept that well in months," Iac says, sitting up in bed, clouds of quilts gathered around him. His eyes are glossed, half closed. He's smiling. An expression so simple, so warm, something utterly without artifice. The taste of honey.

"Do you always wake this early?"

"I like to be back to the workshop before—"

"The others wake. I understand." He rises from the bed, taking the quilts with him. "But Verrocchio surely he knows what you get up to? As a man of similar tastes."

"We never speak of it. I'd be mortified if we did. But how did you know?"

"He's an artist with no wife, who devotes so much of his time to training young, handsome painters. It's not a secret."

He smirks. "The rest of them are eyesores, I swear."

"And you aren't?" Iac steps in front of him and pulls at one of his curls. "No, I know I'm lucky."

He looks down at his hands and rolls on his hose.

"Does he care that you spend some of your nights here?"

He pulls on his tunic, but his belt is missing. "He doesn't say anything. I think he knows he can't, now that I've brought in a commission."

The belt is in Iac's hands. He wraps it around his waist. Clasps it. "Then we'll have to keep finding you work."

HE STARES, THOUGH BY NOW he knows her face so well. Her skin, pale without lead. Smooth, with a certain coolness, like the flesh of a pear. A prick of rose at her cheeks.

He is in a palace a few minutes' walk from his father's house. In a spacious upstairs salon. Him and Ginevra and her brother, Giovanni de' Benci.

The light falls from behind him through a tall, sashed window, spinning Ginevra's neatly pinned hair into gold. Every day, she runs her fingers over it, flattening it. But the foremost strands are stubborn; they curl, gather into wooly nests. He doesn't paint it this way, though. He gives her lovely, tight curls. Like Iac's.

Her dresses have changed, over so many months. He never asked her to wear the same outfit every day. To do so seemed rude, an imposition. Instead, he picked his favorite gown, the chestnut-colored one, with a collar threaded in cloth of gold. The one that best suited her eyes. On the days she wore it, he'd paint her body. The rest of the days—parades of silk and velvet in kermes, sheep gray, or frit-blue—he'd paint her face. And she had so many other gowns; there were so many of these days. She is wealthy, exceedingly so. Her late father worked within the highest levels of the Medici Bank. He was one of his father's clients.

There is, however, a constant to her many outfits: a strip of linen, near-black and simple, that draped over her shoulders and fell to her slippered feet. He didn't know what it was at first; he had to ask her brother. A scapular, worn by the Benedictines at Le Murate. Ginevra was only recently returned from the nunnery. Brought back to her family home. Soon to live permanently with her new husband.

It was the brother who wanted the painting. To remember her like this, before she leaves, Giovanni said.

His brush touches oil. It hovers over her painted eyes. These are what he has looked at the most, what have fixed his attention over so many weeks and months. They're large but quite narrow. Heavy-lidded. The irises sable-brown at the rims, fading to a color he lacks a name for, knows only by the mess of pigment on his stone slab: vine black, ivory, a touch of massicot all smeared together. And their stare: perceptive and steady, and yet so vague in their intention. Better at hiding than any veil.

So many days he has sat here, wondering if he might ask Ginevra how she was feeling, or if she had attended the parade for San Giovanni's Day, or whether she intended to make a pilgrimage to Rome for next year's Jubilee. Banal talk, useless chatter—except then he could finally hear her voice.

Instead, on the first day he thought it would be impolite to ask questions.

The second day, he thought she might be shy, might prefer the quiet.

The third day, and so many days after, he thought it better to give his attention to the work.

And in all of those days, from sketch to cartoon to painted panel, he listened to the preserved silence, for its little transgressions—a cough, a sigh, a servant's footsteps. He waited for an interruption, one in particular. A visit from Lorenzo, who Giovanni said called upon them from time to time, who was quite friendly with the family.

He thought that could be how he'd prove to Lorenzo his talent. Make good on the years-old promise from the courtyard.

But Lorenzo never came. And now he's done with this portrait—he really does have to admit that—though he's drawn out the days by trifling, by trying to make Ginevra's gaze more real. By trying to glean the thoughts behind it.

Sitting here—in a stately palace, beside a woman, young and beautiful—it's been easy to imagine a different life for himself. One where he is a notary, like his father. Or perhaps not even that, but an engineer—who designs walls, bridges, machines. He might have children—two girls, no boys yet. He could be doling out commissions, rather than scavenging for them. He could finally learn Latin and Greek. Lead a fine, respectable life. But living it, day in, day out—it's unfathomable to him. His mind would drift to his fancies. He would wander—back to the Buco, back to Iac. And that would be worse, he thinks. To lie to Iac, to devote only a cleaved heart to him.

The truth is that women exist to him across some chasm. All his time in Florence he's lived a life without them. And even before that, he was mostly with his grandfather at the farmhouse in Vinci. His mother was in that town too—but he was always kept from her. If he is honest, he often forgets about her. To him, she is more myth and story to him than flesh and blood.

Without her, he wonders if he's missed some crucial inheritance. He sees how the world around him exists in male and female. That truth is everywhere: in the Tuscan tongue, in the matching cones dropped by cypress trees, in the songs of starlings nesting on the city walls. All the world has its corresponding sex; life, creation springs from that union.

Against that model, he is a transgressor. Not only in the obvious sense—that he'd never crave the embrace of woman, that he'll never have a family—but in all senses, insignificant but always noticed. How he moved his hands when he spoke and he never chose the right dyes for his tunics, always lilac or rose instead of morello or indigo. How he sat lifeless and bored through jousts or calcio matches.

It's an aspect of himself he couldn't change, even if he tried. Still, it frightens him, to live in this same world of matching parts but never understand how he's meant to exist within it. To carry an essential dissonance with him—in his voice, his appearance, his thoughts—like the tolling of a cracked, misshapen bell. Painting is his only reprieve.

He's tried to find a reason, an origin to all of this. Last year, he went back to Vinci. Said nothing to his father, told Andrea he wanted a few days outside Florence to sketch new landscapes. It was summer, when the cliff stone was warm to sit on and the distant fields were beginning to amber. He looked down on the town he once knew, so small, trapped within low walls. His mother was still there. He wanted to call on her. But she had her own life: a husband and so many children—ones she called her own. What would she have said to him if he had appeared at her door, decades older and dressed in city clothes? Would she have even recognized him? And what would he have said to her? That he was a painter—in a city she did not know, that did not matter to her life? A painter with no work to show to her, with no work to his name?

At least that has changed. He has this, his first commission, wholly his own. And he has done good work, though there's an unsettling quality to what he's made, what he's staring at.

He feels it, a little knife prick: he's trapped Ginevra on his panel; he's rendered, made mimicry, but failed to comprehend. And it is this imperfect, incomplete version of her that will be caged within a heavy frame and hung on a wall in this palace, left to fade in sunlight and gather dust. A private work, rarely to be seen. Something that would one day disappear.

He rests his brush, steps back from the painting.

"What do you think?" he asks.

Giovanni, sitting by a window, sets aside his book and joins Leonardo.

"Beautiful," he says, resting a hand on Leonardo's shoulder. "It really is a marvel."

"You're pleased?"

"Most certainly," Giovanni says, but his brow is furrowed.

"What is it?"

"Her mouth. I can't deny you've painted truthfully. But might you be able to give her a slight smile?"

He looks at the mouth: narrow, pale pink, unmoving.

"I could change that, yes," he says, thinking of another week, maybe two of work, listening to cloth slippers patter against the floor.

"I like it as it is."

Her voice is steady, countertenor. Entirely different from all his imagined conversations.

Ginevra looks at Leonardo with the same impenetrable stare as his painting. She nods, and something unspoken passes between them. Then she withdraws from the room.

"I suppose it's done then," Giovanni says.

XVI

"FATHER, THERE'S BEEN A DEATH."

Salviati opens his eyes. In the muted, early light, the moment expands, a yawning nightmare. He's imagined this moment on so many nights, considered all manner of ways the pope might die. Some sort of apoplexy. A sudden fever. A dagger in the dark. Or simply a normal night's slumber that never ended. It shouldn't be surprising; after all, the pope was nearly sixty. He thinks about the chamberlain, who surely would also not be surprised, who would bend over Rovere's body, trying in vain to avoid his beak nose as he struck him with his silver hammer.

"They've sent a coach," Maddalena says, shielding her eyes from the sight of a priest, naked beneath his bedquilts.

He thanks her, dismisses her. He rises, kneels, prays—but only for Rovere's salvation. He can't harbor any other thoughts just yet. He splashes cold water on his face, dresses quickly in his darkest, blackest cassock.

Only when he is seated in the coach and it lurches ahead does he allow himself to ask the terrible question: What about him? His bishopric still eludes him. It was promised; it seemed so close, but now it would be more distant than ever.

No longer will anyone want to indulge the pope's nephews. And the cardinals certainly won't give a fig about Salviati and what the dead pope had promised him. Yes, the burden of his debt might be gone—but for what? His modest house, his fine clothes—they're frill, they're useless now. Everyone in the Vatican will soon forget him.

The coach groans as it climbs uphill. Inside it, he shakes his head. To stake his whole future on a fat fisherman who never kept his promises? What a fool he has been!

The coach stalls. The ride has been short—too short. The door opens to a hilltop, draped in golden morning light. To the familiar gaudy villa, and not the Vatican Palace.

He understands in an instant, in a hot rush of blood. He begins to laugh—a fit so sudden, so violent, so odd in its sound that the servants waiting outside turn to one another and whisper how touching it is to see Father Salviati so upset by the cardinal's death.

He's shown to Pietro's bedside. The room stinks of sweat and wine. The cardinal's face has already grayed, and his stiff lips have retreated from his teeth. Even in death, Pietro seems to be sneering at him.

"Choked on his own vomit," a servant quietly tells him.

A glutton to the end, he thinks. Then he mutters a quick Ave for forgiveness.

He takes out his purse and fingers the two gold coins inside. Enough to persuade this servant to whisper a different rendition of what has happened here. A more suitable one, like a sudden fit, or even a bout of plague. Something pious, tragic.

He looks at the body, at the nasty mess covering Pietro's chest, at his stomach, rotund from so many banquets. Then he snorts. Swear to God, the cardinal's cock is poking at the quilts, straight and stiff as a lance. An unholy man to his very end!

Yet this man was the cardinal, not him.

He dismisses the servant. Alone, he leans forward and places the two coins in his palm on top of Pietro's closed lids. He kneels at the bedside, hides his face in his prayer-cupped hands as he secrets a smile. He's realizing all of Pietro's offices are now vacant. The choicest selection of benefices is waiting to be plundered.

⁓

HIS RISE IN THE WAKE of Pietro's death startles him. It's stallion-fast, it turns his stomach. Now it is him and Girolamo constantly offering their opinions to the pope so he doesn't need to render his own. It is him and Girolamo guiding—no, coddling—the pope, for he is so morose these days, breaking into maudlin fits every evening.

"It's as if I've lost a son," the pope cries one night. Poor Girolamo has to nod along and pat the Holy Father's shoulder.

Salviati and Girolamo don't speak of the pope's careening moods, just as they don't remark, not ever, on their sudden elevation in the Holy Father's esteem. To Salviati, the cardinal was a man of God—in name at least; propitious as his exit may have been, it was still something to lament. And to Girolamo, Pietro was a brother, supposedly; even to a reprobate, it's unconscionable to speak of his death as an unexpected gift.

But do they both think it? Of course. Salviati goes to bed every night with Pietro's former offices chanting in his head like a paternoster.

The pope, however, seems disinclined to fill Pietro's former offices. For months, he's reluctant to do anything, really, except sob and sleep and sit in silence. When Salviati or Girolamo or even one of the cardinals gently mentions one of the unfilled posts, Rovere shakes his head and shuts his eyes, as if merely the name of this-or-that diocese might summon the ghost of his nephew.

Still, priests continue sniffing about the Vatican, knowing that benefices are being left uncollected. They know the pope must relent. And Salviati watches as one by one, Pietro's former posts are scavenged by bishops, by foreigners, by mendicant priests.

Each time, he presses his hands in prayer. Reminds himself not to covet. Tells himself that his own appointment will come soon.

If the pope notices Salviati's disappointment, he doesn't remark on it. Eventually, finally, he shakes off his heavy pall of grief, and in its place, he seizes upon his building projects once more—and with alarming intensity. Day after day, he meets with builders and artists and engineers; all he wants to talk about are his plans for next year's Jubilee.

Rome shall have its dirt roads paved with stone! he says. Widen the streets and knock down the dusty porticos! Use the blocks from the Flavian Amphitheatre to build a new bridge to span the Tiber! He's even invited his new ally, King Ferrante, from Naples for January's celebration.

It's all so exhausting.

Then, one morning, the pope summons Salviati. Requests that he join him—and only him—for a walk.

They stroll across the palace grounds, between a row of narrow trees and the Vatican walls. Some poor, sweaty servant shuffles alongside the pope, carrying a fringed canopy, shielding the Holy Father from the still-warm autumn sun. Odd as it seems for a man from the seaside, the pope has always avoided the light, even kept the palace windows constantly curtained.

Salviati now understands why. Out of the palace's constant clouds of incense, he can see the olive spots sprawling across the pope's face, like stains of wine on an overused tablecloth. The forehead, plowed with wrinkles. The wiry white hairs along his chin too. He remembers that the pope is an old man. Remembers that every day he continues to give Mass in a church, rather than a cathedral, is a risk.

The pope stops. "I'm having the chapel rebuilt."

Another building project. Salviati smiles, says nothing.

They've reached the edge of a field, half covered in rubble. He doesn't know outside of which halls of the palace they're standing; even after years of walking through its halls, he still can't master its layout. It's a mongrel building: wings added on by each pope, entryways rebuilt, other doorways shuttered, old chambers knocked down.

"The old chapel was such an embarrassment," the pope says. "No more. I want something tall, higher than the trees. Not terribly large though. It doesn't need to be. Doesn't need to be beautiful from the outside either. They can make it from the same stone as the rest of this beast, for all I care. But inside—that I care about. I want it to be a treasure. A sacred place, where future conclaves could be held."

The pope turns to him. Ah, Salviati thinks, he expects him to speak.

"A most holy endeavor," he says.

The pope smiles. "I knew you'd understand. Girolamo, he lacks the patience. He doesn't understand that realizing great things takes years, decades even. But you know this, I think. After all, you've been so patient with me during this trying time. There have been so many posts to fill. I would've given you any of them, if you had asked. But I thought you deserved something more."

Salviati kneels, and the cool, sodden earth seeps through his cassock.

"What do you think of Pisa, Salviati?"

He doesn't think of it, truthfully. It's an unfortunate city. Once was a prosperous port. But the plague killed half its people, Florence sieged it, and then it fell under the republic's dominion.

"I hear its cathedral is beautiful," Salviati tells the pope. "White and shining."

"And it shall be yours. The archbishop has died, and you will replace him."

Not a bishopric, but an archbishopric. After so long, after so much waiting, it doesn't seem possible. He's not worthy of such a thing.

"Having you at my side these past months, it's been such a comfort," he says. "But it is time to send you away so you can serve our Lord. So that, one day, you might return here and stand in my chapel to serve on a conclave. Hopefully a day very far from now," the pope says, letting out a strange, shrill giggle.

Salviati ignores the sound, bows to the Holy Father. The Lord is good, he thinks, looking down at the dirt. He has seen him delivered.

"I knew you'd be pleased," the pope says, beckoning him to stand. "I needed something most special for my Florentine. Pisa is a Primate, you know. Richest benefices in all of the peninsula, after Florence."

The name of his birthplace snags his excitement, tears, quickly, violently through his joy, like fabric caught on a nail. "Will Medici not want to put his own man forward?" he asks.

The pope frowns. He obviously hadn't considered this. "Don't mind that. This is a matter for God, not for bankers."

XVII

SCAFFOLDS OF FRESH TIMBER, TALL AS BUILDINGS. THOU-sands standing, sitting, squatting on every level. Legends retold on banners of lustrous silk, rounding the field; Venus and Cupid, Hercules and the Hydra, Theseus and the Minotaur, all whipping brightly in the raw winter wind. On the tilting grounds, jousters ride on horses capari-soned in fringed taffeta. Round after round, their lances, painted saffron yellow, blood red, darkest black, splinter and shatter.

"How much is this costing us?" his mother asks.

Lorenzo laughs, his breath fogging.

He could tell her he spent thousands on Giuliano's armor alone, but she'd probably throttle him on this dais in front of the whole city. "It's a bargain compared to what the pope's spending on his little Jubilee. Good riddance. A year ago, and it would've been us footing all that nonsense."

It's true—that was all the Pazzi's responsibility now. They're here too, of course; he's sat the whole family across the field from them in the frontmost row. Guglielmo is watching the fanfare with a patient, strained smile. Bianca has slumped in her seat, a goblet of wine in her gloved palms—and not her first of the day, he'd reckon. And then there is Jacopo with his chin in his hand, sitting close enough to the field to see every gemstone and silver-threaded banner, to sum all the finery on display.

"You sound as if you're pleased that you lost us the Curial account."

"I didn't lose it," he says to the veiled, stony outline of his mother's face. "It was stolen."

Clarice sits between them, her typical pout betraying nothing. She keeps her attention on the children in the row below theirs. Lucrezia, the oldest, primly watching the field. Piero fidgeting on the bench beside her. Little Maddalena crawling beneath her mother's furs.

Rare for them all to be out in public together. But this is a special celebration. And for once, Clarice isn't pregnant. The last daughter she birthed survived only a few weeks; he thought it prudent to give her a reprieve.

"The bank still serves the king in England, the duke in Burgundy and in Milan too. There are still our branches in Naples, Lyon, Venice, and the rest," he says, watching Clarice shift her copper hair behind her ear and turn her face toward him ever so slightly. Listening. "The bank has served its purpose. It's made us who we are. Made this city what it is. Look at it. All the work the guilds have done for this, done for us. We deserve this. Especially now that we can count Venice as our ally, along with Milan. It's a modern Triumvirate."

That should set the matter to rest, he thinks. He takes a drink from his silver cup of wine spiced with cinnamon, ginger, clove. But the drink has cooled. It clings to his tongue.

Typical of his mother to ruin a good day—a great one, even.

"And while you've courted Galeazzo in Milan and the doge in Venice, the pope has been courting Ferrante. Successfully," she says. "Losing Naples as an ally? I don't like it. Rome and Naples together? That's a big, provoking mass to the south. A mass with two large armies at its disposal."

He doesn't like this either but agreeing won't keep his mother from complaining.

"This is a time of peace, isn't it?" Clarice says calmly. "I don't see the use in squabbling over these little pacts."

"Hear, hear," he says. God bless her; he could kiss her. Maybe she can be the one to finally shut his mother up.

His mother laughs dryly, and blood creeps into Clarice's cheeks. "If it's really a time of peace, your husband should make amends."

"With Ferrante?" Lorenzo says. "Despite this alliance nonsense, I promise you he and I are still friendly."

"Amends with the pope."

"Enough with that sodding fisherman."

Clarice flinches. His mother glances about. "Mind what you say."

"Why? I saw him in Rome. He's a toothless hermit who can't bear the weight of his own tiara. He'll be dead soon enough, and when he is, we'll make friends with the next pope and become the Curial bankers once more."

"You can't wait for that."

He laughs. "I'm young. He's old. I'll outlast him. Easily."

"Never count on your youth," his mother whispers.

A glint of gold steals his attention. Down on the field, a new jouster has emerged. From this distance, he is small, his face half hidden by a helmet in the old Greek style, with a long strip of steel covering the nose and two teardrop holes for eyes. Giuliano, looking better than David.

He knows it's Giuliano from the white destrier he rides, from the pearls clustered on his cape, from the banner held in his fist: a cloth-of-gold Minerva. And it is not only him who has noticed his brother's entrance. Trumpets sound his arrival, and in their wake, the crowd's murmuring lulls. The thousands lean forward. The stands creak.

On the opposite side of the field, his brother's opponent emerges. He is bulky with steel, carrying his own standard, but one that is dull, that fails to catch the faint winter sun.

The jousters take their positions on the bleached yard. His brother readies his blue-painted lance.

Clarice clutches his arm. "I can't bear this part," she says, looking away.

His mother raises her voice. "Speaking of the pope, I hear you still haven't agreed to his choice for the Pisa archbishopric. That you've ban-died the Signoria into continuing to refuse."

He keeps his eyes on Giuliano. "You've heard correctly."

Hooves thunder on the frozen earth. Shining steel streaks across the field. Clarice's fingers dig into his skin. He doesn't breathe.

A crash. A shattering. A whinnying. Then sharp, feeble crying.

The crowd roars. His brother rides back across the field, sitting high on his horse, the threaded Minerva smiling down on him. Behind him, his opponent is dragged off the field.

Clarice's eyes are still shut. "It's done," he tells her.

He marks his mother opening her eyes too, searching for Giuliano. "You shouldn't be making him do this," she says. "It isn't safe."

"No one would dare unseat him."

"Can you be certain of that?" Clarice asks.

She can go back to staying quiet, he thinks.

"It's all for show. He can't be beaten. He's to be the tournament's champion," he says, watching Giuliano retreat to the distant edge of the field, listening to the crowd cheering him on. "He deserves this. To be celebrated. All his life he's been fed that absurd notion that second sons must enter the church. And now it's come to naught."

"You didn't have to will it so," his mother says. "He's different from you, Lorenzo. He's not so certain of things as you are. There's more of your father in him."

"I know that." He thinks of Giuliano leant over the side of his horse, vomiting onto the street in Volterra. It was why he chose a joust: so his brother felt celebrated, yes, but so he could be toughened too. "Listen to everyone cheering for him. He's a hero."

She leans forward, craning her neck toward him. "There's only one hero for every age."

"Castor and Pollux. Augustus and Agrippa. Cosmos and Damian. There's room for both of us."

She's still bent forward, her body crooked. "You know he'll do whatever you tell him to."

Clarice is looking askance at him too.

He nods. He knows.

"And since he's not to be a cardinal, his future is now your responsibility. You have to give him purpose. He can't simply be your—" She stops, picks a stray white fleck from the dark satin of her gloves. "We'll need to find him a wife too."

"Can't we let him enjoy—" He doesn't finish. Odd, he thinks, that he can discuss such matters with his mother but not his wife.

"I hate to even mention such ugly gossip, but we both know our enemies love to say that Florence is chock-full of sodomites. Best to find him a woman before they start whispering such things about your brother."

"That's base chatter. I'll have you know that I've had the night officers increase their arrests," Lorenzo says. "Besides, Giuliano would never do such a thing."

"Of course he wouldn't. But you two were already married at his age. It's time. Surely you agree, Clarice?"

"He does seem restless," she says, still blushing from the mention of buggerers. "I think it would do him good. Someone to moor him before he drifts too distant."

He wonders: Does she think she's moored him? Surely she knows he keeps other women.

"And where shall we find him a wife?" he asks.

"Where we are in need of friends. Like how you, Clarice, bonded us with Rome."

So much for that bond, he thinks.

"What about Venice?" Clarice offers. "The doge's daughter, to mark your alliance?"

His mother nods. "Lorenzo, you can make inquiries while I'm away."

At the far end of the field, Giuliano's horse kicks restlessly at the dirt waiting to gallop.

"Away?" he asks as his brother's next opponent emerges. Richer armor than the last. A thicker horse too.

"I'm leaving. Tomorrow at first light."

He turns. His mother stares down at the field. Clarice too—willfully so. She knew, he thinks.

"Where?"

"Morba."

He thinks of scarred earth, of white smoke gathering above cratered pools.

"I've delayed as long as I could, but the physicians are insisting. I have a psora that won't heal. The waters should help."

Another bout of revelry blares, and then the tilt falls quiet once more. "For how long?"

Horses rush, steel rattles. This time, he doesn't look. He watches his mother, mouthing Aves. He hears the crash, the cheers. His mother leans back in her seat, and he knows Giuliano has won again.

"Before I go, I need to know one thing," she says, ignoring his question. "When will you relent on the Pisan archbishopric?"

His gaze flits to Jacopo de' Pazzi, shivering, clapping along with the rest of the crowd.

"When I'm feeling generous," he says.

"What more do you want? The pope chose a Florentine. A Salviati."

"Clarice, why don't you tell my mother what your father wrote to you about this Salviati?"

She knocks her knees against his. Dares to glare at him, if only briefly. "My father heard that it was this same Salviati who helped forge this new relationship between the Pazzi Bank and the Holy Father. He's quite close with Jacopo de' Pazzi, apparently. A cousin."

"How curious," his mother says. "Have you met him, Lorenzo?"

"I don't think so. But I don't like the pope putting him just downriver in Pisa."

"You said you don't even like Pisa," Clarice says.

"No one does. You should visit sometime. They can't even build a bell tower properly. But my problem isn't with Pisa. It's the proximity. Especially when this Salviati is clearly a Pazzi lackey."

"You don't know his intentions," his mother says. "Besides, this is a church matter. There's no good in tarrying. You'll have to yield."

"Perhaps. Eventually."

The trumpets sound. Again his brother waits tirelessly on his horse. But Lorenzo and his mother remain turned toward each other.

"When did you stop wanting my advice?" she asks.

The horses barrel down the tilt. Deadlocked. Refusing to break.

"I'm not father. I'm not sickly. I don't need you telling me what to do. And neither does Giuliano." His last words are drowned out by a fresh bout of cheers. He breaks away from his mother's black eyes. On the field, Giuliano is retreating from a riderless horse. "See? He wins again. You worry too much."

"It's a mother's curse to worry," she says, turning away. "I don't know how much more of this I can suffer."

"Then go," he tells her. "No one is keeping you here."

XVIII

THE TOURNAMENT FINISHES. THE CROWD PULSES OUT FROM the scaffolds and into the piazza. The whole city, the entirety of it. Excepting those early years in the country, it's every figure from his existence. Faces he knows. Faces he doesn't know but that strike him as vaguely familiar, as if from a dream.

He sees Ginevra held firmly by a man whose name he doesn't know, who must be her husband. He sees his father too, next to a girl. Not Francesca, who died last year, but his new wife, Margherita, who is so slight of figure that she can't be more than fifteen. And he also sees the artists who have left Andrea's workshop: Sandro and Domenico and a spate of others whose work was clearly unremarkable since he has forgotten their names. He hopes none of them have noticed him, following Andrea across the piazza. Still chained to their master.

On a pole, high above the edge of the field, silk whips in the wind. Andrea's contribution to the tournament, a banner of Venus and Cupid. Andrea did the gods, then left the scenery for Leonardo to finish. He hasn't won any new work since finishing Ginevra's portrait, so he is back to busying himself with tasks Andrea didn't feel like doing himself.

The banner is good but not excellent. Like most of his master's work. Sandro's Minerva, which the Medici brother carried, is the better one. But that doesn't matter. No one, besides him, is looking at the banners anymore. They're useless now, left to shake in the wind, waiting to unravel, fade, and fray until they're as tattered as pauper's rags.

He looks away from them, turning back to the piazza, where he sights one more familiar face, one that sticks his boots to the earth like thick, wet mud.

Iac.

He looks so different, dressed in a tunic and woolen coat. Almost undistinguishable, except to him. He moves the same, though— lithely, easily passing unnoticed by the men hoisting flagons of ale and the women strolling arm in arm. Around them all, Iac's body shifts and twists without effort but full of grace. Leonardo thinks of the parts now concealed by fabric yet so clear in his mind. The freckled pathways, the taut legs.

He is only steps away from him. Close enough to wonder if, in a deep breath, he might catch his particular scent of marjoram. A foot forward, a reach of the arm, and he could feel his hand in his palm.

He considers this, but he doesn't move. And though he's still close, so close that he wouldn't even need to shout Iac's name to turn his head, he keeps his mouth shut.

Besides, what could he say to him here in the sprawl of a piazza? What words do they have to share beyond fatuous pleasantries? He knows only the faintest outlines of Iac's life. A workshop, not filled with paintings but with works of gold, where he still labors as an apprentice. A home, where Leonardo imagines Iac visits every Sunday for supper. Whether or not Iac has a mother who dotes on him, or a long-dead father; whether he is the youngest of his siblings; whether he is an orphan or a bastard or the prodigal heir to some fortune—Leonardo doesn't know. He knows only the spot on Iac's left cheek where a dimple shows when he smiles. That, unlike him, he favors his right hand. He knows nothing that matters. And this is mutual.

Better, then, to let Iac drift into the crowd, into that life of which Leonardo is not a part. To ignore the divine mistake or the error of nature that allowed him to happen upon Iac in a busy piazza. After all, they weren't meant to know each other by day.

As if tugged by a rope, Iac stops midstride. He sees Leonardo, sees how he has spotted him. And then Iac's face broadens into a crooked-teeth smile, one that curls Leonardo's lips too.

Iac steps closer. He says his name. Pats his arm. In his soft grip, Leonardo turns to cool stone. He doesn't breathe, doesn't speak. He doesn't dare to think.

"Did you enjoy the joust?" Iac is asking him.

"I-I—" he stammers. I hated it, he wants to say. But he is worried about sounding embittered. He's afraid he'll say something that will make Iac realize he doesn't like him this way, out of the tavern. "It was quite the spectacle."

Iac leans closer, lowers his voice. "It all seems rather indulgent, if you ask me. But the commissions have kept my master in business, so I suppose there's some good in that. Your master also made something, no?"

"A banner."

"Was it the Minerva that the champion was carrying? Gorgeous, that."

"That was Sandro Botticelli's," Andrea says, stepping forward. His master's voice makes Leonardo wish he could crumple, fold into himself, vanish. But Andrea's words are warm, not bitter. "One of my former pupils, so I'm pleased you like the work."

He watches the error crack across Iac's face. "Signor Verrocchio. Forgive me, I didn't—"

"There's nothing to forgive. But indulge me. You strike me as familiar."

"Iac once posed in the workshop," he says quickly. "Years ago. Just after Sandro left, if I recall."

"Ha!" Andrea slaps him on the arm, slaps Iac on the arm too. "You posed as an angel. I remember. A pleasure to see you again, Iac. You were learning to be a goldsmith, if I remember correctly."

"I still am, though I hope to finish my apprenticeship by next winter." He's embarrassed he didn't know this.

"I wish you the best of luck," Andrea offers.

Iac leaves them then, with a polite farewell and a quick nod. Leonardo says nothing; he only manages to raise a clumsy salute as the boy leaves.

"I'm glad you're enjoying yourself," Andrea says, leaning close to his ear. "You should be. A word of caution, though. Anyone can drop an accusation into one of those boxes they keep at the churches. This is Florence, not old Athens. They'll still jail you if you're foolish enough to get caught."

He meets his master's gaze, too knowing. He doesn't know what to say, if there are any words worth saying.

A breathless page boy interrupts them, sparing him. The boy asks his master if he is Andrea del Verrocchio. He tells him that Lorenzo de' Medici has requested his presence.

"Of course," Andrea says, with a straightened back, a courteous smile—the man he recognizes, not the man who was just whispering to him of boys.

But then he touches Leonardo's arm. Winks at him. Says, "Go, enjoy yourself tonight."

The page boy sees this, Leonardo thinks. He's watching him, making judgments. Then the boy turns back to Andrea. "Is he your apprentice? The one named Leonardo?"

"Former apprentice, yes."

"Lorenzo would like to see him too."

TO THE TILT. TO THE FAR END of the field, spotted with manure, with blood. To the dais at the front of the scaffolds, where the two Medici brothers sit side by side. Tables, heaving with gold platters of dates, pears, and colored jellies, beside heaps of roast capons, rolls of goat's cheese, and coils of sausage arranged around them. Fingers of rich merchants and veil-hidden noblewomen pick at the food; they cajole one another. In their shadows, nervous-eyed servants and slaves remain carefully in reach but out of the way.

Lorenzo sits, wide-armed, in the center of it all. Like a Christ in a fresco.

He won't remember him, Leonardo thinks. He can shake off the past, can introduce himself again—this time as a master painter, as someone who was commissioned by the Benci family.

Then a smile breaks across Lorenzo's face. "The giant slayer!" he shouts, rising to his feet, turning every head.

Leonardo bows. "An honor to meet you again, sir," he says, the words half lost to the wind.

"I don't know what it is about jousts, but they make me ravenous." Lorenzo slides a thin slice of cured meat between his teeth. "You must try some. Please." He waves to a servant, who rushes the platter before them.

Leonardo too easily recalls the look Lorenzo gave him the last time they met, the way he smirked at his clothes. He won't repeat that mistake. He takes the meat and swallows as fast as he can. Still, the fat lingers on his tongue like a stain.

"Your work was exquisite, Andrea. As always," Lorenzo says. "My brother agrees."

The man beside Lorenzo nods, but his eyes are trained somewhere behind him and Andrea, beyond the ring of the scaffolds. He looks starkly different from his brother. His face, gentle and long. His hair, falling in dark ribbons. Features all working in harmony.

"Giuliano has told me he wishes to make a commission himself. He was most impressed with your banner. But he is in desire of a painting, not silk work. Isn't that right, Giuliano?"

"Yes." The brother's voice is smooth, much deeper than Lorenzo's. "A devotional."

"I told my brother he should speak to Sandro, but I hear he's occupied with some altarpiece. Then I was at the Benci house, and Giovanni showed me a portrait of his sister. She's a fine girl, isn't she?"

"She is," Leonardo says, though he doesn't think he sounds convincing.

"It's a captivating portrait. You're registered at the guild, yes?" He says this with the air of a merchant thumbing a bolt of silk, assessing its quality.

"I am."

Lorenzo raises a glass, though neither he nor Andrea has one. "Then we shall draw up a contract."

OUTSIDE THE SCAFFOLDS, Andrea pulls him into a sudden embrace, and Leonardo finds himself wrapping his arms around his master, bringing his teary face to Andrea's shoulder.

"Hold on to this moment," Andrea says. "Don't ever forget how it feels."

How could he? It's like the first bite of a pear soaked in spiced wine. Like afternoon sun on bare, river-wet legs. Like waking up under heavy quilts beside Iac. A feeling so golden that he no longer cares about his earlier embarrassment, that Andrea knows of his habits. What did any of that matter now that he's been commissioned by the Medici?

But Andrea's hands are pulling away. He's peering at something over Leonardo's shoulder. Stepping away from him.

Approaching them is Giuliano, alone.

"Leonardo, yes? I'm glad you're still here," the brother says. "I had some thoughts on the subject matter. Seems foolish to wait and find another day to discuss it when you're right here."

A laugh, nervous and unexpected, slips from his mouth. "Of course."

Giuliano's eyes flit to Andrea, beside him. "I was hoping we might be able to speak in confidence."

"Say no more," Andrea says without hesitation. "I'll leave you." He bows to Giuliano, then walks away, back toward the workshop.

Giuliano turns to him, and Leonardo sees how his eyes are wider than his brother's, warm brown instead of nearly black. "You'll have to excuse me. I've been terribly rude. Were you on your way somewhere?"

"Home," he says, but then he realizes he doesn't want Giuliano to know he lives in Andrea's workshop. "My father's home, near the Palagio," he adds, even though he hasn't visited there in months.

"Would you mind if I walked with you there?"

"It would be an honor," he says, borrowing a phrase he's heard Andrea say to countless clients.

They walk westward toward the lolling sun saying nothing. Just a few streets separate them and the revelry at Santa Croce, but here the only sounds are shutters creaking in the wind, their boots padding the dirt. Giuliano's gait is uneven; he walks with a slight limp.

"I was good until the third course."

"I couldn't tell. You looked magnificent."

"That's all due to the likes of you, isn't it? The gold and silk and steel. I should be thanking you. You gave me a reason to escape all of that . . ."

Giuliano's voice trails, his feet slow.

"My brother is at ease among a crowd. He was born for it. I thought I was to join the church, so I learned to prefer a quieter life. But now I am to remain in Florence. I am to marry. And this is why I wanted us to speak privately." He lowers his voice, though the street is empty, the houses on each side all darkened. "The painting is for a girl. A woman, I should say. I want to present it to her as a gift. And I want the subject to be something honorable, something that conveys my sincerity and my intentions. Nothing presumptuous, though."

"A Madonna, perhaps?"

"Yes," Giuliano says eagerly. "But not in some manger. I want her to look like a queen."

His mind is already turning. Flashes of women posing, gentle-faced and knowing. A heavy jewel hanging from her neck. A babe in her arms, maybe? A flower in her fingers? Yes, that would be good.

"I could paint her dressed in silks. With the infant Christ cradled in her arms, if you wish. A simple, pious image."

"Excellent."

"Is there a family emblem I should include?"

Giuliano's mouth opens, closes, then opens again. "No. She's from a family of more modest means. But the heart cannot be denied. You're an artist, a man of feeling. Surely you understand."

"I do," he says, though he could never say how.

Giuliano stops, turning on his heel. "I should return before they complain too much about my absence. But it's a rare pleasure to be able to speak like this. I'm grateful to you for it."

"And I am grateful for the opportunity. I won't disappoint you."

"I know. I'm trusting you, Leonardo." He says this with a smile and a soft clasp of his gloved hand, and then he leaves. In his absence, a chill slips beneath Leonardo's tunic, stealing away the too-brief comfort of his success, the feeling now mottling brown, like a bitten apple, abandoned on a table. The sun has withdrawn behind the homes to the west. Ahead, his father's house casts a bladelike shadow over the small piazza.

He searches the upstairs windows for a madder glow, but they're all gray and blank. Like every house on this deadened street. He's alone, surrounded only by the dead leaves dragging across the dirt. Left only with a heavy, unignorable sensation: the dread of the work to be done.

XIX

HE STANDS ON HIS STONE PULPIT. HE WAVES HIS ARMS, BLESSES his congregation.

Through the censer smoke, he watches them genuflect then turn their backs to the altar, drifting toward the far end of the nave, dissipating like ghosts.

There was a time not so long ago when they would loiter near the transept as he retreated to the sacristy and changed out of his vestments. Young parents, wiry of frame, or broad-shouldered craftsmen, failing to conceal their tears. When he reemerged, they asked him for prayers: for a sickly daughter, for a bountiful harvest, for him to pass their blessings on to the Holy Father too.

Now, the nave promptly empties after his masses. Even devout Beatrice, with her white halo of hair, leaves with the rest of the flock. No longer does she bake him ubriachelle.

He looks out at the hazy expanse. The fissured stone floor. A cracked glass Abraham in a narrow, leaded window, his colors muted by grime, a trail of damp stone down the wall beneath him. He smells the must underneath the frankincense. It's all more like Christ's tomb in Calvary than a church. Certainly isn't a marble cathedral in Pisa.

His vision darkens. He stumbles down from the pulpit and staggers toward the sacristy, where he collapses onto a chair. He has only eaten one mouthful of holy bread today. He has been fasting for months now. No food at dawn, no meal in the afternoon—only the sparsest morsels after sundown. No meat, no cheese or milk, no wine either.

It began as his Lenten sacrifice. Each day, he felt weaker. He waited to feel worse. He wanted a glorious emptiness, an annihilation. But it refused to arrive. Those forty days have come and gone, yet he keeps his fast. After all, he is still in Rome and not in Pisa. He must have done something wrong to incur God's punishment.

He's prayed too—oh, how he's prayed. For strength, to endure this trial. For Medici to change his mind, for God to show him the path to righteousness. For the Lord to grant the pope wisdom or boldness, or both. For patience, for forgiveness, for hope. He confessed to bishops, cardinals, monks. Listed every one his sins. Expiated.

Nothing has changed.

A hand clasps his elbow, stirring him. His vision still wavers, but he can discern one of his young acolytes, holding a silver goblet. "Drink, Father," he's saying.

He obeys, weakly lapping at the wine. He wonders if it's the same wine he blessed during today's Mass, if he's drinking Christ's blood. Either way, wine or blood, it restores him. He rises, still unsteady on his feet, and the acolyte helps him pull his vestments over his head. When they fall to the floor, he sees how they're speckled red.

He turns to the acolyte, waits to be handed his cassock. But the young man is standing agape. Looking back at Salviati, at his chest. At his hair shirt.

It's a short-sleeved thing, made of coarse fur. Looks less like a garment and more like the discarded carcass of some farm animal, which it is—a goat, he'd guess. It scours his chest, makes his skin raw, his nipples bleed. And he deserves this, he thinks. If he's not yet in Pisa, then the Lord must think he's not yet penitent enough.

The sight of the garment has frightened the acolyte. Wearing such a thing—this isn't how the young man has envisioned his future in the church. That was true for Salviati too. He wanted to remain like the man standing before him—pious and dutiful and patient. What did he do it all for—the borrowing, bartering, conniving—if only to be robbed of what he most desired? What sort of story was that? He'd trade it all back, the fur-lined cloaks and his Trastevere house, to once again be nothing more than a simple servant to God.

He grabs his cassock out of the acolyte's arms. Hastily pulls the dark wool against his stinging skin. He has to stifle a cry. "God be with you," he mutters to the acolyte, and then he hurries out the sacristy.

But there's a lonely figure wandering the otherwise empty nave. Someone out of place, dressed in garish yellow silk.

"So this is where you preach," Girolamo says, glancing about the dark nave, which he does briefly, as the decorations are sparse. A triptych of the Passion. A waxy-looking Christ on a crucifix—repainted before Easter, given a lighter shade of skin this time. "Must you spend so much time here?"

"I prefer to keep busy."

"Or you're a glutton for punishment."

Both can be true, he thinks. "Come to confess something?"

Girolamo's laugh echoes off the bare walls. "I thought it would be good for us to talk, away from the palace."

"So talk," he says. He's being sour; he knows it. He wraps his arms around his chest and feels the coarse, stiff hairs scratch his skin.

"We both know my uncle's attention is not where it should be."

Yes, he thinks, it should be on Pisa.

"First it was the Jubilee, which was permissible. Then it was his library. Now it's this chapel. I think the architects see him more than we do these days. The cardinals are starting to complain. They say he's distracted. I'm sure you hear the whispers too."

They weren't whispers. Everyone in the Vatican heard the discontent. But that's how it always is. The pope indulges, the cardinals complain, and no one ever does anything. No one can.

"For all my uncle's talk about the Turks, all he's done is name a bishop to be his legate for the 'restoration of peace.' As if a priest can stop the infidels. I keep telling him that he must let me raise troops, that we should attack first, that we cannot let them put a single boot, or whatever it is they wear, on the peninsula. But all he does is nod. How good at nodding he is!

"He's weak. And everyone sees that now. Milan, Venice, and Florence, all allied against him. Medici ignoring his orders. And here I am, ready to raise an army to defend him if he asked. Yet he prefers to loiter about his roofless chapel."

Salviati nods and nods, hardly listening. Once again feeling uncertain on his feet, feeling empty. "But what is there for us to do?"

"Where's the fight in you?"

"You're the captain. I'm only a priest."

"Priests were never my preferred companions. You were the exception. You used to be a wily man."

"Perhaps I shouldn't have been."

Girolamo sighs. "You can feel it, can't you? This peace—it can't last. The animosity has grown thicker than fog. Something is going to change, and we need to be prepared for it."

"I don't need to do anything. I'm waiting, as the pope asked me to."

Girolamo shakes his head. "And what will you do if my uncle falters? What happens to us then? Everything I have I owe to him. And so do you."

A fat lot less though. "At least you have Imola."

"And if anything changes here, Florence will march on it the very next day."

"Not with you married to Sforza's daughter."

"Bastard daughter. Would Medici really care?"

He feels a prick of pity for Girolamo. "There's nothing to do but pray. I wish I could do more. But I can't."

Girolamo turns, takes a step. Then he stops. "Do you ever wish you could start it all over?" The words are barely a breath.

"Never." It's the truth.

"Not even to do things better? The right way?"

But what decision could have altered his life? He had always been marked as different. That was his curse, from the moment he slipped out from between the legs of a servant girl, just as it had been her curse to be sold from somewhere distant and south.

"As soon as we're born, it's too late," he says. "Original Sin. It's what we've inherited that's the issue."

"Then how do you address the mistakes?"

You can't, he thinks—but that's not what the Scriptures say. "That's why we have baptism. A cleanse to purge the wrongs. Only then can we be reborn."

Girolamo pouts. "Must you always speak like a priest? I'm not talking about our souls. I mean the daily mistakes. What we've done wrong."

"There's always confession."

"Be honest with me. Has it ever really made you feel better?"

"Sometimes it helps to let your mind speak aloud."

"But you can do that with anyone. It doesn't need to be a priest."

"The Holy Father would disagree."

"My uncle disagrees with me on many things. Sure, I can go to a priest and ask forgiveness for what I've done. But whom am I supposed to blame for what's been done to me?"

God, Salviati thinks.

He waits to feel a pang of guilt for such a thought. It fails to arrive.

He should tell Girolamo that they could both pray—together. He should tell him that God will listen; that he, Salviati, would listen too. But how would that be any different from these months of punishing himself, from the years he's spent enduring this rotten man?

Sympathy, to him, is a currency as crucial as the florin. It needs to be given just as it needs to be received. Some have more of it, others less. But there is a finite amount of it in the world. If he spent all of his on pitying a rich fool like Girolamo, what would be left for Maddalena, for Beatrice, for the mendicant and needy—for himself?

This man is God's problem now, he thinks. "If you'll indulge me in preaching just a little more, Christ would say to forgive those who have done you wrong."

"I don't know if I can," Girolamo says. "I'm no savior."

"None of us is."

"Would you forgive?"

He thinks of white robes and a priest's hand at the small of his back. He thinks of sinking into a marble font, cool water flooding his face, an oil-slick thumb striking a cross on his forehead.

That could be peace, he thinks. The cleansing of everything wrong.

A vision swarms, wretched and red, radiant and beautiful, like shining, faceted garnet. A great black cloud roams over the loamy earth. It churns, it rolls over the Tuscan hills, to Florence. There are good people there, holy ones praying. The cloud passes over them. It crawls instead into the courtyards of palaces, swirls around sculptures, climbs up stairs. It finds the men in silk and sable, and it chokes them. Their mouths fill with foamy spittle, and they fall to the floor, grasping at their throats. Then the cloud lifts. In its place, a massive sun appears. Brighter than anything ever seen. Glowing the city's homes umber. Turning Santa Reparata's bell tower to ruby and emerald, its dome to fire. Lighting bright the palace on the Via Larga, where Medici lies on the ground, putrefying lemon yellow and anise green.

A purge, he thinks. To wipe away the sins.

"No," he says. "I can't."

He lurches away from Girolamo. Leaves him gaping in the nave.

Outside, the sun glares, the streets bake. The hair shirt tears. He staggers—down the hill, over the river, back to his house. He heaves himself up the stairs, crawls across the bedroom floor. He hangs his head over his chamber pot, breathing in lye and faint filth. He sticks his sweaty fingers into his mouth. Out, he begs the ugly thoughts, out! He sputters a pale liquid, and he slumps to the floor.

Sideways, prone, he presses his slick fingers together in prayer. He asks God for forgiveness, again and again. He wants this unholiness gone.

XX

HE RETURNS TO THE PALACE, WHICH IS MUCH THE SAME AS IT was four years past. Except today the sky is the color of untreated wool; everything seems less brilliant, more brutish. Shadows brood in the arcades. Donatello's David swaggers but fails to shine. Still it is graceful and slight and bold. The statue is even better than he remembers. It reminds him of Iac. So many things do now.

For the first time, he steps inside the palace. An attendant leads him up a stairwell and through so many rooms, wide and long. The windows are mostly shuttered, the light is faint, the air trapped and thick with dust. There are rolled-up rugs, chairs hidden under bolts of undyed linen. Any color comes from the various devotional paintings hanging from the walls not unlike shackled prisoners. He passes at least three Madonna and Christs—but this attendant is fast-footed; he cannot pause to see if they're any good. He wonders if anyone ever stops to look at them.

More rooms. Another hallway, a door at its end. A knock and they're told to enter. Giuliano is grinning at him, surprising him with a quick embrace. He tells Leonardo he's been looking forward to this day. He then dismisses the attendant, carefully shuts the door behind him.

This salon is different from the others. The shutters are open, the windows overlooking a garden. The furniture is handsome, painted and carved, its varnish lustrous. There is a silk-threaded screen, detailed as a tapestry, that Giuliano is now shifting, folding.

"Please allow me to introduce you to Fioretta."

She is full-faced and button-mouthed. Her hair is palest honey; she has it pulled back from her face in a simple, tight braid. But her eyes are what most fascinate. Under heavy lids, they are wide and gray. They shine, they put him at ease.

"Fioretta," Giuliano is saying, "this is Leonardo."

He is already leaning forward, bringing his lips to her gloveless fingers. Her cheeks bloom at this, a bright red, unabashed. She titters, and when she does, she fails to cover her open mouth.

"I've never been painted before," she says, her voice light.

"You're in the best of hands," Giuliano says, running his hand over her unveiled, plaited hair. "He'll capture your likeness better than anyone else could. I promise it."

Leonardo steps back, watching, noting, committing to memory—how her long fingers trace the line of Giuliano's jaw; how she looks up at her love, her gaze serene, almost sleepy; and then the mouth, so small, not quite smiling.

The sight turns his neck hot; in him is an urge to turn away, a sense that he is a trespasser here. But they're too absorbed in each other. Entranced, if only for a moment. Unconcerned with him, with the differences between their lives, with everything beyond this quiet room.

This is love, he realizes. A rare thing to see, right before the eyes, so earnest and unveiled and uncomplicated.

He sets down his supplies. He prepares. If Giuliano wants her likeness rendered, he'll need to capture this, her adoration. She cannot be alone, a Madonna waiting solemnly for an angel to arrive or her son to return. She'll need to have her child, the object of her affection, in her arms.

Giuliano places a cushioned stool beside Fioretta. He looks over at Leonardo, at his papers, his pens and charcoal, his knives and ink. Eagerly, like a boy eyeing sugar-dusted cake at a feast.

"Thank you, again," he says. "You honor me by painting her."

"It is my honor," Leonardo says.

Giuliano searches the room. He frowns. "We're in need of wine. Some Trebbiano, perhaps?"

Leonardo waits for Fioretta to speak, but she's looking at him, expectant. They both nod.

Giuliano is already opening the door, stepping through it. "I'll return. You two can acquaint yourselves. You'll be spending plenty of time together, after all."

The door shuts, and then there's only the hearth's soft crackling.

Here he is, alone with a woman. He glances at her. She's turned away, toward the folded screen.

He trifles with his pen, fingers his paper. Already, he senses he's ruining this. Making the same mistakes he did when working on Ginevra's portrait. Already, he has promised too much—a scene, instead of a simple portrait. A moment, and a world, made only by his hand, his oil blends, his brush. In all his hoping for a commission like this, he neglected to consider what would happen to him, to his career, if he fails.

He steps to the window, looks down on the garden, shaggy with green hedges and trees. Pocketed with rare color too: pale yellow lemons, fallen from branches and rotting in the soil; the blood-red bloom of a carnation peeking from beneath a thicket of emerald leaves. Something else shining too—in a cooler shade, one of bronze. His younger self, kept the same over the years, save for a slight tarnishing of the shoulders. Him as David, still striving to be—failing to be—heroic.

Behind Leonardo, Fioretta is waiting, sitting patiently on her stool. Straight-backed, legs tightly crossed. She dangles a shoe—a loose, simple clog—from her toes. Without Giuliano, she looks so uncertain, so unaccustomed to this place. And he must look the same.

"It's kind of him to find us wine," he hears himself saying. "Though truthfully I couldn't tell you the difference between Trebbiano and Vernaccia."

"Such luxuries are lost on me too," she says. "But he told me your father is a notary. I would've thought you grew up with such things."

"He is. But I was raised out in the country," he says, returning to his papers. "And I began my apprenticeship shortly after I arrived in the city."

"He must be proud to have a son with rare talent."

"I think he would have preferred a son who could have followed him into his business."

"Perhaps we have that in common, you and me. My father is a professor and lacks sons to teach." She meets his stare. She is unafraid, he realizes. "You have sisters?"

"No sisters, no brothers. But perhaps that may change soon. My father's wife is newly with child."

"A blessing. My congratulations."

He says nothing.

"You are fortunate, you know. To get to make something that you'll leave behind."

"All I do is mere imitation. Copying, not creating," he says. "I'm envious of that in women. To truly bring something to life. It amazes me when I think about it."

She laughs. "A child? I'd prefer not to. I know why I'm here. I know better than to believe it could be anything more. Thinking otherwise, letting oneself dream—that's when trouble begins." She runs her palms across her thighs, smoothing the wrinkles in her dress. "I like my life as it is," she says, her voice quieter than before.

"I suppose I do as well."

But he also thinks: I've always been a dreamer.

He brings pen to paper, and he begins to trace her features.

THIS BECOMES HIS DAY, a day that multiplies, that unspools to many weeks, to months. Sometimes he comes here, to the palace. Some days he goes to her father's house, east of Santa Croce. Once, he even journeys to a villa north of the city, where he paints her before a portico.

The streaks and outlines are quick to coalesce. Fioretta dissolves and his Madonna becomes real, her oil cheeks seeming to warm with blood, her silk-covered chest heaving with breath. It is already better than his portrait of Ginevra. It is beautiful, he's beginning to think. When he finishes, it might even be great.

By day, he works relentlessly. Every evening, the panel glistens. And nearly every night as it dries, he returns to the tavern, to Iac.

"WHAT DOES SHE LOOK LIKE?" Iac asks.

The question surprises him. He never talks about his work here; it feels wrong to do so. He and Iac, they have an arrangement, its nature made clear by the coins in his purse. Terms explicit, roles defined.

He sounds like his father, he realizes. God help him.

He sits up in bed. Beside him, Iac looks up at him from beneath a mess of curls. He is smiling. Curious. He truly wants to know.

He slides his arm behind Iac's slender back and pulls him against his chest, feeling both the knobs of his spine and the smoothness of his skin. He wraps Iac's fingers inside the palm of his left hand, extends the pointing finger.

"It's difficult to describe," he says, guiding Iac's finger as if it were a brush. "She sits in the middle, in a dress. Blue, of course. There's silk and gauze, folding, creasing everywhere, making so many little shadows. Her sleeves are carnelian with a hint of saffron so it looks different from the carnation"—he jerks Iac's finger downward—"which has deep red petals, lifting from a thin yet sturdy stem at the very center of the painting." He lets go of Iac's hand, rubs at his face. "The Christ child will be reaching for the carnation. But I haven't started that yet."

It's beginning to frighten him, this part of the painting. A large, cream-colored splotch on the right side of the Madonna's lap, where the infant Christ is meant to be. The child who eludes him, whom he can't yet paint. He knows Andrea sees this, that his gaze remains on this void, while Leonardo fusses with adding layer upon diaphanous layer to the Virgin's sleeves. Remember the carp, Andrea has told him—more than once. And he knows Sandro and Domenico and even less skilled painters like Cosimo Rosselli are now whipping up one, two, three devotionals in a single year. Meanwhile, he keeps mincing his brushstrokes, leaving the others to collect commissions that he, too, could be competing for, commissions that will sustain them into the next year, and the one after that.

He shifts, rolling onto his side to face Iac.

Don't dwell on the work, he thinks. Look at this boy, lying beside you. At those arms, faintly dusted with hair. He needs this—Iac's heat, his herby scent.

"You're doing it," Iac says.

"Doing what?"

"Staring at me like I'm a painting."

A subject, not a painting, he wants to correct.

"Your nostrils flare when you're doing it."

"My nostrils flare?" He touches his nose.

Iac laughs. "I swear it," he says, then he swats his hand away and kisses his nose. "One notices such things, after so many nights."

Something about Iac's gentle grin coaxes the words from his mouth. "Sometimes I still see the boy who posed for the workshop. I think I'm still an apprentice. But—"

The words snag.

Wasn't he still that apprentice, in so many ways? Still working for his master, still living under his roof, still waiting to make his own name? All that had changed was that he now has his own work and owes his yearly dues to the guild. That he sometimes is afforded the freedom to come here, to the Buco.

Fingers, on his chin. "I like when you stare, mind you," Iac whispers, mouth to ear, every word hot against his skin. "I've never known anyone else to look at me the way you do."

Blood pounds. Thoughts babble and blare. He pulls away, rises from the bed, tensing at the sharp autumn air. He gathers his clothes, dresses quickly.

"Would you ever draw me?" Iac asks, behind him.

The words stop him. His belt trembles in his hands. "I don't need a model."

"Not as a model. As a subject."

"No," he says, still turned away from Iac. "You don't even know if I'm any good."

"I've seen a sketch of yours, remember?"

He could never forget. "That was only an exercise. A portrait is something different, something more. It takes time. Devotion."

"I can be patient," Iac says. "And I promise to judge the work fairly once I've seen it."

"But—"

"But I'm a whore?"

"That's not what I was going to say." He pulls on his boots. He doesn't know what he was going to say, truthfully.

"I don't intend on doing this work forever, you know," Iac says. "It's only a means to an end, until my apprenticeship is done."

"I know," he says quietly, turning back to him.

Iac is sitting on the edge of the bed, arms stretched widely behind him. Leonardo can count his every rib, their ridges and shadows. He can mark the exact spot where his hairs begin to curl, just above his navel. Where they begin to thicken and darken, leading down to his cock, soft and pink-tipped.

And Iac is so at ease like this, naked before him. Like this, he can imagine him in a thousand scenes. On fields, in deserts, atop ruins. Iac watching a joust or standing in the door of his own smithy's shop. Iac in bedrooms different from this one. Palace bedrooms, farmhouse lofts. A bedroom they could share, a small upstairs room for just the two of them.

It is nice to dream of such things, impossible things.

But they must live their separate lives. He will never have the luxury of choosing the subjects he paints. This city has its tastes, after all, and they're not for Achilles and Patroclus nor Jupiter and Ganymede. They're for Christs and Madonnas, for saints and their suffering. It is all he knows how to paint: virgins and angels and wives to be. He's never painted a flesh-and-blood man. He doesn't know if he can.

"One day, perhaps," he lies. "Once I finish the Christ child."

XXI

HE RIDES AWAY FROM HIS BANKERS AND THE PRIORS, AWAY from his uncle, away from his letters, from their noise and every ill tiding, away from Florence. Not in a coach but upon a saddle on his favorite black-haired destrier. At a canter, his body jolting against the dirt roads, his seat still bruised from his last ride.

He rides not knowing where he'll end the day. Sometimes it's not so far: to Fiesole, where he can still see his city while he strolls through his gardens. Other times, he goes to Careggi, charging his horse past the ghosts of the men who came with daggers for his father. Usually, though, he goes farther—to his villa at Cafaggiolo.

He likes it here in the misty green valleys of the Mugello. It feels right for him to be here; after all, they were his ancestral lands. A place where his family were once knights, where legend had it that one such forefather slayed a giant.

He sees no giants today—only the rise of the familiar, red-roofed clock-tower, the white, crenellated walls, the sprawling gardens that his grandfather had built. He has Sigismondo with him to hunt; together, they'll slip hoods from falcons' heads and watch them seek out their prey. He has Agnolo with him to write letters back to the city—to Nori and the bank, to the priors at the Palagio, to his brother too. He'd like it if Giuliano was with him, but lately he always seems to be missing his brother.

He stops his horse at the stone-arched doorway. Climbs off, strokes his mane. He breathes in the untroubled air, cooler and autumn-sharp. On it, the rustling of brittle leaves and scant birdsong. There are no servants here to greet him, for he told no one he was coming. He prefers it this way, to slip in and out without notice. It keeps the letters from finding him for a little while longer.

"Find the stable boy, will you?" he asks Agnolo and Sigismondo. He leaves them with his horse.

Inside, he kicks off his boots. His hosed feet leave a trail of damp prints on the rose-colored floor. Now he feels it: the throbbing of his lower back, the aching in his knees, his feet. Feels, too, how his riding shirt is soaked through. He takes the stairs to his chambers slowly, bracing himself against the wall.

Upstairs, he hears distant muttering behind a closed door: the servants with their daily duties. He stops at a window along the hallway to his bedroom. Looks out at the long, walled garden, at the bronze statues.

He'll stay here until the couriers come. Sometimes he'll have a week. Two, if he's blessed. But the letters will come. Missives from the Signoria complaining about the cost of wine or the sodomy accusations piling up in the churches. Reports from his bankers in England, whining that King Edward owes over thirty thousand florins. More of the same from the bankers in Bruges, fretting about Burgundy's debts. And then there were the letters of warning: from his mother, as always, but also from his ambassadors, even from Galeazzo in Milan. The duke told him, told his brother to be on guard. That they had made too many foes.

He disagrees with this, of course. Relationships may be strained with Rome, and Naples too—but he does not have any enemies. Except for the Pazzi, of course. And that was their own making. Besides, they were just bankers. And here, away from Florence, he won't let them disturb him.

He walks to his bedroom, opens the door.

A sharp scream. Clarice, in an armchair. Flush-faced, hand clutching her bosom. "I didn't know to expect you," she says, after regaining her breath.

He feels his own blood rushing too. He thought she was at Fiesole with the children. She certainly had told him she was here; she was unfailing in sending him thrice-weekly missives about her days in the country—so dull, she called them—and her reports on the children: Lucrezia and Maddalena always well-behaved, Piero always a trouble. He wouldn't call these letters nuisances, but he sometimes chooses not to open them. He gets so many letters, after all.

Instead, he tells her, "I wanted to surprise you."

"I'd think the doctors might say surprises aren't good for me at the moment." She rises slowly to her feet. Waddles toward him. Brings him into a quick embrace, her domed belly keeping them apart. "You stink of horse."

He wouldn't know. "We rode fast."

"Your brother's with you?"

"Just Sigismondo and Agnolo. I hardly see Giuliano anymore."

She turns away, but he catches her coy grin.

"What?"

She eases herself back into her chair, rests her hands on her stomach. She smiles. "You really don't know? Your brother has a lover."

He laughs, shakes his head. "He's a man in his best years. I doubt it's just one."

"Oh, I heard differently. That one girl in particular has caught his attention. I don't know who she is though."

"And how did you hear this?"

"You should listen to the servants' chatter. They're always about. They strip our sheets. They know everything."

Her eyes hold on his, a brief challenge.

There was nothing to say to this. She was with child. Certain accommodations were necessary. Expected, even.

"I've been trying to find him a decent bride," he says, hoping to redirect the conversation. "I suppose this explains his reluctance to commit."

"What does your mother think?"

He imagines her in Morba, gurgling in a hot spring. "I haven't asked."

He walks to the large cassone, carved and gilded, at the foot of his bed. He opens it, searches through the folded clothes inside.

"While you're here, might I ask you about something?" Clarice says.

"If you wish." He pulls out fresh linen.

"This Pisan matter. When will it be resolved?"

He turns, saying nothing.

"I don't wish to interfere with your affairs," she says, her words quickening. "I know they're difficult, far beyond what I could comprehend. But what I've heard worries me."

"Did my mother write you?"

"I don't hear everything from her, Lorenzo."

"So your father, then."

"No," she stammers. "If you're so insistent on knowing, it was Bianca. She was here, a week past. She's troubled by all this squabbling with the Pazzi. What it means for Guglielmo. For her family."

"Why is she speaking to you of this? She's my sister. She should know she can come to me with her concerns," he says. "Besides, I've taken no issue with Guglielmo in any of this."

"But surely you can appreciate how he must be vexed by it. You, his friend, his wife's brother, on one side of him. His uncle and his brother on the other."

"And if he tried to remedy the situation, I'd welcome it. Instead, he said no word but mum while his brother snatched away the Curial account."

He strips off his still-wet riding shirt and throws it onto the floor. He unclasps his belt and pulls down his hose.

Clarice brings a hand to her face, averts her gaze. "It's not my place to offer advice to you. I know that," she says softly. "But I don't like us being at odds with the church."

He dresses in crisp linen. Rolls on soft, dry hose. "Your feelings aren't material here."

"I want to be able to go back to Rome, Lorenzo. To visit my family. For our children to meet their grandfather."

He considers her belly. Wonders if he'll have another son. "Nothing is preventing that."

"Is that so?"

She looks up at him with a lancing glare.

He turns to the floor, finds his belt. Clasps it around his waist once more. "I'm pleased to see that you are healthy, so I won't trouble you here any longer. I'll see you again once you're returned to Florence."

Her face turns steely, her lips purse. "Lucrezia and Piero should be back from their riding lessons soon. And Maddalena is in the nursery."

"You'll give them my love, won't you? And tell Piero he's to begin lessons with Agnolo when you're all in Florence again."

If she's surprised, she hides it well. "Be careful," she says.

Another warning he doesn't need.

THEY LEAVE, HE AND AGNOLO AND SIGISMONDO. They ride, farther still. Not back to Florence, but westward. Over ambering mountains and along streams with leaping trout. The sky bruises, then dims as they ride into Prato, their horses slavering. They find an inn for the evening, and Lorenzo leaves his companions once they've settled into their rooms, roaming the empty streets until he comes upon a brothel. Inside, he makes his selection quickly. Spends an efficient hour caressing unfamiliar curves, enjoying the comfort of a woman who doesn't speak to him about church appointments or bank balances. Who only asks him what he wants for tonight, and tonight alone.

In the morning, he is the first on his horse. He sits in his saddle, waiting for the others, listening to the city chime with bells. A group of women walks toward him, all in brown mantles with white scarves wrapped over their heads and scapulars dangling from their shoulders. The nuns' faces are crinkled, their cheeks ruddy. They pass him without a word, make their slow way across a wide piazza to a small, plain church.

Agnolo and Sigismondo come beside him. "To Florence?" Agnolo asks.

"Not yet," he tells them, ignoring their frowns.

They continue riding west, then south. Over more mountains, through more hamlets and towns he has never heard of, that don't matter to him: Colle, Anchiano, Vinci. They meet the Arno once again—not the narrow, murky serpent that ripples through Florence, but here a wide, white-capped river busy with barges. They ride all day, then under a dusky, torn-sheet sky, Pisa appears before them.

The harbor is silty and half empty. The cathedral is marble, yes, but it is so much smaller than Florence's. And then there's the bell tower beside it, still crooked.

So many letters, so much arguing. And for this?

"The proverb about Pisa," he says. "What is it?"

Agnolo laughs. "'Better a death in your family than a Pisan on your doorstep.'"

"There's truth in that," he says with a grin. But if he were to let this Salviati fellow have Pisa, then he wouldn't be on his doorstep in Florence. He'd be here, in this bad air, swarming with biting gnats.

Let him have it, he thinks.

XXII

EVEN IN SLEEP, THE MADONNA IS THERE WITH HIM. GAZING down at him with her lips budded in the smallest of smiles. He meets her soft gray eyes; he can see the love in them. He knows what he is meant to be—her creation, her hope.

But he cannot see it himself. He tries to reach a hand forward, to see his puffed baby fingers, but nothing is there. When he looks down to glimpse his naked body, there is only the cushion on which he, the child, is meant to be sitting. It is ochre velvet, patterned with crystal balls; it is empty. He is only a blank gash on gessoed poplar.

His heart jolts.

He blinks, and the Madonna vanishes. He sees only the tavern bedroom.

He thinks: was there such a thing as velvet, back in the age of Christ? Perhaps hemp or worsted would have been more accurate. Duller, though. Certainly less magnificent.

The truth is that he could look at any single stroke and quibble with some detail. Look at nearly any Virgin in Florence, and she is wearing a soft blue robe. Could a carpenter's wife really have afforded her robes to be dyed with expensive indigo? He doubts it, yet the Madonna in her blue is more than accepted—it's expected.

He turns to Iac, watches his bare chest rise slowly, fall quickly. He lays his hand against it, feels his body at work. "When will I see him?" he asks.

Iac opens his eyes, turns to him. "Who?"

"The Christ child."

Iac doesn't laugh at this. He doesn't shake his head or rub at his eyes. He simply says, "I don't know. How do other artists paint him?"

"Terribly." He laughs. Every frescoed or paneled infant is hideous. They had ghoulish faces, skin looking like melted wax, exceptionally full heads of hair, scowls of old men. The reason is simple: no artist paints them from life. They cannot use their familiar models who pose as their saints and virgins. Instead, they contort what has come before, creating new monstrosities.

"Do you have any relatives you could draw?"

Not yet, he thinks. "I have no one."

Iac leans away from Leonardo and pulls the quilt over his bare body. "When are you meant to finish it?"

"It's already overdue," he says softly.

Iac's brows furrow. "My sister is with child. I'll ask if you could paint the child, when it comes."

Leonardo shifts off the bed. "I couldn't impose like that. On your family," he says, facing the lone, cloth-covered window, threading his fingers through his tangled hair.

He hears Iac throw off the quilts, hears his bare feet touch the floor. "I'm sure you'll see the child eventually," he says from behind him.

"Will I?" he says, turning around.

Iac is leaning against the bedpost, his bare chest puckered, his arms folded behind him. His stare is steady, almost steely. But his mouth, wrinkled, betrays his hurt.

Leonardo's left hand twitches. An idea glints, transporting him. He sees a desert, flat and harsh. A man tied to a post. Martyred Sebastian, pelted with arrows. The ropes are fraying, they're falling to his bare thighs. This Sebastian moves toward him, across sunbaked sand.

"I need to tell you something before you go," Sebastian is telling him, prying apart his restless fingers, unfolding them into his hands. His lips graze his palm, its creases ink-stained. "I'm to register at the guild by summer. My master thinks I'm ready. And I've nearly saved enough to find my own space."

He pulls his hands away. Sebastian disappears. The desert is gone.

He's taken too long to speak. "I'm pleased for you," he manages to say. He means it.

"We could still visit each other, even if we won't have this bedroom."

"I'd like that," he says. But he knows that is just another dream. He and Iac can't know each other outside this bedroom. When Iac leaves this place, he will vanish from his life; and Leonardo—he'll remain in the workshop, taunted by his childless Madonna. Andrea will tire of his tarrying. And Giuliano will forget about the commission, forget about him.

Everything will continue on, without him. Unless he paints the Christ.

A CHILD IS BORN. An occurrence that truthfully happens every day. But this child, its arrival, is exceptional to Leonardo. For many reasons.

He goes to the baptistery. He knows this building only from the outside. Its stripes of marble, from Carrara and Prato. The bronze doors, to the north and south, with panels of Christ. To the east, facing the cathedral, that other pair of radiant doors painted gold and cast with stories more vivid than they ever were on paper.

Dante and his Beatrice, Donatello and Sandro, Lorenzo and Giuliano, and Andrea beside him—every child born in Florence has been carried through its doors and baptized at its font. But him, a country boy? He's never stepped inside.

He had thought the interior would be dark and austere with bare walls of drab, smoothed pietraforte like the inside of Santa Reparata. He's pleased to see he was wrong—very much so. It's a riot of patterns, of tesserae and marble and stone. There's a mosaic devil surrounded by serpents; men being stoned and men being eaten by snakes; he even spots a man with his bare ass hanging from the devil's mouth.

He stifles a laugh, and a priest glares at him from across the marble basin filled with water. He turns away, looks at the other side of the dome. There's a throned adult Christ, larger than anything, arms outspread, palms turned outward. A provoking gesture.

I will paint you, Leonardo wants to say back. If only you'd come to me.

Sometimes he wonders if the Christ refuses to come because he so often fails to go to Mass. If he's being punishing for a perceived lack of faith. It's not that he doesn't believe in Him. He simply has questions he'd like answered. Like where all the water disappeared to, after the Flood. Or how rotted Lazarus was before Christ raised him from the dead.

"Your father's drawn quite a crowd," Andrea says.

"He has." It's true—though there were few familiar faces in this room. Andrea, of course, whom he's glad to have with him as company. And there's Giovanni as well, standing toward the doors, though it is odd to see him without Ginevra. But the rest of the men in this room—friars in brown robes, merchants and bankers in finer stuff—must all be clients of his father. Men he doesn't know, men who don't seem to know him either. Why would they? Even he does not look like himself today in this lifeless gray tunic and beige wool cloak, thirsting for more vibrant dye. They make him feel as if the years have vanished and he's a boy again, new to the city. And like he's that child, he has secreted a notebook beneath his clothes, against his hip.

"Do you know if it's a boy or a girl?" Andrea asks.

"No," he says. The letter from his father was only an announcement. Likely the same that the rest of the men here received. Yes, he could've run to his father's house as soon as he read it. Ten minutes is all it would have taken him. But he was reluctant. It would have been an intrusion, he told himself. Besides, the baptism would be held within days. Waiting risked purgatory. The child could catch cold or burn with fever. There could even be another plague.

But he's prayed—a rare act for him—that he has a sister. He'd like to have a woman in his life who was more than story to him, who existed beyond his painted panels. Someone he could one day ask the thousand questions that rest in his mind about what is different for them.

It's a selfish hope. He knows his father wouldn't dote on a daughter. He'd complain about the eventual expense of her dowry.

A brother—that would be simpler for his father. Far more complicated for him though.

White washes over the ceiling. The mosaics glint and glow. The doors have opened, and his father is walking down the aisle, cradling a bundle of wools and furs. From the swaddling a hand reaches up with stubby fingers. He has to remember this, he thinks. His Christ child must have the same hands.

His father looks down at the child in his arms. He's smiling.

So it's a boy.

His father continues toward the font, passing his firstborn without even a nod or a glance. At the font, the priest begins reciting his incomprehensible Latin, that tongue he was never taught and has no desire to learn. At the basin, brimming with water, his father unwraps his son from his nest and gently rubs the infant's forehead.

Leonardo touches his own hair, the long curls that his father never knew how to tame. Beneath his tunic, a rivulet of sweat runs down his side, where his notebook is hidden. He wants to rescue those papers. He wants to pull the charcoal from inside his boot and draw.

The infant is in the priest's arms now, and he raises the child high, revealing him to them all. The fleshiness is what surprises him. The rolls of fat at the belly, on the arms and legs. The almost jowly swell of the cheeks. That's where all the others err, he thinks. The face must be round.

Remember this, he tells himself.

Then the priest reads his brother's name. Antonio di Ser Piero da Vinci.

He dips the infant into the water, and Leonardo shuts his eyes.

Antonio—it was his grandfather's name. The man who raised him on that hillside in the country because his father was always a long day's ride away, ingratiating himself with the city merchants. His grandfather— who was kind, who was patient with him.

Look, he always said to Leonardo.

At what? he once asked.

At everything, he'd said.

So he always looked. At the green of the rustling cypresses. At the swirls of glassy creek-water around a cluster of smoothed, pale blue stones. At a tuft of cloud tinged gray on its underside, as if it had been dragged through dust.

He supposes his father had always intended to name his firstborn after his own father. That Leonardo happened upon his father's life too early and unasked for was only a tiring obligation for the man. For so long, he had thought his father might one day acknowledge him as more than a bastard. All he had to do was draft a simple document, send it to the council—a document his notary father had written for scores of other men who made the same mistake as him.

He's a fool for not knowing it sooner. Leonardo could paint for kings and still couldn't change this truth.

The infant is brought up from the water, dripping, screaming. Every limb is kicking, the head is shaking back and forth, the hands are balled into pink fists. He's rather ugly. A red tadpole. This, too, is where the other painters have gone wrong: infants are never still, unless they are asleep. They are twisting, full of motion.

It's too good a moment to waste. As for what his father will say? He no longer gives a fig. He knows what his father will do after this: deposit the child in the wet nurse's arms, retreat to his office, to his ledgers and contracts. He'll wait, impatiently, for the boy to be weaned, for him to crawl, to walk, to speak. Then he'll mold him into the good son, the true son, the one that will follow him, become a notary, carry on his name.

Leonardo? He has no part in that. His own name, it will vanish with him.

But his work? By the grace of God, it might continue on. If it's good enough.

He frees his notebook, finds an empty page. He grabs the nub of charcoal blistering his ankle. He ignores Andrea's widening eyes, ignores his father's grim glare. He draws: the pulsing movements of the infant, the shadows cast by his fatty legs. His motions are quick, mere outlines and hasty shadings. He hopes it will be enough.

XXIII

EVENTUALLY, RELUCTANTLY, HE MUST RETURN TO FLORENCE.
No matter how fast he rides across Tuscany, letters from the city always
catch up to him: the priors, asking to meet before their term is finished;
Nori, sharing his concerns over the bank's balances; Clarice, wondering
when he intends to spend time with their newborn son.

Truthfully, he has tired of life on the road. His backside is red and
pimpled, saddle sore. His back aches from lumpy inn mattresses. And
while Agnolo and Sigismondo do their best to keep him in good spirits,
they are always reserved with him, infallibly obsequious.

He'll be honest: he misses the company of his brother.

He arrives unannounced. The courtyard's setts are slick with springtime rain. He wipes his muddy soles on the way up to his chambers.
Quietly retreats to his bedroom, where he kicks off his boots, thumbs
through the thick stack of letters on his desk, his wet fingers blurring
their ink. None of them important.

Then he hears the muffled cry of his son.

He follows the sound—out of his bedroom, through small rooms
and wide salons, past shuttered windows and rolled-up rugs and divans
covered in sheets of linen. The sconces are lit only where necessary. The
house has a transient quality now—more like an inn than a palace.

Clarice's room is cool and curtained. When he enters, she quickly
shoos her handmaid and draws a cloth over her bare, swollen breast.
"You should have written," she says.

He steps next to the bed. Her cheeks are full and rosy. Her hair is oily,
pulled into a long, tight plait. At her breast, little Giovanni makes a quiet
sucking sound. He has more dark hair than when he saw him last. He
carefully leans over his son and pecks Clarice's forehead.

"You're well?" he asks.

"I'll be better when he stops teething."

"So call the wet nurse and spare yourself the discomfort."

"I gave Piero to the wet nurse and now he gives us nothing but trouble. If I had—" She stops, wipes the sweat from her brow. "How long will you be home?"

"A week. Perhaps longer."

Her wide face remains placid. She shifts the babe, grimacing.

"How is he?"

"Good. Healthy."

He watches his son. His soft, small chin moving up and down. His wide, dark eyes, staring at nothing. Perhaps he can do better with this one, he thinks. There's still time.

"May I?" he asks, reaching for the child.

"Not now," Clarice says, flinching. She pulls Giovanni closer. "You're filthy."

He pulls his hands away, chastened. The sleeves are splattered with mud.

"I'll come back after I bathe," he says, walking away. He stops at the door. "Is Giuliano here?"

Her lips curl. "He is. And I think he has company."

GIULIANO IS SMILING, HE LOOKS almost boyish, when he opens the door. Then he sees Lorenzo, and his face falls and mottles. His brother bashfully glances at the woman—fair-haired and unfamiliar—retreating toward the wall in small, slippered steps. She is not the only other person in the room. There is another man here, whom he vaguely recognizes. Tall, with a strong nose and eyes that linger.

"You remember Leonardo," Giuliano says.

"Our David." He laughs.

"A pleasure to see you again," the artist says, a tremble in his voice.

"And who is the lovely woman?" he calmly asks his brother.

Giuliano goes to her, takes her hand. He brings her back under the candlelight.

"This is Fioretta Gorini," his brother says.

"It's an honor to meet you, my lord," she says, curtsying in her green wool dress.

He studies her face. She's a beaut, he'll give his brother that. Small, pert lips with blonde lolling curls. Even in her plain dress, she strikes quite the contrast from Clarice, with her straight mouth and chastely braided hair.

"A delight to finally meet you, Fioretta. Gorini, however—it's not a name I'm familiar with. You're from Florence?"

Her cheeks, her forehead, even her nose turn as red as a cardinal's robes.

"She lives in Santa Croce," Giuliano says. "Her father is a professor."

"A professor? How interesting." He gestures to an easel, standing in the center of the room. "And what is this?"

"A painting I commissioned from Leonardo here."

Lorenzo circuits the easel and comes to stand between his brother and Fioretta. He looks at the painting: a woman and child. She wears no halo, but it's clear she's the Madonna. Her hair is a riled sea of curls, her face peaceful, but maybe plaintive too. And in her lap, an infant rendered as real as his son nursing just a few rooms away. But he must be Christ. His arms are reaching for the delicate flower between the Virgin's fingers.

"Isn't it exquisite work?" Giuliano says.

"The babe," Lorenzo says. His fingers hover over the infant. Like Clarice, the painter flinches. "How did you do it?"

"Painting from life."

"You have a son?" Lorenzo asks.

"No, my lord. My father was recently blessed with a son."

"Congratulations." He cannot recall the artist's family name, and it's driving him mad. "You're from a large family?"

"No, my lord. Just my father, his wife, and now their son."

"And you, of course," Lorenzo says.

The painter says nothing; he glances at his painting again. Lorenzo considers it again too. He's enjoying this—the tension in the room, knowing it's like a taut rope he holds firmly in his grip.

He waits. He looks at the Madonna's clean fingers gently pressing against her child's flesh. The skyward, wide-eyed gaze of Christ. The cushion beneath him, with the pattern of his family's crest. The painter knew what he was doing.

Except this Madonna looks ordinary. She is beautiful, yes, as is the woman in this room. But there is no golden ring around her head. She is lacking that holy glow.

"Why doesn't she have a halo?"

The painter frowns. "I wanted her to seem more human, a reflection of her modest upbringing in Nazareth. Like a woman you might see at the market."

"And the flower?"

"A carnation. A reminder of blood, Christ's fate."

"But he's reaching for it."

"Because he knows what will be asked of him."

"What a curse," Giuliano mutters.

"Strange," Lorenzo says. "I'd find that a relief, to know the greatness promised for you."

The painter nods.

"You've done good work for my brother. I think he's proving himself to have the better eye out of the two of us." He turns to Giuliano. "Where shall we hang it?"

Giuliano says nothing at first. He paws his chin, face fixed to the painting. "It's meant to be a gift."

"To Fioretta here?"

"Yes," his brother says.

He sighs, heavy and long. "You can't hang this in a professor's house, of all places. I say this with the utmost respect," he says, nodding to Fioretta. "You understand, don't you?"

"Of course," she says, dabbing her forehead with a trembling handkerchief.

"And you, Giuliano?"

His brother grips his hands together. Cordlike veins cross his forearms. He'd dare Giuliano to strike him. To speak out against him. But he knows he won't.

Giuliano turns to Fioretta. "Would you mind leaving us?" he asks softly.

She demurs. "It was an honor," she says again, before vanishing from the room.

When the door closes, Lorenzo turns back to his brother. "Is she why you've tarried with every proposal I've brought to you?" His voice is louder now, sharper. "It's one thing to be fucking. It's another to be gifting paintings. Be sensible, Giuliano."

For a moment, there is only the sound of heavy breathing and the rain outside. Then he remembers: there's still another person here. The painter, standing like a sentinel beside his work. "You must forgive us," Lorenzo says to him. "It's a trying time."

"I'll take my leave, if you wish," he says, neatly bowing his head.

"Before you do," Lorenzo says. "If this painting ends up not hanging here after all, foolish as that is, could you do us another?"

"Another Madonna?" the painter stammers.

"Not necessarily. Perhaps not, actually. We have so many. But something Biblical, certainly."

"What about a martyr? A Sebastian perhaps?"

He doesn't care, not really. "That could work. Yes. Do that."

"Thank you," the artist says, bowing once to him, once more to his brother.

"Wait," Giuliano says, stepping to his writing desk. From a drawer, he collects a small bag of buffed leather, tied with string. "Please forgive me for all of this," he whispers, giving the purse to the painter, who stutters his profuse thanks as he feels its weight. Then he nearly bounds out of the room.

It is only the two of them now.

"You humiliated me," Giuliano says, not looking at him. "You humiliated both of us."

"I did?" He scoffs. "You brought your mistress here, to my house. And if you think you've been discreet, think again. Clarice knows what you've been up to. There are places for such things. Brothels, for one."

"She's not a whore."

"Did I say she was? Still, there's no denying that she is a professor's daughter. Nothing can change that. She can't ever be anything more."

"She can be whatever I want her to be. Whatever she wants to be," Giuliano says, his voice growing louder. "I shouldn't have to say this, but I'm not your servant, Lorenzo. I'm not your secretary. I'm not even a prior. I'm your brother. You can't keep me under your thumb. The least you could do, after everything with Rome, is to allow me the dignity of making my own choices."

"You can keep seeing your girl, for all I care. But you're to choose a wife who is appropriate for the family, one who comes with a dowry that befits your status."

"I don't care about the dowry. We're rich enough."

He laughs. The sound is familiar, jagged, and bitter. "You only think that because you spend your days entertaining painters. The bank's bleeding money, Giuliano."

"And my marriage will change that?"

It won't, he thinks. "Mother agrees that it's time for you to be wed. Of course, I could write to her, if you'd prefer. Explain your situation."

"You wouldn't—" But his brother doesn't finish.

"I wouldn't?" He shrugs. "No, I won't bother her with this. Not yet, at least. You want to make your own decisions? Go ahead, here's one for you to make: do you want to be a part of this family, or do you want to keep fucking about?"

He takes a step toward the door. Looks at the painted babe reaching for the thin-stemmed carnation. "There are more pressing matters for me to deal with, so I'll leave you with something else to decide: what you'll do with this painting. Such work deserves to be hung somewhere respectable. Any less would be a disservice to that painter. So I hope you'll choose wisely. On both counts."

XXIV

"I WANT TO PAINT YOU," HE TELLS IAC.

He runs his tongue over his chest, tasting wine and sweat and seed. Tonight, they hurried their hands over each other's bodies; they panted, took turns fucking each other. Iac conjured up a dusty fiasco of wine, and they drank it in bed, from the bottle, plum streaming down their chins, their necks. They've let themselves be stupid, ebullient. Drowned out the thought that they might soon no longer have this place.

"Is this you trying to tell me that they liked the painting?" Iac says, smiling down at Leonardo whose chin now rests over his navel.

A playful laugh. "Yes."

"This is only the beginning."

"I know." He does. He's not yet twenty-four; he has so many years ahead of him, decades to paint for kings, for dukes, the pope. He's young enough that he may even paint for two popes.

"They want another too. A Sebastian." He widens his legs, straddles Iac's narrow frame. He holds his freckled face in his hands. "And I want you to pose for it."

Their lips meet, and then they still. Iac stares into his eyes, and he stares back. In them, he sees amber and umber and siena earth.

"Can I draw you now?"

"Here? Like this?"

"Exactly as you are," he says, already off the bed, pulling his notebook from his sack.

"How should I pose?" Iac asks, flushing. A rare sight.

"Standing, if you don't mind. With your back against the bedpost."

He's sitting on the floor now, a wet pen in his fingers, his notebook splayed open on his thighs. Iac rises from the bed. He fingers his curls, and his feet patter against the floor. He takes his pose, and Leonardo looks down at the blank page in his lap.

He pauses. Wonders if he's too giddy from the day's success, if the wine has made him too reckless. He knows if he does this, he'll be taking Iac beyond this room. Transforming him into something else.

He looks up. Iac breaths in, his ribs lift. He grins. "I'm a poor martyr without any arrows."

He laughs and drops his pen. "You have to let me concentrate."

"Me, a distraction?" Iac puts a hand to his chest. "I've never heard such a thing."

"Go back to the way you were. Hands behind your back, leaning against the post. Prop your right foot against it too."

Iac rearranges himself, and Leonardo sketches. His eyes flick, paper to boy, boy to paper. The first touches: the lines proudly display the shoulders, the slight twisting of his torso, and then downward, to his slender legs.

He looks up at Iac's face. He's smiling. Radiant.

"Are you comfortable?" he asks. "It's not too cold?"

"No," Iac says. "Do I look small?"

He smiles. No, he certainly doesn't.

His pen races across the paper. Now for the notches of detail: his small nipples, the carved lines of his abdomen, the gathering of trimmed hair at his groin. There will be no swaddling of cloth around his Sebastian's waist. He will be bare; the saint likely was, he thinks. It might be provocative, but so was Donatello's David—and that still stands in the center of Lorenzo's courtyard.

His fingers are moist and blackened when he stops. From the bed, Iac tries to peek at his work, but he keeps the page hidden.

"Let me see!"

"I never share—" He stops. He looks at it again. He can see pen lines becoming brushstrokes. Pale paper becoming panel, filled with so many colors, blurring together, edging into shadow.

No, he thinks. This is different.

He stands, flattens the notebook, hands it to Iac. "It's just a first sketch," he blurts. "If you think it's good, and you're willing, you could let me do it properly, by daylight. I think I can find my own space now. They've paid me enough."

More than enough, really. Gold florins, too many of them to count. A sum that can sustain him for years.

"I've never— I can't— I don't understand how you realize so much, in so little space," Iac says. "How do you see so much?"

He wraps his arms around Iac and buries his face into his neck. He feels it, alongside his thudding blood: a question rolling onto his tongue. If he asks it, he'll be surrendering himself to his father's silent sneer, the midnight whispers of the other apprentices, the wink of Andrea's eye. What he's always wrestled against. To be reduced to a single, ugly word.

But he has a purse fat with gold. A commission from the city's most important man. Now, he can do whatever he wants.

"When I leave Andrea's, when you register at the guild—what if we were to find a workshop together? A space large enough for you to cast and for me to paint. With rooms upstairs for us and whatever assistants we choose to hire," he says, breathing the words into Iac's neck. "If that's what you want, that is."

Iac's fingers stroke his chin, shifting his face until they're looking at each other, their eyes like glass in the dark.

"Yes," he tells him.

———

IN A FEW BLURRED WEEKS, he brings his Sebastian to life. It's as wide as his outstretched arms, as tall as he stands. Bigger than anything he's painted before. Large enough not to look small in Lorenzo's palace.

There's the grand, rocky desert. A hazed sunset to the left. In the center, an old tree, knobby and leafless. Sebastian stands against it, his arms pinioned behind the trunk, his blond curls spun into the wind. His—Iac's—chest writhes; it's thick with muscle, freckled, bronze from the sun.

So far, he has not touched his jar of lac red; he has yet to wound his subject. But he has been dwelling on having the arrow pierce the chest, its head digging into the heart. To paint the martyr's last breaths. A violent act, to choose where the arrow will strike.

Whenever Iac can give him the time, he visits the workshop. He notices Andrea's smirk, and then he forgets about it. He hears the tittering of the apprentices, and he turns to face them with a smug and certain smile, silencing them. And when he's finished his work for the day, he leaves the workshop without a word and walks across the city. He strolls past palaces—Vespucci, Strozzi, Pazzi—more families for whom he might also soon work. He walks into churches, into San Lorenzo and Sant'Ambrogio; into Santa Maria Novella, where he finds Sandro on scaffolds painting a fresco. He's noting every blank-walled chapel in every church; he's thinking of his next commission, after he finishes the Sebastian.

He walks to find a space to rent too. Somewhere he and Iac can move to, once his apprenticeship is finished. In San Giovanni, he strolls through a former smithy with a soot-stained ceiling, and he thinks about Iac soldering gold necklaces. By the Arno, he visits a shuttered wool shop with empty, dust-laden tables, and he imagines every surface covered by paintings, his own apprentices scrambling about. He even looks at a disused taproom in seedy Baldracca, and in its wide, empty space he wonders if he might free the fantastical ideas he's tucked away in his mind: designs for vehicles, for waterwheels, for wings.

When he finally tells Andrea he wishes to discuss his future, his master rests a hand on his chest. He smiles. He says he knows, that he's been waiting for this day, that he's happy for him. But he also says he needn't hasten his exit, that he is welcome to stay as long as he needs, as long as it takes to find the perfect space.

His life glides. He is abandoning his burdens, his concerns, for they no longer serve the work. He buys new pigments, the choicest ultramarine. At the Mercato Nuovo, he orders new tunics, dyed rose or violet. He even indulges himself with a pair of hose patterned with tiny spinels. Passing priests stare, butchers on the bridge cup their mouths and laugh—but Leonardo doesn't see any of this. He walks through the city blinded by the thought of waking up beside Iac, morning after morning to come.

SO WHEN THE OFFICERS ARRIVE, he doesn't notice them. They slip in just before dusk, before the night's candles have been lit. Coming out of the shadow, carrying no lanterns. Their faces are deeply lined, their hair threaded gray and white. They approach an apprentice gathering the now-dry day's work from the table at the front of the shop. Then one speaks his name in a heavy, certain voice.

This, he hears. He turns away from his Sebastian, his brush in his left hand. He sees the apprentice, his face flushed and pained. His arm is extended, his finger pointing—at him.

The officers are walking toward him, past dye-stained tables and half-carved busts. He hears fast, light feet, another apprentice running to find their master. He hears a growing hiss like a nest of snakes.

The officers approach him. They ask his name, and he tells them. Then they look beyond him to the Sebastian on its easel, and their faces rivel.

The officers do not need to say what he has done, what they will do with him. He follows them toward the door, his brush still pressed between his fingers. Andrea approaches him, clutches his hands. He waits for Andrea to say something to him. To speak to the officers in his courteous, beguiling way. To talk of error. To mention for whom he paints. To shout, even. Protest.

Then he feels Andrea's fingers pry open his fist, and his brush leaves his palm.

Part Three

THE MARTYRDOM OF SAINT SEBASTIAN

1476–1478

XXV

GO TO THE HAPSBURG COURT UP IN THE ALPS AND ASK SOME-
one how to say sodomite. *Florenzer*, they'll tell you.

It's not difficult to understand where this name originates. All it
takes is a close look, an open ear. By evening, behind a curtain of steam
at the baths, where a silk trader's soft hand crawls between the legs of his
neighbor. Or beside the moonlit Arno, where one of last term's priors
kneels in the soggy dirt and buries his face in a butcher's groin. Even
mid-afternoon, in the shadows of a transept after mass, where two boys
make their own communion.

Such actions aren't confined within the walls of Florence, of course.
Sodomy exists anywhere there are men with cocks and men with holes.
Which is everywhere, really, except for the convents—and there the
nuns have their own methods. But does anyone condone it? Certainly
not. These are Christian lands.

Florence preferred to present itself as a tolerant place. Here, they
prided themselves on their more learned ways; they had studied the
Greeks, so they knew what the Greeks, from Achilles to Alexander, once
practiced. Youthful impulses deserved some sympathy, especially in a
city where most men weren't married until thirty. It was understandable
to a certain degree if a man needed to satisfy his urges before that time.
Better if it was with a woman, of course, but sometimes a man had to
settle for the nearest orifice.

Peccadillos are one matter, but the city's pride is another. When Florence had begun to be mocked at courts near and far, at pulpits in cities and hill towns, the priors said an effort—a gentle one—was needed
to rein in the city's most undesirable habits. They established a police
committee, placed letter boxes across the city, in Santa Reparata and
Orsanmichele. How they work is simple: scrawl an indecency on a scrap
of paper and name its perpetrator. The committee, the Officers of the
Night, would take care of it.

Who decided this? Lorenzo's grandfather. Cosimo and the priors
claimed their punishments were fair. Only a fine on the first offense: a

reasonable fifty florins; more than a year's wages for the average wool weaver, but certainly preferable to being flayed. Only the brazen—the ones found underneath other men, the ones who the priors said forgot they were men—faced a more severe punishment. Only these men were sometimes put to death.

Lorenzo hasn't altered this tradition; he's continued it with aplomb. More men are being convicted than ever before. He finds great fun in reading the officers' warrant lists, in seeing which prior's son or which pious merchant was foolish enough to get caught. He says he's cleaning the scourge of the city, making its marble shine again.

Little changes in Florence. Men fuck and are fucked. Hands write indecencies and names on torn paper. They fold them, slip them inside brimming letter boxes.

And on one of these shreds, Leonardo's name has been written.

—

THIS IS HIS PUNISHMENT, he thinks.

Being blinded. Waking in a windowless cell, drowned in purest lamp black. Covering his eyes with his hands, nothing changes. Turning his head back and forth, everything is the same. All nothingness.

This is worse than being jailed, beaten, starved. How can he paint, if he cannot see? And what is he, if not a painter?

A sodomite, he thinks.

How long has he been in here, he doesn't know. Day and night are one. A single, tough-crusted nub of bread is all he's been fed. He ate it greedily, bits of earth crackling between his teeth, the taste of copper staining his tongue.

He smells blood too, matted between his nose and upper lip. Not strong enough to mask the bright, pervading scent of piss and the low funk of mold. In an awful wave: his own filth too. Inescapable.

He kneels, sharp pebbles grinding against his scabbed shins. Rests his forehead against slick, cold stone, his brow meeting the soft fur of moss along its grout. Pads his cheeks with stiff fingers. Skin, tacky and tender. Drags the fingers farther to his eyes, watery and cool. He blinks, over and over again. Still only darkness.

The hours unravel into the void. He has only this time, an unknowable amount of it, and his mind—a dangerous pairing. There are so many questions to ask. To start: Who accused him, and why? He conjures up names and explanations, reasonable and absurd. Perhaps it was one of the apprentices, who somehow learned of Leonardo's midnight habits, who was disgusted by them. Or it could have been another painter in the city, one with trifling work, jealous of Leonardo's favor with the Medici.

No. In the dank and silent cell, he can believe only one explanation. His father put him here. After all, his father often works for the Bargello, where the officers held their trials; he has served as their notary for years. His father knows how this city operates, knows that a sodomy accusation in this city can bring shame and a hefty fine, sometimes banishment, but rarely anything worse.

He rolls to his side. Digs his shoulder into the padded dirt. Gathers his aching knees to his chest, clutches them.

More than a decade has passed since those hushed days when he lived with his father, when he taught himself never to ask questions, to be meek, little more than a shadow. He was a country boy then—curious, knowing little. A child who hadn't yet allowed his gaze to rove over boys' narrow backs at the baths, who hadn't wandered the reeds of the riverbank, who hadn't touched lips with another man.

He'd thought he had escaped that house before the telltale signs became obvious. He was wrong. His father has always known. In Leonardo, his father saw it—some unnamable, leprous quality. He saw it in the way he stepped, how he favored walking on the balls of his feet. He heard it in his voice, better suited to a woman than a man. He saw it in the way his eyes hovered too long on everything.

They all must have known: his grandfather, his mother too. Why else would she have kept herself a stranger to him?

As for his father, he only endured Leonardo's presence because he lacked any other boy to call his son. For a time, before his difference was too glaring, his father might have been able to pretend. Leaving that village, coming to Florence; working ceaselessly by daylight and candlelight—his father did it all to build a legacy. Now he has a son, one by true blood, one to carry his name. Leonardo? He's not only an inconvenience, but a liability too. Something that could, and did, bring shame. Something to discard and forget.

A charge of sodomy? It was what his father needed to finally disavow his bastard.

He shakes. Boxes his ears. Shuts his eyes. But now he begins to see—visions he tries to push away; that in the blackness, cannot be escaped. He sees a man, golden hair falling against the side of his smooth face. Pale lips rounding, howling a cry. A bare, broad chest with wine-colored nipples. Sees him writhing against a post of splintered wood.

A thrum, and his body jerks. An arrow, meeting the flesh, just above the navel. Steel tip tearing, skin washing red. More arrows, thigh and arm and heart. His body twisting, jolting. Then under rippling gore he stills.

The martyr's eyes are long-lashed and shut, as if he is sleeping or lost in a pang of pleasure. But then the lids open—not a flutter, not a slow rise, but a single, immediate flicker. They stare, brown and wet. Then they grow wide with confusion. They harden with pain. Then he hears words, though no lips move: *Draw me.*

Now the tavern, the bedroom. Here is Iac, stepping out of his hose. Approaching him, fingering the hem of his tunic. Lifting it, pressing their bodies together, warm becoming hot. Iac bringing his mouth to meet his, Iac taking his hand and guiding it south. Their bodies shifting, their—

"Iac," he says into the darkness.

No one answers.

He runs his hand over the packed dirt beneath him. He remembers where he is. In a flush, he feels how his cock has turned stiff.

He's a fool, a craven creature. Spineless, desperate. So many wasted nights at that tavern. Sketching a whore, when he should have been painting saints. He deserves this, to be here, alongside the ravishers and murders and thieves. He's a base sort of beast.

But the painting was good, a softer voice says. He could still make it great.

There's something to fix though. It should depict the moment after the first arrow pierces, the next being slung. The stare should be a challenge—to look at him, at his weeping wounds, at what he's done to this man.

He draws, there in the cell, with his finger and the dirt floor. Traces his Sebastian in the coarse-grained earth, blending by spitting onto dirt, smearing it. He finishes, but he can't see his work. He sweeps over it with an open palm, begins again. Draws until his nail splinters and his fingertip chafes.

Then something streaks, deep orange, across his vision. He sees it again: a flickering, thin and warm, to his right. Growing closer. For the first time, he sees the iron bars before him, the close, stone walls veined with trickling water. The light coalesces into a flame atop an uneven pillar of wax, planted onto a dented candlestick, held by a jailer whose mail casts starry reflections all around him. There's a wooden bucket in his other hand. The man grunts, unlocks Leonardo's cell, pushes the bucket forward with his foot. Water slops onto the dirt floor, running over his drawing, erasing it.

"Get yourself clean."

Leonardo rises onto one leg, then the other. His knees buckle. He rises again and staggers toward the bucket. Floating on the murky surface is a brush with dark, crooked bristles. He takes it with one hand, then undresses, turning away from the jailer. Shivers, as the soaked brush dribbles icy water down his back. He scrubs. The bristles are stiff, needle-sharp, but he doesn't stop. The longer he takes, the better.

He knows what waits for him. To be questioned by the officers. To face trial. A public humiliation. And despite all the time he has had in this cell, he hasn't given a single thought to what he'll say, if it's even worth trying to defend himself. If the officers ask him about the particulars, what does he say? Is it better to be honest with the council, lest they catch his lies? Or will he disgust them by telling them it was not just once but a thousand times? That he hasn't merely fucked a man, he's let another man come inside him, has taken his cock in his mouth, has tasted his seed?

He drops the brush. Brings his shaking hands together. Prays—a plea that it is only himself whom his father has condemned. That Iac remains blameless.

He reaches down, recovers the brush. Scrubs harder. He can't be angry, can't be indignant. He knew the laws; he had been warned. He is guilty of what they'll say he's done. He loosens the dirt, the blood, the filth. Scours his skin. His arms ache, as if he is an apprentice again, diligently polishing bronze.

"That's enough," the jailer says.

Leonardo kneels to collect the crumpled sark.

"No. You'll get your clothes back when you leave."

"Leave?" The voice doesn't sound like his own. It's rough, deep.

"You're lucky to have a friend who wants you out. He's waiting for you."

He steadies himself against the bars. He can't have his father see him like this.

The guard raps his gloved knuckles on the cell door. "Come along. The other one's already out there."

The thought of seeing Iac is a salve, however small. It stirs him, moves him to take a fretted step forward, and then another. To follow the jailer as he marches him past a row of cells, past gaunt phantoms and sunken-eye stares. To step behind him into a new room, brilliantly white, blindingly so.

He stumbles, and someone laughs.

Now he sees outlines, darker shapes blocking the lead white daylight. There's the guard, two other men too. One naked, one wearing a cloak. He can't manage his father's stare, not yet, so he looks at Iac.

First he sees skin mottled with dirt. Then hair, dark like poplar, across the chest and sprawling over a loose stomach. This isn't Iac. This man hopelessly trying to cover his groin—he doesn't know him.

"This isn't to happen again," the man is being told. The voice is familiar, sharp and nasal. "I've seen to it that you won't see him again."

He stifles a cry. Everything is wrong. He feels his skin being pulled off. He feels every beautiful thing ripped away, gone. His feet tread backward. He wants the darkness again, to be blind.

His naked back meets the jailer's mail, and he's shoved forward. His feet tangle, and he falls. On the floor, beside his hands, are two boots of perfect, supple, black-dyed leather. They step back from him. A handkerchief, embroidered with laurels, wipes at the dust settled on the vamps.

He wills his gaze up from boots to white hose to kermes doublet. He meets Lorenzo's face, that awful chimera.

XXVI

THIS CATHEDRAL IS HIS. THIS NAVE, LIGHT-FILLED, WITH marble walls striped white and black. This pulpit, rounded in intricate reliefs of the Nativity, the Adoration, the Last Judgment.

These cassocked priests, not acolytes, bringing his gilt-edged Bible, his silver chalice of ruby wine—they are his too. So are the boys, white-robed, singing a plangent Miserere. As are all these people standing before him with billowing sleeves of velvet and jewels at their throats. In the transept—his transept—there is his cousin too.

He listens to the sung psalm, listless. He climbs the stairs to the pulpit, tired. Reads from his lectern, bored. He speaks about Christ mounting a hill in Galilee. Repeats the words of Christ's sermon, that we should love our enemies and pray for those who persecute us.

Rovere had said the same, back at the Vatican, when he informed Salviati that he was to take his post, here in Pisa. The Lord was, at last, rewarding him for his faith, his patience, Rovere told him. But Salviati hadn't listened. He was distracted—by the pope's beet-red face, by the sweet reek of his holy sweat, trapped beneath all his pelts of ermine and lynx. He didn't thank the pope; he failed to kiss the wet, pudgy hand that was presented to him. Instead he asked the pope what had changed, why Medici had relented.

Do not question His ways, the pope spat.

He felt no elation when he left the Vatican. He still doesn't, months later.

He leaves his pulpit, returns to his plush cathedra. Harmonies are sung, they fail to stir. He thinks about his old church in Rome, where he had no choir, no precious relics. He was more comfortable there, ensconced in the shadows. He thinks about the widow Beatrice, prays for her health. He stares at a pillared candle, melted down to a nub. The wick, black and twisted, threatening to extinguish.

And then the Mass is over, and Jacopo is waiting for him.

Outside the cathedral, they embrace, holding on to each other longer than they need to. They walk across the emerald lawn toward the bell tower and his palace. He wants his cousin to see it all.

But Jacopo doesn't gaze at the cathedral's blind arcade or at the baptistery. He only looks at him. "I hoped to see you sooner," he says. "Christmas has passed, Easter too. It would've been my honor to host you."

"Next time," he says. He sounds unconvincing. "You know I haven't been back, not since before——" He swats at a gnat. "Has it changed?"

"Not in any visible way. The baptistery doors still shine. The cathedral still lacks a marble front."

"Still?"

Jacopo nods. "But I imagine you'd find Florence different for you now," he says, pointing to his purple zucchetto.

He's not so sure.

"It was a gift to see you give Mass. And in such a beautiful church——"

"Cathedral," Salviati corrects.

"How does it feel?"

The sea-tinged breeze is steady. It shakes the grass and stings the eyes. He wishes he could say he felt gratified, revived, holy. Better than saying that he feels hollowed out, the absence of something essential yet vague. "I only regret that it didn't come sooner. And I can't keep myself from wondering what it might have felt like if I hadn't been stopped."

"But you're here now. That's what matters."

"Is it? That year, stuck in Rome——it was awful, interminable. I thought coming here would revive me. There's still so much I want to do."

Jacopo's steps slow. "That ambition——that's the Florentine in you."

"I'm not a Florentine any longer. I haven't been for a long time. The city made that clear when they kept me in Rome."

"Not Florence," Jacopo says. "Just one Florentine."

"You act as if there's a difference."

"He did you wrong," his cousin says in a quick exhale. "If it's any comfort, relations are no better between Florence and Rome since you were allowed to keep your appointment. My bank now has the Curia's alum mining rights, and Lorenzo was sore to lose those."

"Congratulations," he says glumly.

His cousin pats his back. "Come now. We must enjoy our successes when they come. They're all too rare."

Before them, the bell tower rises. Column upon column of brilliant marble, each ornate layer reaching higher, dazzling brighter—then faltering.

There's something indecent in the way it tilts, he thinks.

"I want to stop it. From leaning," he says. "To make it stand fully upright."

"A noble endeavor."

He doesn't hear his cousin. His thoughts are loud, he wants to shout over them. Words are brewing, bubbling up his throat. "I have to say it. We'd all be better off if it were you leading Florence."

Jacopo's mouth puckers. "I don't disagree," he says, still looking at the tower.

He breathes deeply, smells the cut grass, sharp. His awful thoughts—he has never spoken of them aloud, not even to a priest. He was too afraid, and for no reason. Look at him! He's still standing out in the field, his cathedral isn't crumbling, his palace isn't burning. God has not smitten him!

"Have you ever considered it?" Salviati asks.

"Of course I have."

"You know the pope thinks highly of you. He'd welcome such a change, if it were for the Christian good. Which it would be."

"There's little use in discussing the impossible."

"But what if it was possible? What if it all could be made right?"

"Stop this talk. Only a fool would ruin the peace we have. Especially if the Turks do invade."

"You sound like Rovere."

"And I would think you of all people would know to listen to the Holy Father. Besides, what would we do? Pay some mercenaries to throw Lorenzo in a cell? Exile him? That didn't work with Cosimo, and it certainly won't now."

"So we're meant to suffer his slights? Continue to let that godless imp lord over Florence when he's done nothing to earn that right?" He shuts his eyes, recovers his breath. "Didn't you once tell me that the city was fading? What if you could change that? A cleanse could restore Florence. Make it once more the city you remember it being."

"What has possessed you?" Jacopo says, quickly and quietly. "This is dangerous talk. Foolish. Unholy, even."

"Says the banker."

"And what of Guglielmo? Have you thought of him in any of this? They're his family too."

"That didn't stop you from seizing their accounts."

"Which you delivered into our laps."

"Francesco did that. Not me."

"Don't think me a fool. I never believed that. Francesco, he lacks the ingenuity for such a plan. There was a reason I wanted you to work for me all those years ago. You have it. The guile."

"Guile?" he sneers. "I've only ever wanted to serve. That's what would've made me a poor banker. I've only ever done what's best for the Church. And that is why I'm saying this to you now. What if it is for the greater good? What if it is what God wants?"

"You think God wants this? What about the Gospel you just read on the pulpit? What about being struck on the right cheek and offering the other?"

"Yet Exodus says an eye for an eye, a tooth for a tooth."

Jacopo shakes his head. "Look at me. I'm blessed. I've prospered. My bank is growing richer than his. You know why? Because I know when I should be satisfied. I know my place. So should you. You are here now. That is what matters. Forget the past. Forgive him. Thank him for honoring you with this appointment. Send him a gift, even. You'll be a better man for it. You'll feel better."

"It's not right."

"No. It's not. But that's a matter for God to address."

FORGIVENESS—IT IS THE CHRISTIAN WAY. He feels sick at having to be reminded of this by a banker, of all people. But if he seeks God's forgiveness, perhaps he can smooth away this brittle feeling inside him. If he forgives Medici, perhaps he'll feel holy again.

He'll listen to Jacopo and give Medici a gift. Quite the task, since the man enjoys every luxury. But there's one thing Pisa has that Florence lacks: the sea at its fringes. Here, Salviati indulges on the freshest fish, while Medici must wait for his trout and herring to be salted and carried upriver by barge.

This will be his gift. A hundred sea bass caught by the shore under dawn light, brought to his palace, then sent on to Florence. He'll pay a driver to race his cart across Tuscany, to ride through the night. To have it delivered to the city by the end of the next day. A rare treat for any Florentine, even Medici.

He tells his kitchens to arrange this with the fishmongers, tells his footman to be ready. In the meantime, Salviati will write a letter to accompany his gift. Something trite and gracious.

He sits at his desk, unmarked paper before him, dry pen in his hand. Words do not come. The fish has been brought from the sea, the cart waits in the courtyard—and he does is listen to the bell tower tolling over and over.

Keep ringing, he thinks. Maybe it'll crack the marble. Maybe one day he'll step outside and find all its columns have collapsed. Then, at least, he'd be able to repair the tower.

The sun retreats, and he decides to write the letter at first light. Prayer and sleep will restore him. The fish will not spoil yet. He'll pay the courier an even larger sum, have him ride even faster.

He prays. He sleeps. He wakes. He prays again, asks God for strength. He looks at the paper on his desk. His fingers ball. His ankle itches. Yet another gnat bite. He dreads the looming summer months of red welts and foul, humid air. He scratches at the bite, and the skin begins to sting. Little red splotches bloom on the white of his hose.

He opens his Bible, parses its pages for guidance. He turns to the Gospels, to his reading from Mass. Then he reaches the words Jacopo spoke to him: if someone strikes you on the right cheek, give him the other.

He pauses here, his finger tapping the thick, leathery page. So curious, he thinks, how specific these words are; how it's the right cheek that is struck first, how Christ doesn't say to offer the same cheek again, but the other—the left.

He laughs, alone in his bedroom. He understands now. The Savior had a sense of humor. He's telling a wicked little joke. To offer the left cheek is to force the aggressor to strike again—this time with their other hand, their left hand—the hand one uses to wipe the shit from their ass. To offer the left cheek is a provocation.

There's always comfort to find in the Bible, he thinks.

Now he knows he can write his letter. But he will do it later. He shall enjoy his day. He will ignore the servants hovering. He will eat his breakfast, he will give another Mass, he will walk his grassy, beautiful grounds, he will sup, he will pray. A good day's work.

After supper, his cook approaches him, asks if he would like the bass soaked in brine or cured in salt. Salviati smiles at him. Heavens no, he tells him. The fish is perfect as it is.

He enjoys another sleep. At dawn, he dips his pen into ink, scratches a few quick lines to Medici.

Now, at last, he walks out to the courtyard, into a dank cloud of salt and seaweed. He approaches the crate, its once-pale wood now soaked through and dark. He peers through the slats, grins at the hundred dead, glassy stares. He deeply inhales, and he holds it in, sweet and ripe.

His footman waits in the arcade, shaking a hand at the troublesome flies. Salviati goes to him, hands him the letter. He tells him to take the fish to Florence.

XXVII

HE HAS REMAINED IN FLORENCE. HE THOUGHT IT PRUDENT TO stay, to more vigilantly be his brother's keeper. So many months has he kept out of reach and out of breath, and now he has stillness. He no longer aches. His letters are constant and immediate.

But nothing here has changed since his return, save for the days creeping longer, hotter. He thought he'd finally feel rested by staying at home and sleeping in his own bed, by never missing a hearty meal. Instead, he remains tired—tired of waiting, most of all. For the cool relief of evening. For Giuliano to break his silence and come to his senses. For a letter with some word that could change his fortunes. News that another hill town has mutinied. That the Turks have come ashore. Or, hell, even that Siena or Rome or Naples have invaded his lands. He craves it, a chance to prove himself, for his great life to resume.

He stands, walks to the blue porcelain ewer next to the salon's windows. He dips his linen handkerchief into the now-tepid water, dabs his forehead and neck. Everyone seems so languid. Clarice, drowsy-eyed, waves a fan with one hand and rocks the wood cradle with the other. Little Lucrezia and his toddler Maddalena are sprawled on the thick embroidered carpet conspiring with each other. Piero, now somehow a boy of four, slouches on his toy horse and saddle.

Lorenzo walks to his daughters, huddled over a writing board. Lucrezia draws wide, careful words on a single piece of paper while Maddalena watches, mesmerized as if her older sister is performing witchcraft. He kneels beside them.

"What are you writing, little one?"

His oldest doesn't look up from her paper. "A letter," she says. "To Grandmother."

To want, willingly, to write to his mother—he can't fathom it. "And what are you telling her?"

"It's private," Lucrezia says, matter-of-factly.

"Lucrezia," Clarice scolds. "Be respectful of your father."

His daughter looks up at him. A distant, skeptical stare. "I'm telling her that we miss her, that we want her to come home."

He pats her head. "Of course we—"

His infant son lets out a flustered cry, trampling his words. Piero has abandoned his toy horse and is leering over the cradle, laughing at his brother. He shakes a wooden rattle with golden bells, keeps shaking it even as Giovanni wails.

"What are you doing?" Clarice says, snatching the rattle from Piero's hand. "Apologize to your brother."

Piero says nothing, only grins.

"Lorenzo, say something to him."

His son's smirk vanishes.

"Listen to your mother, Piero. Apologize to Giovanni."

His son glowers at him. "Why? He doesn't understand."

He stands, and his son takes a step back from the cradle. "If you won't listen to me, you can spend the rest of the day in your bedroom, studying your Latin."

Piero pushes aside the blond hair hanging over his forehead. His eyes brim with tears, but he doesn't let them fall. "But—"

"To your bedroom," Lorenzo shouts. "Now."

His son stomps out of the room, followed by one of the nurses. A hush falls once more, and Lorenzo joins his wife on the sofa. When Lucrezia resumes scrawling her letter, Clarice turns to him.

"His behavior is becoming so poor."

"I'll speak to Agnolo. Ask him to make more of an effort with his lessons."

"He needs to learn from you, not a tutor," she says, letting the cradle still. "There's much he could learn from how you conduct yourself."

He has nothing to show him, he thinks. Not until something changes. "Unless he wants to learn about marriage negotiations and sodomy charges, I think he'll find it all rather dull. He's still too young for such talk."

"I should say so." She checks that all of the children are occupied. "Speaking of which, I heard one of your mother's nephews was found in flagrante delicto."

"How did you hear—"

"Your sister."

"You two shouldn't be talking about such sordid things."

"Everyone talks about it, Lorenzo."

And that was the issue, wasn't it? People once were sensible about such behavior; they showed discretion, they kept such habits a private matter, in private places. Now, people are so blatant in their craven ways, fucking in alleys just steps away from the Mercato Vecchio. No one has any self-restraint.

Clarice fusses with Giovanni's swaddling clothes. "They're talking about your brother too. About his little amour. I say nothing, of course. But I thought you should know."

"Giuliano and I remain at an impasse."

"Still?" The gossip stokes a flicker of mischief in her eyes. "What did he say to the proposal from the Borromeo girl?"

"He told me there's only one woman in Florence he'll wed. That he's in love."

"Love? I didn't think him so naive."

His daughter still scratches away at her paper. "It's a sizable dowry too, which would be useful at the moment."

Clarice's hand drifts from the cradle. "Do we need to be concerned?"

"Of course not," he lies. Never before has he had to think about his wealth—like a fine wool cloak, he merely wore it; he didn't need to consider the shepherd who sheared the sheep, or the dyers who fixed its color with alum. But now his man in Avignon says the bank's branch there is teetering toward insolvency. On top of that—and far closer to home—there are the Pazzi, like thorns in his ass, stealing his remaining accounts, one by one.

Unfortunately, maddeningly, there is little he can do. He's only a citizen, after all. He's learning too well that it's the title that people respect: pope, king, duke, count, or marquis. If he and his brother and one day his son were the city's princes, the Pazzi wouldn't dare take his accounts, for they'd know it would be treason. The pope? He wouldn't dare try to turn him poor. That'd be an act of war.

He turns to Clarice. Opens his mouth, hesitates. But he asks. "What should I do?"

Her face clouds. "What ever do you mean?"

"With my brother. I know he still resents me. And I've tried to make amends for what happened with Rome. I've tried to make something of him. But would it be better if I gave up? Let him do whatever he'd like, even if it's with this professor's daughter?"

His wife's mouth hangs open. She blinks, then shakes her head. "I'd never presume to tell you what to do."

He feels her hand tremble when he covers it with his own. "I'm asking you. I can't speak with Sigismondo or Agnolo or Guglielmo, for they're his friends too. And Tommaso? He's useless. You're the only person with whom I can talk about this with any honesty."

He searches her eyes—so inoffensive, so appeasing. "You know best, Lorenzo," she says, turning away.

He walks to the ewer again, wets his face once more. Foolish of him to think she had the answers.

"Father," Lucrezia says, and he turns. She's holding up her paper, now folded inside a small coverture. "Would you add this to your letters?"

"Of course," he says, taking the paper, kissing her head. At the sight of his daughter's trim, delicate writing, he realizes to whom he, too, must send a letter.

HIS MOTHER'S BEDROOM IS COOLER than the rest of the house, its air more still. Here, there's a white skim of dust on every surface. Unlike his room, the windows face outward, not on the courtyard. She gets to look out at the city, at the sprawl of roofs tapering to western fields and, farther yet, hills. He can see the long stone nave of San Lorenzo, where his grandfather's bones lie in a crypt, where his father's body has been nestled inside a porphyry tomb.

A peculiar view for his mother to have. To write her letters at this desk, overlooking all the family's dead. She's like Proserpina, he thinks. No wonder she has spent so much time away.

The garden, below the window, is a pleasant view, though. Fountains and now-fruitless lemon trees, bronze sculptures nestled between them. There's Judith with Holofernes, there's David with Goliath's head at his feet. His sight catches on this, on Verrocchio's boy warrior. The boy faces away from the window, as if he's ashamed.

That painter should consider himself lucky. He had to intervene to see his cousin pardoned—he obviously couldn't have a convicted sodomite in the family—but choosing to free the painter too? That was a kindness, a generous one. Though, he also didn't want the priors whispering that Giuliano was hiring buggerers to decorate his bedrooms. His brother remains unmarried, after all. Such circumstances can so easily breed ugly rumors.

Quite the embarrassment for the painter, he thinks. No one pretends to have morals anymore. Sodomites fuck out in the open, kings act as if their debts don't exist, even the pope's a cheat. And all of them have wronged him, stalled his many plans.

Four years have passed since he sat at his desk and wrote the record of his life. How has he fared since then? Well enough, with what he inherited. He holds a tight grip on the Signoria—more than his forefathers can say. The bank's business, albeit faltering, means that the thrones of England, of Burgundy, of France all look kindly upon him. And within the peninsula, he has turned Venice and all her ships from adversary to friend. There's still Galeazzo in Milan too; they are so intertwined that Lorenzo is godfather to one of his children. No matter the money, these are his protections, stronger than any armor. He has done some good.

And yet, under his eye, the bank lost its largest account.

His brother will not speak to him.

Ferrante is no longer his ally.

The pope belittles him, again and again.

He is not a prince.

Something has to change, he thinks. Or he has to change something. He's not his father. He's not his grandfather either. He has time—an abundance of it.

With his palm, he sweeps the dust from his mother's desk. There is still clean paper, a covered inkpot, and a long-dried pen too. He writes the letter quickly, keeps it brief. A simple appeal for advice, a prayer for a new beginning. He ends it no differently from the rest of his letters: I commend myself to you.

He doesn't read over his words. He folds the letter before the ink has fully dried; he wants it out of his hands. He opens the desk drawer, searching for wax. Loose sheets of yellowed paper shift about. Correspondences, most of them. Mainly from nuns and artists, old widows and monks. On one paper, he sees the familiar, gently curving letters of his mother's hand. They cover the page, top to bottom. A rather lengthy letter.

Carefully, he slides out the page. The first sentences—clearly not the beginning—are disorienting: mentions of a drought, sand-swept camps, Assyrians. At the name Nebuchadnezzar, he realizes what this is: a story. This must be how his mother spends her afternoons: penning Biblical fantasies. He indulges himself in reading it—how could he not?—pulling dozens of pages from his mother's drawer, following holy Judith as she enters the Assyrian camp, as she severs the captain's head and hands it to her handmaid. Say nothing, she whispers.

It's not a comforting story. When he finishes, he hides the pages in his mother's drawer. He finally finds a half-gone stick of red wax, holds it to a candle's flame. He seals his letter, waits for the wax to harden.

He has questions. Of all the bronze statues that line their gardens, why was this the story she chose to write? It was so violent—especially for a woman. Then again, his mother was not most women. If she was in the Assyrian camp, she wouldn't hesitate to pick up the sword in the captain's tent. He wouldn't either.

He looks through the window at the statue in the garden. It's been there for at least a decade, unbothered, unquestioned; he's never thought much of it. He can see the blade in Judith's hands, sharp and gilded. But he can't see her face. She's hiding it from him.

The seal has dried. He stands, his letter and his daughter's letter in his hand, and shuts the curtains so his visit here remains a secret. He walks through the salons, and there's not a servant in sight. No distant footsteps, no creaking doors. Odd.

Downstairs he goes, out of the house and into the garden. He strides, gravel crunching beneath his boots, down the hedged pathway toward the fountain. The bronze Holofernes sits above the trickling water, Judith towering over him. She's grasping his head. He's leaning away, his eyes shut. His neck is bared, supple, waiting to be hewn. There's no surprise, no anger. He looks pliant, resigned to this end.

Lorenzo circuits the fountain, squinting from the cloudless daylight, from the metallic shine. Now he sees Judith's face. Surprisingly small, but with a hardness to its every feature: the slender but firm nose, the prim mouth pressed shut. No anguish, no guilt in those wide-open eyes. They're vacant. This is a grim woman, set on her plan.

He rubs his eyes, looks once more at the letter in his hands, the paper now wrinkled. He walks back up the pathway, his feet quick. At the archway toward the courtyard, he turns back, tries to glimpse Judith one more time, wanting to glean something, anything from her stare.

Another statue blocks his view. Verrocchio's David, cocksure with flower-petals over his nipples and his hand on his skirted hip. A smug grin on his youthful face, as if to say, I killed the giant, and I didn't even need my sword. And Goliath's severed head at his feet—not some monster, just the sad face of a man too large for his world.

It's not right. He needs to get rid of it. Sell it, to the Signoria. They can decorate the Palagio with it. Such a statue would fetch a nice, fat purse.

Satisfied, he leaves the garden. To his surprise, there's a group gathered in the courtyard, near the carriageway to the street. Here's where his household has been hiding. Staring at a large wooden crate. He walks toward them, and they quit their cupped-hand whispering. They step out of his path. Some are grimacing, others won't look at him at all. But they're all clutching at their noses or their mouths.

There's only the low noise of summer, the constant buzz of flies.

He approaches the crate. Something catches the light. Almost shimmering, like marble. Maybe Giuliano's now gifting his mistress a statue. He wonders how many hundreds of florins this is going to cost him.

No—what's inside can't be marble. It's many-colored, iridescent.

He steps closer, brings his face to the slats, hears a servant gasp. Between them, he meets the faded stare of fish eyes. He sees flesh turned a yolky yellow, gray sludge leaking from gills.

He staggers backward. The servants stare, as if he's the one who must have an explanation.

"Where did it come from?"

Agnolo says Pisa, which doesn't make sense. Not a terribly long journey by horse. Not long enough for fish to fully rot.

"Who sent it?"

Agnolo reluctantly hands him a letter, already opened. The script is clean but unfamiliar.

If the fish is not worthy of you, nor of my desire and debt, I apologize, since fishing is a game of Fortune, and She often does not satisfy our great longings.

Then he sees the signature: Francesco Salviati, Archbishop of Pisa.

He casts aside the wicked note, turning away before it hits the setts. He says nothing to Agnolo, says nothing to the servants. He has no words for this.

As he leaves the courtyard, someone says they'll do something about the smell.

Back in the palace, up one long flight of stairs, then another. The letters for his mother are still in his hand, though his is badly creased, Lucrezia's even worse. He's angry, yes—spiteful, even—but there's an unexpected satisfaction in knowing he was right about the archbishop. He was indeed a pawn of the pope, a lackey of the Pazzi. They are all swarming around him, a black cloud of gnats stealing his blood, little by little.

To think his mother, his wife told him to acquiesce, to seek friendship with Rome.

Enough of patience, of compromises, of kindness.

He heaves at the top of the final flight of stairs, but he does not stop. He walks through the loggia, into the kitchens, where his appearance startles the staff preparing supper. He is never up here, has no reason to be.

He asks a cherry-faced cook where the oven is. He goes to it, peers into the steady fire. He tosses one letter into the flames, then the other, watching as the paper blackens and curls, as the wax bleeds.

XXVIII

AT THE WORKSHOP, HE KEEPS TO HIS BEDROOM—A DISUSED larder, narrow and windowless, smelling of pine nuts and must. He lies in bed for all his hours, morning and night, rising only to piss and pick at bowls left at the door by Andrea.

He hasn't spoken since leaving the prison. He hasn't opened his notebook or touched his pen. He's only stared, blankly, at the ceiling, the larder's damp cool making him feel as if he's lying in a half-dug grave.

He's petrified, afraid of so many things. That cell, those guards. His father. Any stranger's whispers.

And then there is the thought of Iac.

"You have to get up."

His eyes open to see Andrea standing over him. The bloody sunset catches every crease, every fold in his master's wizened face. The wrinkled nose and the mouth puckering with pity. Suddenly he looks old to him. This change in his master's face, it's not from some long passage of time. He still doesn't know how long he spent in the Stinche, but clearly he was not gone for a significant length of time if the days were growing longer. This evening's late sunset makes it clear he's simply been ignoring the details—a rarity for him.

Leonardo shuts his eyes and waits to be alone again. But an arm slides beneath his damp back. A hand is grasping his fingers, the nails still crusted, wine-colored. He is brought to his feet, which provide no resistance to this intrusion. Out from the sheets, he can smell himself—sour, stale. He wants to retch.

Andrea slowly, carefully leads him away from the bed. When he hesitates at the doorway, he's told, "I sent the boys away for the evening. It's only us."

On the neglected, weedy patch of land behind the workshop, the tub where they usually washed their clothes has been filled with clear, steaming water. The evening is balmy, but Leonardo still clutches his arms after he pulls off his limp, soiled tunic. He doesn't try to conceal his naked, lean body from his master; he can't summon the effort to care what he sees. He climbs in the tub, hugs his knees to his chest. Andrea begins to wash his back with a soft, soaked cloth. There's an awkwardness to his touch; he's using his right hand, careful to keep his left hand, wrapped many times over in a bandage, dry. He doesn't remember Andrea injuring himself.

Eventually, Leonardo submits, letting his eyes rest, feeling Andrea run the cloth along his neck, shoulders. Andrea lifts his arms, scrubs at their length, even washes the whorl of hair in his pits. He wonders if his mother ever bathed him this way, when he was still a babe.

After his skin has been scoured, after the bath water has turned from clear to cloudy dun, Andrea crouches beside the tub, resting his elbows against its rim. "You're safe now. All the charges were annulled."

His own murky reflection meets him in fragments. A grim mouth, half hidden by a burgeoning beard. He notes the absence of any elation; he sees only exhaustion. Perhaps it's not even himself he's looking at, perhaps by some magic, he's slipped into a stranger's skin. But no—he still feels the familiar ache of the one question that has festered in his mind for so many days.

"And Iac's charges?"

"His circumstances were different. I don't know if you knew this, but he's been accused before. Still, they gave him his life. Banished him from the city."

"Gave him his life," Leonardo whispers, bristling at the careful words, the audacity hidden within them.

"He'll be safer, away from here. He'll find a beginning in another place."

Where? he wants to ask. But what place could be different from here? Where could be better? He can't conceive of the world beyond the green hills of Tuscany. He has been told of so many places, of course; he's pored over many crinkled, faded maps. He knows of Rome with its avaricious bishops and crumbling churches. Half-drowned Venice, where they burn men like him. Give him a map, and he can point to Naples and Genoa and Mantua, can paint the mountains and the malarial marshes between them. But these places have been presented to him only by pen and paper, or by mouth; they're no more real to him than the myths of Minerva and Leda, Romulus and Remus.

Knowing where Iac went: what good would that serve him?

"And the Sebastian?" he asks.

"You need to think about what's next. Find yourself a new project."

He turns around to face his master. Andrea doesn't understand.

"Did the guards take it?"

Andrea looks away, hesitates. "No."

"Do you still have it?"

"Yes," he says softly.

"I want to see it."

"What good is there in that?"

"I have to see it. Please, show it to me."

"I don't think—"

"Show me!" The words erupt—loud, a shout. At the sound of them, Andrea retreats from the tub, and Leonardo covers his face.

"Dry off. Dress yourself," Andrea says, passing him a towel. "I'll have it ready inside."

THE PANEL, HULKING AND DARK, waits on an easel with a tarp crumpled around its base. He hesitates at the sight, but at this distance, it's nothing more than a featureless form. Without a candle, it's too dark to see the desert, the bare chest; he's too far to glimpse that face.

He approaches the panel with skittish steps as if he's lurking to sight someone unawares. A butter-yellow glow wavers against the tall ceiling. It builds, burns into saffron. He sees the brief shine of his many-layered oils, but then the candlelight leaps; it plays tricks. His work is gone. The panel is a void.

He steps closer. He reaches out. At his touch, the paint crumbles.

It is no longer his. A monstrous black streak tears across the surface, layer upon layer of pigment flaking away. All that remains of his work are its tallest reaches, where a few sparse colors remain, clouded by soot. A golden lock of hair. A splash of freckled skin. A lone brown eye, the skin around it wrinkling with pain.

A sound, an awful, guttural one, comes from within him. He presses his face to the scarred surface, feels its grain. He breathes in, searching for the fresh-needle scent of linseed. He smells only char.

Andrea's hands pull him back. He fights them.

"I tried to stop them. I told them whom you were painting it for. They either already knew, or they didn't care. They said it was proof. That it had to be destroyed. After they left, I pulled it from the fire. It was still too hot to hold. I tried to salvage it, I did. I tried . . ." His voice dwindles. He rubs his eyes, clumsily, with the side of his bandaged fist. "I shouldn't have let them take you."

"You had no choice." He realizes he doesn't believe the words as he says them.

"I should've protected you. It's so wrong, all of it. Insidious."

"You gave me a life. A home. And I ruined that. I brought this on myself."

"No." A shove, sudden and hard. "Don't say that. Where's the fight in you?"

"What is there to fight?"

Andrea stares at him, breathing heavily, his cheeks streaked. He can't bear it. He looks away, back to the painting. To its one watchful eye.

"I have to leave," he says, the words firm and clear. "I can't have this taint you or any of the apprentices. I can't be your burden."

He expects his old master to argue, to tell him he should find new work before leaving, or to say that every artist has good periods and bad ones. Instead, Andrea retreats to a locked cabinet, opens it.

"I made sure they didn't find this, when they searched through your things."

He walks back to Leonardo and places his purse on the table beside him. "You have to make me one promise. Don't stop painting. Not now. Not ever."

He promises.

HE DECAMPS TO THE FAR SIDE of the river, to San Frediano. The western fringe of the city, beside the gate to Pisa. The corner he knows least.

It's a quieter place, with plots of wide-leafed cabbages. In the early morning, before the carts roll, he can hear the Arno rush. What few towers rise into the sky end abruptly, half-finished, looking like crooked teeth. By afternoon, the whole hamlet sits in shadow beneath the tall pietra serena walls that surround the city.

Here, he rents the first space he visits. A former apothecary's shop; the pleasant scents of sage, pennyroyal, and nettles still remain. He buys a narrow bed for the upstairs quarters, haggles for iron pans at the forge up the street. From lumber, he builds a long rack to hold his jars of pigments, which he carefully orders. Lac to indigo, ivory to his myriad blacks. He counts the coins in his purse after every purchase. There are still so many florins remaining. Enough to last him years.

Sometimes he wonders if a letter will arrive. If Lorenzo will ask if his Sebastian is finished. If Giuliano might, in secret, ask him for another portrait of Fioretta. Then he remembers how that's all impossible now. He's told no one, not even Andrea, where he's living. He simply left one afternoon, heaving his sole chest of clothes and belongings, and never went back.

For days, weeks, months, he paces in his workshop. The disused space seems to brood. On a table beside a window, his brushes wait for him—bristles paling, growing stiff, lines of dust gathering on the handles.

It will be a year before he touches them again.

XXIX

TO MILAN, BRIEFLY. A PUGNACIOUS, CROWDED CITY, HALF-lost in a thick scum of smoke. The city gates are shut, out of fear of the plague brewing in Pavia, just to the south. Merchants and peasants alike are growing restless, but the city's work carries on. The shouting of the newly raised price of flour at the market. The clanging of hammers against anvils at the smithies. The screams of hot steel plunging into water at the armories. And then there is the sound of whispers, spoken alongside all this work.

They are telling a story about this city's duke.

The morning was a snowy one, they say. One that briefly turned the city more white than gray. Within the walls of the brick citadel, inside his castle, Galeazzo Sforza—Duke of Milan, friend to Florence, father-in-law to the pope's nephew—was tired, reluctant to get dressed. He didn't want to go to Mass, but his privy advisors told him it was necessary. So he barked at his servants to bring him his warmest clothes. They outfit him in twilled wool, with a sable-lined cloak. But no chainmail, not on this day. It was too heavy, and he was too tired.

The duke was clothed, fed, then wheeled in his coach over the drawbridge and to the Church of Santo Stefano. With courtiers at his sides and guards at his back, he trudged through the padded snow toward the church—a squat and simple building of few windows and palely stained glass.

Inside, the nave was crowded, unusually so. There were nobles and ambassadors, priests and the duke's many mistresses—and all of them were waiting for him. He stepped down the aisle, and men swooped before him, their heads bowing and rising, as if they were pigeons, and he was a nub of bread. The duke endured these clumsy obeisances for some time. He tried not to grimace as his knuckles grew wet from their many kisses.

Then a man genuflected directly before him, his knees almost coming between the duke's legs. The duke only vaguely recognized him. So as the man babbled about an abbey, the duke did not listen—he tried to move past him.

The man rose. There was a shout. A brief shine in the dim. A thrust of an arm.

The duke, bleeding, pawed at his wound, which was embarrassingly around his groin. Then he was stabbed again.

More bodies gathered then, more daggers too. They snatched at his throat, at his head, at his back. The duke stumbled to his knees and tried to summon his final words. They were uninspired but accurate: "I'm dead."

That was indeed the end of their duke of ten years. But why had he died?

Some say he had fathered at least seven bastards. Others claim he once starved a priest to death for auguring that he'd have a short reign. Almost everyone agrees that he prodigiously fucked his way through court—not just his councilors' wives, but his ambassadors too. Man or woman, he did not discriminate. And if anyone ever tried to refuse him, he raped them.

So there was good reason—an abundance of it really—as to why someone might want the duke dead.

However, some say the duke, as a person, wasn't the problem at all. That there was a group of thirty nobles gathered in that church who wanted to stage a coup and expel the duchy, who wanted Milan to become a republic, like its friends Florence and Venice. These men were meant to leave the church and lead the attackers to safety. They were to proclaim to the people that they'd been liberated from their oppressors.

But these nobles did no such thing. They simply gawped, transfixed by the sight of the duke's body—deflated, contorted, trampled by the escaping crowd.

The ending to this story is predictable.

One of the attackers was killed in the church. The other three were quartered within the citadel a few days later. The duke was buried, and his widow is now their regent while they wait for the late duke's firstborn to come of age.

Perhaps it is because of this ending, guessable and neat, that the whispers quickly dwindle. The voices who told this story have already returned to their iron-forging, their herb-grinding, their clothes-starching. There is not much for them to ponder. Yes, they've lost their duke—but how did that really matter to their lives?

This death, however, will still find a second life. In the hands of couriers, riding down the Apennines to Florence, farther south still to Rome. There, the story—fractured and incomplete—is only beginning to be told.

XXX

"PEACE IN ITALY DIED TODAY," THE POPE SAYS. HE TAKES A long look across the dining table—one to Girolamo, then one to Salviati. With such pompous gravity that Salviati must hide his smirk in his wineglass.

Here's the truth: if the duke's death killed the peace—a specious claim to Salviati—then it's been dead for over a week; by now, it'd be reeking, festering with flies. Northern, snowy Milan is so far from Rome; it's taken days of day-and-night riding for word of the stabbed duke to make it here. Who and how and why—these details must wait for future letters.

Besides, what was this peace? For all the talk about it, he's never seen it. There might be no cavalry stomping at the gates, but he's witnessed plenty of violence in his life: men trampling over each other for a single soldo, women left to hemorrhage in the red wake of birth. Peace be with you, he says at every Mass—but he's never felt it.

"Pray on this," the Holy Father says, shuffling out of the room, his white cassock dragging on the carpet. His attendants follow. One stoops beneath the table to retrieve the pope's silk slippers he had abandoned beneath his chair.

The door shuts. They are alone. Girolamo pours himself another glass of wine, pours one for Salviati, who drinks deeply. The flavor is piquant; it livens him. For so many months, he has sat in Pisa, mumbling through his Masses, waiting to feel something, anything other than the dull itch of red welts on his arms, his ankles. Then an outbreak of plague spurred him from Pisa back to Rome. And now this news of the duke's death has struck like a bolt of lightning. It has flashed, brilliant white, over all his life, letting him peer into every once-shadowed void. Now he sees it all, he understands. The duke's death was a sign of the Lord.

He knows now how their God has a temper, no matter what the pope likes to preach. He tired of peace and let Satan into His garden to make life far more interesting. He drowned the world, save for a single boat. He demanded His own son's head to be torn by thorns, his back lashed by whips, his palms and soles pierced by nails. And now, in Milan, God has seen the awful duke punished for his crimes in the most gruesome of ways.

Now he wonders: what would He like to see done about Florence?

Girolamo taps a fingernail against his glass. "Why do you think they did it?"

"We all know what was said about your father-in-law. Rumors I wouldn't dare repeat here, of all places."

"Ha!" The glass jolts in Girolamo's hand; wine dribbles onto the table. "I thought you were going to say we should hold vigil for his soul. Pisa's changed you."

"I'm the same man who left Rome," he says, trying to ignore Girolamo's grease-streaked chin. "No matter what was said about her father, I do grieve for your wife's loss."

"Save your prayers. She's useless to me now."

"Not true. She still carries the Sforza name."

"And what does that matter, if they're all run out of Milan by a mob?"

He nods with a pensive pinch of the brows, a soft frown—an expression he's perfected from listening to so many confessions. A face that loosens lips and promises understanding.

Girolamo slouches in his chair. "Whether they stay or go, I'm still ruined. Galeazzo kept Medici from having Imola. He gave me that countship. With him gone, what is to prevent Medici from striding in and taking it?"

The room is darker now, all shadows and deep orange splashes. The wine in Salviati's glass has gone from ruby to plum. He swirls it.

"You're assuming the worst. Consider it another way. With Galeazzo dead, Florence has lost their best strong arm. Medici may want Imola, I agree with you on that, but he can't attempt to take it from you without an army. And where's he going to get one without the help of the Milanese?"

"He has Venice as an ally."

"They're too worried about the Turks to spare any men."

"There are always condottieri."

"Sure, at one time, Montefeltro would've said yes to Medici for the right sum. But your uncle invested him as duke. He wouldn't dare strike against you now."

Salviati stands, steps around the table. The thin candle flames waver as he passes, swaying the room from orange to black. He grabs a chair and drags it next to Girolamo. Close enough to smell the camphor on his neck.

"The way I see it, your uncle has his own army, with you as its captain. He has Ferrante as an ally, along with his army in Naples. And if that weren't enough, he could call on Montefeltro too. You're worrying about Medici, but he's the one who's vulnerable. Especially now. If Florence were to turn against him, he'd have no one to protect him."

"This is pointless talk," Girolamo says. "You know my uncle. If I ask him to do anything—even to defend my own land—he'll press his palms together and say he has to pray on it. Then he'll go back to building his chapel, hoping God will do his bidding for him."

God has, Salviati thinks. It's the only way to make sense of it all.

Below the table, he grabs the hem of the tablecloth, dries his hands on it. "You're the head of your uncle's army. It's your duty to God to protect him. I worry, and I think you do too, that your uncle . . . He can be too cautious at times. He was always worried about ruining the peace. But now he says that peace is dead. Perhaps this is the moment to take action."

The nearest candle on the table extinguishes, its wick drowned by melted wax. The room dims. Smoke wafts across the table, masking Girolamo's face.

"My uncle won't start a war."

"I would never argue for one. It's unnecessary. Look at Milan. All it took was a few men and some daggers to bring down the duke."

Silence. A long one. In it, a fear creeps in: he might've misjudged. He could be wrong—about all of it. Girolamo could go to the pope, tell him how Pisa has turned the archbishop into a wicked, untrustworthy man. He could be cast out.

A glint in the dark. Girolamo's gold-ringed fingers reach for more wine.

"I won't deny having Medici gone would certainly solve my problems," his voice lowers. "Some of my uncle's too. But there's no use in discussing it. He'd never consent. He's an ambitious man, but not a bold one. Why do you think he spends so much time on his building projects? He knows he hasn't done anything that will give him a legacy. But if he builds a grand enough bridge or library or chapel and chisels his name onto it, then he can live on."

Salviati inhales, holds the breath. This is it, he thinks. He could quit this talk right now, tell Girolamo he's right. Girolamo could return to Imola and Salviati to Pisa to suffer its plague as his punishment. They could both never speak of this night again.

"You're right," he says, but the next words catch. Why was he a child of Florence, why did he work so hard in Rovere's service, why was he kept from his rightful prize in Pisa for so long if not to act here, tonight?

"You're right," he says again, but this time the next words are different. "Your uncle wants his legacy, his monuments, even if he does nothing more than nod along to the builders' plans. So let us be his architects. Let us make our plan and find the masons to do the labor. Then we can go before your uncle and present it to him. Something so beautiful he cannot refuse it."

Girolamo pushes back his chair, stalks down to the far end of the room, where the lone surviving candlestick rests on a mantel. He grabs it, carries it back to the table. Now Salviati can see Girolamo's face once more—his wide, hungry grin.

"How would you see it done?" he asks.

—

A YEAR PASSES. A year of dodging plague, in Pisa and in Rome. Of letters written in code, of weeks-long waits for couriers to return northward from Naples, southward from Urbino. Of more Masses for Salviati, recitations of God killing every firstborn in Egypt, of Him casting sulfur and fire down onto Sodom and Gomorrah, of Him stilling the sun so Joshua could slaughter the Canaanites.

Now they've come once more to the Vatican, to the pope's presence chamber. He, Girolamo, Francesco from the bank, and also Giovanni Battista, the head of the papal guard. All of them kneeling, with the pope before them—the man who is essential to their plans, who has hovered, unseen, as they've made every recruit, the man whom they say this is all for. Like God, he supposes.

In truth, it had been easy to avoid him. The pope has kept himself busy making cardinals, stitching mozzetta, summoning titular churches from the ether. Pietro's death was like pitch to his dynastic ambitions. Having two nephews in the church? That wasn't enough, not nearly. Now he has nephews, grandnephews, and even more relatives of dubious relation joining the college. Cristoforo and Basso della Rovere, along with his new favorite nephew, Raffaele Riario—all made cardinals in a single year. Domenico della Rovere later this year, if he can manage it.

The presence chamber is silent—no gurgling censers, no rustling flabella. The servants have all been dismissed, the doors shut and bolted.

"A motley gathering you all make," the pope says, smiling from his wide throne. "Tell us, what is it that you wish to discuss?"

Girolamo rises to one knee. "Florence, Your Holiness."

He coughs, wipes phlegm from his chin with a fist. "Why?"

"It has turned backward, to the past, and become a godless city. The people are praying to gold and not to Jesus. The artists are painting pagan gods and not our Lord. There are sodomites everywhere you look. And Medici lords over it, allows it all."

"Is this true, Salviati?"

After all these years, he's still his Florentine. "It saddens me to say that it is, Your Holiness. I've been horrified by the reports I've received in Pisa. Hundreds convicted of sodomy in the last year alone. And those are only the men so unrepentant as to be caught."

The pope's eyes widen. "This is most concerning. It sickens me to think this could be happening on our holy peninsula. But what are we to do about it? We could pray for them, but as you've said, they're a godless people."

"We could restore the city, Your Holiness. Bring it back to His Light."

"But how, my child?"

"By taking the people out of Medici's clutches," Girolamo says. "By replacing him with someone who will guide the people of Florence back to God. Someone who will be a friend to you."

"Who?"

"I'd suggest Jacopo de' Pazzi. As your banker, he's proven himself a loyal friend. And his family stretches far back in Florence's history. Much further than the Medici. The people would see this as a restoration of their glory days, him as their savior."

The pope turns to Francesco. "And your uncle, he would do this for us?"

"If Your Holiness asked," he says. "He would do anything for the Church."

What bollocks, Salviati thinks. More likely anything for the coin.

But what Francesco's said isn't a lie, not precisely. When Francesco approached Jacopo with their plans, he balked. Said it was foolish, that it'd see them killed. But if the pope blesses such a plan, he knows his cousin couldn't refuse.

"It is not only within Florence that we'd have support," Girolamo says. "King Ferrante has told me he would send troops to support any cause you deemed holy. So has his son in Calabria, who has a sizable army. As well as Duke Montefeltro. That's soldiers from Naples, Calabria, and Urbino, all willing to fight for us."

"What of Milan and Venice? Surely they'd come to Florence's aid." The pope shakes his head. "No, we would not wish for war. Even if it secured us Florence."

"None of us want a war," Girolamo says. "And we would not need one to seek a change in government. All we would need to do is invite Medici to Rome, for Easter perhaps, and detain him, allowing Jacopo to oversee the city in his absence."

The pope tents his fingers, nods slowly. "And what if the invitation were refused?"

"Then some of us could go to Florence," Girolamo says. "See that he relinquishes control of the city, one way or another. Even if it costs him his life."

The Holy Father's face is like that of a falcon that's just had its hood pulled off. Clear-eyed. Predatory.

"We wish death on no man," the pope says, "not for any reason. It's not appropriate for our office to consent to such a thing."

Salviati's head sinks. It's done. He was a fool.

"But," the pope continues, "Medici behaves ill toward us. He is a villain."

Salviati looks up, watches the words whistle from the pope's lips, one by one, barely strung together. "No," the pope says. "On no account would we wish to see him dead. But a change in government, yes."

This back and forth is better than any *jeu de paume*. He has no mind of how to respond to it. Girolamo, however, is a seasoned player; he is unperturbed. "We could deliver you this change, and we, of course, would do everything we can to avoid Medici's death. But should he die, God forbid, would you forgive those responsible?"

"You're an animal," the pope says with a single, throaty laugh.

"I only—"

The pope holds up a hand, silencing him. The hand is pudgy and supple, yet where the fingers meet the palm the skin is darker, scarred from his former life and its long days of rowing.

The pope looks from Girolamo, to Battista, to him. Salviati craves a judgment in his gaze, to see the eyes soften with satisfaction, or even narrow with disgust. But they remain unchanged, unknowable. Maddeningly vague.

"We'll say it again, to all of you. While we don't wish the death of anyone, we greatly want change in Florence. Take the government from Medici's hands. He's a scoundrel and a wicked man and has no respect for us. Once he is out of Florence, we can do whatever we'd like with the republic. Bring its best artists here. Send our most devout men there to return its people to God." The pope turns to Salviati, nods. "Yes, this would all be most pleasing to us."

He cannot believe these words.

Girolamo reaches up, clasps his father's hand. "Your Holiness speaks the truth. All the continent will long to be your friend with Medici gone. Every artist will fight to paint for you and your chapel. God will shine down on the peninsula, all of it. Know that we'll do everything possible to bring this about."

God as his witness, the pope coos.

"Do what you want, my child. But know we cannot wish for death."

This divine prolocution—it dizzies, confuses, turns the stomach. He can't make sense of it. He needs certainty, he needs to know that he's staying on God's path. He brings his hands together in prayer.

"Holy Father," he says, then he stops. He cannot speak the act aloud—not directly at least. He searches for more delicate words. At the sight of the pope's roughened palms, he knows what to say. "Are you content with how we'll steer this ship?" he asks. "That we'll steer it well and toward a good and safe harbor?"

The pope turns to him. He's smiling.

"We are content," he says. "God be with you."

Part Four

THE
ALTARPIECE

April 26, 1478

XXXI

A SUNDAY DAWNS IN APRIL. A WINDLESS MORNING, THE ARNO'S surface smooth and specular. Along the river's rocks and reeds, paupers are rising. Chewing on ends of days-stale bread. Cupping handfuls of brown, cloudy river water and washing the grime from their faces. Stripping off their shifts and pulling on their least-dirty smocks.

One man has yet to rise. He lies, blanketed, near the water's edge. His open, vacant eyes stare at the hours-dead bonfire.

A girl with broad, sun-blistered cheeks approaches him. She extends a foot, her toe protruding through the slipper's frayed tip. She prods the man's shoulder. She crouches, and the reeds prick her thighs. The man's blanket is rather well-woven; it could keep away the cold at night. She grabs the nearest edge of the blanket and pulls it away from the body.

The man's arm is pockmarked—hand and fingers turned the darkest shade of black she's ever seen, from the wrist down to the nails. She drops the blanket, stumbles backward. She cries out.

The women come first. They know what a lone scream can mean. They look at the startled girl, then at the dead man. No one knows his name, but who he was doesn't matter to them. They shout to the men to grab the ashy logs from last night's fire. They snap off dry reeds and toss them onto the body.

The girl stands alone, and no one stops to comfort her. A gray-haired woman is walking past her; the girl squeezes her bony arm. Why can't they let nature take care of the body, she asks. Could they roll it into the water and let the river take it away?

The older woman shakes her head, looks at the girl's flushed face, her flat chest. Only now does she see how young she is. Too young to know. She walks past the girl, saying nothing.

The makeshift pyre is lit, and the gathering disbands. Some head to Mass, others to scavenge in the alleys behind the bakehouses. The older woman walks away from the reek and the embers, then stops. She looks over her shoulder at the girl, still beside the fire with her eyes unblinking, despite the buffeting smoke.

"Best not to dwell on it," she calls to her.

XXXII

THE WORKSHOP IS WIDE, SILENT, AND EMPTY. HIS JARS OF PIG-
ment are all corked and full. His brushes rest on a cloth, their bristles all
rigid. The tables, the floors are in need of a good dusting. But his apprentice left him some weeks ago. Told him he was tired of having nothing
to work on, nothing to learn. He couldn't blame the boy for wanting to
go. A mistake to have hired him at all. But he was such a pretty, curious
thing. Better that he's gone now. He gave him dreams that by morning
made him feel guilty just looking at him.

He thought living alone might be a blessing. That it might free him,
fully, from distractions: no more questions from his apprentice to break
the stillness, no gossip about other artists to remind him of all the work
he has not won, no more dangerous thoughts causing his cock to swell.
With a newfound focus, he might finally have time not only to think
about the painting that is to be done but also to indulge the other fas-
cinations lurking in the recesses of his mind: the ways water flows; the
building of an unsupported arch; the logic of the body's blood, organs,
muscles, sinews—how they all work together.

Instead, alone, he finds himself listless, waiting to be stirred. He now
fails to remember the day of the week, forgets when rent is due, finds
himself without ink or fresh firewood.

Into his leather sack, he places his notebook—a small quarto, battered, threatening to tear at the spine. He packs a purse with tinkling
denari, along with a fresh stick of charcoal and a blade to sharpen its tip.
The coins are all he really needs, but he never steps outside without charcoal and paper. Even if there's no work he wishes to do.

He slings his sack onto his shoulder and opens the door to blooming
peony and jacinth.

This is his morning walk, always the same. First, away from the
river, up to Santa Maria del Carmine. Sometimes he stops here, not to
pray but to look at its frescoes—Masaccio's Adam and Eve, in particular. The couple leaving Eden in shame. Eve's howling mouth, her palpa-
ble anguish. Adam's perfect naked form, his face buried in his hands.

He always prefers to paint in oil, but this fresco is special. It makes him wonder what he might accomplish with an entire wall.

Today is too beautiful to spend in those shadows. The unclouded sun hints at warmth to come. He continues his daily walk, back down to the Arno. On this side, the banks are hushed, empty. It is across the river that tents and bonfires are nestled together in the mud beside the reeds, below the spires and towers and domes of the city center.

He crosses here, on the Ponte Santa Trinita, uncrowded and clean-stoned and curving. Never on the Ponte Vecchio, with blood from the butchers running between its stones, with its far end spilling so closely, too closely, to the streets of the Baldracca. Never there. He hasn't walked those alleys in two years.

Sometimes he wonders what for.

On some days, he pauses at the midpoint over the bridge. Looking east, toward the shops on the Ponte Vecchio, to the oratories and the homes on the Rubaconte. He's drawn his own design for a bridge, more graceful than any of these. But, as ever, he's too late. There's no use for another bridge to span the Arno within the city walls.

Onward, now—to the Via Por Santa Maria. Here is a familiar neighborhood, the one where he lived with his father all those years ago. Where he'd walk through the streets admiring the shops selling ivory combs and lace veils and pearl-capped pins. He always wanted to step inside, purchase some fanciful accessory to decorate his unruly curls. But there were only ever women inside, so he never did.

The shops are closed today. The many goldsmiths too. Now he notices the absence of creaking cart wheels and clopping hooves. Instead, he hears the constant chiming of church bells in their place. He's a fool. It's Sunday. The market will be empty.

Nonetheless, he strolls through the piazza, between the shuttered stalls, down aisles with gashed, overripe pears resting in the dirt. He keeps going, following the old, northern road to the baptistery and Santa Reparata.

This is his daily turning point: the narrow gap called Paradise in between the baptistery and the cathedral. Where the bronze doors gleam by morning light and the bell tower spars with the cerulean sky. He'll stand here—sometimes for an hour, more—and admire these panels, each of them so ornate. The dozens of soldiers swarming Jericho. Cain, bringing down his sword. Abraham, halted by the angel. And then, when hunger stirs, he will retrace his path, buying bread at the market before returning to his workshop where he pretends that he's working.

Today, the passageway is thronged. Bells summon from high towers. People flood through the nave doors. He, too, should go to Mass and pray. But there are so many things he should be doing. Cleaning his workshop. Visiting his father, his stepbrother, his infant stepsister. Frescoing chapel walls like Sandro, painting more family portraits like Domenico, sculpting fountains and saints like Andrea.

Most of all he should be working on his altarpiece. Another Madonna, of course. For the priors' chapel within the Palagio. A decent commission, one that arrived unexpectedly just after his apprentice left. It's a miracle that he won the work, even if he's merely the substitute for its original painter. He doesn't quite believe it, but no one has said a word of his past. Clearly his father didn't know, if he recommended him for the job.

He still hasn't gone to thank him for putting forward his name. He doesn't want to have to explain to his father why three months have passed and he still hasn't started the work. His father won't understand why painting another lapis-robed Virgin fails to inspire him. And he certainly can't tell his father he's afraid to pick up his brush after so long, afraid of what he might see when he does.

A commotion turns his head. Beyond the cathedral, up the Via Larga. A procession with fluttering banners in mustard and crimson. Dozens of trotting horses, caparisoned in taffeta.

He abandons his daily path and follows alongside the procession. He sees guardsmen with swords, tonsured priests in black cassocks, a cardinal in crimson, a bishop in the most terrible shade of purple. The bishop's gaze roves—over the ruts in the road, over the crowd passing by.

Leonardo's feet still. He's standing across from it. That palace.

It's unchanged, in all this time. He glances up at the many windows. One is open, its curtains pulled aside. A familiar face is looking down at the action below. And Leonardo, in turn, stares at his dark, wavy hair, at his long nose, his strong jaw.

Giuliano's eyes meet his; they widen. The smallest curve appears at the corner of his mouth. He raises his right hand to him, and Leonardo salutes back. Then Giuliano turns around. He disappears.

Perhaps he's been wrong. Perhaps there is still a chance—if not to paint for him again, then for these churchmen he's hosting. But he would need work to show these men. Even if it's unfinished. Some answer to what he's done in these last two years.

His feet quicken—away from the palace, back down the Via Larga. He walks in front of the cathedral, passes it. He does not turn to look at the baptistery doors, he does not slow his steps, not until he's standing beneath the craggy rise of the Palagio.

Today, he'll begin again.

XXXIII

HIS BROTHER STANDS AT A WINDOW IN A LINEN CHEMISE, damp at the underarms and hanging loosely below his waist.

"You're not dressed?"

Giuliano turns toward him and takes a jagged step. His left hand clutches his thigh, wrapped with a poultice. The knee below is marbled red and purple.

He had fallen off a horse on the road to Fiesole, where they were meant to host a banquet for one of the pope's cardinal nephews. Lorenzo had wanted to ride to the villa a day early; he had asked Giuliano to join him. But his brother demurred, said he had an obligation in the city, that he'd come later. So Lorenzo took the coaches with Clarice and the children by day, and his brother stupidly left Florence well into the evening, taking the road by horse under sparse moonlight. What happened next was predictable: the horse spooked, his brother tumbled. Giuliano then turned back to the city, absented himself from the next day's events. And now Lorenzo must host another banquet here in Florence, must suffer once more the cardinal and the odious archbishop and all of their friends.

"Let me help," Lorenzo says, conscious of the hour. He shuts the window, draws the curtain too. "They're arriving. We can't keep them waiting long."

He steps behind his brother. Gently grabs the hem of his chemise and lifts it. Giuliano silently obliges, raising his arms, letting Lorenzo pull it over his head. His brother's back is broad. Sparse freckles trail from his shoulders to the base of his spine. Firm muscles course beneath his pale, hairless skin. It's a body worthy of sculpture, far better than his own. But Giuliano has time for leisure; he doesn't have to waste half the day sat at a desk, dictating letters.

He fetches his brother's outfit, laid across his cassone by a servant. Hose in black velvet and an emerald doublet embroidered with leaves in cloth of gold. A silk shirt and a mail vest of steel chain to wear underneath.

He hands him the hose, but Giuliano staggers as he tries to put his feet into them.

"Here," he says, setting aside his brother's garments, guiding him to a chair.

"I feel like Father," Giuliano says, wincing as he lowers himself onto the seat.

The thought crossed his mind too: all those days sat at his father's bedside, staring at his hands, his feet, turned red and swollen by gout.

"Don't say that," he says, grabbing the hose dropped to the floor. "That'd make me Mother."

They both laugh. It's been some time since they've done that.

"Do you think she'll come back soon?"

"She wants to, judging by all the letters she writes. But she's also building herself a villa beside the springs. So perhaps she knows she can't."

Giuliano frowns, cupping his hand over his hairy groin, hiding his ample cock. Lorenzo kneels, not turning his gaze away, rolling the hose over his brother's high-arched feet and up his tensed calves.

"This is why you need a wife," he says, stopping at the knees. "Much better than having me do this. Mother says Semiramide is not only a lord's daughter, but a kind woman too. She'll take care of you."

She's also coming to his brother with a healthy dowry, even larger than the one Clarice brought him. And new income for the family is dearly needed.

With a grimace, Giuliano hoists the hose up to his waist.

Lorenzo hands him the mail vest.

"Must we?"

"Until the Signoria permits us to have our own guards, yes, we must."

In truth, it was a promise to his mother.

"Even to church? That seems extreme."

Like an answer, a fresh swell of bells washes across the city.

"Come now, dress yourself. We don't want to make the cardinal late for his own Mass."

"Which cardinal is this again?"

"Raffaele, a nephew on the Riario side of the family," Lorenzo says. "I think so, at least. Hard to be sure. It seems Rovere will make anyone a cardinal these days."

"Except for me," Giuliano mutters. He's gazing down at the steel in his hands, mouth wrinkled. "There's something I need tell you."

"Now?"

"Please don't be angry."

"Just say it."

"Fioretta—she's with child."

The silk crumples in his grip. "Christ, Giuliano. You're affianced. You agreed to the Semiramide girl."

"I'm well aware of that."

"How long have you known?"

Giuliano says nothing.

"You saw her, didn't you? The other day, before your fall."

He still says nothing, but this time he flashes a guilty, wet glance.

"That matters not. Tomorrow, once the cardinal and the others are gone, we'll take her to an apothecary," he says, the words spinning faster. "There's one near Santa Maria Novella that Nori has used before. They have herbs. They'll know what to do. We'll manage it, and your bride-to-be and her father will be none the wiser."

"It's too late."

He drops the silk, the doublet into his brother's lap. Leers over him, resting one hand on the back of the chair. "We need that dowry, Giuliano. Galeazzo's death hurt us badly. With him gone, we're never going to see our debts in Milan repaid. We might have to shut the Avignon branch, maybe London too."

"I didn't know," his brother mumbles.

"Of course you didn't. While I've been working to keep the bank solvent, you've been out chasing cunt."

"Just give me this peace," Giuliano says.

"Peace?" he whines, grabbing his brother's chin, pulling it up to face him. "You've only had peace because you've left it to me and Mother to find you a bride. You've only had peace because I kept your secret from her. No more. You need to fix this, Giuliano. I don't care how."

Giuliano catches his hand, tugs it away from his chin. Squeezes the fingers tightly until they shade deep pink. "No, Lorenzo."

"No?" he says, freeing his hand, wringing it. He laughs. "No?"

He walks to an ewer at the bedside and dips a fresh, folded cloth into its water. He tosses the soaked linen to Giuliano, who doesn't catch it, who lets it slide down his taut abdomen and over his side.

"Wipe your face and get dressed. I'll keep our guests entertained while we wait for you."

"No. I'm not going," Giuliano says, his neck flushed.

"It's Mass. You have to go."

"I don't have to do anything, Lorenzo."

He stomps his foot. "Really? You won't come? Leave it, as always, for me to manage?"

His brother shakes his head. Stretches his legs long before him. Settles more deeply into his chair. His strong, bare chest heaves. It glistens. The silk and steel gather at his waist like a loincloth. Like he's some rich Christ.

XXXIV

HIS WORLD IS HAZED, CANTED, HALF LOST BEHIND THE DUST kicked up by the horses. In the brown fog, faces appear and dither: paupers in sarks and traders' wives in unbleached mantels and artists in palely dyed tunics. He searches their faces, all of them—looking to recognize someone, for someone to recognize him.

They all rush. Darting in front of the braying horses, not minding the heaps of dung scattered on the street, not granting him or the cardinal or his cousin a bow or even a nod. He watches it all, biting back bile.

He expected this feeling to ease as they entered the city gates, as everything at last hardened from hypotheticals. He had only returned to Florence for one purpose, and it would be met before sundown. Then, he'll leave. Back to Pisa, or back to Rome. With a beatific calm, knowing he'll have fulfilled His vision, seen to God's plan.

His stomach heaves. It's this fetid air, he thinks. The same as it was all those years ago. Filling his mouth, his nostrils. Catching in his throat like ash. He feels it in him, his body fighting it like a poison. He wonders if there's something to be understood in the sensation, if he should pull on these reins and ride back out the gates.

No. This is one of His tests. He must remain devoted.

"An odd homecoming, is it not?" his cousin says from the horse beside him. His face has taken on a papery quality, his brows have silvered.

"I thought it'd be different, coming back."

"I know you did," Jacopo says. His sky-blue eyes drift from Salviati's embroidered palladium to his purple robes, down to the rings on his fingers, gold and garnet and peridot. "And you didn't have to return. You didn't have to do any of this. But here we are."

"You'll make this place better," he says.

"Pray for it." Jacopo looks to the palace looming ahead. "I should leave you here, yes?"

Salviati nods. "I'll see you at the Palagio."

Jacopo grips the reins, turns his horse. "God be with you, cousin," he shouts, then rides away.

With that, it begins.

THEY DISMOUNT IN THE COURTYARD. A handkerchief is passed; they all wipe their boots.

"This will work," Battista says. Ever the guardsman, he scans the courtyard: the tables laid out for the afternoon's banquet, the barrels piled in the arcades, the tranches waiting to be filled with geese and pheasant and rabbit. "If we're blessed, we won't need our swords. The wine will do."

Salviati isn't listening. He's distracted—by a statue of a buggerly boy cast in bronze, preening with a sword in his hand. It's a David. He knows this. But a depiction like this is sacrilege. A boy like this never would have brought down the giant. He's too much of a fop. They should melt this bronze when the day is done, he thinks. Recast it into something more suitable. A Messiah, perhaps.

The others don't seem to notice it. Battista is watching the archway. Francesco is leant against a pillar, his veins pulsing at his temples. The rest of their party shuffles in the arcades, feigning boredom while they wait for Medici to join them. There are two priests, both from the republic: Stefano, from Bagnone; and Maffei, from Volterra. And there's Baroncelli—a gaunt-faced, jittery man so indebted to Jacopo that he's pledged to do anything they might ask of him, as long as his loans are forgiven. An awful bargain, Salviati thinks. Then again, he made one himself not so long ago.

Battista touches his arm. "It will be over soon."

It has to be. There are dozens of hired swords lurking in the streets; in the hills, there are hundreds of Montefeltro's men waiting to attack. They have no choice but to act.

Footsteps from the stairwell. Medici strides toward them, affecting a smile. The young Cardinal Raffaele scurries across the courtyard, so eager to greet him that he nearly trips over his robes. It's too much fabric for a stubby, sixteen-year-old boy. A terrible color too. Brings out the rosiness in Raffaele's cheeks, makes him look like a sliced beet.

They both kneel to each other, Medici and the cardinal. They laugh at this.

Him? He'll do no such thing.

"I hope I haven't kept you waiting too long," Medici says to them all.

"Where's your brother?" Francesco asks, too brusquely.

Salviati puts a hand on Francesco's shoulder, squeezes it. "I hope his injury doesn't still ail him," he says.

"Alas, he remains bed rid, I'm afraid," Medici says, his face darkening.

Beneath his hand, he feels Francesco's arm tighten. "Still? I thought it was only a small riding injury. He can't see us, even for a short moment?"

Medici shakes his head.

"Not even for Mass?" Salviati says. "Surely he must take Communion."

Medici pouts slightly. Looks at his robes, as if he's weighing how much sacrilege he can speak to a priest. "If he cannot join us, he can take to the family chapel, inside the palace."

"I hope he can at least still sup with us after the Mass."

"Unlikely, given the state he's in," he says, falling silent for a moment. "But I'll commend to him your thoughts and prayers."

"Oh!" Raffaele exclaims, his voice cracking. "We brought a gift for you both. A small gesture, for your gracious hospitality." He waves a scarlet-draped arm to a cask, placed beside the David.

"A Trebbiano," Battista says. "From the Holy Father's cellars."

"Well this is certainly better than getting fish from Pisa." He smirks at Salviati, then smiles to the cardinal and bows his head. "Thank you, Your Excellency. To bring this all the way from Rome—it is far too much of an extravagance. I'll be sure to write to the Holy Father with my sincere gratitude." He claps his hands, turns to his broad-nosed secretary, hanging in his shadows. "We shall all enjoy it this afternoon. Agnolo, would you tell the servants to serve it with supper?"

He wants to shout, to distract, to intervene. The wine is a waste if the brother isn't to join them.

"Shall we to Mass?" Medici asks, and Raffaele nods, wide-mouthed like an eager dog. The cardinal has been so easy to keep unaware of their plans. That was a blessing, until now. But there's no time to reassess, let alone think. Medici's arm is around the cardinal's back. He's already guiding him out of the courtyard, toward the cathedral.

Salviati and the others follow. There is nothing else they can do.

They walk onto the Via Larga, the thoroughfare that threads together every part of their plan—what was their plan, at least. Ahead, the cathedral where the cardinal would be honored. Farther on, the Palagio, where Jacopo will proclaim himself as Florence's new leader.

With everyone already in the cathedral, the street has a desolate, unnerving quality. Dirt-ridden and well-worn, it looks like a drought-dry river. He feels caught by its dusty riptide, drawn against his will to the Mass.

Francesco clutches his elbow, slows him like an anchor. Beside him, Battista lags too. Medici and the cardinal are far ahead, engrossed in each other's company.

"I can go back to the palace," Francesco whispers. "Tell the servants Lorenzo requested Giuliano join him at Mass."

"Will they believe you?" Battista says.

"Would they dare question it?"

"Is that a gamble we can afford taking?"

"Can we risk not taking it?" Francesco says. "We need them together, by any means necessary."

"And what if, after Mass, Giuliano asks his brother why he forced him out of bed? We'd be found out."

"So we'll do it as soon as they're together. In the cathedral. When the Eucharist is raised and everyone's heads are bowed. It will be crowded in there. Dark. No one will know what's happened."

Salviati's feet falter. Ahead, beyond Francesco, Battista, and the others, the cathedral's bulk carves the surrounding piazza into slices of sun and shadow. He waits to feel Battista's hand on his arm, to hear him say that this is the only way. But Battista has stepped back; he's silent.

"Keep walking," Francesco snarls to the both of them.

"Inside a church?"

They are his thoughts, but Battista's words. Two priests and him, an archbishop, are in their party—yet it's the guardsman who has balked. He wants to turn away from these men. To find a shaded alley to kneel. To pray. He has to know what God wants him to do.

"We h-have the Holy Father's blessing," Francesco stammers, his voice low. "The die's already cast. We're set on this, one way or another."

"Not like this." Battista takes another step backward. "That's adding sacrilege onto it all."

Francesco throws up his arms. A flock of pigeons startles and takes to the air. "You all do what you wish. I'm going to fetch the brother so we can finish this." He points to Baroncelli. "You—with me."

Salviati watches the two of them turn, watches their feet, so fast and determined, tread back up the Via Larga.

When he turns back to the piazza, Battista is gone. Medici and his retinue, the cardinal and his servants are well ahead, all standing beside the cathedral. Only the two bearded priests have remained at his side. Waiting for his word.

He says nothing to them. He drifts across the piazza, to the baptistery doors.

Everyone in Florence was baptized here. He was baptized here. Medici was baptized here. And they are not so different in age, when he thinks about it; their baptisms must have been just a few years apart. Their families—they weren't so different either; they both existed in this city long enough that they must share some blood. Even though Medici was born an heir and he a mistake, baptism, here in this building, was meant to cleanse them of their differences. Make them the same in God's eyes.

What a lie!

The voice is small and terrible. It rings in his head. He can't shake its sound.

His hand is trembling. He reaches out, grips the sun-warmed metal. He searches the panels, their sculpted scenes. The same stories he tells in his Masses, verses he knows by memory. Adam, Eve, Moses, David. There had to be some parcel of truth in them, however small.

He reaches for Abraham, climbing a rocky, gilt Moriah. So pious, so loyal. Look at him, nearing the heavens, ready to burn his son. A sacrifice, a terrible one, demanded by God. A test of faith stopped only by the arrival of this angel in a swirl of radiant bronze.

Stop me, he thinks. Please stop me.

Fingers graze his elbow. The two priests are still with him.

"They're going inside," Maffei says.

Past the priests, Medici is striding up the cathedral steps, the cardinal following with his head upturned. Salviati follows his gaze up to the dome's very peak, where a bare cross reflects the distant sun. The clouds above the cathedral are thin and ribbonlike, as if the dome has torn open the firmament.

He shuts his eyes. He waits, feels the air still. His breath held, he hears the softest fluttering, drawing closer. The flapping of wings. It's here, he thinks. A miracle. The golden angel, come to save him.

He opens his eyes. It's a pigeon, scavenging crumbs in the narrow pathway, between the baptistery and the cathedral. He watches it peck uselessly at the dirt.

He wipes his face, looks back to the priests. "My father once told me that, centuries ago, the city's dead were buried here, beneath the piazza," he hears himself saying. "He was a good talker, my father. Knew how to spin a story, to make someone listen, to make them desperate for his next word. I always envied that about him. I wanted to have that ability. I suppose that was when I first started thinking about becoming a priest."

He kicks at the dirt. "So my father used to say that there was a different church standing where the cathedral is now. A smaller one. And there wasn't enough room in the crypts for all the dead. So they began digging them into the earth out here, in this little strip between the church and the baptistery. Paradise, they called it."

His feet are leaden. He can't will them to lift from the paving. He thinks about the bodies, the thousands of them, deep below these stones. Bones snared, flesh long gone. Souls waiting for Judgment Day.

"I can't go inside with you," he tells the priests. "I—"

Maffei lets go of his arm. "Say no more, Your Excellency." He parts his cloak and moves his hand to the hilt of a dagger, belted tightly to his cassock. "If Francesco returns with the brother, we'll be standing next to Lorenzo, ready to act."

There is surely something he should say. Some proverb from the Bible. Some lesson to impart. But the three of them, they're priests. They know all the sacred advice.

So he nods and watches the priests walk away, into the cathedral.

XXXV

THEY ENTER THE CATHEDRAL. HE AND THE CARDINAL AND the many men in their service. The doors shut behind them, and he is briefly blind in the dim. How like a cave a church nave can be. So much stone, so much shadow.

Unlike a cave, the nave is crammed with bodies. He can see them now, face to nape, shoulder to shoulder—the number of them is impressive, almost frightening. His hand slips beneath his cape, drifts across the downy velvet of his doublet. He presses, and, yes, here's the reminder of steel against his ribs. He reaches down, finds another comfort: his sword-sheath, inlaid with mother-of-pearl.

He wades into the crowd. Down the nave, toward the altar. Past peasants and publicans, by farmers, foremen, and carpenters, who then give way to wool-weavers and spice-traders as they carve their path to the altar.

A boy, to his right. Pupils ringed with green, widening when he sees him, taking in his yellow doublet and his long cape, dyed with kermes. The boy pulls off his cap, crumples it against his heart. He bows.

So does everyone else. All of them, parting for him. He may not be a prince by law, but look at this—he is to them. They all owe thanks to him. The paupers love him, because he keeps the price of bread low. The textile guilds? His bank lends money to their businesses. And as for the old families? He lets them hoard their wealth at tax time.

All of them know it: how he, how his money, makes this city turn.

This walk through the nave is long; it's slow. It would've been much quicker to enter through the side doors, at each end of the transept. But every step here is a reminder to the cardinal, to the archbishop, to all the pope's men: he has something they never will, something better than the allegiance of an army or the devotion of the congregation. He has the adoration of an entire city. The greatest city.

He looks over his shoulder. The doors through which they entered are now lost in the incense haze. He sees Agnolo and his footmen, sees the two priests who came with the cardinal too. But they've lost

Francesco de' Pazzi and the archbishop in the crowd. Good riddance, he thinks.

They reach the octagonal choir. In the chancel, acolytes are swinging censers in wide arcs, casting thick smoke across the altar. Above them, the boys' choir is singing up on the lofted marble galley.

He genuflects. Here, the cardinal leaves him, stepping into the chancel, taking his cushioned seat, faced away from the congregation. Lorenzo walks to his usual place in the southern transept, far less crowded than the nave. The rest of the cardinal's men follow him.

He and Agnolo step beside Sigismondo and Nori, who claps him on the shoulder. "Giuliano?" he mouths.

Lorenzo shakes his head, motions to his leg. Nori nods with a frown.

The Mass begins. The congregation kneels, Lorenzo among them. He looks out onto the crowd between prayers, searching for familiar faces. He sees his sisters; Nannina praying with her eyes shut, Bianca, like him, keeping hers open. He sees Ginevra de' Benci, sees Lucrezia Donati. Women he once fawned over, women he's fucked.

Opposite, in the northern transept, he sees a few of his many bankers, he sees men who once served as priors and whined to him about fatuous problems that no longer matter. He sees Guglielmo, who also is scanning the congregation, who must be waiting for Francesco to join him.

There are so many here today. Tens of thousands, he'd guess. Enough to think that all of Florence has joined him to honor the cardinal: every noble, banker, merchant, artist; every wife, mother, widow.

Everyone, it seems, except Clarice, who remained at Fiesole with the children. Except his mother, away in Morba. Except his brother, who refused to come.

They don't matter, he thinks. It's everyone here who does. And look at them, how beautifully they fulfill their duty, how they stand and kneel to the cardinal in a single wave, ebbing from the altar all the way to the distant western doors. It's a miracle how they know when to kneel, given that the cardinal's words are barely audible, that half this crowd hasn't even studied Latin. It must be an instinct, then, to know when to kneel. To know whom to kneel to.

He catches the cardinal glancing upward. Not to God—to the dome, rising above the altar.

His grandfather once hosted Pope Eugenio here in the cathedral. He told Lorenzo it was the best day of his life. And his grandfather had much to boast: the bank that served the Curia and enriched Florence; the cathedral's countless bricks and marble slabs that he, in part, paid for. How he carefully cultivated his city, perfumed its air with possibility, spun visions of impossible domes.

What had that pope thought, when he came to consecrate the cathedral, with its newly built dome? When the pope looked at his grandfather, the man who had invited him, how did he see him? Surely not only as a banker.

He looks up. The dome swells perfectly into the air—and yet its underside remains an unpainted white nothing. He knows that it was meant to be painted gold. How spectacular, how radiant that would've been. Instead, it's been neglected for decades. Left to look like a pasty tit.

Maybe the cardinal has noticed it. Noticed, too, how he's clinging to a decades-old pride. How this cathedral is like a treasure box with nothing inside. No mosaics, few frescoes. Gray everywhere one looked. So much of it left to be finished.

Perhaps the cardinal will say this to the pope, and that old sack will nod knowingly. For here Lorenzo is, underneath a fifty-year-old dome, his own achievements picayune to what was done before.

It's not all his fault. Look at his inheritance: a city scarred by plague; a father too weak to lead; a massive bank, yes, but one that was slowly bleeding. His grandfather? He oversaw the bank at its peak. He lived in this city alongside its greatest minds—Brunelleschi and Ghiberti and Donatello. He enjoyed its most glorious days.

Yet Lorenzo has still found magnificence—that cannot be denied. And he still has years ahead of him, decades to take this princely air and turn it into something grander than gold and tougher than steel, to etch it into law. This Mass for the cardinal? It is a single stone in the bridge he's building to that vision.

Building. This is what he needs to do. He's wasted so many days trying to win over the ever-changing priors, lost so much money trying to maintain the favor of fickle, foreign courts. Better, then, to make something that lasts. His grandfather knew this. He understood the power of a monument. They stand larger than a man ever can. They endure.

Yes, he could still have the underside of this dome painted gold. Yes, he could finally finish the cathedral's marble facade. But he also needs something greater than all that, something of his own. Not just for himself but for Giuliano and Piero and the rest of the family too.

A sudden shaft of daylight, across the northern transept. A wooden groan outsounds the cardinal's dry words. Opposite Lorenzo, across the altar, a door has opened. Parishioners shift as someone wades through the throng.

His brother limps to the front of the crowd. His face is pallid, his curls damp. Even still, in his green doublet, he is a vision, one that gives Lorenzo a golden feeling. He wants to call him over, to have him stand at his side—but the altar separates them, and the cardinal is still muttering his prayers. It's all right. His brother is here. He has done this small thing for him. He's glad for everything still to come for them both.

The church organ blares, startling him. A buzzing swells across the nave, like a swarm of cicadas. He hates that low noise, an indefinite din that hovers in the ears. But it's only the congregation chanting the Credo.

He joins them. He says he believes in one God, he genuflects at the mention of the Annunciation, he speaks of Pilate, of the Crucifixion, of the ascent into heaven. Of a baptism for the remission of sins, of the resurrection of the dead, of a world without end.

He says he believes all this, but he carries his doubts. He keeps these a secret; he knows even his closest friends would chide him for such sacrilege. It's Christ with whom he struggles. What was the point of it all—of raising Lazarus, of turning water into wine—if only to allow Himself to be crucified in the end? To just let that happen?

He knows what the priests would say: His sacrifice forgave our sins! He did it for us! But was that true? The apostles seemed to carry on more work than Christ ever did. Mary, too, he supposes. And for what? Men, his own ancestors, had ridden for the Crusades, and now an infidel sultan lords over Jerusalem. Popes sit on the throne of San Pietro and squabble over land. Priests join the church simply to enrich themselves.

Artists paint Madonnas for coin. What was the point of it all? What was still holy?

He looks back to his brother across the altar. Their eyes meet. Giuliano's are hard, unfeeling.

He shivers. It's damn cold in here. Too much stone, too few windows. What little light does bleed through the narrow panes is mired by the colored glass.

The cathedral quiets again. The congregation listens to the cardinal.

He speaks of bread broken, of body and blood.

Bells chime gently from the altar.

The Eucharist is raised.

Lorenzo feels warm breath against his neck and a hand grasping his shoulder.

He turns, sees one of the cardinal's priests, his teeth digging into a blanched bottom lip. "Traitor!" he shouts.

There's a glint, a dash of silver catching the candlelight.

The priest's body collapses on top of him. His throat goes hot. It somehow feels watery, startlingly so, and then he feels cold again. Another man lunges forward—there's a dagger in his hand.

He understands what this is.

Someone is shouting. He can't tell if it's near or distant. His feet fumble beneath him, slipping on the velvet trail of his cape. He spins, he falls away from the blades, down onto the floor.

A commotion is above him, jostling limbs and clashing steel. He can't hear the cardinal anymore, only the staccato shouting of men, the tenuto screams of women. Then, a different sound: a horrible keening from across the altar.

He has to get to his feet, climb out of this madness. He must find Giuliano. They must leave this place.

A figure falls to the ground beside him. Nori's face splits open against the floor, his mangled tongue slipping from his mouth like a lazy dog's. Lorenzo is crawling on his hands now, the floor slick beneath them. He has to get across the altar and find his brother.

A hand on his elbow. He recoils from it. But it's insistent. It's lifting him up, getting him to his feet. It's Agnolo, pushing him away from the men with their daggers.

He touches his side. He has a sword! He remembers this now, pulls at it. But his hands are shaking, and the jeweled hilt is so hard to grasp. The sword clangs against the stone floor before he has a chance to swing it.

Agnolo is pushing him again, toward the altar. Yes, he wants to say. They must find Giuliano. No words will come out of his mouth, not a shout, not a cry. It's all so confusing. Guglielmo is running to his side, shouting in his face. I knew nothing! he seems to be saying, though it's hard to hear him over all the screaming. Nothing of what? Lorenzo wants to say, but his words are drowned. His mouth is wet, very wet.

All the yelling becomes one constant roar. The panic of ten thousand voices. Someone says the dome has collapsed. Everywhere he looks, people are clambering, shoving, trampling. Trying to escape.

He wonders if it was an earthquake, if the cathedral has split open from nave to apse, hundreds of bodies falling into the crypts. If they might fall deeper still—into the earth, into one of Dante's dark circles. Which one, is the question.

No, that can't be. That doesn't explain the priests and their blades. And here, look at this stone floor. It's solid and unbroken. It spins beneath his feet. He feels a deep swell of nausea, but he can't be sick, not here in front of so many. He stumbles. He tries to ask for help. The fingers around his arm grow tighter.

His head swings to the right, and Christ looks back at him, wooden and crucified, above the altar. No sympathy in his eyes, only anguish. There's a mound of scarlet on the cathedra—yes, the cardinal. He's standing on the chair, his face green, his mouth a black hole.

What will he say to the pope now?

No time to think. Agnolo is speaking to him. Don't look, he's saying. Don't look. At what? he wants to ask, but they're moving too quickly, he can't catch his breath, every exhale is leaving a foreign, rusty taste in his mouth.

To his left, there's a figure knelt on the floor, the face unrecognizable. A crown of brown curls broken into gore. An emerald doublet shredded.

His eyes flutter. He doesn't understand.

Now they're at the wooden doors of the sacristy, to the northern side of the chancel. Agnolo hurls him inside. Other men follow, sticky with sweat, with blood. They're shouting—there's still so much shouting. But he still can't hear his brother.

The sacristy door slams shut. Somebody bolts it. His brother is here, then. They are safe. He looks around the room. Sigismondo is barricading the door. Agnolo is crying.

Where is Giuliano? Again, he tries to say it, but the words won't come, they're getting lost somehow. He touches his neck. It's hot, wet. His fingers are tipped with bright blood.

He looks down. There's a flood of it, running over his ribs, across his abdomen, trickling down the sides of his body.

His head rolls back. The ceiling is unfrescoed, unspecial. Yet another thing unfinished. He shuts his eyes to it, welcomes the black.

XXXVI

HIS BOOTS HIT THE GROUND. HEAVILY, WITH THE CERTAINTY he lacks. Loudly, as if he's trying to scrape away the Sunday stillness. The city, however, is reticent. The few who aren't at Mass are either too shamefaced to be out, or they're hidden away in fragrant kitchens, toiling over preparations for the afternoon's supper. It's only him in these streets.

And the condottieri, he supposes. Jacopo and Battista too. But he can't think about them yet.

Before him, the curling roads and crossing lanes are familiar. The details—the grimed grout between the palace stones, the ever-present fug of stagnant water, the slender brick towers dashing the daylight— all of those are unchanged, all of them too readily remind him of why he left.

He drifts down the Via Ghibellina, away from where he should be going. Away from the Baldracca, where he'll meet the disguised condottieri. Away from the Palagio, where he's meant to distract the gonfalonier until Jacopo arrives. All of that—it must wait for after the Mass.

Shadow falls over him, and a draft follows it. Ahead is a high and windowless building of mismatched stone. A low buzzing joins the soft patter of his feet. A soupy, fly-swarmed moat circles the base of the imposing prison before him.

The Stinche. Yes, that was its name. A place for whores and thieves and sodomites. Traitors too. He knows the sight of this building— knows it too well. When he was a child, he could see it from his bedroom. His stepmother would grasp his arm and make him stand at the window. Told him if he kept misbehaving, he'd end up in that prison. He'd stare at it, imagining the men inside—men in heavy manacles and soiled sarks, men with long hair, flattened by grease and grime. Despite his stepmother's threats, he couldn't conceive what he'd ever do in life to end up like them.

He turns toward the house he grew up in. A plain, gray-brown building. The street-level stones are rusticated, but poorly done, as if a blind man took a pick to them. A palace, some might call it, though that belied the mold-corniced hallways, the upper-floor rooms with walls stained piss yellow from unrepaired leaks.

His eyes drift up to the second-floor windows, where his father once slept, and his stepmother likely still sleeps. If she's still alive, that is. In all these years, they haven't spoken. A mutual, tacit severance. He wonders what she'd say to him now, if she were to see him in his purple robes. Nothing, probably. She'd glare, thinking he's some swindler. Even if she believed his transformation, she'd wag a pudgy finger in his face. Tell him he didn't belong in the church. The Stinche—that was for him.

He looks up farther, at the row of stubby windows on the third floor. He counts them. Stares at the familiar fourth window from the right. His bedroom. A small room, next to the kitchens and the servants' quarters. From where he's standing, he can't see inside it—though it's likely empty.

Iron scrapes, wood shudders. A woman steps outside, hefting a clay pot. She's young, slender-hipped, wearing a linen shift and a well-worn, stained apron. He doesn't recognize her.

Her brown eyes meet his, widen. She's startled too. She considers his hair, his face, his robes. Above the droning of the flies, he hears her strained breathing. He wonders if he should say something, explain who he is.

She steps out onto the street. Leans over. Tips the chamber pot forward and lets a thin brown stream seep into the dirt. Her eyes flash to his again. Then she steps back into the house's shadow, carrying the emptied pot. She shuts the door, and he hears an iron bolt slide into place.

The flies, fat and persistent, gather around the mess, trickling toward him. They dance in the dirty puddle, they land on it with their little legs, they frolic. Some of them hover around his ears, distracted by his camphor-dabbed skin. He swats at them, retreats from the filth.

He returns to the Via Ghibellina. To his left, the street continues, long and straight through low-roofed Santa Croce, out to the city's eastern walls. He could walk that way, out the gates, hike to the hills. With a few florins, he could buy a simple linen tunic from some villager, along with a grizzled, sturdy horse. He could ride up into the Apennines. Steal away.

But then what would he do? Word of his disappearance would be carried back to Rome. He would be called a traitor. Girolamo would send his soldiers to hunt him down. Worse, the pope would name him an apostate; he'd never be a priest again. And if he was not that, who was he?

He looks right. The road slices westward, not curving, not veering, but deliberate in its path back to the center of the city—to the Palagio. To the killing and the work to be done.

"HIS EXCELLENCY, THE ARCHBISHOP OF PISA, requests an audience with the gonfalonier," Braccolini announces. He is a respected scholar, a tutor to the cardinal. A man of good standing in Florence, yet one who is sympathetic to their cause. A helpful presence in gaining access to the Palagio and then securing it.

The bushy-browed attendant frowns at Salviati. "I'm sorry, Your Excellency," he says softly. "The gonfalonier and the rest of the priors are taking Mass within their chapel."

Bracciolini eyes him askance. They should have anticipated this. They're here too early. They were supposed to come from the banquet, after the Mass, after both brothers had sipped their wine.

Salviati finds a courteous smile. "As they should be, for they are a most pious council." He slips his hand within his cloak, pulls out a letter, fastened with the papal seal. "May I wait for the gonfalonier somewhere inside? I'm to personally deliver a message from the Holy Father."

The attendant skews his head, peers at the impressive train of gray-cloaked men behind Salviati. He ushers them into the Palagio. What few guardsmen they pass don't care to check what lies underneath the cloaks of his supposed servants.

He's taken, alone, to the gonfalonier's salon—a rather plain room with a pair of modest wooden chairs and a small table. No framed devotionals, no cushions of silk. It's small—so small that Bracciolini is asked to wait for him in the hallway, and the condottieri are guided to an empty chancery.

He chooses to sit in the cardinal-style chair across from the open window. In his hands, he holds a cup of wine that a page boy brought for him. He drinks from it—slow, even sips—thinking about a knife scraping a whetstone. Praying for the gonfalonier to join him soon.

Bells, tolling. First, the smallest ringing from a single church. Santi Apostoli, perhaps. Then, more bells. From all across the city. And one toll is louder, heavier than the rest. Santa Reparata. If the Mass is over, the brothers must be dead.

His wine is gone. The page boy hasn't returned.

A hangnail curls from his thumb. He bites at the skin.

The door opens, and he stands, pulling his hand away from his mouth. The thumb throbs.

"My sincerest apology for having kept you waiting, Your Excellency," the gonfalonier says, making an obeisance—a rather shallow one. "My attendant only found me after I had supped. Had I known you were here, I would've had you join me."

"It's forgiven," he says, his voice airy. "You weren't expecting me."

"This morning has been full of unexpected visitors. But this is a welcome one," he says, taking the chair by the window.

Salviati sits back down across from him, by the door. He looks at the gonfalonier, then looks past him, to the open window. Jacopo should be riding through the streets by now. He should be rallying the people to proclaim him as their new leader. But, outside, there's no sound of horses, no cheering.

The gonfalonier follows his gaze to the window. "A lovely day."

He should say something here, he knows this, but he is thinking about the silence in the piazza. What it means. What it would mean if the brothers weren't killed. What he is meant to do with this man until he knows for certain. And he's thinking about this hangnail, aching terribly and blooming with blood.

The gonfalonier leans forward. "You bring word from the Holy Father?"

He's brought word that the pope demands a new government in Florence, that the gonfalonier is to instruct the priors to accept Jacopo as the city's leader or suffer an invasion by the Duke of Urbino's armies. But he can't tell him any of this—not yet, not until he hears his cousin in the piazza below, not until he has confidence that their plan has worked.

"Yes," he says, trying to summon some scenario to mind. "You have a son, yes?"

"I do, in Rome."

Thank God he got that right. "The Holy Father has taken an interest in—" The boy, he almost says, but he truthfully has no idea how old he is. He swallows. "Him."

"I'm grateful." He sounds concerned though. "You're hurt," he says, pointing to his hand.

He is. His pesky hangnail has kept bleeding, and now his dry, cracked fingers are tinging red. He lets out a shrill, startled laugh. "Nothing serious."

"Are you feeling well, Your Excellency? You look quite pale."

He glances past the man, out the window again.

"I'll ask the servant for some wine and some smelling salts," he says, standing.

"No," Salviati says, suddenly on his feet.

"It's no bother. I won't be gone a minute."

Salviati catches the gonfalonier's arm as he passes. "Don't," he tells him. "The feeling has passed," he adds, too late—for a sound has carried on the wind. A woman's scream, sharp and unmistakable.

Nothing follows, and both men watch the window, their breathing halted.

Another scream—throatier, more prolonged. Then a third. A growing chorus.

The gonfalonier's eyes roll over his body, from his mud-specked boots to his tonsured, coiled hair.

He cannot balk like he did outside the cathedral. This time, he has to act. He shoves the gonfalonier, knocking the man to the ground. He dashes out of the room, through the open door. Behind him, there is a shout for guards, for someone to sound the alarm.

He runs—down the hallway, toward Bracciolini. He grasps him, pants. "Get the men."

Bracciolini leads them through an open doorway into a high-ceilinged room with stark, unpainted walls and a row of bright windows. Through them, the cathedral's dome rises above the roofs, red and angry.

To their left is another door, ajar. To the right, a closed door. Bracciolini fumbles with the knob. He batters the door. "Open it!" he screams to the condottieri inside.

The brass knob rattles, the frame splinters, but the door refuses to open.

Steel boots march in the hallway.

Bracciolini faces the approaching footsteps, reaches beneath his cape. Blue sky streaks across his blade. But Salviati? He has no sword, not even a dagger. And his hands are shaking too violently to be of any use. He's an archbishop, not a soldier.

"God be with you," he tells the tutor.

He leaves him. Runs, through the only door left, hoping for a stairwell, a servant's passageway, any place he can hide. But the next room is almost identical to the first. Windows mocked by the dome's scale. Another open door.

He rushes toward it.

Marble is under his feet now instead of drab stone. This new room is different. Dim and windowless. A gold foil book—a Bible, he sees— shines on a small altar. He's come to a chapel.

Earlier today, he would've taken this as a sign.

To his left stands a young man dressed in a belted tunic. An open notebook rests in his hands.

XXXVII

HE CAME TO THE PRIORS' CHAPEL, A NARROW ROOM LINED with marble, and squatted by its small wooden altar. He wanted to understand where his work would live. How light might fall into the room through an open door. Where shadows might cover the altarpiece when it's lit only by thin candles.

All he's managed to do is open his notebook and make a hasty sketch of a manger, with vague outlines of the saints approaching the Madonna. Their faces all float in his mind, reluctant to be put to paper.

He could easily copy what he's done before, paint another Madonna with Fioretta's face. As for the shepherds, he could steal their features from any of the lackluster altarpieces he's seen around Florence. He could replicate it all: the same prayerful hands, same timber manger, even the same bleating rams. The priors would be none the wiser.

They all knew this story, after all. Year after year, they heard it at Mass. So he doesn't see the point in retelling such a tale, centuries-stale. What he cared about was how the sunlight should color the shepherds' cloaks, the particular grain of the timber, the white-gray whorls of each ram's coat. This was the only way he could suffer painting such a trite story—to find something real, however small, previously overlooked.

He's made little progress today. But that's not entirely his fault. He has been plagued by distractions. First, a servant kept him waiting in an empty salon for nearly an hour. It's Sunday, the servant had said reproachfully, the chapel was in use. Didn't he know the priors take Mass inside the Palagio and not at the cathedral?

He didn't, but even when the priors were done and he was at last ushered into this cold box of a room, one damned interruption followed another. Servants scurrying through the adjacent rooms. The overzealous ringing of bells. Windows groaning open only to be shut, loudly and suddenly, not ten minutes later. And he couldn't close the door to the noise. The attendant had made that very clear. The doors were self-locking, he'd told Leonardo. A unique design of the building. For the priors' safety.

He had thought the attendant was telling a poor joke.

The distractions continued. An absurd number of footsteps. Clanging. Shouting, even. Maybe he should've found that concerning, but it was just irritating to him.

Now this. A bishop, of all people! It's laughable, really. If he were more devout, he might think it providence.

The bishop is panting. He is still and frightened yet primed to bolt, a startled hare. When he steps inside, he shuts the door behind him. There's a loud metal clack.

"I hope you have a key, Father."

The bishop doesn't seem to hear him. He's turned away, the shining bald spot of his head staring at Leonardo like an unblinking eye. "The doors are self-locking," he says.

The bishop turns to him now. Hazel irises, a thin face. Heavy robes in an ugly shade of plum. He saw this man earlier on the Via Larga.

"That explains it," the bishop says. Then he laughs. It begins as an airless chuckle but builds into something hysterical. Leonardo sees his purpled tongue, his yellowing teeth. He has to look away, to the bishop's hands. He's running one over the other in a constant motion. The fingers on his right hand are mottled a pale red. Sometimes Leonardo's hands are stained that shade after grinding lac. He has to scrub at them with a stiff, goat's hair brush to wash the color away. If he doesn't, it looks as if he's been in a fight.

He shuts his notebook, holds it to his chest. He shifts away from the bishop, presses himself against the wall.

His companion notices this.

"I can leave," Leonardo offers. "If you have a key."

"I do not," the bishop says. He sits on the floor, his back against the door. "Were you praying?"

"No," he says, too quickly. "Sketching. I'm a painter. I'm meant to make an altarpiece."

"Meant to?"

"I haven't made very much progress," he says. "Should we call for someone?"

"I don't think that would be wise." The words are slow and faded, but they quicken his blood. "What will it be? Your altarpiece."

His questions are tiresome, but he can't ignore a man of the cloth. "A Madonna with shepherds approaching to honor the Christ child."

"A holy subject. Why does it trouble you?"

He didn't say that it did, but he also shouldn't lie to a priest. "I've painted Madonnas before. But this one, I can't grasp it."

He doesn't tell this priest that in his visions the Madonna scowls at him.

The bishop nods slowly. "I read the Bible every day, and yet I don't know what the Virgin looked like. None of us do. Who's to say if she had blonde hair or brown? Whether she was thin or tall?" His voice grows faint, and he thumbs the crucifix at his neck. "Whether she even existed at all? So why trouble yourself over it?"

Odd words for a bishop to say, he thinks.

"I know there's a simpler way," Leonardo says. "That I could imitate all the versions that have come before. What we all imagine when we summon her to mind. The blue robes. The haloed head. But if it's what's familiar, why bother making it at all? What good is there in offering that to the world? Where's the truth in that?"

"Who are you to decide what's true and what's not? Anyone can believe what they want. Neither you nor I were there with her in Bethlehem."

"But I have to believe that some part of it is real. Otherwise, what is it all for?" There's an edge to his voice. A heat to his cheeks. He turns away, to the small, wooden altar.

"The eternal question," the bishop says. "One that none of us has the answer to."

"I know what's true, at least. I can't explain how I know it, but I do. I feel it, when it's there. And it's missing in this piece."

He looks back and finds those hazel eyes still watching him. Goading him. "And you, why are you here?"

The bishop blinks. "In Florence?"

He meant the chapel, but he nods.

"I was raised here. Not ten minutes from where we are now. Across from the Stinche."

He thinks of his fingers drawing in dirt. His last painting, scorched and flaking.

"I left for Rome, entered the church. Over a decade ago now. And I liked Rome—how ancient its traditions were, how it was a city crowded with priests, like Florence was with artists. I had a church there. A simple one, not in the best of neighborhoods. But my parishioners were honest people. There was this widow who always approached me after Mass wanting a prayer for her sons, for her granddaughters. She only saw me as a priest. Not as—" He stops, his mouth hanging open. "Forgive me."

Leonardo keeps his gaze low.

"It was enough. I should've ignored everything else. But I coveted a bishopric. I wanted more. My cousin, he said that was the Florentine in me. I don't know. By the time I was sent to Pisa and given a cathedral, God wasn't there. So I came back here, even though I didn't want to. I thought it was what God wanted for me. I thought maybe He wanted me to return here so I could be redeemed. Perhaps He'll still see to that. I hope so. But I think I might have erred somewhere."

The bishop stares, blankly, somewhere beyond the altar. A tear streaks down his cheek. He wipes at it, quickly, then looks down at his lap. He runs his hands over his robes, smoothing its creases.

"May I ask you something? Not as a priest," he clarifies. "Just as one man speaking to another?"

Leonardo nods.

"Do you believe in forgiveness?"

He thumbs the pages of his notebook. "The idea of it, yes."

"But in practice?"

He sees Iac's freckled face, framed by golden curls. "The Bible makes it seem like an easy virtue. But I've never found it to be so simple. I know we all err, we all do damage, and sometimes I wonder what the purpose of it all is. What's the use in seeking forgiveness from someone who could never give it?"

"That's the rub, isn't it? We can't expect anyone's forgiveness. Even God's."

"So what are we meant to do?" Leonardo asks.

"Do you want the Bible's answer or my own?"

"Yours."

"Pray on it. Rely on yourself. Others, they only taint you."

Shadows gather in the crevasses beneath the bishop's cheeks. His wet eyes look like a polished stone, the color striking. He imagines it on his slab. Verona and umber.

The bishop rises to his feet. "Could I see your drawing?"

Leonardo flinches at his outstretched hand. But this man needs some solace, however small. He hands him his notebook.

The bishop's fingers drifting over his ink marks. There's no change in his searching eyes, no feeling. He knows he sees it: the work is false.

"You have talent," the bishop says.

"Few here seem to appreciate it."

"So why do you stay?"

"You said it yourself. The painters are here. Florence is the destination. Why would I leave?"

"You could paint anywhere. A city is just four walls and some gates. One is as good as any other."

"And every city has its lords, its merchants, its churches. What would make another place any different?"

"Nothing. Everything. Only God knows. But if nothing else, another place is a new beginning. I somehow forgot that."

He gently tugs the notebook back from the bishop. He looks at the manger and the saints, the ghost of a Madonna—all of it too peaceful. The work is worthless.

A solitary bell tolls. A low sound, like a moan from deep within the earth. He feels it, the wall quaking against his back, the floor trembling underfoot. The pealing continues, the sound running over itself, waxing, growing louder and louder.

"The alarm," the bishop shouts over the clanging, turning back to him. "It wasn't meant to ring. My men, they seem to have been trapped by these door locks you mentioned. The people should have been gathered outside by now, but I don't think they've come."

He moves away from the bishop, away from the door. But the chapel is so small.

"Our time together may be coming to an end," the bishop says. "Don't fret. Whether it be friend or foe out there, I'll see that you're out of this safely."

He backs into the most distant corner of the room.

"Could I ask something else of you?" the bishop says. "Whatever happens after this, will you pray for me?"

"Yes," Leonardo says, though he's not sure what good it will do. God never seemed to listen to his prayers, however few he made.

The bishop smiles meekly, then turns toward the door. There's rising din coming from the other side. Shouting. The clatter of metal, steel against steel. Leonardo drops his notebook at the sound, shuts his eyes, balls his fists, presses them against his ears. Prays, not for the bishop, but for this all to stop.

His eyes open at the sound of a key fumbling in the lock. There's a metal snap, and then the door opens. A guardsman, sword unsheathed, with two more men behind him. He steps inside and grabs the bishop, who is limp in his hands, who lets himself be brought to the ground without a sound. The guard grasps his skull, slams it against the floor. His face is twisted, silent but full of hurt.

"What are you doing?" Leonardo shouts. "He's a bishop."

The guard turns to him. "Take him too," he orders his men.

The other guards push inside the room. At the feeling of cool iron on his wrists, his limbs turn loose, he falls to the floor.

"He's a painter for the priors," he hears the bishop say, the words muffled. "He has no part in this."

A guard spits on the bishop's face. "You claim to be a man of God. Out there, a man said he was a tutor and took his sword to us. Doesn't seem like we can believe what any of you claim to be."

He feels a tugging at his arms. He's being dragged across the floor, toward the door. His notebook is splayed on the marble. Sheets have come loose, drawings of gesturing hands and designs for bridges, for wells. He knows he should be trying to gather those pages. To pull away from the guards and rescue his notebook.

On a creased sheet, apart from the rest, he sees his charcoal manger, his day's work, retreating from view.

Leave it, he thinks.

XXXVIII

FINGERS AT HIS THROAT. HE STIRS, TRIES TO BAT AWAY THE villain forcing the life from him. Every breath rip his throat, burns. When he shouts, no words come out, and he feels as if his mouth has been filled with hot soil.

His eyes flutter open. Blurred silhouettes hover above him, bracing his arms, chanting his name. Anonymous hands cradle his back and lift him from the floor. He's leant against a wall, carved with reliefs that dig into his shoulders. The hand at his throat loosens, the silhouettes retreat. Something warm trickles down his chest.

The hazy figures are reluctant to coalesce. He first sees wood, its high polish caught by the light falling through a window of colored glass. Too vivid, and too bright. He shuts his eyes again, preferring to drift back into the darkness. There, he felt nothing, heard only reverberant whispers. There he didn't have to think about what had happened. He wonders if Christ felt the same way when he woke in the cave. Did he even want to return to the world outside? Did he consider staying in the dark, waiting for death to take him again?

No, he thinks. He would've felt the crusted blood at his crown, the throbbing stigmata in his hands and feet. He would've known what had been done to him, known that his resurrection was a miracle.

He opens his eyes again, blinks until the light becomes a less painful presence. The nearest outlines sharpen into the faces of Agnolo and Sigismondo. He sees there are others too, but their faces are drowned by too much light.

"Where's Giuliano?" he says, but no one replies. "Is he safe?"

His words are barely more than a croak. He wants to touch his mouth, his neck. But his arms are leaden, too heavy to lift.

"You were attacked," Agnolo tells him.

His memories are shards: a priest's white lip; Guglielmo's shrill cries; a tattered green mound.

"Who was it?" he says.

Agnolo shakes his head, but Sigismondo bends down beside him. "I saw Francesco de' Pazzi. And there were two priests behind you. Likely others."

"Where are they now?"

Agnolo takes his hand. "It was—is—chaos. People were trampling one another. They thought the dome had collapsed."

He frees his hand, props himself up on one arm, then the other. "I need to get back to the palace. Send letters."

"What you need is a surgeon," Agnolo says.

He shakes his head, winces at the motion. "Help me up."

Sigismondo and Agnolo hesitate, look to each other. Then they nestle themselves underneath his shoulders. As they lift him, his vision tunnels. He tries to fix his eyes on the walls' wooden reliefs, where carved infants play along a twisting vine. They're grinning, like they're trading secrets about him. Look how he bleeds, they whisper. Hear how he whines for his brother.

"Where's Nori?" he asks.

"He fought the priests who attacked you. One of them—" Agnolo stops.

"They'll pay for it," Sigismondo says.

"So he's gone. And—" He tastes blood on his tongue. "We should leave."

They unbolt the sacristy door, open it slowly. The wood creaks, and a blade of light cuts across the transept. There's blood streaking the floor, the shine of an abandoned sword, humps of bodies.

The door behind them shuts, and the light retreats. The pillared candles have burnt out, gray wisps still stemming from their wicks. From the chancel, there's a hushed gurgling, like a babe sleeping fitfully in a crib. Censers, nearly empty.

They cross the transept, quiet and tentative. Their movements are coordinated and cautious—then, without warning, their footsteps hasten. Lorenzo's heart beats fast, turning his stomach. He wants to turn back, to see who might be chasing them. But another set of footsteps never arrives; there's only the patter of their own.

He cranes his neck, tips his eyes. Sees a familiar green doublet. A body, supine on the floor and thatched with too many wounds to count. A head cratered in its center. A face like a wilted carnation.

A savage sort of sound falls from his mouth.

His friends' shoulders dig into his sides. His feet are dragging across the floor now; he can't will them to step. Sigismondo and Agnolo keep trudging forward with him between them.

Stop, he tries to tell them. But they push onward, out of the cathedral. His brother vanishes from sight.

The piazza reminds him of paintings he's seen of battle scenes; it calls to mind his ride through Volterra, years past. There are cloaks strewn on paving beside tossed, scuffed chopines. People prostrate and still, people bandaging gashes with torn strips of linen. He sees a chubby-cheeked girl next to the body of a man; she's wailing into her vacant-faced mother's shift.

A bell rings, its sound distinct. A heavy, long tolling. The alarm at the Palagio.

They tense. The crowd looks around, panicked. Some of them are already struggling to get to their feet and hasten away. They all know the alarm is a call to arms, a summoning of every able-bodied man to grab whatever weapons or armor he owns and walk, ride, run to the Palagio, to call for an emergency council.

And this council—it could pledge to protect Lorenzo, make him its fulcrum. Or it might think to repeat what was done to his grandfather and exile him from the city.

"Make haste," he says, and they hurry up the Via Larga, not stopping, not resting until the palace is in sight, and only then do they slow their pace. But it looks the same—the stone clean, windows unbroken. No one is loitering in the courtyard. The chairs set out for the banquet are empty.

They take him inside, past servants who clutch their faces at the sight of him. Up to his apartments, where he's carried toward his bed.

He plants his feet on the bedroom floor. "Not yet," he tells them.

"I think you should rest. Gather your strength," Agnolo whispers into his ear.

"There's no time for that," he says, and he moves his arms off his friends' shoulders. He wavers, blinks furiously, but he stays upright. Sigismondo steps out of the room, bellows for someone to fetch fresh clothing—and a bolt of clean linen.

Lorenzo fingers the tender slit at his neck. The wound pulses with a pain that courses through his whole body, yet it's small enough to cover with his thumb. Surely it will scar. But what does that matter? Giuliano is the handsome one.

His mouth droops. His breathing sharpens. Agnolo places a hand on the small of his back. He shakes it off.

They help him undress—an unexpectedly humiliating affair. He'd rather his mother do it.

Oh God, what will he say to her? What will she say to him?

Around his throat, Agnolo wraps a strip of white linen like a neckerchief. He's buttoned into a doublet, black velvet. No one remarks on the color.

"Walk with me," he says, and he holds on to Sigismondo's arm with one hand. Staggers forward, out the bedroom door.

"Where are we going?" Sigismondo asks.

"They need to see me," he says. His throat burns beneath the cloth.

They walk, slowly, with Agnolo behind them. Through one room, and then another. Until he is back where he stood that morning, beside the window, in his brother's bedroom.

Giuliano isn't here. His bed is still unmade, a pillow on top of it with a shallow depression from where his head had rested the night before. The armchair where he dressed is empty. The vest of mail lies in a silvery heap on the floor.

He stumbles. Sigismondo steadies him.

Then, a commotion. Shouting from the hallways, fast footsteps, the slamming of doors. His hand shifts to his waist, but there's no sword there. He takes one step back from the doorway, then another.

Guglielmo charges into the room. Three of Lorenzo's servants are chasing behind him, grabbing at his arms, trying to stop him.

"Get your hands off of him!" his sister screams from farther down the hallway.

Guglielmo falls to his knees before Lorenzo. "I didn't know," he says, the words half sobbed. "I promise on my life I didn't know." He shakes off the servants' hands, reaches up, clings to Lorenzo's knees. "Spare me, please."

Lorenzo doesn't move. He stares down at his brother-in-law—at his snot-smeared mouth, at his doublet torn at the shoulder, at the hay stuck to the soles of his boots.

His sister pushes past the servants into the room. A single cut arcs across her cheek. "There are mobs out in the streets. They went to our palace. Broke all the windows. Dragged Francesco out with them. They would've taken us, had we not hidden in the stables."

He turns to the servants. More have gathered outside the doorway. "Take them outside," he tells them.

"What?" Bianca says as his men wrestle Guglielmo away. "Did you not hear me? They'll kill us if they find us!"

"Her too," he tells the servants.

They approach her gently, but she thrashes at their touch. "Don't you dare touch me!" she scolds. She pulls away, falls in front of Lorenzo. Reaches for his stockinged feet. "Lorenzo, please."

"Our brother is dead," he says. He feels a tearing in his throat, a fresh current of blood. "Your family did this."

Bianca stills. She surrenders to the servants, lets them guide her out of the bedroom with their hands on her elbows.

Sigismondo looks blankly at him. Agnolo faces away, toward the empty bed.

Lorenzo limps toward the gilt-framed mirror opposite the window. The reflection, his own, makes him grit his teeth. His black eyes are somehow faint, like a garment that has been washed too many times. His cheeks are gray and damp, while his mouth is wine-red, startling.

With the clean black doublet, he no longer appears wounded, only sickly. He looks like his father, who died in this same house, leaving behind a shit-stained bed and a litany of problems.

"No," he says. "Take this off."

"You'd prefer another?" Agnolo asks.

"Get the old one."

"But it's stained."

"Get it," he says firmly, and Sigismondo steps out of the room.

Agnolo places a hand on his shoulder. "You saw the state of him,

Lorenzo. He can't have known. He would've come to you the second he heard of it. He would've stopped it."

"He didn't stop it when his family took the Curial account, or any of the others after that. So how can you be so certain?"

Agnolo falls silent. The two of them stand, saying nothing, until Sigismondo returns. Then they help him out of the clean doublet and into the other, its yellow brocade ruined by a bib of red brown.

He looks back at the mirror. Better, he thinks.

"A glass of wine too."

"A good idea," Agnolo says, and soon a glass with a modest pour of red wine is in his hand. He brings it to his mouth, sips it, then tips the cup over the clean linen at his neck. He pours the wine on himself until his front is fully stained.

Now he's ready.

He steps to the same window his brother stood at that morning. He parts its curtains. Unlatches the window, opens it. Down on the Via Larga, men are rushing, some with swords and shields, others with only supper knives. He leans out the window, and the wet linen clings, pleasantly cool, against his throat. The men below look up, they stop.

"My neighbors, my friends," he says, the words but a whisper. He swallows and it burns. He tries to speak louder, to tell the men below to save their strength, that they have been attacked from within and will now surely be attacked by foreign armies. But no more words will come.

Down in the street, the men are still looking up at him; they wait with puzzled faces, cocked heads.

He pulls a smile, raises his hand, waves to them.

They begin to chant, to roar his name.

His stomach riles. He steps out of view from the window and falls forward onto the floor. Quickly, violently, he vomits a loose red mess. He gasps for breath on all fours like a dog as he listens to the crowd outside cheering his name. Forehead on the cool stone floor, he waits until the chanting grows distant, until his breathing calms.

He's carried back to his bedroom, put into bed, but he won't let his friends cover him with quilts. There's work to be done. It must be his account of the day's events that first reaches the courts of Europe.

While a surgeon cleans his wounds and gives him medicine, he dictates to Agnolo letters that will be carried to Milan's regent, to the doge in Venice, to King Louis in France too. Reluctantly, he abstains from sharing his suspicions of where the attack originated, instead emphasizing the sacrilege of an attack at Mass. And, most importantly, he implores for the aid of troops.

As these letters are drafted, men gather in the palace courtyard, pledging their arms. Some are sent to the Palagio to fight off whatever insurrection may be unfurling there. Others are asked to remain here, to serve as guardsmen until the council's intentions are known.

Then, by late afternoon, the Signoria finally writes. They send good news: they've imprisoned several men who tried to take control of the Palagio. They have some two dozen condottieri locked away in a room. They ask Lorenzo what he'd like done with them.

Agnolo lists the names.

Bracciolini.

Pazzi.

Salviati.

This last name spurs him, sends him staggering back to his feet. "This was the pope's doing," he says. "All of it."

"Think on what you're saying," Agnolo chides, glancing at Sigismondo.

His friend leans in. "It could be like Milan. It might only have been a few malcontents."

"Only a few malcontents? Who came to the palace today? The pope's archbishop, from Pisa. The pope's bankers, from Rome. Those priests who attacked me. Even the sodding head of the pope's guard. This was all the pope's plan. It's the only way to make sense of it."

"And you may be right. But is it not wisest to exercise caution until you have a confession in hand?" Agnolo says.

His mind is fogged with labdanum, but his anger burns through it. Agnolo can't understand—he is not family; he cannot fathom what has been done to his name. He and Sigismondo don't see how he must now be sharp, decisive, and ruthless. There's only one person he knows who can comprehend what has been done, who will want to wound.

"Send a coach to Morba," he says. "Bring my mother back here."

"One to Fiesole too? For Clarice and the children?" Sigismondo asks.

"What? Why?" He shakes his head. "Send some men to the villa to keep them safe."

"You wouldn't rather them here?"

He thinks of little Lucrezia, of Piero leering over him from his bedside, staring at his bloody neck. "No. Better to keep them away for now."

"And what of the Signoria? How do you want to reply?"

"The hired swords should be killed. There's too many of them. It'd be a risk to keep them in the Stinche."

"I agree," Sigismondo says, and Agnolo nods along.

"As for the rest of the prisoners?" Lorenzo says. "Let's give the city a show."

Agnolo's face stills. "What of the archbishop?"

He thinks of his crate of fish, the countless, rotting stares. "Him too."

"You can't execute a man of the cloth. It's sacrilege."

He meets Agnolo's gaze, holds it. "I can't?"

"The pope will be furious," Sigismondo whispers.

"Good," he tells him.

XXXIX

LIBERTY.

He hears the word on the wind. He leans forward; his chains rattle. He hears it again—Jacopo's voice, resounding from the piazza below.

He thought it was over, but now he can hope. Francesco was surely with his cousin, the two of them riding through the streets, gathering support. Battista must be somewhere down there too. And there are still Montefeltro's mercenaries waiting in the country. They might not even need the Neapolitan or papal armies, for the crux of their plan has already succeeded: the brothers are dead. The guards said so as they wrangled him upstairs.

He was foolish, cowardly to ever lose faith. God would see them freed from these chains.

He and Bracciolini stand, arms and legs fettered, on a terrace of old, uneven stone, high above the city's roofs, surrounded by priors and guardsmen. In chains, they've suffered this purgatory of waiting—but that is over. Now, he's ascendant.

A chant begins. A single word, but he can't understand it. The priors hear it too; they're wandering to the terrace's edge. The gonfalonier gives him a hateful scowl as he passes, but he doesn't care; he'll even pray for the man once they get through this day.

When the priors peer down at the piazza, the cheering swells, a hundred voices as one massive drum. Then Salviati hears it: they're roaring for the Medici.

The manacles tear the skin from his wrists.

Clattered footsteps sound from the stairs up to the terrace. Not soldiers, but civilians carrying dull swords. They say they were sent by Lorenzo. More armed men follow onto the terrace, and the group becomes a rabble. An object is passed among them—something short, something no one wants to touch. They shove it forward, in front of the priors, and it crumples at their feet. So bloodied, so matted with grime that it looks more like a half-butchered swine than a breathing man. Francesco.

Salviati chokes on a laugh. He doesn't know why; it's not amusing.

Someone is telling the priors to kill him, but they're shaking their heads. They can't do that, the gonfalonier says. Not yet. Not until they've heard from Lorenzo.

Salviati leans back against the brick wall. He turns away from the group, looks instead toward the turrets. The painter is over there, standing by himself, in a pale yellow tunic that doesn't even cover his knees. An alien sort of man.

The painter looks at him. His brown-eyed stare is exact, it claws beneath the skin. Salviati doubts he can rely on his prayers any longer. He must now have faith in God alone.

His fingers curl, his clotted thumb throbs once more. He wants to shout across the terrace and explain it all to the painter, tell him how his intentions were holy, how he thought he was doing something good, how he's nothing like the rest of them. That he was following God's plan.

The priors retreat down the stairs, back inside the palace. The guards chain Francesco beside him. A hush falls on the terrace. He strains to hear something, anything more from the piazza below. But there's no clash of metal, no cannon fire—they all wait in silence.

Hours pass like this.

He must confess, he decides. Try to make them understand. Tell them that he was trying to save them. They'd have seen that, if the plan hadn't faltered. Whatever penance they demand of him, he'll do it. He'll prostrate himself. Admit his many errors. Plead for mercy. For forgiveness.

A small bird, auburn-winged and white-bellied, lands at his feet. It flits around his boots, never still. It trills pleasantly. He reaches toward it, but shackles tug at his wrists. The bird flutters into the air, hovering over the parapets, then flies away, chirping above the piazza, its song becoming distant as it swoops over the countless homes, flies for the arrogant rise of the cathedral's dome.

In the birdsong's absence, he hears the voices of people gathering in front of the Palagio. Their voices build until they're almost humming, sounding like a troop of untuned lyres.

The priors return to the terrace. They huddle together.

"I wish to confess," he shouts to them.

They don't turn. They won't look at him.

The gonfalonier speaks to the guardsmen, softly enough not to be overheard. Then, the guards approach, they untie him and his companions from the tower's fixtures. They try to make them stand, which Salviati does—he wants to remain dignified—but Bracciolini has already fallen to his knees, mumbling, and Francesco's body has slumped to the floor. A guard lifts Francesco by the pits, slaps him, once, twice, three times—but still his head rolls.

They need a silver hammer, he thinks.

One of the priors produces a snuff box, hands it to the guard. What follows is an odd sight, really—the guard holding a delicately carved wooden box in his gauntlets, opening its little lid beneath Francesco's bloodied nose. The banker wakes, startled, tumbling backward in his fetters. Two of the guardsmen help Francesco stand again, the other returns the snuff box to the prior, who wipes its surface with his scarlet sleeve before hiding it away.

"What's happening?" Francesco says to him.

A stupid question, he thinks. Francesco says it again. "Now would be the time to pray," Salviati tells him.

Guards emerge from the clock tower dragging thick coils of rope. They carry them to the parapets, fasten one end to iron fixtures. The other ends they shape into nooses. They tie the knot quickly, its shape familiar to them. A small mercy for his companions.

He wonders what they'll save for him. While, to them, he's done grave evil, he's still a bishop. There's reverence paid to that, even in Sodom. They might even let him live out his days in a guarded room in the country, with a narrow bed. Or perhaps they'll put him in the Stinche, make his stepmother's prophecy come true.

To pass his remaining years in a cell? There are worse fates, he tells himself. There's even something pleasingly ascetic about a life with no more Masses, with no more eyes on him. Just a bed, a Bible, and his thoughts. Maybe pen and paper, too, once he proves himself trustworthy. It wouldn't be so different from a life in a monastery. He could even fashion himself as a new San Girolamo, making translations, writing treatises until the end of his days.

The guards push him aside as they take Bracciolini. The tutor blubbers mercies over and over again as he's dragged across the parapets, knees scraping against the stones. When he reaches the edge, he cries out again, says he doesn't want to die.

It's an obvious statement. A futile one.

Salviati has never feared his end. He thought he was different, that one day he'd welcome it. He had lived a holy life; he had the comfort of knowing what was promised to him: paradise, unending and free of the scum who had plagued his years on this earth.

At the arching parapets, one of the guards brings Bracciolini to his feet, hoisting him around the midline like a stable boy grabbing a bale of hay. They drape the rope over his neck, they tighten it. The precise moment is sudden. An unannounced push, without fanfare. Too quick to say a single prayer. The vanishing of a silhouette. The whirring of the cord. And then a ravenous cheering bellowing from below.

The guards return, but they don't stop in front of Francesco; they stand before him instead. They hesitate. One of the guards stares at the golden crucifix hanging from his neck.

Now he understands.

He turns to the painter, but the man's eyes are shut. He prays he'll be seen out of this awful place.

The guards' steel gloves bore into his arms. He wrestles against their grip. He jams his heels against the stones.

"But I'm a priest!" he hears himself scream. "I'm a priest!"

He's twisting, writhing with each forced step. He can't let them take him to the parapets. He can't have all those thousands of Florentines gathered below see him like this. They will point at him, like he's some beast in a menagerie. They will jeer. Shout hideous words. Tie curses to his name. Make him the monster in some fable they'll tell their children.

He sees a widening, cloudless sky. A sea of tawny roofs. He hears the roar of the eager crowd.

His toes meet the building's edge. He keeps his gaze high, even as they lift the noose over his head. They place the rope around his neck, gently, like it's a necklace of rare gemstones.

A sibilant slip. The knot tightens. It's heavy and thick.

He waits for the push. He looks ahead, above the crowd, the noise. The sky is perfect, the cleanest cerulean. A yolky sun hangs halfway toward the westward horizon, washing the distant green hills with gold.

He stares at it, lets it singe his eyes, lets sweat run over his lips and leave the taste of salt. The city's houses, palaces, churches all fade in the light. Nothing stands taller than him.

A hand on his back.

A jolt.

A brief rush of air.

His vision pulses and stars. His neck burns, his lungs strain. He wants to hang somberly, like a wooden Christ on the cross, but his body fights against him, convulsing. His teeth grind and bite. The rope creaks, the crowd jeers.

An eternity passes like this.

A red blur streaks across his waning vision. He's pelted from the side. Skin presses against his face, smothering him. Dirt, sweat, twine. His body keeps shaking, his mouth clawing for breath. And then there is an unfamiliar taste. His tongue laps at something gristly and hot. The blood of Christ, he thinks.

He drinks.

XL

FOR HOURS, HE SAT ALONE ON THE SOUTHERN SIDE OF THE terrace. The Signoria had conferred, decided he was truly a painter; they ordered the guards to unshackle him. The gonfalonier himself walked over, carrying Leonardo's leather sack, and apologized.

"You're free to go, of course," he told him, "but trust me that for now, you're safer here. The crowd below is growing violent."

Leonardo wanted to laugh in his face. It was violent below? What about his bruised wrists? What about the bishop and the two other bloodied men fettered not twenty paces from where he was sitting?

He said nothing. He stayed. He peered into his bag, saw that his notebook wasn't inside and felt nothing at the discovery. He stared at the building's details, one by one. The hard-edged, gapped crenellations like the blade of a crude handsaw. The motley stone, each slab textured differently from the next. The stone's awful color, a dunned umber that he'd never want to see smeared onto a panel.

When the ropes were brought out and the nooses made, he averted his gaze, found new sights beyond the parapets. Sharp spires, rusticated palaces, rambling, low-roofed homes. Haughty, defiant Santa Reparata, rising above it all. At its peak, Andrea's gold-leafed orb dazzling like a comet.

He wished he could go back to that day when the orb lifted into the sky. That feat had mesmerized him; in the days after, he filled page after page of his notebook with drawings of pulleys and levers. It had made him wonder what else might be possible.

He'd have told that boy not to err. To become a man who builds rather than paints. To spend his childhood sketching tools and bridges, rather than angels and virgins. Had he done that, then he never would've come to the Palagio to paint a useless altarpiece. He wouldn't have had to hear the prisoners' snotty pleas, the crowd's glee, the sharp whipping of ropes. He could have made more useful things than pretty, little decorations.

When he looked away from the orb, the priest was gone from the terrace. The ropes were all stiff. They tugged at the iron fixtures along the parapets.

He always noticed these details; it was his curse. Everything he sees brands itself onto his memory.

He prayed then—for the priest, for forgiveness, for his memories to fade. Before his silent words were finished, the guards brought forward more chained men and led them to the edge of the parapets. This time, he didn't close his eyes; he didn't have time. There was no tying of ropes. The men were pushed off the edge, one after another.

He stood, ran to the priors.

"I want to leave," he told the gonfalonier.

The priors shook their heads. "They're rioting down there," one said.

"You said I was free to go." He tried to keep his voice from quavering. "Take me down."

The priors relented; a guard walked him down unlit, dark-spotted stairs. Down here, to the Palagio's courtyard, crowded with sculptures.

Now he stands, stonelike, distracted by a familiar figure. Gleaming, slender legs and a crown of neat, cropped curls. A boyish face, his younger reflection staring back at him. His own casual smile mocking him.

He thought he'd never see the David again. Assumed it would sit amid weeds in Lorenzo's garden, its skin losing its sheen with each summer's rain. But here it—he—is, in the Palagio. Sold, he presumes, by Lorenzo.

Goliath's head has been moved. In the garden, it sat beneath David's sword, as if it had been hewn off not moments before. Now, it's straddled by the boy warrior's legs, a presented gift. Like the boy is bragging about what's he done.

He nods farewell to the boy and the bodiless giant, and then he finally leaves the Palagio.

In the piazza, he has to push himself through the massive, shifting crowd. Sudden shouts of awe and bawdy laughter pepper the air, as if today were a festival day and a colorful parade were about to bisect the square. He wonders if he's imagined the day's horror. His father did always tell him he was prone to ridiculous ideas.

Something tugs on his foot. There's a gray cape on the ground, still clasped around a neck, bent at an impossible angle. The skull looks like a rotted plum fallen from a tree. Blood, brain, and bone. Hideous yet fascinating.

He looks left, he looks right. Bodies litter the ground. Dozens of them.

He threads his way into the thick of the crowd, where the air is hot, where it smells of ale and horses and oddly of sex too. The people around him, they're all facing the Palagio. They're giddy, they're squealing with delight.

He follows their eyes, up the dark stones, up past the colonnades and the scattered windows of the apartments above, up, up to the parapets.

Three men. Unmoving but huddled together, like a sculpture carved from a single slab of marble. The necks are red and raw. Their hands haven't yet drained of color. Their faces are contorted, as if they might cry out at any moment.

The bishop is the worst of them. His robes are bunched, revealing black-hosed legs, oddly slender, something almost delicate in the way his feet point to the ground. But his face is different. It's washed with blood, from nose to chin. His teeth are buried into the bare chest of the man beside him.

This he knows he'll never forget.

He moves through the crowd, pushing against hard leather jerkins, elbowing arms draped in mail. These Florentines carry daggers, swords, maces, more rudimentary tools too—hammers, hoes, even heavy iron pans. He doesn't recognize these people, this strange fever that's taken hold of them. He doesn't understand it.

He needs to get out. He pushes southward. For the first time in years, he weaves into the Baldracca. Even these slim, maligned alleys are crammed with drunks stumbling around corners, and merchants lifting up their tunics to press their bodies against women made taller by their chopines. That it's Sunday, that there are three bodies hanging, not two minutes away? No one seems to care.

He walks faster, toward everything he's avoided, toward the one place he once felt safe. The years, the fear—they don't matter now.

The Buco appears around a corner, the building gray and lifeless. There's no orange glow coming from the windows; they're boarded with wood. Gone is the signboard that hung above the door, that creaked all through the night. The door is padlocked, and weeds now sprout from its stoop.

He stops, rubs at his eyes. How stupid he is, to think it would remain unchanged, to expect it to wait for him to return. All that remains is a ruin. He should've sketched it—painted it, even. He wonders why the good memories are the hazy ones, their details bleached by each passing day. Why couldn't they remain vibrant in the mind, resting ready on a slab like prepared oils?

He can't think about him. Not now.

He keeps walking, to the riverside, where he climbs down to the muddy banks and heads upstream. He holds his gaze directly ahead, fights the usual urge to let his eyes wander to whatever fascinates—the river splashing against thick piers beneath the bridge, a tree across the river, clustered with pink buds. There could be bodies floating in the river, corpses hanging from those branches.

Ahead, a familiar sight. Vagabonds, huddled beside bonfires. They're farther east than he remembers, and their number has dwindled. There was a time when the camp sprawled from bridge to bridge. Now there can't be more than two dozen of them here.

He walks through the camp, and no one minds him. This aspect, at least, hasn't changed. They mill about, hanging clothes damp with river water, dusting off their makeshift mattresses with brooms made of reeds. Today is an unremarkable day for them. They're fortunate that way. Foreign troops could've flooded through the city gates, and still these people would be sitting by the river unawares.

He sits by an ashy-faced girl on a dry patch of soil, alongside the splintered planks of an abandoned bonfire. He tries to ease his breathing. To forget.

But he spoke to the bishop. Heard his voice, marked the careful way he gestured, and saw his proud gait. Told him he'd pray for him.

He glances at the girl beside him. She, too, is staring out at the quiet, untroubled river. Steady-eyed, somewhat wistful—she'd make a good Madonna. He'd sketch her if he had his notebook.

The dusky chill raises the hairs on his nape. He can't stay here—not unless he wants to scavenge a rank blanket and lie before a bonfire. But he can't bear the thought of treading back into the streets, into that rabble. Of seeing just a glimpse of the Palagio again.

Perhaps it'd be better to abandon the altarpiece. That Madonna, those shepherds were lifeless, they were false. Especially now. He saw the glee, plain and terrible, across so many faces in that piazza. And it wasn't just today. He's smelled the damp stink, the filth of starved bodies, bare and bony in the Stinche. He knows the truth: this is an ugly city, gilded by altarpieces of saints and bell towers clad with marble in delicate hues. And he's lived alongside it—worse, he's made himself complicit, because this place turns to its artists to paint over the rot. To distract with bold kermes dye, with rare ultramarine.

He was right in telling the bishop that Florence is the city for artists. It's the city for those who willfully blind themselves.

But he could leave. The bishop was right about that. There's little keeping him here. He isn't so different from these forgotten souls roaming the riverbank. Perhaps he should learn from them, simply pack his papers and panels. Heave them onto a cart. Leave. To go where? That didn't really matter. There would always be rich men wanting portraits of their virgin brides, monks wanting frescoes of Christ. His skills, he can take them anywhere. Rome or Naples, Milan or Avignon, even as far as Constantinople.

But carts cost coin. A new city means a new workshop, introductions, and letters of recommendation. A move—it must be planned. His workshop can no longer remain a wasted place. He has to search for work again, and with a renewed vigor. He has to paint his way out of this place.

INTERLUDE I

May 26, 1478

XLI

"IT'S A MONTH TODAY," HIS MOTHER SAYS.

"I know."

They sit in a coach, their knees knocking together with each rut in the road. After her long absence, she's once again a near-constant presence. At his brother's funeral, clutching his hand. Across the table at every supper, slicing her meat into the smallest of morsels. In the corner of a salon, silent but seen, each time the councillors came to tell him that another one of the attackers had been caught: first Jacopo, then the two priests, and finally Battista. He had Jacopo hanged, had the priests castrated, the guardsman beheaded.

But there was still Baroncelli. A month has passed, and he's not been found.

And he and his mother, in this same time, have said little—if anything—to each other. There was always an audience, someone listening or watching. If not the priors or his friends or his uncle, then the guards, who now trail him everywhere he goes. Even into his bedroom. He's never alone; no one will allow him to be.

Inside this small coach—it's the first time they've had a moment of privacy. They're by themselves, for however long this ride will last. Then the doors will open and the guards will once again be waiting for them.

"Will you return soon?" he dares to ask. "To Morba?"

"I don't think that's wise," she says quickly. Despite their little talk, she's kept her voice honed like a blade.

"What of the villa you were building there?"

"I'm having the foreman write me with his progress," she says, distracted. She's peering through a gap in the curtains, up at the rise of the Palagio. "When are you going to cut them down, Lorenzo? They're rotting."

He glances. They are.

"I thought you'd want to see them punished."

"I did. And you have punished them. Clearly. But that's done now. I want to see you safe."

"Safe? One of the attackers is still out there."

"And the pope lives too. Do you aim to hang him as well?"

"Don't tempt me." But he wouldn't hang the fisherman. He'd gut him.

"Where does this end?" Her voice is softer now. "That you've banished your own sister. I still can't—" She coughs into a soot-black handkerchief.

"She should consider herself fortunate that she and Guglielmo aren't locked away in Volterra like the rest of the Pazzi."

She shuts her eyes, the skin bunching together. "It's my fault. I should've been here. I warned you—Yes, I warned you. But I didn't make you listen." She reaches blindly, clasps his hand. Her skin is scaly and cold to the touch. "You can't keep provoking the pope. We can't afford war."

The coach slows. He frees his hand, but she leans forward and clutches it again.

"Cut down the bodies. Please. We've already lost too much."

He ignores her, staring through the gap as the coach veers eastward. On a quiet, narrow street near Santa Croce, it slows. Mutts, their ears twitching, sleep beneath louvers. Bees drone between lilies, sprouting from a weedy garden patch.

The coach stops in front of a narrow, two-story house, no different from its neighbors.

"Where have you brought us?" he asks.

"To a new beginning, if you'll allow it."

They're ushered inside the house by a man with an unshaven face wearing a wool tunic. He bows, deep and long, introduces himself as Gorini, then leads them upstairs to a hot room, an infernal one, with the windows shut. The furniture is faded, splintering. A long, bare nail protrudes from the wall. Bloodied linens lie in a heap beneath the foot of a canopied bed. And hidden behind the bed's curtains, he can hear something shifting, someone's jagged breathing.

"Thank you for coming so quickly," Gorini says, his voice barely rising above the crackling, overworked hearth. "She'll be in God's hands soon."

He pries open the bed's curtains.

Lying in the bed is a woman, barely stirring. She is sallow-skinned and pale-lipped. Blonde curls are matted to her forehead. Her round, fogged eyes move only to blink. Still, he recognizes her.

Movement, in her arms. A babe sucks at her breast.

He looks away, flushing.

"I've been blessed with a healthy grandson," Gorini says. "Loud lungs on him."

"Him?" he hears himself ask.

Gorini places a hand on his shoulders, the gesture too familiar. "I am an old man, but you still have much of your youth. Your family can give him a far better life than I could ever hope to."

He turns to his mother. "Clarice—"

"I wrote to her this morning. She'll understand."

Not even a month returned from Morba, and she's already infesting his plans.

She sits down on the edge of the mattress, runs a finger over the babe's impossibly small hands. She leans close to the woman's wan cheeks.

"Only if Fioretta wishes it."

The dying woman looks up at his mother, gives her a tired nod.

"We'll take him to be baptized tomorrow," his mother says.

"What will you name him?" Fioretta asks, the words slow and labored.

He watches his mother kiss the babe's downy head. "Giulio," he hears himself say.

His mother stills. Fioretta smiles weakly.

"There's another matter. A small one," Gorini says, lifting something, small and squarish, from the bedside. He faces it toward them, and there she is: the Madonna, still plaintive and radiant. The child in her arms still reaching for a blood-red carnation.

It feels as if the fire has burned up all the room's air. So many arguments he and Giuliano had over this woman, in front of him now twice-over, alive and dying. All of them pointless.

"Please take it," Gorini says. "So Giulio might one day know what she looked like."

"No—"

His mother speaks louder. "You honor us with such a gift," she says, rising from the bed. "It's fine work. Do you know who painted it?"

The fire crackles. The babe coos. He looks at the infant, at his eyes—large and brown and wide, just like his brother's.

"No one of importance," Lorenzo says, looking away.

INTERLUDE II

1478–1479

XLII

THESE ARE THE SCENES HE DOES NOT PAINT:

THE HEAD OF THE POPE'S GUARDSMAN, piked from the parapets of the Bargello. Framed on each side by the two priests who attacked Lorenzo. Their bodies have been stripped of their cassocks; their ears have been shorn, their noses too.

A PACK OF BOYS with scabbed knees, grinning, jostling each other. Behind them, the rain-darkened pietraforte of pointed Santa Croce burnishing in a shaft of sun. The piazza dirt still soft from rain, the mud flicking their small limbs as they play calcio, not with a leather ball but with the festering head of Jacopo de' Pazzi.

OUT OF A NOW-UNNAMED PALACE, slaves carrying a sofa in sky-colored silk, plates in etched silver, a barely worn cape lined with sable. A man standing beside the gathering riches, one hand shielding his eyes from the stubborn sun, the other lifted high, its fingers pointing. "Pazzi pearls for five florins!" he is calling. "An oak bed for twenty!"

ORANGE-TIPPED FLAMES sending off sparks. Thick panels of poplar splitting, crumbling to glowing embers. The painted faces of Jacopo, of Francesco, of already-forgotten ancestors streaking black, becoming char.

PAPERS, THOUSANDS OF THEM, lifting into the air like gulls above the empty steps outside Santa Reparata. Words, printed with the pope's new press. They say Lorenzo is a heretic; they excommunicate him. They say Florence is a godless city, and they announce an interdict against it. The church bells are stilled. No longer can they take Communion, confess, hold Mass for their dead.

THE HAZE OF CANNON SMOKE in the southern stretches of their Tuscan country. Sun-sliced steel and scimitars. Bucking horses and screaming soldiers invading from Naples and Calabria and Siena, all of them blessed by the pope to siege Florence and its lands; to starve, pillage, and take.

A LONELY FIRE in a piazza. A widow, balling an oil-soaked handkerchief to her reddened nose, trying to snuff out the stench of burning hair, the reek of plague. Pyres are everywhere now, pockmarking every street. Bootprints of soot wherever one walks.

SIX GUARDSMEN, their arms extended and faces trickling with sweat, pushing the city gates closed. To keep them safe—from plague or from war, no one is sure.

BODIES BOBBING ALONG THE ARNO. Bubonic corpses festering in gardens, in alleys, in the shadows of churches too. There is no longer any timber to burn. The gates are still shut.

TWO WEEKS OF RAIN. The Arno rushing and rising. The river sweeping away the tents along the banks. The water creeping higher still, slipping beneath tavern doors in the Baldracca, soaking sacks of flour on the floors of bakehouses, warping the linen looms in the workhouses.

IN THE ARTISTS' WORKSHOPS, candles burning, all through the night. Knives to be sharpened, oils to be mixed, panels to be prepared. They are busy, wildly so, despite war and plague. Andrea is carving wax effigies of Lorenzo, and Sandro is making murals of the hanged men, is painting votives of Giuliano too.

And Leonardo? He is not hired for any of this work, nor does he chase it. He thinks it's cheap, dishonest. What he is painting are the poorer commissions abandoned by Sandro, Domenico, and the others. Madonnas mainly. Before the year's over, he begins two of them.

THE MEN WHO ASKED for these devotionals vanish. The first falls to plague. The second is luckier—he survives—but he's decided he can no longer ignore the city's clearly inevitable demise. He gathers his family, tells them to fill chests with their finest clothing, with anything, everything valuable. With the coin meant to pay for the painting he no longer needs, he bribes a guard to let them slip through the northern gates.

Now these half-rendered virgins lean against the rear wall. Leonardo doesn't delude himself into thinking he'll finish them. He doesn't even bother buying new pigments or more linseed. Florence is changing and him with it.

No—that's not right. If, amid the dying and the bloodlust, Florence has finally revealed her true nature, then he supposes he has too. No longer does he consider himself a master painter—for was he ever truly that? He decides he is done with making mothers and martyrs.

Now, in his mind, he indulges all the curiosities that for so long he's shooed like flies, that in Andrea's words, were a distraction from his painting.

He considers how smoke rises from a bonfire, different from fast-moving steam, from sluggish fog; how it dissipates in the wind.

He hears talk of battles in the Tuscan hills, and he wonders how captains make themselves heard to their men over the thunder of lit gunpowder. If it might be possible to design an instrument to better project one's voice.

At the news of sieges outside city walls, he imagines covered ladders that protect their climbers from projectiles thrown from above.

Armies encroach on Florence, and he resolves to make work suitable for the moment. Now he sketches crossbows, mortars, cannons. He draws bloody war.

Part Five

THE
ADORATION

1479–1483

XLIII

HIGH UP THE BARGELLO, HE HANGS, BARELY SWAYING IN THE steady wind. His cheeks and eyes are sunken. His nose protrudes, beaklike, pointing down toward the earth.

He is—was—the last of the assailants from that awful day. A man called Baroncelli. Found in Constantinople, the market rumors said. Leonardo believes them, for his clothes are exotic: blacks striped with red, a blue coat lined with what looks like fox fur.

Leonardo sits across from the building, his back to a wall. The dirt beneath him is frost-hard; it refuses to grant any comfort. He shifts, sweeps at the pebbles, shifts again. He cups his hands and brings them to his mouth, blows warm breath into them. He cradles his notebook between his crossed legs, cracks its spine until it splays flat. On the ground next to him, he rests a small inkpot. Reluctantly, he dips his pen.

He has avoided this kind of work for over a year now. Remained alone in his workshop. It wasn't so difficult living only on his father's allowance when he no longer had to buy expensive pigments. When he only worked in paper and ink, drawing weapons and ladders and wells. But then, yesterday, his father asked him to come to his office in the Badia. Sat him down, told him he was expecting another child— meaning a third legitimate child. Said he needed to be more mindful of his expenses, with another mouth to feed. Leonardo's allowance? No longer could he afford such an indulgence. Surely, though, Leonardo was successful enough not to rely on such a thing, no?

In truth, he couldn't begrudge his father. It was a miracle the payments had lasted this long. So he told his father he understood. He even shook his hand. Then, through the window of his father's office, he saw a small crowd gathering across the street, below the Bargello. A man in mail was walking the building's parapets, carrying rope.

He knew then how he might win more work.

HE LOOKED AT SANDRO'S MURALS before sitting down to draw. Foolishly thought they'd be good to study, that he might glean something from them. The bishop, the banker, the cardinal's tutor, all drawn on the wall of the custom house. Gaping mouths, no tongues to be seen. Noses, flat and hastily sketched. All of it colored in garish shades of poppy red, saffron yellow, anise green.

His attention caught on every mistake. The bodies looked light as dried leaves when he remembers how heavy they seemed, how little they shifted in the wind. The eyes seemed to burst, seemed so hateful, when he can still recall the bishop's panicked stare.

He imagined what that man must look like now: his purple robes stained and sun-paled, his bones cleaned by the vultures. He knows he's still there, still tied to the same fraying rope. Rotting through rain, hail, and snow. In the streets, he's heard men—well-dressed ones, informed ones—say that if Lorenzo had cut down the body, there never would have been an interdict. Rome and Naples never would've declared war.

But the body remains, though he hasn't seen it, won't dare look on it again. The war continues, through storms and floods and plague. Enemy troops near the city, and he stays, trapped, in Florence with an ever-dwindling purse.

HE DRAGS QUILL ACROSS PAPER. Draws the outline of the body, its pinioned arms, the little bootless feet. He sketches the bony face, marks its shadows. He even draws the thin leash of rope extending above the man's head and fastidiously notes each article of the man's clothing, its color, its material. He won't have his drawing be like Sandro's. If he must make a mural of such a wretched subject, he'll make it terrible and true.

Sketch done, he looks at his hands, the fingertips blackened, waiting for the ink to dry. What's next will be worse, but there's no use in tarrying. Another artist could easily win the commission if he's too slow, and then he'll have drawn this ugly thing for no reason at all. No use in writing an appeal, either. He needs to present himself, his sketch in hand. Only his work can outshine his past.

If he wins this, it would be an opening. If his sketch impresses, so might his designs to save the city. Triple-barreled cannons that can fire twenty-one shots, all at once. Rotating blades to mount on the city walls. Inventions, unlike anyone else's, that could not only earn him enough to leave but also forge him a new reputation to carry abroad: not as a painter, but an engineer.

He stands, back stiff. Walks northward through shafts of faint sunlight and bitter-cold shade. The Epiphany is only a few days away, but the homes are all darkened; no slender candles glow through their window glass.

Even Santa Reparata's bell tower looks dim today. No nativity scenes huddle outside the cathedral doors. No bells toll, no hymns are being sung; there will be no feasts or parades or celebrations. The rumors are the only thing left to listen to in the city, and they say that enemy troops have taken the Mugello, that they're camping in the hills, just to the north.

Cities are meant to be loud, he thinks. Frenetic. To see Florence emptied, hushed—he finds it unnerving. It's the expectant stillness of a final, held breath.

The palace on the Via Larga rises before him, too big and too proud. He wonders if his Madonna is somewhere inside, a prisoner in a salon that hasn't seen guests in over a year. His best work made useless. He imagines a different version of this same city, one where it was Giuliano, not Lorenzo, who survived. Perhaps they never would've gone to war. Perhaps it would be Leonardo and not Sandro making painting after painting for the Medici. Then he remembers: even Giuliano didn't give him any more work after his arrest. In any version of this city, he'd still be workless. Except for the one where he never went to the tavern.

He looks at the mouth of the courtyard, where two guards are stationed. He prays—he doesn't truly pray, but he hopes—for this drawing to be the escape he needs. He grips his notebook in his left hand and approaches the guards. He tells them he's a painter with new work to present to Lorenzo.

The guards turn to each other, surprised.

"You say he knows you?" the taller of the two asks. "You've worked for him before?"

"Yes, I painted a Madonna and Child for his late brother."

The shorter guard nods to the other, who retreats within the courtyard.

He's gone for some time. Long enough for Leonardo to imagine Lorenzo seated, spread-legged in an armchair, ranting. To conjure all the words Lorenzo would use to berate him: *reprobate* and *degenerate* and *delinquent* and *buggerer*.

And those were all true, weren't they?

The guard returns, flanked by a servant. Then, before he can steady his breath, before he can understand what is happening, he is being led up the stairs from the courtyard and into the palace.

He is taken to a different apartment from last time, through a series of rooms overlooking the rear garden. Ushered into a salon, warmer than the rest. He smells her first; almond oil and rosewater—that particular perfume of a wealthy widow. Then he sees her, sitting beside a hearth.

He approaches, bows. With a stiff wave of her arm, she commands him to sit, and he obeys.

Her nose is a long flute. Her forehead is broad, half veiled by lace. Her eyes are familiar—black and crystalline. They watch him, but he looks anywhere else, waiting for her to speak. To the handsome poplar desk, piled with letters. The sounding gong beside her chair. A painting on the opposite wall: an old man, his cheek resting on his chin, his fingers listlessly paging through a book on his desk.

"San Girolamo," Lucrezia says. "One of my late husband's acquisitions. Not my favorite, if I'm honest. He had such a rich and wild life, yet here he's painted translating the Bible."

"I understand, my lady. I prefer him as the desert wanderer."

She nods. "My husband saw the value in a painting or a sculpture. The effort that went into it. But he rarely considered its effect, whether it had merit or not. Lorenzo is much the same. Giuliano, however, was different. He saw the value, the meaning, and the beauty."

She runs her crooked, red fingers along the bare patch above her breasts. The skin is crinkled, like paper wetted then dried.

He considers the years. His mother could look like this now. Simpler, of course. In a smock, darkened with sweat. Hanging over a steaming pot in a bare-walled farmhouse. Listening to the chatter of her sons and daughters, each of them now with children of their own.

"He had commissioned you, yes? For the Madonna."

"He did, my lady."

"A fine work. A pity she's gone."

"Gone?"

"The girl. Fioretta. She passed, last year. Not long after . . ." She quiets. "Before the interdict was announced, at least, so she still received a proper funeral. A minor blessing."

He thinks of Fioretta's stare, bold and gray. What did she tell him on that first day? She preferred not to dream—yes, that was it. She liked her life as it was.

"If I may ask," Lucrezia says, her voice softer now. "What was he like in those months?"

He feels a smile sneak across his face. "It was a good time. He seemed happy. Radiant, even. To have found someone who saw him not as his name. Someone who simply knew his true self, his generous spirit. The Madonna, such a holy subject—that was intentional. He devoted himself to her." He blinks. Says in a soft breath, "It was love, I think."

He finally meets her eyes. Two small currants, dark and dewy.

"Thank you," she says. "Hearing this, it's some comfort, at least." She rubs her palms together, smiles curtly. "But we have yet to discuss what brings you here."

"I wanted to offer my services for a mural." He pauses. It feels vulgar to say such words now. But he is here. "A condemnation of the man hanged at the Bargello. Like the ones done by Botticelli."

"I know the ones."

He opens the sack next to his feet. Pulls out his notebook, begins flipping through its pages. He looks to her, eager to please.

"I don't need to see anything," she says sharply. "I know your talent."

He nods. "Thank you, my lady. If it is not too forward, I also have designs, I'd like to share with you. For weapons and defenses. Tools that could help your son toward victory."

"Let us hope we won't need those," she says. "But I will write to Lorenzo and share with him what you've offered me today."

"Write him?" he hears himself say.

"You weren't aware?" she says, with a gentle tilt of her head. "He is away. It may be some time before he returns."

XLIV

YES, HE LEFT.

By dawn light in a coach with its curtains shut. Before the market stalls had stretched open their awnings, even before the country farmers had saddled their mules. Across the Ponte Vecchio, past the butchers not yet open and the dyers who had closed for good.

He watched his dead city through the smallest gap at the curtain's edge. He hardly recognized it.

At the Pisan gate, the doors were opened without question from the guardsmen. This was an unremarkable event, after all. Everyone seemed to be fleeing Florence. Agnolo had left him. Sigismondo too. Clarice and the children he kept ensconced in the country. He even has a new son, one he's barely met.

Only his mother had remained by his side in Florence.

Freed from the city, he pulled back the curtains, revealing the Tuscan hills, meandering on. He watched the frost melt. Watched the morning mist burn away and reveal a scarred landscape of blackened trees and hamlets reduced to rubble.

Losing this war was an outcome he hadn't considered, one he hardly understood. He was the one wronged, after all. He thought there would be battles worthy of a sprawling triptych, one he could hang on his bedroom wall. Brave captains, raised lances, rearing stallions, and the like. Instead, war had proved tedious, full of waiting. The troops that came to Florence's defense from Milan and Venice fought against those invading from Rome and Naples, Calabria and Siena. He remained in his palace, reading letters that announced the defeat of his armies, battle after battle—not even in grand massacres, something tragic that could still be painted. Only small, sad losses. Countless, creeping retreats.

His mother called his plan mad. She pleaded with him to send ambassadors, send Tommaso, send anyone else from the war tribunal. Warned him he could be imprisoned, tortured, killed.

She didn't understand, and he couldn't explain. Something had happened, unbidden and unspoken, on that April Sunday, nearly two years past: a transubstantiation that turned his blood into the city's soil, his bones its stone. He had become Florence; Florence had become him. The paupers in the street saw it; that's why they cheered his name. The priors saw it; it's why they no longer refused him. And the dukes, kings, the pope—they saw it too.

This was the crux: if the city fell, so would he. And he knew what that would look like; he remembered Volterra. Florence would be ravaged, the marble chiseled off her facades and carted to distant castles, her best artists sold like whores to foreign courts, her riches divvied up by fat-fingered men. The pope in Rome and the king in Naples would split up his lands, just as they'd order his body quartered, shredded to scraps.

And now that Galeazzo's brother, Ludovico Sforza, had taken control in Milan and seemed disinclined to send Florence any fresh troops, this was no longer a distant prospect. Especially now with the enemy in the hills, just to the north.

He had one final recourse. Not so long ago, he and King Ferrante were friends; Naples was Florence's ally, instead of her enemy on the battlefield. If he could win Ferrante's favor once more, then perhaps Ferrante could persuade the pope this war should end.

So he took to the coast, followed only by his latest secretary, his servants carrying chest after chest of gifts. He stepped onto a galley with the flag of Naples fluttering at its stern.

THE CASTLE RISES STRAIGHT from the harbor, seeming too massive to be half resting in the sea. It is somehow both beautiful and imposing, the kind of fortress he'd one day like for himself. Inside, the throne room is elegant, its floors and walls all perfect squares, its ceiling star-shaped with a tiny aperture open to the winter rain.

Waiting for the king, along with some of the many gifts he's brought with him, he tries to recall the last time he saw Ferrante. Sometime between his grandfather's death and the attack on his father. Another lifetime ago. When he still raced Giuliano through the alleyways for sport.

Yet Ferrante is as he remembers: ursine, tall, and broad-shouldered, with a bowl of hair that sweeps over his forehead, nearly reaching his brows. No doubt, he has aged—he must be near fifty now—but he's remained fierce, defiantly brown-haired.

"Lorenzo!" he shouts. He still has the same booming voice too.

Before the king, Lorenzo brings his knees to the floor. He leans forward, prostrating fully, his chin resting just before the toe of Ferrante's pointed shoe.

"Up, up," Ferrante says. "What is this nonsense?"

He rises and sees the smug pleasure in the king's wrinkled face.

"I'm humbled by your hospitality, Your Majesty," Lorenzo says. "All of Florence is."

The ones not dead at least, he thinks. The rare few who haven't starved or succumbed to plague or fled.

"And we are glad you are here. Matters have so swiftly become too wild, don't you think?"

"It warms my heart to hear you say that. It makes me think of Augustus, prizing peace above all else."

Ferrante smiles, without teeth, as if he's sucking on the stone of a ripe apricot.

It has been so long that Lorenzo has forgotten: he's good at this, at careful words and gentle flattery.

"There are lessons to take from the ancients, aren't there?" Ferrante says. "To keep a watchful eye on the east, for one. The Turks will try to invade the peninsula—it is an inevitability. And our kingdom holds the peninsula's southernmost lands, much of it close to the sea. We know they'll come for our lands first. It makes us wonder whether it is wise for us all to be bickering with each other."

"I share this concern," he says. Truthfully, he doesn't give a fig about the Turks. Florence is so deeply inland, it would be one of the last places the sultan's armies reach.

"How did we get here? We were allies not so long ago."

It was the pope, he thinks. You sided with the pope.

"At least we are together again now, in this greatest of castles."

"We're glad you think so. We may not have your artists, but we have still found hands to make this place beautiful."

It's an opening. "I know my city would be honored to share its artists with you, should we find—"

Ferrante shakes his hand, silencing him. He's leaning to his side, peering over Lorenzo's still-knelt body, at all the gifts behind him. He smiles. "There will be plenty time for such talk. Tell us, what have you brought us?"

THIS IS HOW EVERY AUDIENCE GOES. He walks to the castle, passing underneath its arch of brilliant white marble. He scans the crenellations, searches every window. He wonders: was his mother right? Has he been stupid to bring himself into enemy territory without guards, without an army his back? Will today be the day Ferrante orders him captured and sent up to Rome to be killed? Or, just maybe, will today be the day he wins peace for Florence?

But no arrows shoot from above; no chains ever appear. Morning after morning, he comes before the king. Genuflects, kisses his hand. Compliments him more shamelessly than a whore to her punker. For some time, they speak of legacies, of peace. Then Ferrante asks for his gifts.

He came prepared for this. Ferrante thinks Florence a rich and splendid place, and Lorenzo is keen to remind him of its generous spirit. He has come to Naples with rare books from his library, with bolts of silk from now-shuttered shops. He gives Ferrante majolica plates, silver urns, and when he runs out of his lovely objects, he freely gives him gold too. He does not limit his generosity to the castle walls either. He holds court within the palace that houses the bank's Neapolitan branch, one of the few still open. From there, he pays guildsmen for carnival displays, he donates to hospitals, he even funds the dowries of swarthy peasant girls.

This wealth, he doesn't summon it out of the ether. The bank's reserves were now dry wells to draw from. So he mortgaged the villa at Cafaggiolo. Siphoned several thousand from his cousin's inheritance that was trusted to him. He emptied the last of Florence's coffers too— though the Signoria needn't know this yet.

Sixty-thousand florins in total. And he spends it all.

Ferrante keeps him in Naples as his honored guest, teasing him of peace, like a lustful but chaste bride-to-be. Every night. Through Christmas and Epiphany. Into dank February, into Lent. The entire winter.

His stay in Naples tires him; it drags on his soul. He entreats, he grovels, he kneels on cold palace stone and damp garden earth. But it doesn't matter how he debases himself. Not if he returns to Florence with peace.

To the king, he shows none of his displeasure or impatience—not even the slightest pout. He bows, smiles, nods, and laughs. He tries to feel nothing, tries to carve out any discomforting sensation inside him as one spoons out the messy seeds from a gourd. But he can only maintain this for so long.

At night, when he returns from the castle, his body reminds him of how he's belittled himself. His bones rattle with every small movement as he undresses. And when he rolls down his hose, his knees are marbled with bruises. Beneath the skin, they feel worse—like they've been ground to a fire-hot powder.

By the end of February, he cannot continue.

"Arrange a ship for the day after tomorrow," he tells his secretary. "I'm tired of this place. Of the damp. My whole body is aching from all this blasted kneeling. I can feel my bones whittling away."

He puts his head in his palm. He thinks: I sound like my father.

"Write to my mother and to the Signoria so they know to expect us. And say nothing of the peace. I'll make a final appeal in the morning."

WHEN HE MAKES his last obeisance, he doesn't falter. In the throne room, he kneels on stone cold and slick from overnight rain. He doesn't flinch, doesn't shiver. "Your Majesty," he says kindly. "With your blessing, I hope to leave for Florence tomorrow."

"So soon?" Ferrante says, but his countenance does not shift. "You've been good to indulge us for as long as you have."

"I will not forget it. Your kindness, most of all."

"And we will think fondly on our continued friendship."

He looks up at the king's wide face. "If you would permit me a last entreaty, Your Majesty. We are friends, yes, but I want our lands to once more be friends too. I do not wish more for battle when I return to Florence."

"Of course you don't. If Milan doesn't send you more troops, you will be defeated. We both know this. Even if, by some miracle, Ludovico proves as loyal to you as Galeazzo was, even if he does decide to recommit to your cause, you still will lose this war."

"I will not deny it," Lorenzo says.

"We admit: we, too, are tired of this unnecessary war. My son, however, likes battle. He'll be hard-pressed to surrender his army, especially if he cannot keep the territory he has won."

My territory, he thinks.

"But surely he will listen to his father, of all people?"

"Perhaps," Ferrante mutters. "The pope, however, is another matter. He won't see this finished until he has your head on a pike outside Castel Sant'Angelo."

"We do not need him. Let us commit, here and now, to peace for our two nations. Without Rome. The pope cannot keep up this fight without your men. It is you who can bring peace."

The king shakes his head. "We are all Christians. On some matters, we all must kneel to the Holy Father."

"And if the Turks do come to your shores, do you think he'll come to your defense? God forgive me for saying this, but he cannot be trusted to act beyond his own interests. And those are not God's; they are strictly his own. What he did to my brother, a man who wished to enter God's service, is proof enough of that."

A sharp pain sparks from his knees, curdling his stomach. He grits his teeth.

"Harm has been done, we will not deny that," the king says, running a finger across his lip. "But if we are to bring peace, you will eventually have to look past the Holy Father's errors. You know this."

Errors, he thinks. What a word.

He opens his mouth slowly, afraid a cry, a curse will slip out. "Your Majesty is wise. You can see how badly I crave peace. And I hope you also know that however costly that peace may be, I can suffer it."

"We will think about this carefully," the king says, motioning him to stand. "And we wish you a safe return to Florence."

XLV

HIS WORKSHOP CHANGES. THE MADONNAS ARE COVERED WITH a tarp. His pigments have grown clotted in their unopened glass jars. The tables, crowded with paper, are pushed aside, close to the walls. In their place, there are now planks of unvarnished wood, hammers, saws, and spools of rope. Above them, iron winches hang from the rafters.

Only rarely does he let the old stirrings slip in: a quick sketch of a bear in silverpoint or a charcoal of San Girolamo wandering his desert. Otherwise, he devotes himself to his machines, keeping himself ready for Lorenzo's return from Naples.

He sits on the floor, amid wheels and axles. He scavenges these parts from broken carts, abandoned in the tall grass near the city walls. He carries these pieces back to the workshop one by one, lumbering, panting. Then he tries to rebuild.

He doesn't hear the knocking at his door. He is busy fingering small gears, greasing them with olive oil—an unexpected knack from his time at the tavern. He is meshing the tiny teeth together, not listening to whatever noises are coming from the street.

The knocking continues—quiet, persistent, pestering. An unfamiliar sound, when everyone is either sheltering or fleeing.

He thinks: no one has called on me in months.

He thinks: maybe it is a courier, carrying a letter from Lorenzo.

He bolts upright, and the gears clatter. He runs to the door. The knob slips between his slick fingers.

Outside is a boy with coppery, curled hair. Old enough to be working, to be a letter bearer. "Are you Leonardo da Vinci?" he asks.

"Yes," he says, wiping his hands on his tunic, his fingers eager to grasp the sealed paper.

He waits. He notices the boy has no letter in his hand, that he's carrying no satchel.

"My name is Atalante Migliorotti." His voice breaks. "I wish to learn to be an artist like yourself."

He pulls his fingers through his hair, forgetting that they're dirty. He wants to shut the door on this boy. Return to his machines, thinking only on the parts scattered on the floor. The beautifully clean science of whether or not they'll work together.

The boy's eyes remain fixed on him, unflinching. They're sunken, colored like acorns. "You are a painter, yes?"

"I am registered at the guild," Leonardo says, trying to inch the door closed. "But there are others you should go to—Botticelli or Verrocchio or one of the Pollaiuolo brothers. You'll learn much more from them."

"I went to Verrocchio. He told me he no longer paints. He said no one in Florence is better with a brush than you." Atalante smiles, an unexpected, playful grin—one that, against his better effort, makes him smile too.

The boy is standing tiptoe, peering over his shoulder into the workshop. His eyes widen at the mess. "You have no apprentices?"

"Not any longer, no."

"I'm hard-working," Atalante says. "I can play the lyre, and—"

"No," he says tersely. "I have no need of an apprentice at this time. It would do me no good."

The face before him sinks, the head bows. Curls fall onto Atalante's forehead in tight, perfect spirals.

"I understand," Atalante says, turning away from the workshop, his soles scuffing the dirt.

And then he is alone again. From his own doorway, he looks back at the storm of his work, a refuse heap of broken devices and half-rendered ideas. All of it utterly still, the quiet so severe that he can hear his own thudding heart. He thinks about the day he tried to install the winches on his own, how he fell, hard, from the ladder. About all the many times he's cursed not having someone to help him carry a wheel or lift a long plank of wood. And then there is the simple comfort of having company. How long has it been since he's had someone to talk with over supper? Months? Years?

He takes one step backward, and then another.

He runs to the end of the street, where the boy is walking along the Arno.

"Atalante?"

The boy turns. He nods, beaming.

"I must be honest with you: I am not a sought-after painter. I work with machines now. Inventions. I have no commissions, and I have no way of paying you until I win a new one. And with all this talk of war, with this plague, I cannot promise you I'll be in Florence for long. But for a little while at least, I can offer you a room of your own, upstairs in the workshop. I can see that you're fed, if you don't mind forgoing meat. And if you can help me with my designs, some days I might be able to see that you learn something about painting too. What do you say to that?"

THE BOY DOES PROVE USEFUL. Diligent, attentive, and thoughtful too.

One morning, Leonardo finds all his papers have been ordered into stacks. "Here are all your designs for weapons," Atalante says, pointing to the first neat pile. "Here are your ladders, then your water mills, your vehicles." He hesitates before the largest collection. "And this is everything I wasn't certain how to categorize."

He isn't looking at the stacks. He's looking at the bare surfaces of all the other tables, now free of paper.

"Did I do something wrong?" Atalante asks.

"No," he tells him. It's simply that, with the clutter gone, it's terribly obvious that he has no real work.

The boy is helpful in other ways too. In the mornings, he hands Leonardo a woolen cloak before letting him step outside for his daily walk. When he returns, Atalante assists him in lifting wheels onto axles, in carefully oiling gears, in handing him a screw before he can think to ask for it. In the evenings, Atalante dusts and tidies and washes their dishes, and then he plays his lyre by the hearthside. And he not only plays skillfully, but he sings too. Carnival songs, bawdy ones that make him blush and gape at this boy singing with a winking eye.

He tries to remember every note of every song. So little did he hear music anymore, with the churches shut and the festivals suspended. He wishes there were a way to preserve sounds in the same way that he commits what he sees to panel with paint. Until he can find some way, create some kind of memory device, he'll keep himself content with having this handsome little songbird alongside him in his workshop.

Yes, he knows—he needs to be careful. He feels how his heart strains when he listens to Atalante play his music. But he has learned to control his impulses; he doesn't allow himself to draw this apprentice.

Besides, Atalante is so patient with him. He never asks if he has found a commission—which he still hasn't. Instead, Atalante gently informs him of the artists' rumors traded at the market alongside pigments and ink: that Sandro has painted more portraits of Giuliano; that Perugino, who slept in the bed beside his at Andrea's, has returned to the city; or that Andrea has entered a competition for an equestrian statue—a commission, should he win it, that would take him to Venice.

"I can't imagine him anywhere but Florence," he says when he hears this. "He's always worked here."

"Perhaps he's looking for a change," Atalante offers, clasping his lyre. "Or simply an escape from the plague." He plucks a single, plangent note. It hangs in the air. "What an adventure it would be to see a new city. You want to leave too, don't you?"

He nods. "I'd like to see more of this world. Somewhere different, if—"

If he had a good reputation.

If he could afford it.

If he had work.

Any work.

Any work, at all.

"I'd like to see mountains," Atalante says. "Snow banked taller than giants."

He smiles, surprising himself. He'd like that too.

"How about Venice?" he asks.

"Perhaps."

"What about Rome?"

Atalante shrugs. "Too old."

"And Naples?"

"Too south. I wouldn't want to be there if the Turks invade. I don't think the infidels would appreciate my lyre playing."

"You don't know that," he chides. "They might be a music-loving people, for all we know."

Atalante laughs, and then he is laughing too, the sensation foreign. He can't remember how long it's been.

"Do you know anyone who has left?" Atalante asks, his fingers drifting over his silent lyre.

"Yes," he says quietly, surprising himself. "Only once. A friend."

He wants Atalante's still hands to curl, wants him to strum the strings and kill the quiet.

Instead, he looks up. Asks, "Is he glad to be away?"

"I don't know. We haven't spoken, or written any letters," Leonardo says. He travels back to that room smelling of marjoram. Of so many nights of soft conversation like this one. He wonders where Iac is now. If he is somewhere safe. What he might be casting, if he's making gold-chain necklaces for young brides like he always hoped to do. If he's found someone to keep him company at night. If perhaps, like him, what they shared, what they did, was something he's tried to leave in the past.

"He didn't want to leave," he continues, the words slow, barely more than a breath. "It was my fault. But I hope—" He gets to his feet and walks away from the hearth's warmth. He looks back at Atalante, now stacking the day's sketches, careful not to disturb their order. In the dying firelight, hazed by smoke, his unbelted tunic billows around his small frame. He catches himself noticing the growing strength of Atalante's calves, how the sinews are thin and taut like his instrument's strings, how the skin is becoming studded with hair.

An ugly, urgent tide laps inside of him.

He can't ruin this boy. He should be his penance. Someone to share a workshop with, someone he could teach not just how to draw or to build, but how to see the world, how to make work that is honest.

He grabs his heaviest woolen cloak and leaves the workshop. He doesn't tell Atalante where he's going or when he'll return.

INTO THE NIGHT-BLANKETED STREETS. Across an empty bridge, down to the riverbank. There are no fires; the vagabonds are gone.

The Arno is unsettled, sudsy waves crashing every which way. He follows the river, against the direction of its steady current. Passes through the lamp-black shadow underneath the bridge. Walks closer to the river's edge, the mud hard, half-frozen beneath his boots.

Under the full moon, the reeds are like strands of quicksilver. He parts them, steps through them. Waits.

Another figure emerges from the underside of the bridge. He's short, broad in the shoulders. He hesitates beside the tall stalks. But Leonardo knows he's seen him, knows how he's simply gathering the will to step toward him.

He finds it. They study each other in between the swaying grasses. Bashful, uncertain glances. The man's cheeks are pale and pockmarked; they remind him of the imperfect surface of the moon. He's younger than he thought, maybe the age he was when he first found this place.

Leonardo reaches a palm to the line of his jaw, draws him in, brings his mouth to his.

They move swiftly now. Lips part way for tongues. Hose are jerked down. Hands climb underneath loosened tunics, roving over muscle and rib, stroking nipples. They're not thinking about the plague, about who might see them; they're not even thinking about each other. They're deciphering the codes of each other's pleasure, translating the skin against their hands until it becomes something lucid, until they're fluent in each other's sighs, grunts, moans, until they near that familiar peak— and it has been so long for Leonardo that it arrives quickly, suddenly, as it does for this other man. Two more streaks of silver in the moonlight, and they're finished.

They pant, make dense clouds with their breath. They become strangers again, Leonardo leaving him with a brief, stilted smile.

He returns to the Oltrarno with steady steps. The pleasure is already gone, without any lingering warmth. It feels only like he's expunged something. All that's left behind is that potent clarity, the stark knowledge of what he's just done, of what he couldn't keep himself from doing.

Back in the workshop, he lights a candlestick. Wanders, to the darkest, cavelike corner. Lifts the pliant tarp, scattering dust into the air. He looks at each shadow-doused panel, pulling out one, and then another. Barely drawn saints and saviors, and half-colored mothers.

He knows it, in an instant: he'll repeat his mistakes if he stays. He already has. He's trapped them, all of them, with him, in a city on the edge of ruin. And these ink-outlined eyes and unshadowed lips are pleading for him to save them.

XLVI

BEHIND HIM, THE SUN, JUST BEGINNING ITS DESCENT. AHEAD of him, his city. The Arno, slow and golden like honey. The glowing ring of the unscarred walls and the huddle of homes and towers and churches within. The pinkish sky above, free of pyre smoke and streaked with bronzed clouds.

Men are walking toward him from the open gates. Rickety, old Tommaso and Giovanni de' Benci and all the men on the war tribunal. The ambassadors to whom he has written so many letters. The Signoria, too, their scarlet robes dragging in the dirt.

He slows his horse, hiding for a moment in a rising cloud of dust. He flexes his throbbing feet, allows himself a grimace. He rehearses the words he will say to them. Then he presses his calves against his horse's flanks and wrestles a smile onto his face.

"Peace!" he shouts, and they cheer as he comes aside them. They kneel, they raise their hands up high, they kiss the hem of his cape. They greet him like a prince.

Then they ask: How did he do it?

He thinks: I almost didn't.

He thinks: I bowed to our enemy. I emptied my purse. I left Naples having won nothing.

But that doesn't matter now. When he stepped off the boat from Naples, his body stiff and his stomach sour, one of Ferrante's messengers was waiting for him like some angel. Holding a letter, proffering a truce. Suddenly, his aches eased, his nausea abated. In that moment, he finally became his grandfather's true heir: a man who turns exile into ascension.

He tells the priors, fluently, what they need to hear. And when he finishes, they stare, they praise his bravery and his vision, say that this is truly a time of miracles, for the plague vanished over the winter too.

He smiles knowingly, as if he's willed this. Truthfully, he had forgotten about the plague while he was gone.

It is a new beginning, he says.

They agree. They are so grateful, they say. And then they ask: What is in this peace?

It is reasonable, he tells them.

He does not tell them that Ferrante decides when their annexed lands will be returned to them, how they must pay a rather substantial stipend to the king's son if they wish him to withdraw his troops. He does not explain how it was Ferrante who strongarmed the pope into peace, that the Holy Father only begrudgingly agreed on the terms that the arch-bishop's mural is erased, the priests' bodies are cut down, and the Pazzi prisoners are released too. The pope's interdict? How the Holy Father refuses to lift it, despite this peace? He neglects to mention this too.

He leaves them then, before they can ask more.

THE PALACE IS ALL DRAWN CURTAINS and closed windows. Salons, entire wings of the palace stand crypt-like, dust-filmed. Lifeless, save for the shadow of a servant.

Clarice and the children are still in the country, though he can now safely bring them home. But his mother—her absence is unexpected, conspicuous. He wonders if she's quietly returned to Morba to soak in her thermal waters. He feels an unexpected pang of disappointment at this possibility.

No, his footman tells him. She's only gone to the Palagio.

Didn't she know I was to return to today? he asks.

She did, the footman says meekly.

Lorenzo curses. Of all days, of all places. He orders a new horse saddled. Back in the courtyard, he wearily steps into stirrups once more.

When he rides out onto the Via Larga, it's to cheers. Farmers halt their mules. Merchants step aside and kneel into murky puddles. Young girls blush and smile.

He fixes a smile on his face. Stiffly raises his hand and returns their waves.

A chant begins—quiet at first, then it swells like a tide. They are shouting his name. Calling him magnificent.

He wants to be savoring this. To grin broadly, sweep aside his cape, and throw lilies to the prettiest girls. He wants to luxuriate in what he's won.

Perhaps she'll hear them, he thinks. Perhaps that is how she'll come to understand what he's done.

He spurs his horse on.

A BLACK SILHOUETTE AGAINST a paler black shaft of shadow. Standing a few steps away from her coach. Looking up at the Palagio walls.

At the approach of his horse, at the growing chorus of his name, she only lifts her head higher, grips some object in her hands tighter. Thin, long, and white—he recognizes it from decades past. His father's cane.

He dismounts. Comes to stand silently by her side while they wait for the distant crowd to quiet, to disband. Above them, the mural is still vivid, despite the deepening evening. He thought two winters of steady rain would have washed away the dyes, would have caused the details to bleed. Instead, it remains defiantly jester colored. Ignore the violence, and it seems almost cheerful.

She speaks without turning her head. "I thought I should see them a final time before you've had them scrubbed away."

So she already knows. Of course she does.

"At least it's done," he says.

She laughs dryly.

"Nothing else to say?"

"What do you want me to say, Lorenzo?" She turns to him, her thin face only a suggestion behind her veil.

"I thought this was what you wanted."

"This?" She raises a hand, gloved and trembling, toward the murals. "I wanted none of this."

"I willed us out of war."

"You surrendered, Lorenzo."

"I saved us."

"Are they so different?"

"It's peace!" he shouts.

"Is it? Your sister is still exiled to the country, along with Guglielmo and her children. And, yes, you can see that fixed—but what about everything else? You're still excommunicated. Florence is still under interdict."

"That's the pope's doing, not mine."

"We can't go to Mass. Can't receive the Eucharist. Can't properly hold Mass for our dead. Can't confess our sins. . ." She stops, tucks away the silver-stranded hairs snaking out from the fringes of her veil. "So you brought a stop to the dying on the battlefields. But what about peace with Rome? People want it, Lorenzo. So they can pray again. So they can have their mistakes forgiven."

"The pope would want me to come to Rome and beg for absolution at his feet."

"Is that so difficult?"

He thinks of the days-long journey to Rome, of more kneeling before thrones. Yes, he wants to say, it would be difficult. He's not sure he can suffer it.

"He still wants me dead."

"And you wish the same for him. So what? He wouldn't move against you, not now that he doesn't have Ferrante's armies to call on."

"It would be a lie," he says.

She huffs. "Don't tell me you've never lied in confession. Said the prayers, feeling nothing. What does it matter, if you ask for penance? They're only words."

"If it doesn't matter, then why suffer it? We've survived this. We have a beginning again. I've already made something from it, and there's plenty more to be done." He turns his back on the murals. "Look at this building. How beastly it is. How old. It's far outlived its purpose, and so has the Signoria and the rest of the councils. Do you hear the crowd? They're chanting *my* name, not the priors'. So why don't we bring this ugly stone to rubble and build something better in its place? A new palace, for us."

"Knocking something down is simple and brutish. Planning, building—that's the harder work. It takes persistence," she says. "This city likes you, yes. But it also likes its traditions. The Signoria has lasted three centuries. You can't simply vanish that. At most, you can overhaul the councils. Make sure anyone elected safeguards our interests. And I agree that would be a wise use of your current popularity.

"But styling us as anything greater? Building a new palace? That would take years. Decades, even. You might have that time, but not everyone does. Besides, Lorenzo, how will you afford the builders, let alone the marble and stone? The city's coffers are spent, and so are ours. And your brother—" She stabs the earth with her cane. "It's no wonder the bank's failing. You never think about the cost."

He looks down, searches for her eyes. She barely comes up to his shoulders now. And her mantle, brown wool too heavy for the mild evening, seems to smother her. He doesn't remember her being this small.

He reaches out a hand and closes his fingers around her arm. At first she pulls away, but then she submits, lets him guide her homeward. For a moment, he can pretend that they've returned to the past. That he's just a loose-limbed boy, following his mother on a visit to some old-blood widow. A boy who hadn't yet had to think about priors or popes, only when he and his brother might have their next riding lesson.

He feels her arm—how it could be so easily snapped, like the branch of a blighted tree. He remembers: his brother is gone. Nothing he can do will change that.

"We can start again, and that's worth more than any sum of gold," he says. "Let's enjoy our peace. The fighting, the compromises—those are behind us now."

Her arm tugs free from his grip. "Nothing is behind us."

SHE'S RIGHT, OF COURSE. But it takes several months and fresh battle to make him reconsider.

The Turks breach the Italian shores. Yes, after years of worry and blustery talk, the infidel army has finally arrived. They capture Otranto, down at the peninsula's southeastern end—past Rome, past Naples. Far enough to be tempted not to care, but Lorenzo knows these soldiers are men of the sultan Mehmed, the man who conquered Constantinople at twenty-one, who breached those city's walls that had repelled invaders for a thousand years. It only takes a glance at Florence's walls to know they won't last a single day of cannon fire. And Rome's? Those hardly work as a sheep pen.

The pope writes to courts, north and south, proffering a new truce. He urges the whole peninsula to take up arms against the infidels. He calls it a new crusade. And Lorenzo's ambassadors hear this and quickly ask: if there is to be a truce, might Florence be restored from its interdict and Lorenzo from his excommunication?

Yes, the pope says, if he comes to Rome.

His mother doesn't tell him to go. But every day he hears her cane pattering down the halls, he sees her stooped figure gasping at the top of the stairs. And every night, he crawls into bed with Clarice and knows she fears she might never be able to return to Rome and see her parents again. And despite the guards at his bedroom door, he still fears more daggers.

He thinks: if it will give them all some peace, perhaps it's worthwhile.

He thinks: he'd like to see this pope one last time, to stare down the hideous face that's brought him so much ruin.

He thinks: this is no different from Naples.

So he brokers a compromise. He will go if it can finally bring an end. And only if he can do so in secret.

XLVII

THE HANGED BODIES ARE GONE, AND SO HE WALKS BENEATH the Palagio once again. The building is unchanged; it's still brute and ugly. The piazza below is hazy today, it smells of woodsmoke and roasted meat. He threads the makeshift bonfires, weaves through the lac-cheeked crowds. They are pouring ale, slurring songs; they're dancing in swirling pools of sage and mustard serge. They will revel past midnight, pausing only to resume with the sun's next descent.

Peace, they say they're celebrating.

He doesn't see it. He sees the same hungry rabble that cheered as bodies fell from the parapets and broke open on these same setts.

He doesn't feel it either.

But he can't begrudge the crowd their merriment. Not entirely. After everything they've suffered, all that now waits for them is a return to their silk-weaving, their stall-trading, their ledger-keeping—to the drudgery of life.

These crowds will tire, he thinks. The city will fade once more. It had already lost its luster; the proof is just to the north, stretching skyward: that terracotta dome, higher than them all. That is the city's pinnacle. There are no new domes, sprawling palaces, or marble towers. He knows that in the years to come, fewer frescoes will wall the churches, dyes will wane, fabrics will fray. That undoing has already begun. War and plague have only hastened the inevitable.

He walks on, eastward, toward once-known streets and corners he hasn't crossed in years. He could turn up one path and find himself back at Andrea's workshop. He won't go there today; he'll spare them both the embarrassment. But he does wonder if his old bedroom still smells of spice. If Andrea is sitting beside some slab of bronze, nursing wine. If he won the commission in Venice.

He knows what Andrea would say to him if he were to visit. To quit toiling and find work, any way he can. At least he could tell Andrea he's taking his advice for once.

He stays on the wide, transverse road leading from the Bargello to the weedy, fertile execution grounds outside the city walls. He thinks of all the men who walked this same path, knowing they were stepping toward their end. Murderers and heretics and traitors. Surely a few sodomites too.

Before he expects it, before he's prepared, his feet near the ridge where the road plummets into the moat that girds the Stinche. There's the stink of shit, the croaking of toads. He wills himself to smell, to listen, to turn his head. The prison's walls are wan and wet. Too tall, with far too few windows—no windows at all, in truth. He guesses at where in the building he was kept. For how many days. He considers what might have happened to him if Lorenzo had not seen him freed. If that might have been the preferable outcome, after all.

He walks on.

"YOU DEIGN TO GRACE US with your presence?" his father says.

He has no excuses to offer. He cannot lie and say he's been busy. That would defeat the purpose of coming here, to his father's new house.

He focuses instead on this salon. The furniture surprises him. It's handsome, detailed. A well-carved poplar table inlaid with mother-of-pearl, and an embroidered rug beneath it. There's even a painting on the wall. A simple, small Madonna, lifeless eyes like blank half-moons, wide pasty cheeks leading to a button of a mouth.

"It was a wedding gift."

He nods. He doesn't care. He didn't even think to give his father a wedding gift.

"Margherita and the children are all in good health?"

"They are. And your workshop, it's going well?"

He searches his father's eyes. Burnt brown, different from his own. Every time he sees him, he does this, hunting for a hint or a betrayal, a shade of disgust—some sign that his father knows the reason why he's not a favored artist in this city. But his eyes remain unchanged, steady in their stare. That familiar, haughty look of tested patience.

"It was," he lies. "Then the plague arrived."

"Yes, it's been difficult on us all. So many deaths."

And with each of those deaths, there was a will for his father to write.

"At least there is peace now," his father adds. "Surely that will mean more work for you."

"That's what I wished to discuss with you."

"I can't give you money," his father says swiftly.

"And I wasn't going to ask for it. I have a single plea. It shouldn't cost you anything. I need work, urgently so. All I ask is that you might mention my name, if any of your clients are in need of a painter."

A sigh, unnecessarily long. "The problem is your reputation, Leonardo. It's sullied."

His fingers grip the silk armrest. He wonders if he was wrong, if he's known all this time.

Steps, quick-footed, break the quiet. A figure, half-height, runs gleefully past the open doorway. His father's son, his brother, more grown than he expected.

"Quit your playing," his father shouts after the boy. He rises and shuts the door, trapping Leonardo inside. When he returns to his seat, he looks down at his fingers, ink-stained like Leonardo's own. "When the Signoria was looking for a new artist to complete their altarpiece, I didn't hesitate to mention your name," he says, returning to his seat. "They paid you an advance of twenty-five florins, if I recall correctly. A generous sum. Yet you never began work on it."

He nearly laughs—out of relief, out of absurd amusement that his father remembers the precise payment for a work he's nearly forgotten. Of course he does. He is a true notary, diligently recording his grievances. A ledger column, now lengthy, of his unfinished work, of every tardy painting, and also every soldo his father has spent since his arrival in Florence on his allowances and his boyhood tunics and even the bedlinen on which he once slept. Investments that long ago failed to yield any personal profit. And he can't fully blame his father for thinking this way, for what did he have to show for his years of training, for the thousands of sketches, for everything he's endured?

"Why did you bring me here?" He surprises himself with the question. "Why didn't you leave me with—"

"Your mother?" His father shakes his head, lets out a single, mirthless laugh. "You've had a richer life here than you ever would've with her out in the country. Life there is slow—too clogged by old ways, old habits. You of all people couldn't have suffered it, living in a house where water drips from the thatching whenever it rains. You never would have painted there, you can trust me on that.

"You're, what, nearly thirty now? Older than I was when you were born. Still young enough to make mistakes, become distracted, go astray. I'll be honest with you. My family raised you out of some sense of responsibility, but I chose to bring you to Florence because I could see that you were clever. You had potential. There was a time when I thought you would've made a good notary. But you were obstinate about doing something else."

I'm sorry—the words are there, on his tongue. But he isn't, is he?

"I appreciate how generous you've been with me all these years," Leonardo says, straining to keep his words level, knowing he has one last offer to make. "I know I've asked a lot of you. That you have a growing family to think about. I don't mean to interfere with that. In fact, I'm going to leave Florence for good once I have the coin. All I need is one more commission, a good one."

Leave? he expects to hear. For where?

His father only sighs. "I've worked with the friars at San Donato for a number of years now. They mentioned to me recently that they intend to commission a new altarpiece for the monastery. If this interdict is ever lifted, at least."

Another altarpiece. God save him. "Do you know what they'd like the subject to be?"

"If my memory serves me, they want a Madonna with the three Magi."

An Adoration. How original, he thinks. Such a trite subject— Masaccio, Perugino, and Sandro have all painted it. He's seen each of them, how similar they are. All of them brightly hued and formal. All with a passive Madonna, cloaked in lapis, with a limp doll of a Christ propped on her knee. All with stiff-looking kings, huddled together.

He should be kind. In each, there's at least one thing that's commendable. Take Sandro's, for instance, one of the city's most recent iterations. His portraiture is stunning. A shame, then, that he was more preoccupied with greasy flattery than holy vision. Search his crowd, and you can find the Medici as kings. You see poor Giuliano. There's Lorenzo, too, made far too handsome by Sandro's brush. And all of this was for a painting that wasn't even commissioned by the Medici.

If he were to paint an Adoration, by God he would do it differently.

"Should the interdict be lifted, I'd greatly appreciate you mentioning my name. That would be a gift, one I could never pay."

His father's face remains the same. "If I find you work, I expect it to be finished this time. What you do or where you go afterward is your concern, not mine. But the work must be completed, and to my client's satisfaction. Most of all, it must be delivered on time. If I am to broker this, the conditions of the contract will be mine, and they are not to be negotiated. You'll accept the terms, whatever they may be. Understood?"

He agrees.

XLVIII

A DELEGATION IS ARRANGED. TWELVE OF FLORENCE'S LEAD-ing men, headed to Rome to kneel before the pope and ask for forgiveness.

He is not among them. Instead, he gathers them a week before their departure. Wishes a safe journey for them, thanks them for seeing that the interdict against Florence is lifted, for bringing certainty to their fragile peace. He says they will be honored upon their return. That he'll be waiting for them.

He doesn't say that he, too, will be in Rome.

He will ride apart from the delegation, always a day ahead of their progress. In Rome, he will lodge away from them, in Parione, ensconced in Clarice's family home. He, too, will meet with the pope—there is still the matter of his ongoing excommunication, after all—but his confession is to be a private affair, a secret mutually kept. It was the only way he'd suffer it.

In the coach, he bites back complaints about the rough Roman roads. He forces a smile, looks at Clarice, half-covered by a sable pelt. He thought it was a kindness to bring her, to grant her this long-overdue time with her family. Besides, he wants no one but Clarice to be there when he returns from seeing the pope. She will not pry. She is respectful. Discreet.

His body is still sore from the ride days after their arrival, when the delegation is finally summoned to San Pietro for their absolution, when Lorenzo separately takes a coach to the Vatican. Without any attendants in tow, without any fanfare to mark his arrival to the palace, he is ushered to an upper-floor salon with windows overlooking the cathedral's steps. From here, he watches the ceremony down below.

He's grateful for these clandestine arrangements; the December air is biting, the wind keen. Outside, the yellow-and-white standards are whipping; his twelve men are clutching their fur-lined cloaks. The delegation stands before San Pietro's ancient doors, underneath the shelter of its many-pillared portico. It'd be a kindness to bring them inside the cathedral, but he's heard the whispers of how the building is barely more than an open-air barn, stone walls leaning precariously, threatening to collapse.

A fleet of cardinals gathers before his men. He thinks one of the more ashen faces might be that of the poor, clueless Cardinal Raffaele who witnessed the bloody Mass. Among the courtiers, he does not, however, see Girolamo Riario. He's never been able to prove his involvement in plotting the attack, but he'd like to think absence is an admission of his guilt. He'd like even more to see the pope's son drawn and quartered, but alas, that would probably spoil this newfangled peace.

Smoke rises, censers shake. The pope emerges. In tiny, white-slippered steps, he drifts toward his purpose-built throne. With a hand braced against a kneeling servant, he eases himself onto his plush purple seat. As if an afterthought, his tiara is hastily fixed on top of his head.

Lorenzo's palms press against the window. The glass grows wet, runs to rivulets. He wants to shatter it. Howl down to those steps. Call the pope a murderer, a villain, a cur. He wants to see his flabby face turn red, wants to see him suffer an apoplexy and expire, right there on the steps.

It's a goodness, then, that he remains away, in the palace. Alone, where he can will his hot blood to cool before his own absolution.

The pope waves his hand. His men bow. His small mouth moves—Lorenzo does wish he could hear this part, whatever nonsense is being spewed—and then the censers begin to swing again. The chamberlain steps forward and hands the pope a rod. Then, one by one, his men kneel, and the pope strikes them, right on the head. This, Lorenzo can hear, faintly, through the window: the thwack, thwack, thwack.

And then the absolution is complete. The pope, flanked by his attendants, is already shuffling away, his fur train dragging behind him like a tail. Florence is no longer under interdict; Rome is no longer their mortal enemy. Now they are supposed friends. This strikes him as disappointing, sad, frustrating too—as if he's been thrown out of a brothel before finishing a good fuck.

Was that it?

No. He remembers: his own absolution still awaits.

He could still say no. Walk out of the palace, climb into his coach, tell Clarice they have to leave, that he cannot remain in this city a moment longer. But what good would that bring? More war, yes—and this time he has no money to spend on an army; he'd be dooming Florence to invasion. And there'd still be the nagging matter of his own fate, the eternal kind. Not only would he remain an excommunicate, but he'd also still have to sit through his mother's daily tirades—that he's damned himself, damned the family, damned Florence too—from now until Judgment Day.

Or, instead of all that, he could make this small, secret confession.

Besides, he can't deny it—some part of him craves a final word with the fisherman.

THE CHAPEL IS TALL AND NARROW. It's full of light, diffused with dust motes dangling in the air. The pope stands just inside its nondescript doorway; he meets him without servants or guards. He's dispensed with his tiara too; now he wears a simple white zucchetto on top of his head.

The pope walks, rather unsteadily, to the center of the chapel, his head turned up to the wooden rafters. Beneath the high, vaulted ceiling, he looks so small, so short, so fragile. It'd be so easy for Lorenzo to rush at him, to crack his white-capped skull against the floor and curl his fingers around the man's wide, sweaty neck.

"Let us pray," the pope says, and Lorenzo reluctantly kneels against the warped wooden floors and brings his palms together. "You have come here seeking forgiveness, have you not?"

Don't say it, he thinks. He is the wrong one, not you. Forsake this man. Out of respect for your brother, if nothing else. He recalls his last conversation with Giuliano. Shouting. The growing redness of his brother's neck. The pleading in his brother's brown eyes—the same eyes with which little Giulio looks up at him.

His brother only wanted peace. He never let him have that.

He clears his throat. "I have, Your Holiness."

The pope leers over him. He remembers this beak nose, these thin lips, but not the sun-spotted cheeks nor his white-stubbled jowls.

"Do you agree that you have sinned?"

"I have."

"Did you lead your city away from God?"

"I did," he says, but what he is thinking about is an itch, insatiable, on his right hand.

"Did you question God's authority, and did you question Our authority as ruler of His lands?"

"I did." It is a maddening distraction, the kind that once noticed can no longer be ignored, like the chiseling of stone in the streets.

"Did you commit grievous sacrilege by ordering the execution of one of His servants, the Archbishop of Pisa?"

Sacrilege? That archbishop was no man of God. He was just a man from Florence, a wayward, hateful one.

"I did." How badly he wants to take apart his prayerful hands and scratch.

"And do you wish to be absolved of these sins?

He shows nothing. "I do."

The pope wiggles out two petite feet from beneath his robes, and Lorenzo knows what he must do. He bends forward, brings his lips first to the pope's white silken slippers, then to his wrinkled fingers.

The pope smiles at this. "Your penance shall be a suspension of taxes on our clergy in your lands, as well as fifteen galleys to help us fight the infidels. Do you agree?"

"Yes," he says, though he has little clue where he'll find the funds to build fifteen ships.

The pope nods gravely. He shuts his eyes. "Kyrie eléison," he half sings, half moans.

"Kyrie eléison," Lorenzo repeats, finally scratching his hand.

"Christe eléison."

"Christe eléison." He feels brief, blissful relief.

The pope's eyes open again. "In nomine Patris et Filii et Spiritus Sancti, we forgive you, our child. We are Christian brothers once more. Now, rise so we can receive you into our bosom."

He'd rather not, but he does.

Now the pope steps away from him, walking farther into his chapel. "It is a shame." His tone is lighter, almost jocular. "We've never seen Florence."

And what about God? he wonders.

"Everyone speaks of the cathedral and its dome. Your grandfather financed that project, did he not?"

"A small part."

"We thought about rebuilding San Pietro. Making it grander. Giving it a dome—one even larger than yours. You must see it, how Rome has changed since your last visit. It's a city made great again. It would only be natural for it to have a monument that spoke to this revival." The pope's head droops, he looks down at the floor. "Ambition is a fickle thing. Without it, we're nothing. But too much . . ." He stops. The last, lisped words linger.

Is the pope apologizing to him? Has he somehow become his confessor?

The pope turns. His narrow eyes are angry and hungry. This man is still a hawk—but one that has begun shedding its feathers. "God is merciful, but even He finds ways to punish those who forget their station." The words are barked with the certainty of a sermon, the lisp almost gone. "Besides, there's little honor in imitation. But we must give credit where it's due: we have learned something from Florence. Give people a sight to marvel at, and they'll speak of its grandeur as if it was made by your own hands."

The pope raises his arms above his head, gesturing at the blank walls. "I want to make this chapel as magnificent as any place on earth. But unlike your dome, I want its beauty born only on the inside. I want frescoes on every surface, the Scriptures brought to life on every wall. Your city is beautiful because you have artists that make it so. Now it is time for them to make Rome the same. In the spirit of reconciliation, we'd humbly ask for a delegation of Florence's finest artists. Four of them. Only the ones most talented with the brush. Whom could you send?"

The request is unexpected, but of all the pope's various demands from the day, this is certainly the easiest to fulfill. He could name any of the city's artists; a papal commission is a life-altering opportunity, and not simply because of the generous payment that will surely accompany it.

He thinks of the paintings in the halls at home, the altarpieces in various churches. The names come quickly. "Sandro Botticelli I'd most recommend."

"Naturally. People speak of his talents here too."

"Domenico Ghirlandaio and Pietro Perugino are skillful painters. Cosimo Rosselli too."

"Good. Are there any others we should consider?"

He thinks of the Madonna hanging in the room that belonged to his brother. He thinks of its painter, standing in the Stinche, naked and covered in dirt.

The past. There it is again. Something to brush away, like dust.

"None that I'd recommend." He's already forgiven too much today.

"Very well," the pope says.

It's a good project, he thinks, with a twinge of jealousy.

The two of them stand in silence. It's uncomfortable, illicit. They are the ones who are left. And look at the pope, Lorenzo thinks. He's indeed blessed if he has five years left in him. He'll spend the rest of his life waiting for this chapel to be done.

The pope finally dismisses him, tells him he'll pray for his safe return to Florence. Lorenzo wonders if there's a threat hiding in those words, but he shoos away the thought.

Go, he tells himself. Leave. Climb in your coach and ride back home, dreaming of everything you still have time to build, unlike this man. Only fools dwell on ends. He knows what the end of something really is: a beginning, yet to be named as such.

He walks across the narrow chapel, his knees grinding with each step. He reaches for the door, and once more his hand itches. He hesitates. He looks back.

The pope stands at the center of his chapel, staring at the great, pale walls.

"YOU'VE GIVEN US PEACE AGAIN. All of us," Clarice tells him. A hearth illuminates her childhood bedroom. Water runs down the window glass. "Thank you."

She kisses his chin, his neck, and he submits. She lifts his chemise. Runs her hands over his belly. Traces the path of hair beneath his hose. She wraps her fingers around his cock. Tugs at it lightly. It remains stubbornly small.

He reaches down with his own hands, tries to will it to life. She watches with barely concealed repulsion.

"Is it the cold?"

"It's been a tiring day, that's all."

"No, Lorenzo. Your hands."

He turns them to the firelight. The backs of his hands are white and flaky, his knuckles swollen and red. A fine pale dust has already speckled the floor.

"What is it?" she asks.

A small blessing she doesn't know. "All will be better when we're back in Florence," he tells her.

He tries to smile. She does not.

—

THEY RETURN TO A RAUCOUS CITY. News of the interdict's end has traveled faster than them. Bells ring incessantly, merry lyre playing fills every piazza, drunken laughter spills down every street. He hasn't seen so many people out since the day of the attack. And none of them notice the sight of the handsome coach rolling past.

When he exits the coach in the palace courtyard, he falls. Clarice cries out, and his guards flock to his side like vultures to carrion. They grab at his arms, push him this way and that, until he's standing again.

"It has been a long journey," he tells them all.

Clarice eyes him warily. As she walks toward the long set of stairs up to their apartments, he gathers his breath. At the steps, he climbs, left foot first, then the right rising to meet it. He does not dwell on how long this takes. Ignores Clarice's raised eyebrows, her slight pout—that muted concern. Or, perhaps, faint disappointment.

"We should see the children," she says, walking ahead.

Upstairs, the din of the household startles him. Servants shuffle overhead, pots clattering, meat is hammered. Through a closed door, one of his daughters is shouting, and another child is wailing. The door creaks open. A small figure races down the hall toward them, stubby legs unsteady, threatening to tangle, a tumble. It is his youngest, his brother's namesake, whom he instead simply calls his little one.

The child slows, stills. He's seen them now. His fat cheeks sink. His eyes are so large and uncertain, so full of thought. Something of a challenge in them too, their inquisitive hold.

"What is it?" Lorenzo asks, crouching to his son's level.

His son says nothing, not even a babble. Clarice hoists him into her arms, but from her bosom, he still stares.

He rises, his hips grating, his feet throbbing in his boots. And then the skin beneath his gloves once more begs to be scratched, and he cannot suffer it any longer—he strides past his wife and son. Quick, jagged steps for he can hear her following him. He pushes through doors, limps past chairs with taut cushions, through one room after another that he hasn't seen in years, closing one door behind him, then another, until he's certain he's no longer being followed. Until he's standing in the doorway of a room he knows well. Stubbornly unchanged despite the lapsing years. A desk, clear of papers. A bed neatly made. Pillows stiff and virgin. A room without any acknowledgment of time, excepting the two faces painted on a panel hanging from the opposite wall. A mother, blonde-haired, pensive. In her lap, the fatherless child.

How prescient, he thinks.

He tugs off his gloves and lets them fall to the floor. He rubs at his hands until his boots are snowed. He rolls down his hose. A single glimpse of his knees—cherry red—and he knows with certainty. He spent so many hours of his childhood at his father's bedside, terrified by the sight of his hands, this same color. Gout turned his father into a bedridden creature. It forced his mother to retreat to the thermal waters.

When he hears the familiar rapping of her cane approaching, he pulls up his hose.

"Clarice said you ran in here," his mother says. "You have her worried."

He says nothing.

"You're not joining the festivities?"

"The journey was long. I lack the spirit," he says, still facing the portrait. "It's done. The excommunication, the interdict—all of it."

"Did he ask for anything beyond what we expected?"

"Only for us to send a delegation of artists to paint his chapel."

She laughs grimly. "I'm almost disappointed," she says. "Of all things to ask for, when he could've demanded anything."

He turns. The sight of her in the shaft of daylight stills him. Her dress hangs limply off her shoulders and falls loosely over her chest. Deep crevasses slice through the white powder dusted on her face, like cracks threading through limestone.

"I shouldn't have gone," he says, reaching out, taking her hands in his. She looks down at them, as if surprised by the touch. "You need to take care of yourself. Rest. Go back to Morba, if you need to."

"And what will you do?"

"Continue what we've started," he says. "Grandfather's best years came after the coup and his exile, did they not?"

Ridges build across her forehead. She's still looking down at his hands. She loosens his grip, splays out his fingers. He tries to pull away, but she's seen the swelling, the redness, the small white dots of tophi in the crevasses.

"When?" she says.

"Only recently."

A tear leaves a darkened trail against his mother's cheek. In all his life, he's never seen such a sight.

She wipes it away, speaks quickly. "Milk baths help. I'll tell the servants to make you one nightly. The springs are better, but you can't afford to be away that long." She looks up, and her eyes are no longer hard and dark things, they are frightful; he has to turn away from them. "Don't let anyone see that you're hurting. Wear gloves always. Perhaps it won't be as bad as—" She stops.

"You've endured it," he says. "So will I."

"This shouldn't have happened."

"It's over now, right? Tell me it is."

"It is," she whispers, a hand on his cheek.

XLIX

"FOUR ARTISTS ARE TO BE SENT TO ROME," ATALANTE SAYS. "A part of the truce."

He looks at the boy, but the boy won't look at him. "What are they to paint?"

"Frescoes, for the pope's chapel. One artist for each wall in its entirety."

He drinks the rest of his wine, dregs and all. A whole wall. The thought surges through his mind, washes away all the drawings around him. Every scene he's ever wanted to paint, all freed onto a single, massive wall. A wall in Rome. An escape—for him, for Atalante too.

His apprentice, always perceptive, always kind, leans forward and fills Leonardo's cup. Atalante's own remains empty.

"Sandro is to go. Domenico and Perugino too."

"We were all apprentices together," he says, thinking of how he might prove himself for the fourth position. That perhaps Andrea could make an appeal on his behalf.

Atalante is still watching him. He still hasn't refilled his own cup.

"And the fourth?" he asks.

"The market rumors say it might be Cosimo Rosselli."

The wine turns acrid on his tongue. What did he expect? A papal commission—that is work reserved only for the greatest of painters, and he is not among them. They had some quality that he lacked—no, not lacked, but lost. He's not even sure he can call himself a painter anymore.

He feels the boy's stare—sympathetic, yes, but also so burdensome. "I warned you that I wasn't a favored artist in this city," he says into his cup.

Atalante reaches for the half-empty fiasco, finally pours himself some wine. He can relax now that he's dispensed this unfortunate news to his master. And Leonardo is grateful for his pupil's delivery, how he never accuses or judges; he simply informs.

"Everyone seems to be leaving. Andrea to Venice. Others to Naples. Now these painters to Rome," Leonardo says. "You should go, if you have the opportunity. I'd never want you to think you were stuck here with me."

Atalante shakes his head. "We'll leave together. I know it."

He wishes he had the boy's certainty, that he could still afford to be naive.

Then he realizes: there is one small piece of good news in all this talk of truces and Rome. With the interdict lifted, perhaps his father's clients might finally want their altarpiece.

HE'S RIGHT. THE COMMISSION ARRIVES from the friars at San Donato.

Atalante is gleeful; the contract's only just been delivered and he's already gathering brushes and cleaning their long-stiff bristles. "What will the subject be?"

"The Madonna at the arrival of the three Magi," he tells him.

"What size will the work be?"

"Large."

"Will you use oil or tempera?"

"Oil, of course."

He knows he's being short. Any enthusiasm he had for this project has been swiftly deflated by his father's contract. It's exceptional, precise. It allows him a strict thirty months to complete the work, and when the altarpiece is finished, his payment is to be given in the form of a property valued at three hundred florins. A healthy sum. Far beyond what he needs to leave Florence. But the contract also states that he'll be expected to fund the dowry of the girl whose father owns that property—a dowry of a hundred and fifty florins.

It's this that stuns him. For while he can wield a brush to render the coexisting yet conflicting light-dark of a scene, his father can arrange words to have two meanings at once. Only at base level is this a contract with simple terms. Leonardo, and only Leonardo, can see the underside of his father's words: how they spite, mock, and judge. Because he failed to finish the Palagio altarpiece, his father has given him a due day for this next project. Because he's a man nearing thirty who has yet to take a wife, his father is making him pay for a dowry, rather than earning one himself.

He tells himself: at least I now know my father's true feelings.

He tells himself: if I finish this work, I can leave this city and never suffer seeing his face again.

So he begins.

HE LETS THE WORK FALL over him like a heavy quilt. It is everything he sees, everything he touches. It turns his breath hot; it constricts him too. It's a sensation he hasn't felt in years, many years, not since before the war, not since the days of another Madonna, when it was a different boy who kept him company.

Every day, Atalante is at his side. Studying his sketches. Fetching him new charcoal when his nub has dwindled away. For the first time, posing for him: faces of surprise, fear, suspicion. Postured a hundred ways: prostrate on the floor, a weary king before the infant Christ; crouched, a foreigner speaking an untranslated warning; nude, faced away, a pagan ignorant of the changing world.

And when Atalante is stood this way, looking away, Leonardo lets himself study his body. A fair-skinned back, narrow at the waist yet broad and strong at the shoulders. A backside, downed with hair and thick with muscle. At some uncertain point within these last months, the boy disappeared. Now there is this young man nearly matching his own height, who sings the tenor, who joins him on his visits to the barbershop.

He wonders when Andrea noticed these same changes in himself. How it made him feel.

He shoos away these thoughts. There's too much work to do.

In his notebooks, figures squeeze beside his old drawings of devices and under rogue, written reminders. He draws until every sheet within his reach is veined with black ink. He leans close, nose nearly meeting paper, and then closer still, until his pen dragging across the page becomes as loud as a handsaw cutting through wood, until it is louder than the echo of his father telling him that he's sullied his reputation.

As much as the contract offends him, it frees him too. He's done with flattery, done trying to appease. If the friars are to pay him in such a ridiculous manner, then they shall indulge his vision. He's painting them something original, an Adoration different from all its stale predecessors. He is wrangling his subject, wrestling from it a quality both beautiful and ugly, holy and chaotic—the truth.

He's upholding only the most basic conventions: he'll have a Madonna, a Christ, and the three kings. But his Madonna won't be in some rural manger. She'll be with a crowd, in a city. There will be bonfires and dancers, horses rearing and soldiers battling. In the background, a pagan temple will be falling to ruin.

She will rest beneath a tree, surrounded by the poor, tired, and plague-stricken. Most of the crowd won't consider her—for, in truth, with no heralding angels, how would she seem different from any other mother? The rich women, they are elsewhere in the scene, gossiping, ignorant of the Virgin's presence. And the men? They're too busy brandishing knives and arguing about their petty conflicts. Only an unremarkable few will see her, and they'll be perplexed but curious.

Then there will be the three Magi—for they must be included—coming to their knees before the Madonna and her savior son. Yes, they will be kings, but they will be bearded and hollow-cheeked. They will be tired—from decades of ruling, from traveling such a distance, from having to bend their weary legs to lay gifts at the foot of an infant. Their eyes, if he can manage it, will be wistful: the hazel-eyed look of a bishop, standing in a chapel, asking if he'll pray for him.

This work proves different from everything he's done before. It makes him see the past as if through spectacles, suddenly close and clear.

He does not pause, not even for a day. No longer is this painting just a means of escape. It becomes his penance, his restoration, his acme. As he moves from paper to whitewashed panel, he's reminded of what he can will with a brush. With each wet pat of pigmented oil, he's forgiving this city that had nearly forgotten him. He's now grateful for every missed commission, for those workless years. He needed that time to gather strangers' faces in his notebooks, to witness the madness of a crowd, to see chisels taken to palace escutcheons, to see stonework crumble and fall.

He keeps nothing from the work. He unleashes it all, breaks the dam. His painting, with its substantial crowd, is amounting to over fifty faces. Quite a task, especially for him, who has never before put more than two figures in a single painting. Some days, he groans, worrying about how the sunlight will fall on each face, how each person in turn will cast shadows onto those around them. At times, the task he's given himself seems insurmountable. He wishes he'd made it simpler for himself. But he also knows this is the only way he can do it.

He crouches in front of the panel, takes a candle close to its glimmering surface. Already the sky is colored with lapis; the scene teems with dozens of silhouettes. He looks to the background, where soldiers skirmish with sword and shield, the violence of change. He peers at the Madonna and her child, at the unfamiliar mob around her. The same face as that girl, beside the Arno on that April day.

Functionally, he knows the scene is complete. He has made Florence, transmuted it to Bethlehem. It is a match to his sketches; once he adds all his colors, it should be done. But something tugs. He feels an absence. Not like the Christ child in Giuliano's Madonna—nothing he can point to. It's a vague sensation: that he has omitted something from this story.

Wax drips onto his fist. The workshop is bruised black, save for the hearthside, where Atalante softly plays his lyre.

"You'll be finished by winter, I reckon."

"Let's hope," he says, sitting beside him, before the hearth. "And where shall we go, when it's done?"

Atalante grins. "What do you think about Milan? I heard the Sforza court is looking for artists." He pauses, then adds softly, "Musicians too."

Milan? Why not.

"Then that is where we shall go," he says, letting his head rest against Atalante's shoulder.

It is a comforting moment, a thoughtless one. Then he remembers himself, sits upright once more. Stares, tight-chested, at the dwindling fire.

From the corner of his eye, the flickering light goldens Atalante's curls. For the briefest moment, he sees that freckled boy, that good and earnest and trusting boy, the one he abandoned.

A log splits, the fire trembles. He stands, rushing for paper, knowing at last what is missing from his painting.

—

SCRATCHES OF INK, SHADINGS OF CHARCOAL, brush strokes of lapis and lead white. Months pass this way. Ask him what he's done today, and he'd say he added an outstretched hand to a man in the background. A few lines with his pen. Nothing to a secretary or a notary like his father. But for him, it's a day's work. Actions that take mere seconds yet constitute so many of his days, weeks, and now months. Actions that, with time, somehow gather and meld and make the work pulse and breathe.

It's not done. There is no finishing point. Even if there was, he hasn't reached it; the panel is still lacking in most of its color. But even half-oiled and part-detailed, the scene has become real. It's both a single breath and a thousand moments. It's the culmination of every painting he's brushed, every sketch he's penned.

It sprang to life when he added himself.

There, in the foreground. On the far right of the panel, a step away from the crowd, as he typically is. Behind him, faces are turned toward the Madonna; they're awestruck, fearful, confused. But Leonardo, he faces away. Looks out, beyond the panel. As the ruins behind him collapse, as the armies battle, as the Savior arrives, he is turning away. He has borne witness, and now he does nothing. Just as he did when the archbishop stood at the parapets. Just as he did when he was freed from the Stinche.

So when the friars write, asking to visit the workshop and see the progress he's made, he doesn't fret. He and Atalante sweep the floor, scrub away the pigment stains from the tables, bring out his long-abandoned works from beneath their tarps.

Two friars come to the workshop. Augustinians—one tonsured, one bald. Both wearing the same drab brown tunics with flaking leather girdles, the same thin sandals on their feet. Leonardo welcomes them both with a bow of the head, kneeling before them.

Then there's another set of footsteps at the door. Heavier. Heeled leather boots, rather than sandals. Still kneeling, his eyes drift upward. He sees white hose, a patinated jerkin. He sees a hard chin, and a strong, long nose.

He rises slowly. Neither he nor his father greet each other. His father instead looks around the room, bemused. "You've been busy," he says.

Of course he has, but he says nothing. His father still has the power to snatch his tongue.

The friar nearest Leonardo, the bald one, speaks: "You haven't been neglecting us, have you?"

"Not at all," he says, trying to muster a smile like he knows Andrea would.

Atalante is standing beside a window, wiping at an already clean table. Does the boy know he's unsettled? Has he noticed his resemblance to this man accompanying the friars?

"Would you like to see it?" he asks the Augustinians.

All three follow him to the back of the room, where the panel is perched on an easel. It's a much larger work than he's ever attempted. It's taller than him. Much wider too. He stalls, letting the friars and his father drift closer to it. They say nothing, so he fills the silence: "It's very far from being finished, of course. You'll have to imagine it full of color. Every face unique. Every outfit a different fabric."

He wonders which details they're drawn toward. The Christ child with his pudgy fingers raised in blessing? The horses bucking in the background? The palm tree giving shelter to the mother and child?

"Is someone holding a knife behind the Madonna?"

They notice this, out of all the little treasures he's nestled in the painting. "Yes," he says.

His father turns toward him, squinting. The bald friar narrows his rheumy eyes. "Why?"

Leonardo steps beside the panel, hovers a finger over its surface, catching a thousand mistakes he dreads addressing. "It's the chaos of the old world," he says, pointing high at the background. He drags his finger downward, over the twisted bodies of the crowd, toward the Virgin and her son, sitting together, restive, in the foreground. "And the arrival of the new world. The birth of Christian harmony."

It's trumpery, yes—but it's easier to lie than to tell them the truth: this Madonna isn't in Bethlehem. She is here, in Florence, alongside them all.

These friars wouldn't understand that. They live by their gospels and psalms; they don't wade beyond. They can say what they like and what they don't, but rarely can they explain why. What they need is a gentle wind to drift them to an opinion, to help them settle upon it.

He glances at his father. Say something, he wants to whisper. But his father's mouth remains shut.

"Let me give you time to study it," he says to the friars. He keeps his boots light, so he might catch a whisper, a sigh, a compliment. He hears nothing.

Beside Atalante, he watches the friars' hands wave about the panel, his father pointing. At what? He can't tell. Whether it's with marvel or with condemnation, he doesn't know.

"What did they say?" Atalante whispers to him.

"They don't understand it. Or they don't want to understand it."

"They can't deny what you've accomplished," Atalante says, putting a hand on his forearm. The hand is small, the fingers long but not very slender. Their touch is rougher than he expected; the tips are calloused. It's a kind gesture. Insignificant. Yet it steals the air from his lungs.

He steps away, and Atalante's hand falls.

He looks up, sees his father. Looking at him.

His father whispers something to the Augustinians. They nod and leave the panel.

"It's quite dark. And very busy," the bald one says, approaching him. "Does there need to be so much happening?"

The other friar speaks before he can. "Have you seen the Adoration in Santa Maria Novella?"

"Botticelli's?" Leonardo asks, trying to tamper his incredulity.

"I'm not sure of the painter. But it's so lively, so colorful. Can't yours be more like that?"

He wrings his hands. He wants to tell them to look at the Madonna's fingers in the painting, how they throttle the chest of the Savior as if she were trying to squeeze the holy air out of Him. Instead, he says, "I think Botticelli did remarkable work, but I suppose we have different visions for the story."

It's the gentlest dissension he can muster.

"It's too violent, Leonardo," his father says, and the friars eagerly nod. "You understand, don't you?"

"The arrival of the Magi is a celebration of a miracle," the tonsured friar says. "What you've started, it's certainly interesting, but it's confusing. It lacks a clear story. Piety too. It's not appropriate, not for a monastery at least."

"What would you have me do?" he says, the warmth dropping from his voice.

"Begin again," the bald friar says. "You have two years left in the contract. Plenty of time to see it done right. But we'll have to hold any further payments until we see a drawing of the new version, to make sure it's in harmony with our needs."

"And what am I meant to do with the work I've already done?"

"That doesn't matter to us."

"We'll leave you now," the other says, tenting his fingers. "And we'll pray for a new vision to come quickly to you."

Leonardo doesn't see them leave, doesn't even hear their sandaled feet patter away.

His father remains. He turns to Leonardo, mouth open, but he only shakes his head before walking toward the door.

"Why didn't you say anything?" Leonardo calls after him.

"And what would you have had me say?" his father says, turning. "I thought you might do right today. I had a small hope that you learned something from your hardships. It's the maddening thing about you. You know what you're meant to do. You're clever enough to know why. Yet you choose this." He shakes a hand at the painting. "You asked me for help, and I gave it. I staked my reputation on your work. And you respond with sacrilege?"

"They didn't understand it."

"What's there to understand?" his father shouts. "Did you ever think about what they would want? No, you only wanted to indulge your own fancies. That's how it always is with you. You refuse to make yourself acceptable."

I wish I could, he wants to say. But that's not quite true, is it? His strangeness, his distraction, his whims—they were the only thing saving him from being entirely unremarkable.

He steps next to his father. Close enough to see the stitching of his jerkin, straining against his paunch. To smell the hoppy ale on his breath. "All you had to do was say you liked it. That's all I wanted."

"It's all you care about, isn't it? The work. No thought about family, or tradition, or what anyone else thinks."

"That's not true."

"It's not? I took you in, brought you here. I gave you a life. And how do you repay that? By begging me to send you to a workshop, to let you become an artist. And I let you, even when I needed your help with my work. Over and over again, I help you get commissions with my clients. What do you do? You ignore their wishes. You finish years late. Or worse, you don't finish at all. And then I hear how other artists are going to Venice or Rome, or they're doing some sculpture for the Medici. None of the others seem to have your troubles. They understand what's expected of them. They don't make a fool of themselves."

"Trust that I already feel plenty humiliated," he says, looking down at his father's boots.

"Humiliated?" His father shakes his head. "When I first heard what was being said about you, I tried not to listen. I knew those accusations were often nothing more than slander. But I couldn't fully ignore it. What I heard, it seemed plausible. I had always wondered. How could I not? The way you dress. Your indifference toward finding a wife. I thought— naively I see now—that it was nothing more than the stupidity of your youth. That I had been too indulgent with you, let you be too soft. That you would, eventually, grow up.

"But you're stubborn. In your work, yes, but also in the way you live. For someone so clever, you're completely blind to the fact that it's so obvious how you're living here. You say you're humiliated? No. What's humiliating is coming here with my clients, with men of God no less, and seeing that, despite all that's been said, you still keep a boy at your side, and surely by your bed at night too. What's humiliating is seeing that you're utterly shameless."

He is Sebastian, struck with arrows, one by one. It's not his father's knowing that wounds—it's how he's held on to the knowledge, kept it like a loan fat with interest. How now, of all times, he's called in the debt.

"You think I live without shame?" he cries. "It's my blood, my air. How could I ever have lived without it when you reminded me every day that I was in some way inconvenient to your life. That I was never going to be enough to become your son?"

He stares at the sweat-wet skin between his father's flared nostrils and his parted lips.

"But don't worry. I won't embarrass you much longer. I'm still going to leave."

"Then you better give the friars what they asked for," his father says.

ATALANTE WHISPERS HIS NAME, but he ignores it. The apprentice has heard every word. He knows every awful thing. He must think him a monster. When he puts his hand on his shoulder, it feels like a cold iron anvil. He shakes it off.

"You'll make another, and it will be even better. I know it."

If only he could believe that. If only he could listen to his father and paint the friars what they want to see—cheery colors, a doting crowd. They want him to paint like Sandro? He wishes he could, in so many ways. Sandro must have two dozen Madonnas scattered across this city, in churches and in homes. Sandro finishes his work—imperfectly, he'd add—and then, buoyant, he moves on to the next commission. What bliss that must be: to be able to stop caring, the confidence to surrender and move on.

He turns to Atalante. Keeping him at a distance? That wasn't a lesson learned. He's still made him a prisoner, chained Atalante to his faltering career. He's still ruined him, like he's done before. Like he's done with anything he's ever given a damn about.

"You should leave," he tells him.

The surprise in his face is like a crack through marble.

"Even if I start the work over, I don't know when they'll pay me again. It could be months, even a year. And I can't afford to keep you here all that time. I don't—"

The words catch on his tongue: he doesn't think he can paint what the friars want.

Painting, real painting, true painting—that now-familiar cycle of obsession, frustration, discontent, and failure—he doesn't think he can endure it any longer. He's disappointed himself too many times, disappointed everyone else too.

Better, perhaps, to put down his brush. To return to his inventions, his weapons, his machines—objects with use.

"I don't need you," he tells Atalante. "Everyone talented is leaving. So should you."

L

WHO WILL YOU BLAME NOW? SHE HAD SAID.

His mother was in a fever—eyes roving, lips crumbed with sacrament, skin shading blue. She thrashed, she choked, she soaked the bedsheets. Whatever force dragged her away from him, she fought it. Of course she did.

Then she stilled.

It made no sense. His mother was an ageless creature to him. Skin of steel, gaze more forceful than a gale. He thought there was time—months, even years. She never complained about the pain, so how was he supposed to know the end was near?

It shouldn't have been a surprise, he tells himself. She had seen over fifty summers. After he had returned from Rome, she was an extinguished thing. She hobbled, she grimaced. Her arms and hands ruptured and scaled. For the first time in his life, she avoided him. She knew what was coming.

He thinks of those words, her last ones. She was barely conscious when she said them. A madness had come over her that morning; the priest had to force the viaticum between her mumbling lips. She couldn't have known Lorenzo was standing beside her.

NOW HE IS ALONE. There is his bed, the quilts neatly draped; his desk, littered with so many letters, red seals flaked and broken like picked scabs. He listens for a knock. Waits for her to swing the door open, to tell him what to do.

Don't keep the people waiting for the funeral, she'd say.

He dresses. Slides silk gloves onto his crooked red fingers. Rolls velvet hose over his swollen knees. He buttons a doublet, black damask. Drapes his shoulders with a cloak lined with lambskin and collared with soft, dark sable. He leaves his bedroom, limps through the house.

Downstairs, his family is waiting for him, all in long blacks. Clarice. Their four daughters, their three sons. Four, if he counts Giuliano's bastard. He supposes he should.

All of them together—he's not used to this sight. Somehow, in the years that have seemed to slip past him, his family had grown. He has more sons and more daughters than his parents did.

He remembers the day of his grandfather's funeral, when they walked from this same courtyard to San Lorenzo. They were fewer in number, yes, but they felt as fierce as an army. The whole city parted way for them—the carts in the street, the people in the piazza, the very dirt beneath their boots, scattering to the hot summer wind. Everything was theirs.

"They'll be waiting for us," Clarice says, stirring him.

"Go ahead. I'll be there soon."

She nods. The children won't look at him. He watches them all amble out of the courtyard without him.

He waits.

He turns to the statue of David, the one he kept. The bronze is dull under the gray sky. He meets the empty stare of the boy warrior with his wide-brimmed hat and long sword. His frame is so narrow, his skin taut and smooth. He's young—probably closer in age to his eldest son than to him. His eyes drift down to the foot resting atop Goliath's severed head. How easy this boy makes it look, to take down giants.

His litter is brought beside him. A small thing: a cushioned chair secured to some wooden planks, with a canopy hanging over it. His father's, once, though he's had it redecorated with new brocade curtains and cloth of gold tassels. It's a more comfortable means of transport for him than his coach, with its wide wheels that find every divot in the road and jolt his bones.

He climbs inside, sits on the plush seat, shuts his eyes. He tries not to notice the labored exhales of the slaves as they lift the vehicle onto their shoulders. Before they leave the courtyard, he snatches the curtains shut.

OUTSIDE SAN LORENZO, HE WON'T have anyone help him out of the litter. He moves, slowly, deliberately, up the church steps.

At the door, he hesitates. The scene waiting on the other side is familiar: a dark, crowded nave. It turns his hands clammy; it makes his joints grate beneath his clothes. He's being foolish—he knows this. That bloody Mass was in Santa Reparata; this funeral is in San Lorenzo. He has a dozen guards with him and heavy mail weighing on his shoulders. No one can hurt him now.

He nods to his men, and the church doors open. The nave is a murky sea of browns and undyed grays. Everyone's finery is drab now. But that's what happens when the wool trade plummets and the factories shut. London is the new Florence, they say. Though some people tell him it is Bruges. Or Venice. Or, damn it, even Rome.

He still looks sumptuous today—of course he does. He and Florence, they remain one; their fate will be the same. Poverty is a dramatic word for it, but what few branches of the family bank are left are nearing insolvency. He, the banker, has had to borrow thousands from Galeazzo's widow in Milan, has had to pull fifty thousand more from his young cousins' inheritance. And then there were all the florins dispersed winning peace in Naples. Money well spent, truthfully, but that doesn't change the fact that there's none left.

Can one put a price on peace? No, he thinks. Everyone would balk at the cost. No one would want it.

At least they still have it. Peace, that is. Part of him craved a grand battle in the end, to see his soldiers fight off the Turks, for him to be a prince in victory. But he was robbed of that chance. The sultan died last year. Poison, most say. Whatever the method and whoever was responsible, the infidels have now been routed from Otranto. The peninsula has returned to squabbling among itself.

At least Florence continues to stand. Unscathed, they say. Although, inside this church, there's a sarcophagus with his brother's rotting body which belies that claim. His empty purse too.

He looks to the nave. So many are watching him, but the congregation seems paltry. It's not enough. It's not even the size of his father's funeral, let alone his grandfather's. His mother deserves more than this. She deserves a funeral in the cathedral, with the prayers of an archbishop, under the dome. But he won't return to that place.

He approaches the bier. Beneath the white linen shroud, her face is rigid, oil-slicked. There are her familiar lips, almost scowling, and her veiled, brittle hair. Her eyes, he'll only glance at. They're hidden behind fine-lined lids. If he stares too long, they might open once more; his mother might sit up, toss off the shroud, bark at him to stand straighter, to be more gracious, to be great.

But what could she truly complain about? The city has gathered for them. They look at him like he is their prince. He has reformed the councils; he keeps them firmly in his grip. Beyond Florence, he enjoys the favor of kings and dukes. He's once more friendly with the pope. This is what she wanted.

So why does he feel like a husk?

He joins his family, standing in the transept. What a motley assembly they now make. Here's his uncle, miraculously still alive. His grim-faced sisters too: Nannina, overwhelmed with her children; Bianca, who hasn't spared him a word since he let her return from exile.

Clarice steadies herself against a stone pillar, their daughters standing behind her. Thankfully, they resemble their mother more than him. Lucrezia will soon be wedded; he's betrothed her to a Salviati, if one can believe it. A better-blooded branch of the family than that archbishop's, of course. It was his mother who had asked for the match, and he couldn't deny a dying woman. She said they had to forgive, and he found some comfort in knowing he could keep the dowry small.

Around Clarice, his boys are gathered like little guardsmen. Giovanni's hair is already tonsured; he is the second son who will go into the church. So, too, will Giuliano's son, if he can manage it. He imagines the Church is more forgiving of bastards than the rest of the world—and he'd like to give him the career his father was robbed of. As for his youngest son, burying his face against his mother's leg, he thinks he's too handsome and sweet for a life in scarlet.

Then there is his heir, Piero, standing beside him. His son now reaches his shoulders, though he still teeters on tantrums. His hair, wavy and hay-colored, falls over his face. Lorenzo brushes it aside with his fingers, and the boy glares at him. Piero is only a few years younger than he was when he stood in this same church, staring at his grandfather's body. He wonders what his son might be thinking, what dreams he might carry for his own future. Perhaps Piero sees only a gouty wreck of a man. If only he could make him understand.

He hears his mother's words again: Who will you blame now?

Days have passed, but he cannot shake them. Yes, he holds blame.

So much of it. It weighs on him like a crown—something he must wear, something he cannot give to someone else to bear. But this blame he carries is not for her. It's for the pope, for seeing him as nothing more than a banker. It's for the Pazzi for stealing away that wealth. Ferrante, for making him poor. And the priors and this city's stubborn traditions too.

The Mass begins; it ends. The congregation swells before him. Fingers, gloved in silk, curl around his own.

"It's over," Clarice is saying. "Come home with us."

The nave is lifeless and smoky, an abandoned battlefield. The congregation is gone. His uncle has departed. His sisters too.

She tugs on his hand. "Come," she says.

He sees Piero watching him, mouth shut and frowning.

"Not yet," Lorenzo says. "Leave me."

Her sigh is sharp and brief. She drifts away, flanked by their children. None of them say goodbye to him.

The nave is silent. The priests, carrying their golden vessels, have retreated to the sacristy—the one his great-grandfather paid for and now lies inside. His grandfather is here too, just steps away, resting below, in the crypt. If he took a hammer, smashed away the porphyry and opened his tomb, what would he see? Does flesh still cling to those bones or has his grandfather wasted away to a vicious black stain streaked along the marble bottom?

His father? He rests in the sacristy, inside a claw-foot sarcophagus. But he should keep that one shut. Nestled alongside his father is Giuliano. Still without a tomb of his own. Waiting for him to join them all.

He counts the dead. His mother, his brother, all his forefathers. He says goodbye to them for now.

—

HE MAKES ARRANGEMENTS, tells only his servants and his secretaries. He sits in his bedroom, still as a corpse, watching as his chests are packed with clothes, soft bedding, as ink bottles are capped and paper is bundled and tied with twine.

The coach absconds under blue dawn light. Out from the courtyard they go, down the wide, empty street toward the cathedral. Its pink, green, and white doesn't yet shine, but something glimmers, as if wet, in front of the doors. Lit by a half-moon of candles, he glimpses his mother's face.

A trick of the light, he thinks.

He sees her again, down another street, on the steps of an oratory. A third time, on a street corner, nestled between bunches of purple-petaled narcissus. He shouts for the coach to stop.

It's a votive. A vague resemblance of his mother's face, hastily sketched on a plank of splintered wood. The nose isn't long enough. The chin is dulled, the mouth posed in a docile way. The eyes are brown and wide. Her gaze has been turned blank. They've made her meek, shaped her into something Madonna-like—mother to all, radiant with love.

How crudely they honor her, he thinks. She deserves better than the hands of novices. He'll turn back to the palace and summon all the city's best artists. He'll tell them to paint her as she truly was: as a fearless Judith with a sword in her hand, or as a sage Minerva with an owl perched on her shoulder. Sandro should paint the Minerva, he thinks.

Then he remembers: the best have all left him. Sandro is still in Rome, painting the walls of the pope's chapel. Ghirlandaio and Perugino and Rosselli too. Verrocchio's heading to Venice soon. Only the second-rate painters are left, and it'd be an insult to offer his mother's likeness to them.

He's wrong. There's the Madonna in his brother's bedroom. The painter he once called David. He has not heard of him in months, maybe years. Perhaps the plague took him. Perhaps a cardinal's snatched him away to Rome. Or perhaps he's somehow remained.

He recalls the name: Leonardo. He knows he could render her stony eyes, her fierce scowl. He could make her a marvel.

He hears his mother's dry laugh. What an honor, she'd have said, to be painted by a sodomite.

Lorenzo orders the driver to carry on. At the riverbank, the morning light warms the houses to the west. The Arno rushes, turbulent and gold. They ride over the old stone bridge into the Oltrarno, where his mother loiters in the doors of smaller churches, crammed between squat, narrow houses. She watches him leave the city, and then she abandons him.

Out beyond the gates, in the dark green hills, there are no more effigies. Here, the towns are untroubled by what's beyond their low walls. They unfurl into one another with their thatched-roof houses and low stone-walled taverns. Hours pass like this. Then the sharp hill of Volterra appears to the west. Its tall walls scar the landscape. Up there, the fortress has been emptied. The last of the Pazzi prisoners freed. It really was over, all of it.

They continue southward, away from the hills, until they reach the black-pooled plains of Morba. The driver treads forward more carefully now. They wind through the rocky landscape, in and out of wisps of sulfureous smoke. Then he sees it: a modest but handsome villa, its stones not yet mildewed. The house his mother built for herself.

His servants unload his belongings. The bed is made, his letters and papers stacked atop a small desk. He knows it's futile to hide from the entreaties and favors and disputes; they'll chase him wherever he goes.

His mother's votives hover in his mind. Too-soft eyes staring. Pink lips slightly parted, as if she's about to speak.

What is it, he wants to ask. What would she have him do? He'd listen this time.

He calls for his secretary, begins dictating while the man's still dipping his pen into ink. When the letter is finished, he asks his secretary to have a courier take it back to Florence straightaway, to find an artist by the name of Leonardo and deliver it to him.

His secretary asks: And the rest of his letters?

He considers the neat pile of fat covertures. He says they can wait until tomorrow.

His secretary nods, bows, leaves. Lorenzo remains in his chair, considering the unused paper on the desk. Perhaps it's time to return to that record of his family, of his own life, which he briefly started after Piero's birth. Here, alone, he can finally resume it. Pick up his pen and submit to the past after fighting its tidelike draw for so long. Now, he can relent. Explain everything to Piero, make him understand what awaits him.

He reaches for his pen, dips. It trembles above the paper. How does he begin? So much has happened. He'll have to collapse the years, the errors into mere paragraphs.

But wasn't that what he had done when writing his own father's life?

He has done more, he thinks. It deserves a full telling. He'll write of his months in Naples, of peace secured, of Florence saved. But then there are the pesky details: the terms of the treaty, his secret journey to Rome. He can ignore those. Or, better yet, he can pass over it all.

The blank page waits. It will be an undertaking, to tell it all, and he's so weary from the day's journey. The record must wait, he decides. He should recover his health first.

He changes out of his road-damp clothes and wraps a silk robe around his body.

A maid leads him outside, her face turned away to avoid the sight of his bare feet. When they reach the pool, round and gurgling, she tells him he will get used to the smell after a while, that everyone does. He nods, and she disappears.

He unties his robe, drops it to the ground. He clutches himself as his limbs become goosefleshed, and he looks down at his purpled toes. At his knees, puffed and shining. Long-dead leaves rustle in trees somewhere distant in the forlorn scenery, hidden behind a brimstone veil. The country house, the plains, his lands are lost in the fog.

He places one foot into the spring, surprisingly warm.

He takes in the riled surface of the pool, the water littered with white flakes of sulfur, as if a thousand letters have been torn to shreds. He places his other foot into the water. His knees bend. His body lowers. Alone, he lets himself cry out.

He wades toward the pool's deep center, the water rising to his stomach, to his chest, to his scarred neck. Thick clouds of steam buffet his face.

He sinks beneath the surface and waits to feel the promised relief.

LI

HIS WORKSHOP HAS EMPTIED. HIS JARS OF PIGMENT, NEARLY spent, are not to be replaced; green from Verona, yellow from Naples—places he'll now never go. Ropes hang from the winches, swaying in a cold draft, tied to nothing. And then there are his papers, cascading from tables onto the floor. Drawings, dreams, machines—he treads over them all.

Atalante is gathering the last of his belongings to take to Milan. His own pens and papers, his lyre, his favorite clay cup, glazed a pale yellow.

"Sforza's not only looking for musicians, he wants artists too," he reminded Leonardo when he told him of his appointment to play his lyre at Ludovico's court.

"The regent is looking for a sculptor, not a painter," he replied.

It didn't matter. He is neither of those things anymore.

He's leaving this space. He no longer needs it. He's using his last few florins to rent a small bedroom in a lodging house. He'll stay there until someone hires him to build the well he's designed. A simple project, but a useful one. Perhaps one day, after more wells and mills and ladders, he'll have enough coin to travel to Milan and hear Atalante play.

He spills his drafting tools into a wooden crate, bundles loose papers with twine. He feels a twinge, the sensation of being watched. He peers over his shoulder, glances at the silhouettes of his half-finished paintings. They're glowering at him.

They remain a problem, one he's ignored. He won't be able to cram them inside whatever dingy bedroom he finds for himself; there won't be the space. But as much as they haunt him, he can't bring himself to hawk them either. They need a guardian, someone who understands what they were meant to be.

HIS OLD MASTER SITS ON an overturned barrel outside the workshop he once thought of as home. His eyes are closed, his face turned up to the warm but tentative rays of early springtime sun. Leonardo studies him for some time before approaching. He's changed very little, despite the years. A bit rounder, perhaps. A little balder.

When his figure blocks out the sun, Andrea's eyes open, and they are as lively as ever. "Finally," he says, rising, wrapping his arms around him. "I thought I'd have to journey over to San Frediano to say goodbye. Why did you pick a shop all the way over there? It's so far."

"Not as far as Venice," he says. "Besides, I'm leaving that space."

His brows rise. "Leaving for?"

"A smaller one, here in the city."

"Truthfully, I thought you'd have left by now. With the others."

"I wasn't chosen," he says as gently as he can.

"Curious choices they made. Sandro, I understand. Domenico and Perugino are skilled too, though you always outshone them. I quite liked the thought of the four of you, up in Rome together. My apprentices reunited. Why they chose Rosselli I'll never understand."

"It doesn't matter now. They have the work, not me."

The sun slips behind a cloud, and the street turns gray and cool once more.

"I thought you're painting an altarpiece for the friars at San Donato. At least, that's what your father told me when I last asked."

He doesn't want to think about that. "I was," he admits. Andrea's mouth curls. His old master remembers his habits.

"Let's go in. It'll be warmer," Andrea says, opening the door, beckoning him.

He hesitates on the threshold. It's the sweet, familiar scent of worked brass—it snatches the years away, sends him back a decade, more. Makes him want to grab paper and create some small piece of work that might earn his master's attention.

"Come, come."

He steps inside. He knows this scene: the flurry of sketching and carving and weaving; the apprentices all so young, all of them moving about so freely, so lightly.

"You're busy," he says, following Andrea to a pair of old stools away from the fray and out of earshot.

Andrea shrugs. "I'm a dog eating scraps."

"So why are you leaving? You've always worked here."

"And how many devotionals and saints have I sculpted? I'm tired. I need a new challenge." He rubs at his nape. "Enough about me. What happened to altarpiece?"

"The friars didn't like it."

"And what does your apprentice say? Does he think you should keep at it?"

He knows Andrea notices the red blooming on his cheeks. "He's going to Milan. To play his lyre for the duke's court."

Andrea lets out a sigh, long and steady like a squeezed bellows. "You know that boy came to me first? I could've hired him. I almost did. But I sent him to you, because I knew you weren't working. And I thought if he was with you, that would change."

He shakes his head.

"Don't deny it. You were pleased with the work you did for the friars, were you not? This is how you've always been, whether you realize it or not. You need a muse."

"Perhaps that was true in the past. But it doesn't matter. I'm not painting anymore."

"You're fooling yourself, Leonardo. You're an artist."

"No. The ones in Rome, the ones working—they're the artists. I'm only a man wasting his time with a brush."

"I didn't spend years training you only for you to quit," Andrea says in the same sharp tone of the angry master. It still strikes fear in him. "When you left this workshop, you promised me you would keep painting."

"And I have. But it's been to little end."

He watches the commotion of the workshop. Two boys with mussed-up hair are play-fighting with thin planks of poplar. A narrow-faced young man is sullenly carrying in the work left outside to dry. And then there is a solitary boy engaged in Leonardo's old habit: leaning over a notebook, etching ink, fussing with details. But there are no paintings in the workshop—only sculptures, drawings, and embroidery.

"They don't know anything," Andrea says. "Lorenzo, and the rest of them."

"I brought it on myself."

"No," Andrea says, running his fingers through his thinning hair. "No, you didn't. That man thinks he deserves all the world's respect without giving any in return. Remember the David? He never paid me for it."

Leonardo looks up, dumbfounded. "That was a decade ago."

"And I've yet to see a single soldo from it. Even though he sold it off to the Signoria."

"You never asked for it?"

"Please. What was I supposed to do? Knock on his door and demand my payment? He knew what he was doing. He did it because he could, and because doing it was a reminder to the rest of us that he could do things we couldn't."

"But you kept working with him."

"Of course I did. You can't get commissions without making offerings at his altar. You know this. Our work—sometimes we do it with pleasure, but it's always at their pleasure. We all have our masters, artists or not. All we can hope is to find a good-hearted one. One that dotes on us." He turns away. "Why did you come here, Leonardo?"

"I need someone to take the work I haven't finished. I won't have the space for them. And I thought you might want them. You could have your apprentices finish painting them. You could sell them off. I only wish that they don't go to waste."

Andrea raises his left hand, silences him. The skin of his palm is disfigured; it looks like many layers of wax. "I haven't held a brush in years. The last painting I touched—it was your Sebastian, in flames. Do you know why I stopped?"

The lack of paintings suddenly makes sense.

"It was you, Leonardo. I knew I'd never paint something as beautiful as what you were making, and you were barely yet a man. And know that I don't say this out of jealousy. I say it because you were my pride."

Tears well. A blurred Andrea stands. "Wait here," he says, patting him on the shoulder. "Please. Wait."

Leonardo smudges his tears across his cheeks. He blinks. Nothing has changed. He's still that precocious boy dreading the end of his apprenticeship, fearful of leaving.

Andrea returns. He rubs Leonardo's fingers between his own. Then he pushes a leather pouch, small but heavy with coins, into his palm.

"I can't," Leonardo says.

"Take it," Andrea says, bending his fingers, closing his palm. "It's not a life-changing sum by any means. I have no need for it. Your father has been telling me to write a last will before I leave. This is simpler, I think.

"And I won't take your paintings, as much as I'd enjoy seeing them every day. The road to Venice is long, and I'm not a young man anymore. I can't be sure that I'll be coming back here. But I do know that you should hold on to your work. And I think you should leave this place too."

"But I have no recommendations," he says, his voice barely more than a whisper.

"So go where you know there's work. Where you can prove yourself."

"I wasn't good enough here. Why would I be better off somewhere else?"

Andrea's hands tighten around his own. "You have always been great. It was this city that wasn't good enough."

HE RETURNS TO HIS WORKSHOP, for there is nowhere else to go. Atalante's chest remains by the door, but the room is still. In the rear of the workshop, where there are no windows, the light is simple and plays no tricks. He sits on the floor and reluctantly lifts his gaze to the painting that is larger, taller, wider, more intricate than the rest: the Madonna, surrounded by the three Magi. Her face is calm and reassuring; her savior son's is solemn and knowing. Behind her are the dozens of figures he wasted months of his life trying to perfect. Mêlées, daggers, horses, and ruins—the chaos he knows well. And then there is his own face in the painting, uncolored and unfinished. Turning away from everything, afraid. Always failing to act.

Daylight stretches into the room. The door creaks. Atalante drops his rucksack to the floor. He rushes to a table, collects something from its surface, brings it to him. He's smiling.

Leonardo rises, takes the letter. "What is it?"

"A courier came here, not an hour ago. He was looking for you. He said he had been sent by Lorenzo de' Medici."

The boy beams, but Leonardo's heart rattles. He grabs the letter from the boy, hastily breaks its seal, tearing the paper at its edge. He reads the neatly written words. Reads them again.

"What does it say?"

"It's a commission." Somehow, he is laughing.

"From Lorenzo himself?"

He nods. "To paint his late mother."

The boy's hands clasp his arms. "I'll stay," he says. "You'll need help."

"No." The sound escapes his mouth, surprises him. The boy's arms fall away. "You have to leave."

Leonardo's fingers tighten around the small tear at the paper's edge. He pulls the letter apart. Tears it into smaller and smaller shreds, until it dusts the floor around them.

"We both do," he says.

—

LOOK AT HIM NOW, sitting on the back of a cart, surrounded by his belongings. A chest, holding softly colored tunics and the papers he chose to keep. A crate, where his many drafting tools jangle about. And, yes, his paintings, wrapped in leather. It's surprising—and slightly sad—how everything he owns and nearly all the work he's ever done can be hauled by a single horse.

The dirt flows beneath his feet as the cart rolls forward. He looks up, watches this place retreat from him. Home, he supposes he should call it. Eighteen years—most of his life—he's lived here. But all he sees in his wake is a parade of his countless errors.

He bids farewell to it all. Goodbye to the distant Palagio, that horror of a building. May he never see it again. Goodbye to what was once the Buco, just a few streets away. He had no token of all those nights to pack alongside his possessions; he wishes he had secreted that sketch of Iac sleeping after all. Goodbye, too, to his father's home, where the man must be leant over his papers, where his daughters and sons run and cry and do whatever it is that children do. He did not visit him; his father would only be smug knowing that he was proven correct, that Leonardo was abandoning yet another unfinished painting. As for the Adoration? He's left it behind; it was too large to carry with him. But he wouldn't let the friars have it. He took it instead to Giovanni de' Benci, told him to give it to Ginevra.

Bronze glints to his right, marble shines to his left. He passes through Paradise, one final time. He'll miss this sight: the blazing baptistery doors, those carved panels telling better stories than thousands of words ever could. And how could he ever forget this cathedral with its dome that rises like a bloody sun? In this city, it will never be eclipsed; this he knows. No wonder the artists were leaving. They knew they could never outmatch it.

On they go, up the Via Larga, the landmarks falling from view. To the west, the plain nave of San Lorenzo, where he once went to a funeral, a lifetime ago. And now, here's Lorenzo's palace. He wishes he could run inside, find his Madonna, take it with him. He hopes it also will one day escape—to Milan or Naples or Rome or anywhere else. As for the man who lives in those halls, who is still waiting on his reply to his letter? He says farewell to him too.

The homes crouch closer to the earth. There are fields; there's a monastery; and then, before he's truly ready for it, they pass through the city gates. Now he's no longer a master painter. Now he's whoever he says he is. He could be a man of science, an inventor, a sculptor, and an engineer too. He could go to Naples and build his machines of war for the king. He could even go as far as Constantinople and build a bridge to span the Bosphorus.

His breath fogs. His body trembles. He hops off the cart, runs ahead to the coach, climbs inside. Atalante shifts to make space for him.

Yes, he's off to Milan. A city teeming with possibility. A city for weapon-making, a city with a large army, a city with a regent he shall try to win over with his designs. It is the prudent destination.

From the comfort of the coach, he watches morning yawn from gray to yellow. He keeps watching until evening bruises from amber to purple. He sees the landscape change, sees it rise from rolling, violet-spotted hills to sharp, snow-laden peaks. Every year, he forgets this: how spring is so unproven and temperamental, how it's always a miracle.

By the second day, they've traveled farther than he's ever been. For the first time in his life, he leaves the republic. Each new valley, each nestled village is a surprising, wonderful thing to him. His fingers flick an imaginary pen; he draws invisible outlines of mountains.

On the third day, they wind downward to Bologna, where the churches and towers are hidden behind heavy rainfall. Here, they'll give the horses rest, hoping that morning brings kinder weather. But when their caravan pulls into the storm-worn stables of a stone hostelry, they notice the thatched roof is leaking. Their clothes should be safe inside their chests, hidden under heavy tarpaulin, but he doesn't want to leave his paintings out in the stables. To the dismay of the copper-nosed inn-keeper, he and Atalante haul them all inside and up to his room.

He decides to make the most of this time indoors, to draft a letter—one he'll send to Sforza. An introduction.

He asks Atalante to come to his room, says he knows he's no longer his apprentice, but can he write for him? This letter is too important to be ruined with the slanting and smudging of his left-handed scrawl.

Atalante sits down at the desk, prepares paper and ink by weakening candlelight. From the edge of a limp mattress, Leonardo begins to list his skills that he wishes to offer to the regent.

He says he can design bridges, ones that are portable, for the use of armies. That he has other machines for sieges too. He knows how to carve secret tunnels into the earth. He can make impenetrable chariots and cannons and catapults. He has designs for naval battles too. And for peacetime, he can design beautiful buildings, both public and private.

He stops, waiting for Atalante's pen to catch up to his words. Then his former apprentice turns to him. His eyes are expectant, his face so hopeful. Perhaps how he himself once looked at Andrea.

Leonardo considers the deep stack of wrapped paintings leant against the wall. He can't see their strokes, but he knows each of them—every holy virgin, every old saint. He thinks about the majesty he's already witnessed on this journey; he sees Madonnas on desolate mountain-sides, baptisms by half-frozen rivers.

Does he dare open himself up to such disappointments again?

"Write that, in painting and sculpture, I can do everything possible."

Atalante's hand is still. His face broadens into a wide smile.

"Well, go on," he says.

Atalante writes the words.

"We can make changes to the letter in Milan, once we better know Sforza's tastes," Leonardo tells him. Atalante nods, blows softly on the ink. He shakes the paper, stands. He sits on the bed, next to Leonardo. Gives him the letter.

It's an unfamiliar sight—to read his own words in another's hand. But the letter is good. It's a beginning. And he's glad to be able to share it with someone.

"Thank you for letting me come," Leonardo says.

Atalante leans close, then—rather unexpectedly—kisses him. His lips linger, warm.

"No," Leonardo says, shifting away. The letter falls to the floor. "It's not you. It's because—"

Because of what?

He reaches forward, snakes his fingers through Atalante's curls, cradles his head. He kisses him. Kisses him again. Wonders why he's waited so long to do such a thing.

They fall back onto the bed. He whispers to Atalante, asks if he's certain. His songbird beams, says yes. They unclasp their belts. Pull off their tunics. Roll down their hose. They admire the sight of each other like this.

Leonardo throws aside the pillows losing their feathers. He curls his legs around Atalante, draws him closer. He feels how this body is hairier, sturdier than the last one he touched. How the hair at the groin nests and bristles. He takes his hand, the one with fingers roughened by lyre strings. He brings it to his mouth, kisses it, wets it with his spit. The hand searches, it finds. Their bodies converge.

When they are spent, when their sweat-sheened chests cease their heaving, he rises from the bed. He collects the letter from the floor, collects also his notebook from his leather sack. He puts the letter on the desk, considers it for a moment. He pushes it aside, making room for his notebook, thumbing to a clean page. He dips his pen into ink. He looks back at the man sleeping on the bed.

He begins, a single stroke.

HISTORICAL NOTE

THIS IS A WORK OF FICTION, BUT I'VE STRIVED FOR FIDELITY wherever possible, with a few exceptions.

First, on the subject of names: Iac, within this novel, is based upon the sex worker Jacopo Saltarelli, whose name is listed in the still-surviving records of the Officers of the Night. Iacopo is a spelling variant of Jacopo; I decided upon the nickname of Iac to differentiate him from Jacopo de' Pazzi.

No records of a commission to Leonardo from Lorenzo or Giuliano de' Medici survive. It's currently unknown who commissioned the *Madonna of the Carnation*, but I've accepted Jean-Pierre Isbouts and Christopher Heath Brown's compelling hypothesis that it came from Giuliano.* We do know, crucially, that the painting eventually found its way into the collection of Pope Clement VII, the assumed son of Giuliano and Fioretta Gorini.

It's often stated that Lorenzo himself sent Leonardo as an ambassador to the Milanese court. No contemporary records that I'm aware of support this claim, beyond the anonymously written Codice Magliabechiano. This codice also describes Leonardo as living with the Medici in 1480. I've chosen to disregard these claims, given that the manuscript was likely written after Leonardo's death and at least four decades after the events of this novel.

Very little survives of Francesco Salviati's biography. For aspects of his background, I drew inspiration from the life of Alessandro de'

---

* *Young Leonardo: The Evolution of a Revolutionary Artist, 1472–1499* (Thomas Dunne Books, 2017).

Medici, who was likely mixed-race and born illegitimate and was either the great-grandson of Lorenzo or the grandson of Giuliano.

One last liberty I knowingly took: no records suggest that Lorenzo ventured to Rome as a part of Florence's truce with the Papal States. I hope readers will forgive me for deciding to imagine how this might have been possible to allow the story a final moment between Lorenzo and Rovere.

ACKNOWLEDGMENTS

MY NAME MIGHT BE THE ONLY ONE ON THE COVER, BUT THIS IS misleading—this book is indebted to the effort and care of so many others. I should first thank Mom and Dad—for reading to me as a child and for never refusing me a trip to a library or bookstore. Also, to Dottie, for showing me how to live with a creative spirit. Audrey, Alan, Alice, and Adam: thank you for your love, your enthusiasm, and for never complaining when I detoured our family travels so I could visit a particular cathedral or see a certain painting.

To my many teachers over the years. Paula Renda, you made me interested in the lives of artists. Kim Casale, you kindly allowed me to stay inside and read during recess. Betty Jipson, you're still my favorite librarian. Danielle de Pazzis, you first told me of the Medici and the Pazzi. Dick Anthony, you taught me how to truly read a book. Lynne McVeigh, you've never failed to give me a hug and creative encouragement. Archie Tait, you saw this story in a very different form, and you urged me to continue it. Maureen Freely, you helped me consider the possibilities of the historical genre. Tim Leach, you gifted me many wise suggestions—most importantly, to nix the first hundred pages.

To every friend who has at some point asked how the book was doing: thank you. I'm especially grateful to Sungmi Choi for pushing me to become a writer, rather than a marketer. To Kaitlyn Kane, Jessica Shannon, Chandler Coniglio, and Evelyn Hu for being brilliant early readers. Krysten Peck, for her artistic wisdom and a clarifying tarot card reading. Vivian Zhu, for many book chats and her social media expertise. Olivia Donahue, for her creative eye. Chandler Bray, the best bookseller. Thank you also to Yasmin Inkersole, Nina Kenney, and all my fellow Warwick students who made thoughtful suggestions on various excerpts of what became this book.

Scholars, historians, and biographers did much of the difficult fact-finding and record-checking so that I could then imagine this story. The work of Christopher Heath Brown, Meghan Callahan, Walter Isaacson, Jean-Pierre Isbouts, Christopher Hibbert, Martin Kemp, Ross King, Anne Leader, Alexander Lee, J. Lucas-Dubreton, Lauro Martines, Marcello Simonetta, Michael Rocke, and Rocky Ruggiero was crucial in this regard; any inaccuracies are due to my error and not theirs. I'm also very grateful to the patient librarians, archivists, and staffers at the British Library, the Département des Arts Graphiques at the Louvre and the Archivio di Stato di Firenze.

I owe so much to the diligence and care from teams at Liveright, W. W. Norton, and Janklow & Nesbit who have helped bring this book into the world. I'm damn lucky to have such a kind and attentive agent in Chad Luibl, who made this all possible, who also—along with the stellar Roma Panganiban—has been such a champion of this story through its every revision. I was lucky again in getting to work with Gina Iaquinta, editor extraordinaire, who understood my intention with this book from the very beginning and worked her hardest to help me realize it. Another round of thanks to Maria Connors, Dassi Zeidel, Jodi Hughes, Jason Heuer, Peter Miller, Clio Hamilton, Nick Curley, and Kadiatou Keita.

I've saved the best for last. Thank you, Andrew, for not hesitating when I said I wanted to quit the day job to write a book, and for always being my first reader. This book wouldn't exist without you.